# DOOR TO A DARK ROOM

## A DICKIE FLOYD DETECTIVE NOVEL

## DANNY R. SMITH

# COPYRIGHT

*For my fellow bulldogs of the Los Angeles County Sheriff's Homicide Bureau.*

*To my beautiful wife, Lesli
and my daughters Jami and Randi Jo,
without whose love and support, this book could not have been written.*

*And for Patricia Barrick Brennan, my dear friend and editor who motivates and encourages me, and keeps me flying straight between the margins.*

*Every scene had its story, and its secrets. The secrets were what kept me awake at night thirsting for answers. Though mostly insatiable, I fed the cravings like an addict, no matter the cost. The fix was always more death. A fresh kill. A new crime scene. Another story that needed to be told and heard. To inhabit a newly christened sacred ground and allow my mind to drift beyond the immediately tangible. To feel the presence of spirits whose secrets swirled, whispering clues for those who listened closely.*

# 1

———

THEY WERE EASY prey. Complacent, like a herd of sheep, unaware of their vulnerability. Oblivious to the presence of a predator.

Concealed in darkness, he watched them. He relished the power he had over them, knowing it was his choice whether they lived or died, not theirs. Not the decision of God or Satan or some bitch named Karma. It was *his*.

He almost pitied them for their weakness.

Almost.

The mothers, busy on their cell phones, unaware that their children trailed behind, babbling, whining, some staring at phones of their own. He could easily pull one into his car and be gone, *whisk*. How long would it take an oblivious mother to notice? The self-centered bitches were ignorant of his grace.

He waited.

Leonard watched them all, women, girls, and boys. He had no desire for mature women, though the idea of young girls stirred him greatly. In prison, he had managed his own sexual gratification, with only the occasional aid of another man. Young men only, though. Those who were new in the system and as frightened and malleable as he had been when he was locked up at age sixteen.

The real thrill had always been the stalking. Creeping through the darkened homes of others, watching strangers as they slept. Death was their houseguest, though most of them never knew it; they were the fortunate ones. Those who did know, only knew for an instant during their final moments.

Leonard didn't always kill; most times he had not. The first murder had been the result of panic—he had been only thirteen. The others were by choice.

An electric thrill shot through Leonard as he thought of the fear in the eyes of his chosen ones. How they begged, squirmed, tried to escape. Their efforts were futile.

His preference was strangulation; it was so intimate. Bare hands allowed him to feel their final pulses, smell their last breaths, stare into their unbelieving eyes. Some of the killings had been more violent, a swift and easy death with a single blow to the skull. Once he had used a hammer; another time it had been a pipe. Each experience had been an education. Though the more violent attacks were efficient, and there had been little suffering, they had been less gratifying.

Leonard was more compassionate than the news stories had painted him. Always, he kissed them goodbye. Most would not have been capable of understanding the intimacy of their death, nor of appreciating it. But he knew, and he wanted to share his affection with these chosen ones. It was his gift to the newly dead.

Leonard had dreamed of killing during his years of confinement, treasuring and reliving his memories of those he had watched, those he had killed. He remembered them all. They were his. They would always be his.

He thought of the first, an elderly woman alone in her bed. He had meant only to observe her, but she had awakened and begun to scream, leaving him no choice. There had been no desire for sex, although he had explored her lifeless body. When Leonard was eventually arrested, three years later, they didn't even ask him about her murder. Nor did they ask about any of the others, not even the five-year-old boy who had lived—and died—right next door. Leonard thought the boy's mother might have been considered a suspect, but he never heard what became of her.

His only arrest had come after he killed his mother. By that time, he had become efficient at killing. His mother had deserved her death, and she had not been entitled to his grace; he did not kiss her goodbye. He turned himself in; what else could he do? It had been just the two of them all of his life, and now she was dead. This he pondered for hours as he sat on the porch, a cordless telephone in his hand and his mother's body cooling inside the house. He knew the call would end the killing.

Or would it?

His lawyer said his mother had sexually abused him, had tormented him physically and psychologically. "What monster would do this to her own son?" the attorney had asked of the jury, rhetorically. They had bought it. They believed the adolescent when he took the stand and allowed the tears to roll down his cheeks. While on the stand, he had kept his head low and softly answered the questions. *Poor boy*. He had been sentenced as an adult, but his life had been spared. He received twenty-five years and was sent off to Raiford, Florida's infamous penitentiary.

Once Leonard understood what was required to survive in prison, he considered his time there mostly tolerable. He had learned quickly.

The last ten years had been wonderful. He had been assigned a new cellmate, Whitey Blanchard. Whitey, a member of the Irish mafia, had been the youngest man ever convicted of a mafia-related murder in Florida. He was a legend in the crime world, having taken out two top hitmen of a rival family. The two mafiosi were known to be vicious and precise, always wary, yet a mere boy had walked in and popped them both as they sat among friends in a crowded diner. Then he casually walked out. Leonard and Whitey were nearly the same age, and, over the years, they had become like brothers. Each enjoyed sharing with the other details of their crimes, reliving and relishing the memories, the accomplishments.

Their last year together had gone by too quickly. Leonard was released knowing Whitey would never see freedom again, having been sentenced to two consecutive life sentences for the double murder. Though freedom awaited him, Leonard shed tears when he told Whitey goodbye.

Whitey had taken care of things for Leonard though. From prison, he had arranged for Leonard to be introduced to upper management of *the family*, and that had led to a sit-down with the boss. The interview was brief. The boss knew of Leonard's accomplishments. He knew of the killing that had landed Leonard in Raiford, and he knew of the unsolved cases as well. Leonard had divulged certain details of each to Whitey, who in turn had fed them to management. Once they were verified through an FBI agent who was on their payroll, Leonard was in. The dirty cop confirmed there were cases just as Leonard described that remained unsolved. The Irish mafia boss admired his work.

No longer confined, he was now a contract killer, a pro. Neat and efficient.

But never had he been as bold as Whitey. He often thought of the story he had heard many times about the hit in the diner. To prove himself, someday Leonard would do something similar. He'd have to learn to shoot a gun though. How difficult could it be? He had always admired Whitey for his courage in walking up to two killers and doing them in front of an audience. That was a different kind of killing than Leonard knew, and because of it, he saw his friend Whitey as the bigger man. Maybe one day Whitey would read about him in the paper and be proud of his friend.

A woman stopped directly in front of Leonard, startling him out of his reverie. She never looked his way. In a moment, she moved on. Leonard let out a breath he had not realized he had been holding. She would have been the one, he thought, as he watched her walk away. If only he were allowed. But he would no longer choose his victims; that was part of the agreement. Leonard had agreed to kill exclusively for *the family,* though he knew that impulses might dictate otherwise.

He refocused on the target and continued to watch, hoping tonight would bring opportunity. He had been supplied with everything he needed to know, which did not include the *why.* That was the agreement: a name, a location, and a death warrant issued by *the family*. It was all he would need, and all he would receive. This one was to have no sexual component, and efforts to conceal the victim's identity would be made. Simple enough. Killing is killing. You needn't hear trumpets to bask in its glory.

# 2

F LOYD SAID, "LOOK it there, he's back."
Mongo looked up from his work.

I STEPPED THROUGH THE BACK DOOR INTO THE SQUAD ROOM, A SEA OF
desks beneath fluorescent lighting where men and women sat or stood or
walked about in business attire. They were speaking into their cell phones
or landlines or staring at computer screens or visiting with other detectives. It was a typical Wednesday morning at the Los Angeles County
Sheriff's Homicide Bureau. No different from the way it had been the last
time I darkened that doorway, though there were several new faces. The
turnover rate rivaled that of a combat post in the Middle East.

But for me, this was no ordinary Wednesday in the office. Not just
another week, another bureau meeting. It was the return from a year's
absence. The return from a traumatic injury, two gunshot wounds that
resulted in the loss of a kidney and a lengthy rehab. Physical and mental.

At times I had silently questioned if I was ready to return. Ready for
the cheerful greetings and welcome backs and handshakes and high fives.

Ready for the questions: How was I doing? How's the wife? What's it like being shot? Cops were direct like that, at least with one another.

How would I answer?

Great.

Wife's gone. Strike two.

Being shot sucks.

I had concealed my concerns about coming back from those in my inner circle, which had been reduced to my partner Floyd, my doctor, and my shrink. I assured each of them I was fit for duty.

It felt different, all of it. As if I were a stranger in this place I once called home. A place in which I'd spent much of my life over the past decade. Much more of it here, with Floyd, than at home.

Everyone seemed to look up at once from their work or conversations, some still holding phones but not speaking, maybe on hold or listening to the party on the other end. For a moment, the room stood completely silent; everything had come to a stop. It was awkward. Almost embarrassing.

My heart beat rapidly and sweat beaded under my hat. Then, suddenly, as if on cue from a director, the characters resumed their activities. They were back to speaking into phones, typing on computers, and talking to one another. The greetings began. Colleagues were welcoming me back. Some from afar, but others approached and gave me hugs or pats on the back. There were genuine smiles and friendly greetings, and I began to feel comfortable again in this place I called home.

My attention was drawn across the room and I locked eyes with those of a friend. My old partner. An ex-wife, I would often call him. Detective Matt "Pretty Boy Floyd" Tyler sat across the room, behind his desk, watching. Studying. Waiting patiently, a burgeoning grin on his face.

---

FLOYD'S PARTNER, MONGO, AS FLOYD CALLED HIM, DETECTIVE MANNY Diaz according to the name plate on his desk, looked up over reading glasses that hung on the end of his nose. He was editing a report that Floyd told him needed to be finished by the end of the day. They had a meeting with the district attorney the next morning and it was the new guy's job to have the case prepared for filing. Mongo had never met his partner's former partner, though he had heard much about him. Maybe too much. Floyd never stopped talking about him, about their cases, about how well they worked together and how everything seemed balanced and cohesive. Floyd often spoke of the night that had become legendary around the bureau, a dark and rainy night in East Los Angeles that resulted in Dickie being shot. Floyd would recount the night, sometimes with a distant stare, and tell Mongo about finding his partner in a pool of blood. He told how Dickie had shot and killed the man who shot him, a convict who had murdered several prostitutes, a big case they had solved. Floyd would recount how he had charged through the back door after hearing the shots, searching frantically for his partner. How he had gone bat-shit crazy and damn near killed the two assholes he encountered on the way in. One of whom was twice Mongo's size, Floyd would say, in both directions.

Mongo had often felt like the new wife who couldn't match up to the former, and he already hated the other woman. He leaned back in his chair, all two-hundred-and-fifty pounds of his five-foot-seven frame, and watched as the man in the fedora walked slowly through the bureau, greeting at least every other detective along the way. Mongo heard the various greetings: "Welcome back," "Great to see you," blah, blah, blah. He watched as some stood and approached the veteran detective, embracing him with a hug or a handshake. Others, mostly the newer guys, sat and watched. It seemed overdone, maybe a bit of a spectacle.

Mongo had dreaded the arrival of this day.

He glanced over to see his partner, Floyd, leaned back in his chair, chewing on a pen and smiling with his hazel eyes, watching as his former partner made his way through the sea of detectives.

Mongo looked back at Detective Richard Jones and saw that through all the greetings and short conversations and distractions along his way, he continually looked in their direction. Back and forth, but regularly, as if he were homed in on Floyd. The two watched each other in the way only best friends or mortal enemies would, as if nothing around them had any significance compared to that which awaited them each.

Soon the man in the hat, Dickie Jones, stood near their desks. He was tall, probably six feet or better, and of average build for a man in his mid-forties. He had a thick mustache that was mostly gray, but hints of red were still there. The room had fallen silent as the two old partners held their gazes. Finally, Dickie smiled at his old partner. Or maybe it was more of a grin.

He let out a breath and looked at Mongo. "You're in my seat."

---

CAPTAIN STOVER WALKED THROUGH THE SQUAD ROOM LOOKING DOWN AT a clipboard he carried in his hand. He was headed toward the podium to start the weekly briefing when he glanced up and saw me watching him. "You're back, uh?"

"Yes sir, and it's good to be here."

He nodded, but appeared skeptical.

I smiled sincerely. We had had our differences at times—that was well known—but I had come back with a new attitude. A new lease on life, so to speak.

Being out on an injury for a year, or as working cops called it, having been on the sick, lame, and lazy list, could definitely change your attitude about work. I had nearly gone crazy from the boredom. You can only read so many books. With Elmore Leonard dead, Wambaugh slowed down, and Connelly doing the best he could but not keeping up with my demand, entertainment had failed me. There was TV, but I could only do so much Judge Judy. COPS was entertaining, but it also made me miss the action. I had avoided the news all together.

I needed to get back to working cases. I needed a fresh kill, a crime scene, a case complete with a suspect on the run and a twisted motive to decipher. A challenge. I always needed to be challenged.

But sometimes you had to be careful what you wished for.

Before he walked away, Stover said, "After the meeting, come see me in my office."

"You got it, boss."

Floyd watched the captain walk away and then looked at me. "He loves us."

"Yeah, right."

"Oh, he does . . . he just has a funny way of showing it. So, how's it feel to be back? You ready to get at it?"

I looked around the room, and then at the back of his partner's head. Mongo. He seemed to be focused on a report in front of him on his desk. Staying out of the conversation, the way a new guy naturally would, or should.

"It's a little weird, I'm not going to lie. But it felt good to get up and shave, put on a suit. Chances are, by the end of the day, I'll wish I'd stayed home watching the golf channel."

"You watch that?"

"No, but I turn it on to drown out the silence. Helps with the naps."

Floyd watched me for a moment. "Yeah, I imagine that sucks. You talk to her at all, since she split?"

"No."

"Maybe you need a dog."

"That wouldn't be fair to the dog. I thought about it, but then I realized once I came back to work, it would be a stay-at-home dog with no kids to raise or work to do. She'd probably start seeing the neighbor dogs behind my back."

He chuckled. "Sluts."

"Exactly."

The captain began speaking from the podium and the chatter throughout the room softened. Floyd lowered his voice and said, "We'll get lunch later, get caught up on shit. You can get to know my partner, Mongo, the madman. Guy's a fucking mule."

*His partner.*

I forced a smile. "Sure, buddy."

---

CAPTAIN STOVER FINISHED HIS PART OF THE MEETING WHICH INCLUDED department and bureau announcements and briefing the troops on administrative bullshit. I hadn't heard any of it; I was too lost in my thoughts as I looked around the room at new and old faces.

Most of the bureau hadn't paid attention; nobody ever did. The cases are what we wanted to know about. New murders.

"Cases?" the captain queried as he looked around the room.

Raymond Cortez stood up from his desk and, with a blue notebook in his hand, made his way to the podium. There were a few jeers and someone whistled and another said, "Oh look, Cortez actually caught a case."

He looked over the podium and smiled at his peers. Like the rest of us, he knew it was a tough crowd, and nobody ever got a pass.

"My partner and I picked up an interesting one in Santa Clarita over the weekend. It started as a missing persons case, but before Missings could do much with it, the body turned up in a parked car in the industrial area near Magic Mountain.

"We believe the victim to be Marilynn Chaney, a forty-two-year-old white woman—"

"Caucasian, you asshole," someone yelled from the back.

He peered over his glasses and smiled, then, returning to his notebook, he continued speaking. "—who was last seen at about nineteen hundred hours leaving a grocery store near her work. She was a real estate agent, and her office was next to a Vons market, off Valencia Boulevard, not far from the interstate. She had apparently walked over to the grocery before leaving work, picked up a few items, and then walked out to her car. The manager knows her and remembered seeing her leave. There was nothing suspicious or out of the ordinary for her stop, what she bought, or how she acted, according to the manager. He was the last to see her alive, as far as we know. Other than her killer, of course."

"Does the store have video?" someone asked.

"Yes, the store has video cameras that cover most of the interior and part of the parking lot. The hard drives were seized as evidence and are with the tech crew now. So far, no word on that.

"I haven't heard of any similar cases, but if you have anything close, please let me or my partner, Jerry White, know. We're checking with LAPD and other agencies in the San Fernando Valley—Burbank, Glendale, and San Fernando—to see if they've had anything like this lately."

"White still works here?" someone asked.

He smiled again. "I'm without a partner, currently, so I pulled White out of retirement for one case. Unsolveds won't miss him."

There was more chatter, a few chuckles, and as another detective made his way to the front with a blue notebook in hand, Ray stood looking across the room. He seemed to have more to say, but hesitated. He appeared to focus on the wall to the south side of the room where the secretaries routinely gathered to listen in on the briefings. I wasn't the only one to notice his reluctance to continue. There was an awkward silence. The detective who would brief the next case stood to the side, waiting. The captain watched, and he too looked around, as if trying to see what Raymond was looking at or for.

Floyd glanced over at me and frowned. I shrugged.

Ray finally said, "There's something else, but this is holdback information, so it doesn't leave this room . . ."

Someone said, "Jesus Christ, he's coming out."

Ray seemed to not notice the comment and began speaking over the chuckles that ensued. He said, "Our victim was decapitated, and her hands were removed—cut off somehow, cleanly. None of the missing body parts have been recovered."

Floyd looked back at me.

"Jesus Christ," I said, mostly under my breath.

He frowned. "Santa Clarita."

I nodded.

Floyd said, "I don't like that one bit."

I took in a deep breath and let it out slowly as I shook my head. I knew what he was thinking. We had always been that way, able to read one another easily. He put two and two together—real estate agent and Santa Clarita—and thought about Valerie, my soon-to-be ex-wife. He knew I'd be on the same track and equally troubled. Neither of us ever took anything for granted. We were both quick to see the worst-case possibility of any situation, and brace against it. Many cops were this way. When normal people called home and the wife didn't answer because she had the baby in the bath or had stepped outside with the trash, they made a mental note to call back in a bit. Cops, however, saw their wives tied and bound or worse, and began orchestrating a plan to rescue them.

"You need to call her."

I nodded.

"How'd you ID her?" someone asked Ray.

"Well, I guess technically we don't have a positive ID. We're going off of the Missing Person report. The vehicle our victim was recovered in belongs to the missing person. Our victim matches the general description of the missing person, so we have to assume it's her at this point, unless something causes us to believe otherwise."

"Sexual assault?"

"There doesn't appear to have been any sexual assault. She was wearing pants and a blouse, panties and a bra underneath, and she didn't appear to have been re-dressed. The autopsy didn't come up with any evidence of recent sexual intercourse."

"Where is this industrial center?"

"The recovery site is in the industrial area near Magic Mountain, just off of Magic Mountain Parkway, if you're familiar with that area. Not too far from the interstate. It's fairly isolated at night, with few businesses having any after-hours activity.

I pictured the scene. I wondered if she had kids. How was her marriage? Any affairs? What's the story on the old man? How did the killer get there? How did he leave? Why was she there? Was she forced to drive there, and then she was murdered? Where did the killer stand or sit? Was he in the car, or outside of the car? Was he next to her, or in the back seat? I had all of these questions but wasn't comfortable asking. I felt like a guest in my own home. It would take a while, maybe, for me to feel confident again. Maybe a couple of cases. Maybe a couple of months.

Ray was a good guy, and a damn good cop. This was an interesting case, a real distraction from my return, my loneliness, my impending divorce . . . I'd ask him more about it later. Hit him up with a cup of coffee and get more details from him. Not that I had an investment in the case, but hearing it briefed had stirred me and made me excited about being back and doing the job.

Cortez was saying, "That's about it, guys, hit me up later if you have anything for me or want to know more about the case."

He walked away with his head down and the ever-present smile on his face.

We clapped.

It seemed odd to me that we did, yet each briefed case was followed by applause. Not an overly cheerful or congratulatory applause, but an applause nonetheless. A colleague would provide the gruesome details of a citizen's violent death, and we would clap when he or she finished.

Further proof that none of us was right in the head.

# 3

WHEN THE MEETING concluded, I rose from my borrowed chair and followed Captain Stover to his office. He paused at the door and looked back. "You need to grab a cup first?"

"Nah, I'm good," I said, thinking maybe an adult beverage would be more appropriate.

We took our seats, the captain in his big leather chair at the helm, and me in the visitor's chair that I had sat in on many prior occasions, none of which had left warm and fuzzy memories. It reminded me of the grade school principal's office where I had accumulated frequent flier miles and earned the distinction of signing his paddle, an honor reserved for repeat offenders.

But that was then. I no longer suffered corporal punishment, nor did I assume a subordinate role with my superiors. It is true that law enforcement operates in a paramilitary fashion with the rank, authority, and attendant discipline, but that was for the kids, in my opinion. The young deputies. The rookies with a few years on or maybe even ten, but still working in a patrol environment. This was Homicide—the big leagues—and those of us who made the rank expected to be treated in more of a businesslike manner.

It was perhaps this attitude, in part, for which I continually found myself embattled.

"What's up, skipper?"

"How do you feel?"

"Like a million bucks. All healed up and ready to work."

He tugged at the knot of his tie. "Before you're back on the floor, you're going to need a release from the department shrink—"

"Jesus, boss . . ."

"You were shot, nearly killed. It's protocol, Richard, not something I pulled out of my ass in order to fight with you."

I nodded.

"The timing also isn't great, in that we're full on the floor for the first time in years. I wouldn't have anywhere to put you right now anyway."

"Where to put me? . . . Why wouldn't I go back to where I was, Team Two, with my old partner?"

"He's training now, and they're full. Every team is full."

I glanced through the window that separates his office from the hallway and watched for a moment as detectives passed by, chatting and chuckling and enjoying the job because they had partners. "So, what are you going to do with me, stick me in Missing Persons?"

He leaned back in his chair and grinned. "Even *I* wouldn't send you to Missings. No, I'm going to put you in Unsolveds for now. They can always use more bodies. If you like it and want to stay back there, fine. If not, we'll bring you out when something opens up—as long as the shrink gives the okay."

How could I argue? Unsolveds wasn't a bad place to be. Most detectives who went there did so in their last couple of years in preparation for retirement. The perks were regular hours, no callouts—generally speaking —and it was less likely you would generate cases that would require court appearances once you retired. The bulk of the detectives in that unit were solid people, men and women I had worked with here at Homicide and in previous assignments.

I also realized he wasn't trying to punish me. It was just business, the way it was. I couldn't expect to come back and step right into my old spot, as much as I had tried to fool myself into believing it was possible.

It suddenly struck me: "Wait, didn't Cortez say he was without a partner? They pulled White out of Unsolveds to assist on that case he just briefed."

"His partner's status is up in the air currently. White assisted him and will work the case with him until his partner is back."

"Okay, you're the boss."

He hadn't expected that. I wasn't sure if he was skeptical, or relieved. He had no doubt expected a fight. But I didn't want to fight; I never had. Most of the time, I regretted the battles I'd have with supervisors. I didn't want to ruin my job. It was all I had left. I had successfully destroyed two marriages now, and it seemed I was only happy when I was busy at work. It was the badge and gun, the chase of the bad guys, the challenge of sending them away in a system that favored the criminals. I needed to keep in perspective that this job was my entire identity. It was my lifeblood.

---

AFTER STEPPING OUT OF THE CAPTAIN'S OFFICE, I PAUSED BRIEFLY IN THE hallway. Coffee to the right, the squad room to the left. But I didn't currently have a home in the squad room, out on *the floor* as we called it. Currently, I was part of the backroom, Unsolved Homicides. Commonly called Unsolveds. It was better than Missings, but still not the floor. The squad room, the trenches where the real work was done by hard chargers, real bulldogs who were carefully selected to work the elite Homicide Bureau because of their investigative skills and strong character. In our department, working Homicide was an honor. We were the highest paid detectives in the county, as well we should be. We had cars and phones and computers all provided to us. The lieutenants were there to fill out schedules, write murder memos, and sign overtime slips. They didn't interfere in our investigations and they didn't inquire as to our whereabouts or progress on any particular case, other than for the purpose of staying informed. In baseball terms, we had made it to *the show*, the big leagues.

I opted for a cup of coffee and then I'd get it over with, walk into

Unsolveds and make my first appearance. See if there was an empty desk or if I'd be relegated to a chair in the corner. I glanced at my watch thinking it must be nearing the noon hour, and though I made it no practice, a cocktail lunch might be in order.

Where the hell was Floyd?

As I poured a cup, the answer came from behind me in classic Floyd vernacular: "Hey, Dickie, where've you been? I saw you streamline into the captain's office after the meeting; you're not sucking his ass already, are you? Jesus."

The musky scent of his cologne drifted over my shoulder as he came to a stop. I turned and handed him the cup I had just filled for myself.

He gladly received it. "Thanks, Dickie. So, what's the deal, where's he putting you?"

"Unsolveds."

"Unsolveds? . . . Jesus, you pussy."

"Until something on the floor opens up, and not until the shrink gives an okay. Apparently, I'm nuts."

"Well, yeah, Dickie, I've been telling you that for years."

I turned with my cup in hand. "How's your partner?"

Floyd drifted to a nearby table, set his cup down, and pulled out a chair. I followed. He smiled at a secretary who walked by, and kept his eyes on her until she was through the door to the secretariat.

"He's good. Came from Lennox, he's a hard worker, easy to get along with. He can also pick up your car if you have a flat, save the time of using a jack to change the tire. The guy's a regular goon."

I nodded.

"What are they going to have you doing in Unsolveds?"

"Working unsolved cases? What the hell do you think I'd do in Unsolveds?"

"I know, asshole. I mean, who are you pairing up with, did he say?"

I shook my head.

"Poodle-head just went back there a few months ago, maybe you could team up with him. That idiot would keep you entertained. Your sister, Beth, she's back there now. That's who I'd pick. There's Lopes, but he'd drive you crazy, going in a hundred directions at any given time, seeing if he can lie about more overtime than Lee. Or, you could do what you're probably more likely to do anyway and just work by yourself. Find a corner and pull your hat down low and mumble about how much you hate everyone."

Poodle-head. The wiry little Irishman with pale blue eyes whose curly hair earned him the nickname. His antics, stunts, and constant clowning earned him a regular following at after-shift gatherings where cops drank heavily and laughed heartily to forget the sights, sounds, and smells of a night's work. Seldom called by his given name, Rob O'Neill, his excellence in gang investigation had brought him to the bureau.

Beth Jones, my *sista* from another *mista*, would be an excellent choice. She was a good street cop-turned-detective after proving herself on the mean streets of South Los Angeles. It would be difficult to find a more pleasant partner, and she would fill the void of female companionship left by the wife. Not that there would be romantic interest either direction, but the company and conversation of a lady might be a nice way to spend long days. If I couldn't work with my partner, Floyd, that is.

Or Lopes, pronounced with one syllable, rhyming with ropes, or mopes. Davey Lopes, but not the former Dodgers second baseman. *Our* Davey Lopes. A broad-shouldered, stocky, former Marine with gray hair and attentive eyes. A tough ghetto cop whose reputation preceded him from the streets to the prisons to the offices of our executives. The only problem was, he never went home. I'd been accused of being a workaholic on more than a few occasions, but honestly, I was a bit tired now, and not sure I could keep his pace. The man had nearly thirty years on the job and still ran circles around the youngsters.

Steven Lee might work. A constant source of entertainment, the small-statured Jewish kid from Chicago, who had a reputation as a topnotch cop, was one of our best investigators. He was also an insufferable asshole, but in a humorous way for those who knew him well enough to know the difference. He could tell a chief or the sheriff how stupid they were while getting them to smile with him.

"Or Torres," Floyd said and grinned.

"Yeah, that'd be great."

Torres and I still glared at each other after all of these years. He was a former gang detective who had been at Homicide several years before me and had been involved in the case of a murdered deputy from Century Station. At the time, I was working as a station detective there, assigned to the Crime Impact Team. My partner and I had developed several good leads on the suspect, and when we passed them along, he dismissed them out of hand. One such lead was a location, and a week or so later someone else came up with information about the same location and they hit it. The residents confirmed the suspect had been there the week before when my partner and I informed Torres of the information we had. Later, we assisted on a search warrant for the same case, and Torres insisted we be delicate with the occupants because, although they were related to the suspect, there was no reason to believe they were at all involved in gang activity. I emerged from my assigned search area with a stack of photographs showing otherwise, pictures of family members posed in gang attire and possessing firearms in the killer's presence. Torres ordered me to leave the photographs, saying it wasn't a search and destroy mission. I tossed the photographs on the ground and walked out mumbling a few nice words for him. Then I waited for my partner at the car and never spoke to Torres again. He should have—and could have—used the photographs to play hardball with the lying family members. Rather, he treated them as respectable citizens. There was little doubt they could have led us to the whereabouts of the killer, had they been properly motivated to do so.

To make matters worse, when I made the list to come to Homicide, Torres had had the nerve to badmouth me openly at the bureau. He didn't know how many friends I had there, nor did he realize it would get back to me. But it did. Fortunately, nobody with influence seemed to care what he had to say about me; I was selected to come to the bureau on the next list. And neither of us ever tried to make it less awkward once I arrived.

"You two would make a nice couple."

"I'd kill him," I said, "guaranteed."

"Who wouldn't you kill? Jesus, Dickie, I think I've spoiled you all these years, made it too much fun for you. Now you're just plain crabby about the whole thing."

I sipped my coffee. "Whatever."

"I have to head out, Dickie. We have some follow-up to do on our dead baby case over in El Monte. Then we're going to grab lunch at Manny's. You want to meet us in East L.A.?"

"Maybe."

He stood. "Maybe, huh? Well aren't you a daisy."

As he walked away, I said, "See ya later, partner."

He said over his shoulder, "Let me know what you decide about lunch, dickhead."

---

I WALKED THROUGH THE FRONT DESK LOBBY AREA WHERE A DESK CREW sat answering phones, transferring calls, taking messages, and receiving death notices. The latter of which is the beginning process of a homicide investigation. The lobby is the main thoroughfare of the office and is centered in the building. One path from the lobby leads to the administrative offices—the captain, his lieutenant and secretary—and further down the hall, the kitchen. Beyond the kitchen is the secretariat where a dozen underappreciated ladies spend their days—and sometimes, nights—typing lengthy reports from dictations from detectives of varying degrees of oratory skills and sobriety. There were two other paths from the front desk: one led to the squad room, the other into a smaller office area wherein detectives who investigate unsolved homicide cases are assigned. That's where I was headed.

Lopes sat alone in Unsolveds. A phone dangled from the side of his head as he leaned back in his chair with the look of a man who had put in a ten-hour shift: his collar was unbuttoned, the knot of his tie had already been loosened, and his sleeves were rolled up. It wasn't yet noon.

He nodded when I walked in. "Hey man, what's up?"

There were five desks other than his. I pulled a chair from one of them and had a seat. "Nothing much, Davey. I guess I'm going to be back here for a while. How've you been?"

He rolled his eyes. "Busy. I've got a wire running on the mob."

"*La Eme?*" I asked, doing my best to pronounce it with a Spanish flare.

He sneered. "Yeah, goddamn Mexican mafia, I can't get away from them."

I smiled. He was lying. He loved working cases involving the Mexican mafia the way the Yankees loved meeting up with the Red Sox, or the Cowboys and Redskins, Republicans and Democrats. He had dedicated nearly a decade to investigating nothing other than crimes of the Eme when he was assigned to Prison Gangs, a Detective Division assignment he had held before coming to Homicide. Nobody knew the structure and players better, and nobody had been more effective at putting a dent in their criminal enterprise through ongoing investigations. Lopes had turned several hardened gang members into state's witnesses, and by doing so he had been able to obtain convictions against many of the ruthless killers among them.

"You'd be lost without the mob."

He nodded and then his eyes drifted away, looking at his desk now as he leaned forward in his chair and spoke into the phone. "Yeah, Hernandez, Little Spooky from Big Hazard. He's in your C-block . . . No, I'll come see him there . . . Yeah, next couple of days . . . Okay, thank you, sir."

He set the phone back in its cradle. "You coming back here to Unsolveds?"

"I guess, for a while. Until something opens up on the floor."

"Good, we can partner up. You up for a road trip?"

"Where're you headed?"

"I need to go up to Pelican Bay, beat this gangster's nuts. Spooky from Hazard. I need to go remind him about what an asshole I can be."

I chuckled. "You're still messing with them, huh?"

"We have a wire up right now, about a dozen cell phones and two pods at the county jail. These assholes are out of control. A lot of people are getting killed and nobody seems willing to talk about it. I think a bunch of the murder cases are mob related. We're looking to solve a lot of cases when it all comes together, if all goes well."

"This guy, Spooky, he a suspect?"

Davey Lopes shook his head. "Snitch. He's supposed to be giving me information on the regular, but he's been awful quiet. Hopefully they haven't gotten to him."

"Is he a made member?"

"Nah, an affiliate. But he's put in plenty of work for the mafia and has a lot of inside information. He's looking to improve his living conditions, cause he ain't ever getting out."

I smiled. "He doesn't realize they'll kill him?"

Lopes returned the smile. "I've got him convinced he'll have it made. We'll put him in Tehachapi where there's a bunch of other punks and snitches. Shit, they've formed a social club there. Everyone gets along and they're not even stabbing each other very often."

Lopes worked the gangs as well as anyone, better than most. He had developed informants in most of the Latino gangs in the county and half of the black ones too. Not all detectives worked informants to solve their cases. Not all detectives even knew how to work informants. I enjoyed talking to him about the Mexican gangs.

"Yeah, shit, why not? What do I have better to do than watch the champ work the mob?"

"Pfft, whatever. Okay, good, I could use the company. We'll leave tomorrow and make it an overnighter. You can buy me a steak and get me drunk, tell me what it's like getting shot."

"I'll do two of the three."

He stood from the desk. "Ok, deal. Let's go get some lunch and a beer, I'll fill you in on the wire. You may want to get in on it, the overtime's unlimited."

"I'll take a raincheck, Davey. I want to find Ray, talk to him about his Santa Clarita case."

He frowned. "What's he got?"

"You missed the meeting?"

"I don't have time for that shit."

Mandatory was not a word that impressed Davey Lopes to any degree that would cause him to alter his agenda.

"Ray briefed a case about a woman found murdered in her car, decapitated and her hands were cut off. Up in Santa Clarita."

Lopes stood pondering, but only for a moment, his eyes scanning the room though likely not seeing anything outside of his head. He was probably visualizing a headless, handless woman in a car. "No shit, huh? Maybe we do have real mobsters out here whacking folks, fucking

Guido and company. You don't see that shit very often, not on the west coast."

I nodded. "It's an unusual case, that's for sure."

He pulled his jacket off of a coat tree and slung it over his shoulder, stopping before stepping out of the office. He looked back at me and said, "Let's leave here tomorrow morning about ten."

"You got it, buddy."

# 4

I FOUND RAYMOND Cortez sitting at his desk with photos spread out in front of him. His partner, Jerry White, sat perched on his chair, crowding Ray. The two of them were studying the photos and conversing as I walked up.

"Hey guys."

They both looked up.

"Hey, partner, how're ya feeling?" asked Ray.

Jerry said, "Welcome back, Dickie."

"I'm okay," I said. My gaze drifted past them to the desk with the photos. "That's her, huh?"

"Yeah," Ray said, "ever see anything like it?"

"Not on a murder case," I said. "I've seen a couple of decaps from train fatalities, guys laying across the tracks to end it all."

"It's a first for me," Jerry said. "It takes some kind of sick bastard to do this shit. Hopefully it's not the beginning—"

"Of a serial killer," Ray said, finishing his partner's sentence. "That's all we need."

"You mind?" I asked, reaching toward the stack of photos that sat to the side of the six or eight that were spread across his blotter.

"Be our guest," Ray said, pushing the pile closer to me.

I sat down in an empty chair near them and put on my reading glasses. Slowly I went through the stack, studying each photo as if searching for hidden clues.

The first dozen or so were the overall scene photographs, pictures taken from the outskirts of the crime scene looking in, capturing not only the vehicle that held the deceased, but the surrounding area. There were rows of uniform slate-gray buildings with subtle green trim on their windows, doors, and eaves. Walkways led from one building to the next, meandering through impeccably manicured grass with elegant landscaping of bushes and trees and red bark ground covering. There were vehicles scattered throughout the background, but none near the lone black BMW. It was the victim's vehicle, and it sat alone in the shade of a tree, parked on the side of a corner building.

I looked back at the photos that showed buildings, checking for cameras. There were none that were obvious from the pictures.

The next twenty photos were victim perspective shots, pictures taken by the photographer as he stood close to the victim's vehicle, shooting outward in a 360-degree series. I looked for surveillance cameras on the buildings and noted the various vehicles parked in lots and on the street. I studied the terrain beyond the buildings that showed undeveloped mountains of sagebrush and wild grass. I was familiar with the area, and knew this vacant land sprawled to the north but ended quickly to the west where it butted against the freeway. I wondered if the killer had escaped on foot, and whether he had gone through the mountains to avoid detection or simply walked down the road. He may have had a vehicle waiting. Likely an unoccupied vehicle. Unless the killer had not worked alone. Apparently, there was no sexual component to the killing. So maybe it had been a team of killers. Professionals? What *was* the motive?

The thought resonated and marinated in my head for a moment though I didn't mention it aloud. *Professionals . . .* Might she have been a specific target? If so, why? A sexual predator often chooses a random victim only for physical attributes or perhaps vulnerability. I wondered which was the case in this killing. Predator, or pro? The answer to that question would dictate the direction of the investigation and measure the difficulty of it as well. A predator would strike again and again, leaving more clues with each case until captured. If it were professionals, they were one and done.

No trails to follow and no evidence left behind. In that case, the investigation would be approached from an entirely different angle. We would work to discover who would have paid to have her killed, and why.

I needed to call Val.

"Was there a purse?" I blurted out without looking up from the photos.

Ray said, "No, and that's something that bothers me about the ID. I wish her purse had been there."

"Jewelry?"

Ray chuckled, "Where would we find it? I mean, there were certainly no rings, bracelets, necklaces, or earrings left behind . . . those items probably went in the shopping bag with the body parts."

"You sick bastard," his partner remarked.

"Bowling ball bag."

"What's that, Dickie? What do you mean?"

I looked up. "The gentle giant. I can't remember his real name, but that's what they called him, that asshole up on the coast killing college girls back in the seventies. He took the head of a victim home with him, carrying it in a bowling ball bag. Years later, he spoke about it in an interview. He said it had been a real trip because as he was walking up the stairs to his apartment, a young couple passed by him, presumably on their way out for a date. Two college kids giggling and enjoying life without a worry in the world, having no idea they were within inches of another college girl's head in his bag. As they passed one another, the couple greeted him, and he smiled in return. I'll never forget, he described the encounter as 'really making the gears squeak in his head.' Can you imagine that?

"Then he took the head in its bag and went into his apartment where he lived with his mother. He got off on that too, having a dead girl's head in a bowling bag inside the apartment with his mother who constantly bitched at him about cleaning up after himself. Now he walks in and gives mom a kiss while holding this bag with a girl's head in it. He ended up killing the mother too, by the way."

"The mom?"

"Yeah."

"Were you involved in that one?" Ray asked.

I frowned at him. "How old do you think I am?"

He shrugged.

"No, but I've watched the interview. If I'm not mistaken, it was an FBI profiler's interview of him. You know, that's what those assholes do, the profilers. They fly around the country talking to the killers we lock up and then they get famous by writing books about it. They tell everyone how hard it was seeing all those victims, all the crime scenes, never mentioning all they ever saw were the photographs."

"Fucking feds," Jerry White said.

"Exactly," I agreed. "What about DNA, you guys?"

"That's on our list," Ray said. "We plan to get something from the missing person's home, a toothbrush or something we can pull DNA from to compare to the dead woman."

Jerry said, "Wouldn't that be a trip, if they don't match up?"

Ray shook his head with his eyes open wide, as if to say, *Don't even think that!*

I didn't reply. My focus was on the scene, my mind spreading the pieces of the puzzle before me and then moving them around, trying to see the whole picture.

I finished going through the photographs and went through them once more, studying each one before moving on to the next. Jerry White had walked away. Ray Cortez was on the phone. People were speaking in the background, but I didn't hear any of their words or pay any mind to the activity around me.

"The seat . . ."

Ray tucked the phone beneath his chin. He furrowed his brow and said, "What?"

I pushed a photo toward him. It depicted the interior of the victim's vehicle from outside of the opened driver's door. The victim sat in the seat, slumped over toward the passenger's side. Her legs were stretched toward the pedals.

"It's back, probably all the way. Her legs wouldn't reach those pedals."

He studied the photograph and then looked up. "I think you're right."

"She didn't drive that car there, Ray."

Captain Stover rounded the corner. "Jones, I need you and White in my office."

"Okay," I said, "I think Jerry's back in Unsolveds . . . I'll grab him."

The captain walked away and I stood from my chair. "Wonder what that's about."

"I guess you'll find out," Ray said. "I'm sure it will be terrific, whatever it is."

I chuckled. "No doubt. Two meetings with the captain on my first day back; what could be better?"

---

I GATHERED JERRY WHITE FROM UNSOLVEDS AND WE WALKED TO THE captain's office together, Jerry asking if I knew what the hell the captain wanted.

I said, "Probably a promotion, or maybe a new car. I'm sure it's going to be great."

Jerry grunted.

The captain didn't look up from his desk when we entered. "Have a seat."

We sat across the desk and waited.

He sat a file down. "Jones, you're going to pair up with White in Unsolveds. Which means you'll get involved in this headless woman case. They can use the help."

White sat with his chin tucked into his hand, indifferent, bored.

I said, "Okay, sounds good boss . . . is that it?"

"No," he said, and shifted his eyes from me to Jerry White, and back. "The sheriff is all over this thing. Santa Clarita has lost its mind, the mayor and councilmen are having the shits over this murder. Shit like this doesn't happen up there, so this case better get solved, and fast. I don't care what you three have to do to get it solved, but you find that bitch's head and find her killer. Got it?"

I nodded and looked over to see White nod too, but just slightly. He wasn't the overachiever type, the hard-charging, stay late, kill-yourself-to-find-out-who-killed-someone-else type. He was in his last few years, and that's why he was in Unsolveds. Straight hours, no callouts, very little court. He barely earned his pay. He wasn't shitting any of us though, it wasn't just that he was close to retirement; he hadn't been that great a decade earlier either.

Stover leaned back in his chair. "Okay, that's it. Let me know if you guys need anything. I'm serious, this is a big priority case now."

"One question, boss."

"What is it?"

"Why isn't Cortez part of this meeting?" I asked. "Isn't he the lead?"

"He already knows. I talked to him first, asked him if he would work with you."

"Why the hell wouldn't he?" I snapped back, pissed at the comment.

He shrugged. "How the hell should I know? You don't seem to get along with just anyone. You and your old partner out there have a habit of pissing people off."

I huffed and got up from my chair. "You're one to talk."

"Just as I thought," he said to my back as I walked out of his office, "nothing's changed with your shitty attitude."

# 5

LEONARD PICKED UP the phone and recognized the scratchy voice on the other end. It was the voice of a man he'd met shortly after being released from Raiford. The nameless, right-hand man of the Irish mob boss, a thin, pockmarked man whose shel-lacked black hair was fashioned to withstand a category five hurricane, and whose eyes bugged out of his head like Marty Feldman's in *Young Frankenstein.*

The boss, Mr. Patrick McFarland, would never be the one to call; he had made that clear during the initial meeting. His assistant would make all necessary contact. Whatever the assistant told him, Leonard was to take it as if it came from the burning bush. Leonard recalled picturing the pock-marked man on fire when the boss had said it. The nameless man had glared back at him with his malicious eyes, as if the stare was meant to intimidate him. The wannabe goombah motherfucker was lucky they were in the boss's office, not walking the yard at Raiford. Leonard didn't like the man from the first time they met.

"Is it done, the job?" he asked.

"Of course it's done. You said have it done by—"

"I know what I fucking said. Do I need you to tell me what I fucking said? No, I don't. I don't need you to tell me anything. Now, do you want to shut the fuck up and listen?"

Leonard didn't respond. He didn't like being talked to this way, no matter who was speaking. He tossed a burning cigarette butt out the window and forced a plume of smoke from his lungs.

"You there?"

"Yeah, I'm here. It was done over the weekend, what, three, four days ago."

"Okay, boss just wanted to make sure it was completed. Can you take another?"

"It's what I do, right?"

There was a long pause. Leonard pulled the phone from his ear and looked at it. The call still showed on the screen. He thought that meant they were still connected, but he wasn't sure, not yet very familiar with cell phones.

His contempt for this assistant could not be concealed. The whole arrangement should be a simple one. Someone tells him who to kill, where to find said target, and it's a done deal. How difficult could it be? The last had been a woman. The client wanted a souvenir. Okay, fine. Leonard didn't ask questions. Whatever you want, you kinky bastard. Done. Next?

After a moment, the assistant said, "You'll get the details, same way as before. Check your box in two days. Oh—hey, you still with me?"

"Yeah, I'm here."

"You got the souvenir he asked for, right?"

Leonard's eyes drifted away from a boy who walked with his mother into a market. He now looked up through the window into a clear blue sky. "Yes, I have the souvenir."

"Okay, send it to our box right away, and don't forget."

Leonard rolled his eyes behind dark sunglasses. "Yeah, I know, you told me."

After disconnecting, Leonard took a swig from a bottle of Cuervo *Especial* he had concealed in brown paper. It was pretty good, after a couple swigs. He hadn't consumed alcohol before going to prison, but there he was introduced to *pruno*, prison liquor made from fruits, sugar, and water, usually in a Ziplock bag. It almost always tasted terrible, but he enjoyed the high he experienced. Now he was experimenting, trying to find a drink that tasted good to him. He didn't like beer—he had tried different ones—so he decided on liquor. So far, he had tried rum, tequila, brandy, and a couple of different whiskeys. He thought tequila would be his go-to.

He waited until the woman reappeared with the young boy. Now she was pushing a cart full of grocery bags. He watched her load them into a car, and when she took the cart away, the boy stood waiting. Alone. Vulnerable. Easy prey.

Leonard started his car. He put the cap on his bottle and set it aside. He looked both directions and then turned in the opposite direction from where the boy stood. As he drove away, it hit him: the bitch had reminded him of his mother.

# 6

THE NEXT MORNING, I walked into Unsolveds to find Davey Lopes sitting at his desk with papers and files scattered about. He looked over the top of his glasses.

"Ready to go?"

"Oh shit, I totally forgot. Let me check with Cortez, see what he has going. I'm supposed to be working with him and White on that Santa Clarita case now, per your captain."

He sneered. "You mean working with Cortez."

"Cortez and White. They caught it together."

"You mean working with Cortez," he repeated, now with a smirk on his face.

"Sorry, I'm a little slow this morning. Yeah, I guess that would be the case."

"That's why Captain put you on it. Otherwise—if it was just him and White—Ray would be working it alone."

"I hear there's a lot of heat coming down from Santa Clarita. The sheriff has his eye on this one."

Lopes stood and started gathering his files, tucking them one at a time into a soft-sided leather briefcase. "You better stay then. Stover will shit a brick if you go for a road trip with me when you're supposed to be helping Ray."

He was right. I had looked forward to the trip and was disappointed that I wasn't going. I enjoyed Lopes's company, and I always enjoyed a road trip, but working a good case trumped all.

"Sorry, buddy."

Lopes grabbed his jacket and started for the door. "No worries, man. Have fun, I'll see you tomorrow. I have a private plane to catch."

WHEN RAYMOND CORTEZ CAME IN HE ASKED IF I WAS READY TO GET started. He said he had interviews lined up with family members of the missing woman. I thought it interesting he didn't refer to the family members as the family of his murder victim. He seemed to be cautious, if only subconsciously, to not assume they were one and the same, the missing person and the murder victim. To his credit, there was yet to be a positive identification to link the two together. The physical evidence would strongly suggest the dead lady was the missing person, but we would tiptoe around the topic with the family when it came up. Which it would.

We loaded up in his sedan, a Crown Vic like most of the cars in the lot. This one was blue. As I settled into the passenger's seat, I asked, "White's not going?"

"I haven't seen him yet. We wait for him, we won't get anything done."

I sensed the underlying meaning and thought of Lopes's comments. "What's up with that?"

He turned out of the parking lot, headed north on Eastern Avenue and moved over for a turn onto Bandini, which he would take over to the Long Beach Freeway north. He glanced over through mirrored shades. "He's a lazy fuck is what's up with that."

There was no reason to argue, or even reply.

"I'm glad you're back, Dickie, to be honest. I figured I was going to be working this one alone. When I heard you were going to be in Unsolveds for a while, I asked Stover if I could steal you."

I looked over at him and smiled. "That asshole."

"What?"

"He made it out to be his idea. Said the sheriff is on his balls, Santa Clarita's lost its mind. He had the audacity to say he needed to talk to you about it first, make sure you'd be okay working with me, like I'm a problem child or something."

Ray shook his head. "You're right about him being an asshole, partner."

Ray Cortez called all other cops "partner" as a manner of speech. Still, it sounded funny for some reason. I hadn't had anyone other than Floyd as a partner for five years. He had been my partner until the day I was shot, which had caused me to be off work for a year. Now it almost felt like I was cheating on him, being teamed up with someone new. Of course, that sonofabitch was cheating first, him and his boy, Mongo. I saw Mongo in my head, looking at me when I approached Floyd's desk yesterday morning, watching me like I was going to steal his donut. There was no way I'd get between that man and his food.

I pictured the two of them in the car, Mongo taking up two-thirds of the front seat and Floyd leaned up against the passenger door, no doubt making Mongo drive everywhere they went. It had always been one of our ongoing arguments, whose turn it was to drive. Whose turn it was to drive and whose turn it was to buy. Those were the arguments we most often had. He always won the driving argument, insisting each time it was my turn behind the wheel, usually heading straight to my car as if there was no need for further discussion. But I usually conned him into picking up the meal tabs, so it all equalled out.

I wondered if Floyd was talking about me or had been. My ears were burning. It was my second day back, and I was teamed up with Ray Cortez working what might be the most interesting murder of the year. Who knows, it could turn out to be the most interesting of the decade, maybe since the Night Stalker case. The gossip in the bureau was not unlike that in a hair salon, and I was certain Floyd already knew about my assignment. I'd missed lunch with him yesterday and he had texted me and asked where the hell I was. I didn't reply, because I didn't want to, and I was never afraid to deny receiving the message. It was one of my tactics that I used on the wife, playing dumb to technology. But I don't think she ever believed it. Floyd wouldn't either.

The wife. Jesus, I had forgotten to call and check on her, see if she had heard about the murder in Santa Clarita, not far from her new place. Maybe she even knew the missing person. Most of the realtors in Santa Clarita would likely know one another.

Ray was saying, "We're going to the house first. The husband's expecting us and mentioned his daughter might be there too."

I pictured my soon-to-be ex as the headless woman in the car, and tried to drive the image out of my mind. This was something I still hadn't mentioned to the shrink. I feared the revelation of such horrible thoughts would make me look less stable. What would she—or anyone else—think about a man who saw his wife in murder scenes? How would anyone understand it? This wasn't something new; it had been the case for years, and it had always bothered me. It wasn't only the wife I would see at crime scenes, it was friends, coworkers, colleagues . . . I wondered if others had this happen, but didn't dare to ask.

"Depending on how it goes, we may want to figure a way to get hubby down to the station, have a chat with him outside the daughter's presence," Ray had continued, taking his eyes off the road several times to glance over at me.

But my mind was still on the soon-to-be ex. I hadn't heard from her for a few weeks. I tried calling a couple times, but she never answered. I finally left a voicemail letting her know I was cleared to return to work, given the okay by my doc and would be coming back this week, just wanted her to know. But still I hadn't heard a thing. I felt my temperature rise as my mind went back to Val as the headless woman.

"Thoughts?"

What had he said? "Yeah, Ray, whatever sounds good, buddy."

There was no way. She lived and worked in Santa Clarita, but there was no way it could have been her. It was the missing woman, no doubt. It was her car at the scene and the recovered body fit the general description of her. This isn't rocket science.

Jesus.

This was just my twisted brain tormenting me. Demons had taken refuge in my mind years ago, playing tricks on me so that I constantly question my sanity. The shrink understood and explained it, once I stopped lying to her. She had said it was part of the psychological trauma that I had encountered on a regular basis for so many years, though she stopped shy of calling it PTSD. She knows the rules, and she knows I would be out of the bureau for sure—maybe the department—if she diagnosed me with Post-traumatic Stress Disorder. But we both knew I had it, and we both knew that we both knew. It was like our dirty little secret.

That was when I started to feel fondly toward her, this shrink who used to give me nothing but headaches and stress. Sometime over the past year, since I'd been shot, she seemed to warm up to me. She seemed to be an advocate for me, not the adversary I had always seen her as before. Was it that she was sympathetic after I had been shot, or was it something else?

"You okay, partner?"

I forced it closed, the door to a dark room where the bodies were stored, their souls turned to demons that refused to leave me. The same demons that mixed it all up for me, putting loved ones' faces on corpses and causing my imagination to run wild when the wife—the soon-to-be ex-wife—didn't answer her phone. This reaction, in part, is likely part of the reason she would soon be the ex. Ex number two.

I hated that room in the corner of my head, and sometimes I would wonder if cops who ate their guns did so trying to kill their own demons. Cops were known to eat their guns when choosing to check out early. Maybe this was a factor. Perhaps they were trying to silence the voices. I couldn't be the only one who suffered this.

"I'm good, Ray, just thinking about some things."

"What about? If we're going to be partners, we have to talk."

I waited, thinking about what I could say. Wondering how much I would reveal to him. I had known him a long time, but we'd never worked together. It's the difference of intimacy. And I wasn't sure I was ready to hop in the sack.

We were now northbound on the Golden State Freeway toward Santa Clarita. We would be going through Burbank soon, my new hometown. I looked over and forced a smile. "I was just thinking about this case, partner, prepping for the interviews. It's sure an interesting one, and I'm glad I get to tag along with you on it."

He returned the smile. "You're more than tagging along, partner; it's your case now too."

# 7

THE BOX WAS in Sylmar, a forty-minute drive north from downtown Los Angeles on the Golden State or Hollywood Freeway, either one. Or he could take the Glendale to the Foothill, which would take a little longer unless the others were clogged with traffic. He learned to use the names of the freeways rather than the numbers. It was different here than on the east coast.

Sylmar is a community within the City of Los Angeles. A predominately Hispanic community, it is the type of place where a thin, wiry white boy like Leonard might find trouble if he hadn't spent twenty-five years in Raiford learning how to posture. Convicts carry themselves differently than those who have never been inside, and they recognize it in one another. Unfortunately, Leonard knew, the cops would also spot a convict in a crowd. Convicts, like cops, are aware of their surroundings and they protect their backsides. They know to show confidence, each trying to avoid being the bitch. Gangsters on the street also recognize the confidence and poise of a convict, even those gangsters who had not yet been inside. For the most part, the gangsters would give any such person their due respect and avoid confrontation. There were plenty of weak ones on the street; it made no sense to mess with someone who's done time and is not likely a punk. Especially when it was a white boy who showed no fear in barrios and ghettos. That sends a message that is generally heard loud and clear.

Leonard showed no fear because he had grown to understand himself and his capabilities once he entered prison. Up until then, he had been bullied at school and in the neighborhood. Even though he had already killed, he had no confidence to stand up to the so-called tough kids on the block or campus. He hated confrontation and avoided it at all expense, though he did keep a mental list of his offenders and planned to someday exact revenge upon them.

Shortly after he went to prison, he realized he must utilize his propensity for violence in order to survive. He learned that not everyone was so capable, even in the joint. It was one thing to fight, and quite another to dismember someone during the course of a fight. Not that he hadn't suffered a few beatings and survived being stabbed once; he had. However, after the first couple of beatings had been dealt, Leonard decided he would no longer allow others to view him as an easy target. He would deter them with a message silently delivered through acts of extreme violence.

The opportunity came one afternoon at the weight pile on Raiford's Medium Security yard. Leonard saw the man making his approach and immediately knew his intent. He had seen it before and recognized the situation as a predator circling his prey. This would be the day he would send the message that he was not to be considered prey. When the man made his move, Leonard was ready. He stepped out of the striking zone as the man lunged at him with a shank in his hand, a prison knife made from a small piece of scrap metal. He used the man's momentum to drive him into the ground, and then Leonard came down on top of him and shoved his thumb into his aggressor's skull through his eye socket. There was no further fight in the now one-eyed convict who lay screaming and blindly reaching to find his eyeball that dangled from a single tendon. The message was yet to be made clear, in Leonard's opinion. So Leonard grabbed a 10 pound steel weight and beat the man until the guards arrived to take him away. The would-be attacker lay unconscious in a pool of his own blood.

Sylmar was Disneyland compared to Raiford.

He stepped out of the gray Ford Taurus and ran his hand through his thick blond hair while taking in his surroundings. It was a habit he'd learned over the years, one that he would never change. Satisfied, he closed the door and walked into the post office and directly to Box 1196 where he retrieved an envelope addressed to L.F. Hammer. He rolled his eyes. Whitey must have mentioned the story Leonard had told his cellmate about killing a man with a hammer. *Leonard Freeman Hammer.* There was no return address.

Leonard lit a cigarette as he departed, again watching his tail while traveling from the Sylmar post office to the San Fernando post office a few miles away. When he arrived, he retrieved from his trunk a shoebox wrapped in brown paper, addressed to M. Feldman at a box in Boston. He entered the post office but never removed his shades. He barely spoke to the clerk—which seemed to be fine with her—only enough to answer the few questions she had: "Are there any perishable items in the package, any explosives or hazardous materials of any kind?"

Behind the mirrored sunglasses and stoic face, he smiled at the thought of the frozen contents, but simply shook his head. He paid in cash and left without accepting the receipt.

As he started his car, he pictured the boss's boy, the bug-eyed, lanky, wannabe wop, gathering the package and seeing it addressed to M. Feldman. He chuckled to himself and wondered if the dummy would get the joke. Then he pictured the two of them from that day in the boss's office, Feldman with his tough guy posture, and he remembered picturing the man on fire. The burning bush with buggy eyes. Shit, he thought, he should have addressed the package to Moses.

Leonard departed and drove east on Brand and then turned right onto a nearby side street looking for a quiet place to stop. He pulled over beneath a shade tree in a residential area and killed the ignition. He started to open the envelope he had picked up from his box when he noticed a steady stream of children filling the streets. Most were walking though some rode bicycles or skateboards, filling the sidewalks on both sides of the street and darting into traffic at will. Leonard was drawn to them, watching and listening as the kids approached in a wave of plaid skirts and khaki pants or shorts, and white button-up blouses or polos. The last time he was among a group of kids this age, he *was* their age. Now they seemed so young.

And vulnerable . . .

Leonard drifted back to his childhood and remembered watching a neighbor girl about the age of these children who would undress with the blinds partially open. She lived behind him, and her activities became his passion. He had a place to sit where he could see into her room, and sometimes he would wait for hours just to see the show. On a rare occasion, the drunk bitch—his mother—would yell for him to return. He didn't care, she had nothing to offer. It wouldn't be as if she had prepared supper. No, she was likely in need of someone to beat on, or maybe fool around with sexually. He hated her, and was glad the bitch was dead.

As the children passed Leonard's car, some glanced toward him, and when they did, they instinctively stopped smiling or giggling or talking. It seemed each suddenly lost their elation. It angered him. They likely thought him a creep, or worse, maybe a weirdo. He watched in the mirror as they continued past and he noticed several of them looking over their shoulders at him. One in particular, a little Asian girl with pigtails who appeared much younger than the others. She seemed to be interested in him.

Leonard turned in his seat to have a good look as the Asian girl broke away from the others, turning onto a walkway that led to the front door of a modest home. She used a key to open the door and disappeared inside, but not before glancing back at him once more.

Leonard smiled at the closed door and then settled back into his seat. He watched his image in the mirror while running his hand around on the seat next to him searching for his packet of cigarettes. He pulled a Camel from the pack, put it to his lips, and picked up the envelope that sat beside his leg. He looked around once more while bringing a lighter up to his face. Most of the children were now gone. There were no more distractions and fewer vehicles driving past him. No cops anywhere that he could see. He opened the envelope to find a photograph. It was a man of about his own age, maybe older, it was hard to tell. The angle from which the photo had been taken rendered the subject's features unclear, and the hat he wore further obscured his face. It was an old man's hat, or the type of hat men wore several decades earlier and now you only saw them on the occasional east coaster or rock star. There was a folded piece of paper behind it that bore a name and an address. Richard Jones. Leonard grinned through a cloud of exhaled smoke. *Dick Jones*. What a name. Then he saw two more notations that erased his grin: "cop," and "30 days." The last line read, "No preferences, no souvenirs."

He dropped the items to his lap and said, "Fucking cop?"

Leonard shook his head. He never expected this type of an assignment. What the hell were they thinking, killing a cop? Were they crazy? You didn't whack a cop without really bringing the heat. They should know that. Then he thought about the cops at Raiford, the only cops he really had ever known. Dirty sonsabitches each and every one. He hated cops, and the more he pondered it, the more he relished the thought of seeing one beg for his life. Leonard knew most of them were pussies when they didn't have that gun and badge, or the upper hand.

With a chuckle, he placed the two items back in their envelope. He looked behind him once more at the house with the closed front door and blinds covering the windows. There was a little girl inside, likely home alone. He tossed his cigarette out the window and scanned his surroundings once more.

## 8

---

**D**AVEY LOPES WAS comfortable walking the drab halls of Pelican Bay. He had been there dozens of times before, there and many others: Tehachapi, Solano, Folsom, Salinas, Kern, and half a dozen others. The former Marine and veteran cop lumbered through the halls of these fortresses without any fear. Anyone who looked into his permanently squinting eyes could see that Lopes was not the type to be trifled with.

He had been flown in on the department's fixed-wing plane and had grabbed a rental car. He would stay overnight and head back the next day.

His escort through the prison was a Hispanic female who was close to twenty years younger than he. She was petite and had a nice smile but spoke the language of her clientele. "The fuck you want with Lil' Spooky, anyway? He catching another case? Seems like the longer he's here, the more cases he picks up. Motherfuckers must be giving his shit up on the streets."

Lopes grinned slightly as he appraised her profile, her ponytail dancing side to side as they continued walking through the slate-gray hall-way. He could smell a fresh, flowery scent of shampoo, and for a moment he pictured her just out of the shower.

"Where're you from, anyway?"

She stopped and looked him in the eye. "What the fuck is that supposed to mean, *where am I from*? As in, where am I *from,* where am I from? Or just, where am I from?"

He chuckled. "You know what I mean."

"I grew up in *The Avenues*, you know—"

"Yes, I'm very familiar with *The Avenues*."

"I'm first generation. My parents are from Nicaragua, and they're here illegal as fuck, I guess, but I'm not sure 'cause they made a few anchor babies, yours truly included. Didn't Obama make that shit legal?"

Lopes just shrugged.

"Well, anyway, that's my story. I lived in a little apartment with my parents, six siblings, and every so often various aunts and uncles and cousins and shit. So, yes, to answer your question, I'm from the hood. No, I didn't bang. Yes, I have kids—two—and no, I can't make tamales, so don't be picturing this little muchacha naked in your kitchen. I'm single but I also don't need no goddamn man, especially if you're married."

He smiled, thinking he hadn't thought of her naked in the kitchen, only the bathroom. Though, since she suggested it, he went ahead and conjured that image as well.

"You're a feisty little thing, aren't you?"

"And don't ever call me little."

They turned and walked the rest of the way to C-Block without conversation. Lopes was thinking she was exactly what he needed in his life and did a mental eye roll as he thought it. Just like all the others had been exactly what he needed, until he didn't, or maybe to be more honest, until they had had enough of his shit. Relationships were not his field of expertise.

She keyed open the door and held it for him. He saw Spooky sitting at a metal table that was bolted into the cinderblock walls. Before entering, he glanced at her chest but there was no name tag.

She noticed. "Lopez. Just like yours, only with a Z. We didn't misspell ours to try and hide our heritage."

Still grinning, he said, "Well okay then, Miss Lo-*pez*. Thank you. I appreciate the escort, and I doubt I'll forget your name."

She turned her mouth up to feign a smile, but it as quickly disappeared. "I'll be waiting for you right out here," she said, and nodded toward a bench in the hallway. "Just tap on the door when you're done."

"Tap it?"

She frowned. "Yeah, the door. It's the only thing you'll be tapping up here in The Bay, that I can guarantee you."

He smiled and entered the room, listening as the heavy metal door closed solidly behind him.

He nodded at the inmate who sat waiting. "What's up, Spooky?"

---

CORTEZ LOOKED OVER AT ME AS WE STOPPED IN FRONT OF THE TWO-STORY Valencia home. It looked like all the others on this block and all the other blocks in the city, with its natural tones and subtle accents. It was the developers' way to pretend there was no harm in cutting down the mountains and trees to build the sprawling and endless tracts of homes. He said, "One more thing about this guy, this is apparently his third wife."

"You sure he's not a cop?"

"No shit, right?"

"Please tell me none of the priors are dead."

"First one's in Arizona, no kids. Second is down in San Diego. They had a daughter together who's sixteen now. I haven't talked to either one yet, just checked to make sure they were alive and accounted for."

"I thought you said he had an adult daughter who might be here?"

"She's apparently the wife's daughter from a previous marriage. That's the best I can figure."

"Anything else?"

He shook his head. "Nah, partner, that's about it so far. Not even sure what he does for a living, nothing came up from the Department of Labor on him. There's a lack of information about this guy."

"That's odd."

"Or a good sign."

I shrugged. "Yeah, maybe he's self-employed."

"Maybe he was the housewife."

We stepped out of the car and met near the trunk. I said, "You mentioned she does real estate, do you know who she worked for?"

"Not yet," he answered, while quickly appraising the neighborhood, "but I bet she made a good wage up here."

I nodded in agreement, thinking about the expansion of the valley over the years. I had grown up in the area when Valencia didn't exist. It was Newhall, Saugus, and Canyon Country. There was Castaic north and west, and Val Verde further west, but nobody cared about either of those two towns back then. Probably still don't, other than to know it's where most of the criminals come from. I lived on a dirt road in Newhall. Lyons Avenue separated us from the farms, Bunny Luv. They specialized in carrots. But the farms were no longer here and the mountains where I hunted quail and dove as a boy were now littered with near million-dollar homes, swimming pools, and garages full of BMWs, Audis, and Mercedes. I couldn't imagine where all the money came from.

I looked up at the home we were about to enter, a two-story with a four-car garage and professionally maintained landscaping. I guessed nobody in these neighborhoods owned a mower. There were probably some residents who didn't own a vacuum. We were up on the hill in the newer tracts, some of which were gated and had contracted security to protect the residents from people abroad, those from Castaic and Val Verde, maybe old Newhall where I grew up.

Though the truth be known, with the major expansion over the years, there were now plenty of mandated Section 8 housing developments which brought their fair share of people who never worked and never planned to work. They worked the system and lived comfortably on the taxpayers' tab, receiving housing and food subsidies and other gratuities for the sins of our predecessors. There were plenty of parolees and probationers now living just down the road from these otherwise safe neighborhoods, and the crime rates would be more reflective of this fact if not for politics. Santa Clarita Sheriff's station notoriously discouraged proactive policing because an arrest reflected a crime, and the once-labeled *one of the nation's ten safest,* would not stand for high crime rates. I wondered if the animal who killed and dismembered the yet-to-be-identified woman was a transplanted resident of this once-safe city.

Which is why the sheriff and my captain were in a dither over this murder. If she had disappeared from Compton and been found in Long Beach there would barely be mention of it, with or without a head and hands. But this was Santa Clarita, the yuppiest city in the county, previously one of the safest cities in the nation, and it mattered. Politics.

We turned to head up the walk toward the front door. I straightened my tie while saying to Ray, "I'll keep the notes, buddy."

"Sounds good, partner. Thanks."

---

LOPES HAD HIS HANDS FOLDED BEHIND HIS HEAD AND WAS WAITING FOR Spooky to start talking. He had just asked the generic *What do you have for me* question, but as he did there was movement that stopped just outside the room they occupied. Lopes could hear keys rattling and the conversation of at least two male guards. When the footsteps continued and then faded away, he nodded to Spooky who sat waiting. "Well?"

"Look, Lopes, you've got to give me some love, man, all the information I'm giving you, and I don't get shit in here. An hour a day outside my cell, and the store comes around once a week but I ain't even got money for a fucking candy bar, eh? Best I can do is trade in a book or two and maybe a magazine for something new to read. And the chaplain, he kicks down pencils and paper, envelopes too so I can send some kites home, but then I don't have no money for the fucking stamps, eh. I need some jack, man, some money on my books, eh."

"I'll put forty bucks on your books when I leave, if you quit whining like a little bitch and get to it."

Spooky squinted his eyes, but not for long as Lopes drilled into him with his.

"Look, I know the mob's been active, more so than usual. The fucking murders are jumping off in L.A., but I haven't heard shit from you in weeks. What the fuck is going on?"

"It ain't like I can call you, eh."

"Okay, man, fair enough. But I'm here now, so get to it. What's going on that has everything so hot down there?"

"Wait, Lopes, I need another favor too."

He rolled his eyes. "Jesus Christ, man . . . what?"

"My little girl, Vero—"

"Vero?"

"Veronica, we call her Vero . . . See, my baby mama been shacked up with Peanut from La Puente, eh, and that homie, he ain't got no respect for his elders, man. He been dissin' me to my ol' lady—my ex ol' lady—and I got that back in a kite from some of my other homies, and that shit ain't right, eh."

They always needed something.

"Get to it, man, what's the problem?"

"It's just that she—Vero—she's just barely a teenager now, like fourteen or thirteen, eh, and I don't want her going down that road too, like her fucking hood-rat mama. Bitch's old man—this Peanut motherfucker—is dealing dope and banging and shit, bringing all that shit around my little girl. I just want him to go away, man, that's all. Can you get the narcs on him or something, put a case on him, man? Eh?"

"I'll look into it," Lopes said as he leaned forward and hovered over his notebook with a pen he pulled from behind his ear. "What's your old lady's name again?"

"Silvia Banuelos."

He wrote it down. "And who's Peanut?"

"Peanut."

He looked up from his notes. "Yeah, I got that, but what's his fucking name?"

Spooky shrugged. "That's all I know, eh. Peanut from La Puente. Motherfucker got a crooked eye. He be looking at you, but he be looking over there too. You ask a motherfucker what he lookin' at, he prolly don't know. Prolly too much PCP or maybe he got shot in the head, I don't know. But that's all I got, Lopes, 'cause we don't kick it with Puente, eh."

Lopes smirked at the gangster. "So why don't you have him taken care of, Spooky? You don't have any horsepower now?"

Spooky slurped his saliva, which would have been considered disrespectful to Lopes in another environment, on the streets in front of other homies or cops. Spooky slouched in his chair and looked away. "He's mobbed up, eh."

Lopes dropped his pen on the table. "You're telling me this guy, Peanut—Peanut from La Puente—is mobbed up? I never heard of him."

Spooky sat up. "Well not like *mobbed up*, mobbed up, you know . . . just more like an associate. He pays his taxes and puts in work for La Eme, eh. All those fools in Puente be puttin' in work, eh."

Lopes studied him for a minute. He glanced at the convict's arms and neck, curious if there were any new tattoos he hadn't noticed. He had photos in a file showing every tattoo the gangster had, a collection from every time he had been booked or interviewed on a case. He never had the black hand, the tattoo of La Eme, and Lopes doubted he had it now either. There was an hour glass on the back of his hand that Lopes didn't remember, but he might not have paid particular attention to it either. He remembered the important tattoos, the ink that told the story of a gangster's life: the number thirteen on his neck, below the corner of one eye, and again on a forearm. Thirteen for the letter 'M', which has nothing to do with marijuana as many will have you believe, but an indication of his gang showing respect and allegiance to the Mexican mafia. His other tattoos, *Sureno, Hazard, L.A.*, were all indications of where he was from: Big Hazard street gang in Los Angeles, Southern California. He had tear drops tattooed from the corner of his other eye that denoted the number of times he had been sent up to the big house. There were four now, and he was twenty-nine years old.

"Okay, man," Lopes finally said. "I'll see about your little girl, and I'll put forty bucks on your books. Now this better be fucking good man or I'm going to beat your ass and give you a crooked eye to match your homeboy's, Mr. Peanut."

"He ain't my homeboy, eh."

"Get to it."

Little Spooky looked around, but there was nothing to see. Habit, or instinct, he didn't want to be seen or heard talking to the cops. He let out a breath and seemed to slump into his chair. He looked Lopes in the eyes and said, "You ain't seen nothing yet, man, the mob's making some big moves, and it's going to get bloody."

"What's it about?"

"Money. What it's always about? Money and power, same thing, eh? But the mob's been taking it to the community, eh, not just fucking around on the streets anymore."

"What do you mean?"

"They're muscling in on legit businesses, taking cuts. Motherfuckers don't wanna play, they be gettin' whacked. These ain't gangsters and dope dealers and shit, these are regular folks, white motherfuckers too. They ain't just sitting down in the hood no more, there's too much money to be made for all that bullshit."

Lopes leaned back in his chair. "Give me some specifics."

"I know they got enough going on that they're going outside."

"Outside, where? What do you mean?"

"You know, man, contracts. I don't know a lot, I only know that it ain't the homies putting in all the work now, eh. They got some of the hits contracted out."

"How do you know all this?"

Spooky sucked his teeth, "Damn, Lopes, how the fuck you think I know, eh? What kind of fucking question is that?"

Davey Lopes came to his feet and lunged at the inmate who instinctively drew backwards and brought his hands up to shield his face. Lopes grabbed his collar with his left hand and held his right hand cocked, aimed at the convict's face.

"Don't you ever suck your fucking teeth at me again, *ese*, or you'll be spitting Chiclets all the way back to your cell."

Still leaned back, his eyes showing regret, maybe apprehension, his hands still guarding his face, Little Spooky said, "Damn, Lopes . . . goddamn, man, I didn't mean no disrespect, eh?"

He released his grip and backed off but not too far. "Let me tell you something, you little asshole . . . You may be bad with your homies, out on the street, packing heat or having backup, but I'd tear you to fucking pieces, rip your skinny little arms off your body and beat you to death with them. I won't tolerate any of that gangster disrespect bullshit out of you. You got it?"

Spooky nodded, looking away.

"This little agreement we have here is that you provide the information, I keep your name out of our RICO. Sooner or later, all your homies are going to know you're a punk. I already fucking know it, and you best not forget it."

Spooky was straightening his jumpsuit, frowning now.

Lopes walked to the door, paused and came back to the table, still watching the inmate, maybe now more than ever. Lopes knew how to handle the gangsters and keep their respect. And it wasn't by being nice to them. He sat down and said, "Okay, let's try this again. What's this about work being farmed out?"

"Huh?"

"You said others were putting in work for Eme."

"Yeah, it's what I heard just the other day. They were talking about it—"

"Who's they?"

"Lemme think . . . It was some of the *eses* on my row, Trigger, Sleepy, Lil' Oso . . . I dunno, some other *vatos* too. Casper from Florence, I know he was one of them talking. I remember him saying something about it. They were all like, 'Who's seen la lista, eh?' and one of the homies said, 'Shit, man, they ain't putting out the list no more, ese, now that they be contracting it out.'"

Lopes narrowed his brows, skeptical of what the gangster said. "You're telling me there's no more list?"

He nodded with just a slight lift of his chin. "Something like that. I mean, they still have the word out on which gangsters or neighborhoods got the green light on 'em, but they ain't putting down any of this other shit. It's too hot, man, the lista seems to always get back to the cops, so they ain't gonna do it for this new deal they got going."

Lopes grinned and Spooky grinned back at him. Lopes knew they were both likely thinking the same thing. The list—la lista, as it is famously known among gangsters and cops alike—would be compromised by gangsters such as Spooky, who would provide it to cops such as Lopes.

*The List* would have names of gang members, and sometimes entire gangs, who were to be targeted for hits. The severity of the hit would be designated by terms such as soft candy or hard candy, which was the difference between an assault or murder. All members of La Eme and their associate gangs—which were almost all Southern California Hispanic street gangs—were to act on the list at any given opportunity, regardless of the circumstances. It didn't matter if the would-be attacker was outnumbered or if a cop was standing ten feet away; if the opportunity presented itself for any gang member in good standing with La Eme to take out someone on the list, they were to act on it without hesitation. If they did not, they too would be placed on the list.

Some of the ways one could end up on the list included snitching, not paying taxes on their dope sales, or violating any other law of arguably the most powerful prison gang in the country, La Eme.

The room was silent as Lopes jotted a few notes. He looked up and said, "Who are they using then, if they're contracting this shit out? The blacks, white boys? . . . They using the A.B.?"

Spooky sneered. "Shit, the mob ain't gonna have no *mayates* putting in work for them, no fucking way. Maybe the white boys, yeah, the Aryan Brotherhood, I dunno, eh."

"Okay, well that's your new assignment. I want more detail on that shit. You've got a month. I'll be back up here in June when the weather's nicer and I can work on my tan, sitting at the pool over in that hotel drinking cold beer."

Spooky didn't say anything. They stared at each other for half a minute. Finally, Lopes smiled.

"What happened to your sense of humor, Spook?"

"Spook-*y*."

"You're getting a little uppity, you know it?"

He didn't say anything.

"One last thing—I almost forgot why I came up here. There was a double murder in El Monte, couple weeks ago . . . what do you know about it?"

Spooky glanced to the wall but then came back. "I heard something about it, I think maybe it was just a rival gang thing, eh?"

Lopes studied him for a minute, looking into his eyes for the truth. He felt Spooky was holding out on him. He got up from the chair and collected his notebook and pen. "You're holding back on me, man. I'm not going to mess around with you on this. I'm coming back in a month for some other shit, and when I do, I'll pull you out for another chat. You'd best have some details for me then, or the deal will be off the table. I want to know about the double in El Monte, and I want to know about the mob contracting shit out and who they're leaning on. Got it?"

The gangster broke his eye contact again and said quietly, "Yeah, got it."

Lopes stepped over and tapped his knuckles against the steel door twice. As he heard the keys rattling on the other side, he pointed at Spooky and said, "Spooky, take care . . . *eh?*"

Lopes stepped past Officer Lopez at the door and heard Spooky say, "Don't forget my little girl and to put some jack on my books, eh?"

# 9

---

LOOKING OVER HIS shoulder, Leonard watched the closed
front door of the house where the little girl had disappeared only
a few moments earlier. He pictured her in a bedroom now,
maybe changing out of her school clothes. He could see the skirt hit the
carpeted floor, and he allowed his mind's eye to wander upward, seeing
the smooth brown skin of her young legs that were tight and toned but
smooth. Then the thighs, soft and silky, maybe just a little damp from
perspiration, maybe even a little sticky. He closed his eyes and drew a
long, slow breath through his nostrils, his eyes now closed. He pictured
her in white panties contrasting against her brown skin, her buttocks
protruding slightly as she turned away from him in his mind. Leonard
adjusted in his seat as he allowed himself to become aroused by his
thoughts.

Forgetting the new assignment for the time being, his fantasy continued. He saw her remove the panties, slowly sliding them down. Oh, Jesus,
she was looking back at him now, smiling, inviting him to join her. The
little slut was taunting him, begging him for it. Home alone, the parents at
work and nothing to do for the straight-A student other than to tease
grown men.

She needed to get it, and get it good. Get it and then pay for her sins, the lustful little bitch. He would let her have her pleasure, but then she would be a filthy little whore who would never keep their secret. So, he knew what had to be done. The play had now been written and only needed to be acted out.

Leonard opened his eyes and looked back at the closed front door once more. He tucked the letter into his pocket, pulled his keys from the ignition, and stepped out of the car. One last look in all directions, and his decision was made. He walked directly to her door.

# 10

———

PHILIP CHANEY ANSWERED the door wearing a polo shirt, khaki shorts, and casual leather slip-on shoes with no socks. He could have fit in at the beach, at the tennis courts, in the mall, and at the country club. His hair was thick and dark and combed back from his tanned and freckled forehead. He looked familiar to me at first, but then I realized he just had that look you see in any catalog selling yuppie clothing or miracle drugs for erectile dysfunction disorder. I pictured him with a sweater tied around his neck and a million-dollar smile, but he wasn't smiling or sporting a sweater.

Ray introduced us as Detectives Cortez and Jones, and waited for him to invite us in. Mr. Chaney seemed to consider the situation for a moment before opening the door wider and stepping aside, wordlessly indicating we could enter. He closed the large, heavy door behind us, and finally spoke when he suggested we could join him in his office.

We followed him to a room that was furnished in dark wood and leather. An imposing desk sat in front of a giant bookcase. Ray accepted Chaney's gesture to have a seat. I ignored it and walked over to study the books. What someone reads can offer a lot of insight to their character and personality. I could feel Mr. Chaney's eyes on me as he walked around and took a seat behind his desk in the large leather chair. It occurred to me his chair likely cost more than what I had paid to have my new apartment furnished with a sofa, recliner, and forty-inch flat-screen television. When Ray spoke, I glanced from the bookcase to see Mr. Chaney's eyes still upon me. He didn't look away when our eyes initially met, but slowly he turned his attention to Ray, who was asking the preliminaries: full name, date of birth, occupation . . .

I drifted toward the unoccupied chair and stood beside it, watching Mr. Chaney and waiting for his full reply. I was very curious about his occupation; his book collection had offered no clues. His demeanor had not yet hinted at the loss of a loved one, and I had a suspicious feeling about the man.

Leaning back in his chair, appearing disinterested with his hand supporting his face, Mr. Chaney said, "I invest."

Ray watched him without responding. The two sat silent as if both were waiting for the other to speak. Finally, Ray glanced down and made a note in the silence. I pulled the chair further from the desk, took a seat and crossed one leg over the other, making myself comfortable. I set my notebook on his desk, moving a framed picture to do so, but with purpose. Chaney watched me and I could tell it bothered him, but he wasn't going to mention it.

After a moment, I looked over at Ray and said—as if I had forgotten, "Oh, sorry, partner. I told you I'd keep the notes." I retrieved my notebook from Chaney's desk without putting the framed picture back in place.

Ray looked over and I nodded.

He continued: "May I ask what type of investing you do?"

"What does that have to do with my wife missing, Detective Cortez?"

I noted that he remembered Ray's name without being provided a business card. Some people were just good at that; I wasn't. Usually the people who were good at that were people who had attended courses that teach you to be good at that. Like salesman and politicians.

"We don't know what information is going to be relevant to our case," Ray said. "It's likely that some of the answers to our questions won't provide any relevance at all, but we never know. Especially in the beginning stages of an investigation."

Chaney bounced the back of his chair back twice and then came to rest in an upright position, moving his arms onto the desk in front of him. "Look, Detectives Cortez and Jones, I am more than willing to answer your questions, but I would also like to have an honest dialogue about the woman who was found murdered in the industrial area over the weekend. There were photographs in the newspaper and it appeared to be my wife's car. There's no word on my wife and the Missing Persons unit passed my case over to you gentlemen at the Homicide Bureau. I am not ignorant of your methods and processes, and I assume you are considering me a suspect until you can prove otherwise. As such, I have notified my attorney of the situation, and against his advice, I am willing to speak with you. But make no mistake, I realize you will consider me a suspect in my wife's death, so please let's speak as adults and not play games. Now, what may I tell you that will allow you to not waste more of your time or mine, so that you can proceed with your investigation?"

Ray looked over at me and then back to Chaney. Raymond Cortez, who was warm and friendly, the type of person for whom you'd want to buy a drink or whose hand you'd want to shake when you met him. This time, his tone was much more like the tone I would use.

"Okay, let's get to it then. Start with your first date and bring it up to the last time you saw her, and don't leave anything out. How's that sound, Mr. Chaney?"

---

BACK IN THE CAR, I REACHED FROM THE PASSENGER'S SEAT AND TOOK control of the air-conditioning. Ray seemed to be unaware of the stale heat that had awaited us inside the dark sedan.

Ray made a U-turn at the next intersection, the tires squealing against the concrete gutters that ran across the asphalt. As we slowly drove back toward the Chaney residence, both of us were staring at the house. He said, "I don't like this guy at all."

I was just about to respond to that statement when I saw a black four-door sedan pulling up to the curb and parking in the spot we had just vacated. Two men in shirts and ties, both wearing aviator sunglasses, stared at us as we continued creeping along past the home. Ray and I were both locked onto them, and as we passed, Ray said, "Copy the tag, five,

Frank Edward Tom, three two nine. Five, Frank Edward Tom, three two nine."

I repeated it as I wrote it in my notebook, "Five, Frank Edward Tom, three two niner . . . What was it, Ray, a Taurus?"

Ray was watching in his side-view mirror now as we approached the stop sign just a few houses away from the Chaney home. "Yeah, partner, Ford Taurus."

I looked over my shoulder. Both men were pulling suit coats over their white dress shirts, standing on either side of the black sedan as they seemed to watch us. I didn't see any badges or guns, but I might not have been able to at that distance. To me, they looked like feds. "Who the hell are those guys?"

"We're going to have to find out, partner," Ray said. "They look like feds to me."

"Yeah, that's what I was thinking too. What the hell would the feds be doing here? They don't have jurisdiction on anything we have going."

Ray accelerated away from the stop sign and glanced over. "They sure don't, partner, but that never seems to deter them."

I closed my notebook and leaned back in my seat, pulled my seatbelt on and adjusted the air vent to blow directly toward my face. I removed my fedora and placed it on my knee, loosened my tie and unbuttoned my collar.

Ray followed my lead and put his seatbelt on too. We were both old-school cops who had worked patrol back in the days when seatbelts were never worn by cops working in fast-paced areas. We were always more concerned with getting out of a radio car fast than being ejected from one during a crash. Being shot at or suddenly finding yourself in a foot pursuit was far more likely to happen than being hit by a bus, or anything else with wheels. Most of us were accustomed to only strapping in once we were out on the main streets or highways, or in a high-speed pursuit.

"What'd you think of him?" he asked.

"Chaney? I think he's a pompous ass."

Ray nodded. "What else? What do you think of his lack of emotion?"

"I found several things interesting, Ray, if you want to hear it."

"Of course I do, partner. By the way, are you hungry?"

"I can wait, unless you're starving."

"Fine with me, we'll wait."

"Well, first," I said, "his lack of emotion, as you pointed out, was very odd given the situation. When you explained the circumstances of the dead broad, pretty much laying it out that we believe it is his wife who was murdered but can't prove it yet, I studied him, looking for anything I could read about him. There was nothing. I don't think I'd want to play poker with that asshole, I can tell you that."

Ray accelerated up the onramp to the southbound Golden State.

I continued: "His book collection was interesting."

"Yeah?"

"Yeah, I think so. He has textbooks on psychology, sociology, anatomy, physics, history—"

"So, he's probably educated, that kind of goes along with the impression I had of him."

"—everything from world history to American wars and even history of western civilization."

"He's well read."

"But then he's got books on gambling, everything from cards to the roulette wheel, books on odds and books on strategies—"

"Okay, and he gambles . . ."

"—casino guides and gambling vacation resort destinations. Books on race horses too."

Ray stole a glance behind his shades, then looked forward again. "Race horses?"

"Then he had this collection of novels. From the looks of it, every single Louis L'Amour and Elmore Leonard. The L'Amour was a collector's hardcover set. The Leonard books were paperbacks, but it looked like he had them all, from the early days of Westerns to his last books, the *Raylan Givens* series."

"Raylan? Never heard of it."

"You've seen the TV show, *Justified?*"

"Yeah, I've seen it. Good show."

"That's Leonard's character from some of his last novels. Deputy U.S. Marshal Raylan Givens. The show is based off of those books."

"Gotcha. I don't read much other than reports or the daily racing forms."

"He also had Hemingway, Twain, and Edgar Allen Poe, for the love of God. You bet on the ponies, Ray?"

"I do, but I'm no high roller. So, what are you making of all this, partner? I'm not sure I'm following you about all the books."

I picked my hat up and turned it a quarter turn each direction, checking its shape before placing it back on my head now that I had cooled down. "Nothing. He's just an interesting cat, that's all."

Ray chuckled. "Okay, partner. I thought you were going somewhere and I was lost."

"Sorry."

"No, it's okay, partner. Just didn't want to be lost here. No offense, but I'm way more interested in the dudes in suits that showed up than I am his book collection."

"Me too, Ray. Me too."

# 11

---

**L**EONARD WALKED CASUALLY out of the home into the back yard and around the side of the house. He stood for a moment at the gate leading to the front yard, looked over to see nobody around, and then quickly returned to his vehicle. He drove off immediately, but casually, so as to not draw unwanted attention, and worked his way over to the 210 freeway taking side streets. Then he headed south and east toward Pasadena where he would drop down the Glendale freeway into L.A.

He cruised along in the number two lane, going with the flow of traffic, blending in with his environment as he always did.

Leonard thought back to the Asian girl and retraced his steps in reverse. He walked through the gate into the backyard where he found the sliding glass door open, a sheer drape gently flapping outside from the flow of air. He remembered feeling that breeze when he came downstairs. It was the first time he noticed the open windows. It now occurred to him he could have as easily removed a screen and snuck in through the window, though ringing the bell had worked just the same.

He saw himself walk in through the open sliding glass door, proceed through the dining area, the living room, and up the stairs to the second room on the right. He stood at the threshold and saw her there on the floor where he had kissed her goodbye. She was still, at peace now, and there were no signs of violence to distort her beauty. He saw his hands closed around her neck, and he remembered squeezing tightly and seeing panic and excitement in her eyes. They were face to face, close, and intimate. It had been beautiful. He heard himself telling her not to fight it, to just let it happen, and soon she had. He grabbed her as she had gone limp and eased her to the floor.

Leonard reached into his pocket to double-check—unnerved for a moment as he didn't recall if he remembered to take them—and he drew in a slow, easy breath as he felt the soft cotton panties with his hand. It excited him, and he now felt anxious to get back to the privacy and security of his home where he could close his eyes and give the memory the attention it deserved. They would be together forever now, and she would never be tainted by others, such as disgusting and horny little Asian boys.

# 12

F LOYD WALKED UP behind me in the bureau. I was sitting at my desk eating the tacos Ray and I had picked up from King Taco on the way back to the office.

"What are you up to, Dickie? You missed a good lunch at Manny's, and holy shit you should see the little cha-cha working there now."

I leaned to look past him. "No record, Ray."

Floyd glanced over at Ray and back to me. I held up a taco. "We grabbed King Taco."

"Yeah, but dude, I'm telling you, man, you should have seen this little—"

"Hey, aren't you still married? I'm the one that should be checking out these single women."

Floyd said, "I was just helping you out, scouting new talent. I'm like the scout sniper of Homicide Bureau, but instead of looking for the enemy, I'm trying to make friends. See?"

Ray, sitting at the computers along the wall behind us, and apparently not listening to anything Floyd was saying, said, "Well, shit, what do you make of that?"

I swiveled my chair to face his back. "What's up?"

Ray glanced over his shoulder. "No record on file for that plate, Chaney's mystery guests."

"I guess they remain a mystery. Still think they're feds?"

"I don't know. Don't feds register their cars?"

"What are you two idiots up to?" asked Floyd.

Ray was saying in the background he thought the feds registered their cars as I said to Floyd, "This Santa Clarita case, the husband is a strange one—"

"Yeah?"

"When we were leaving, two suits show up."

"Feds?"

"That's what we thought, but the plates come back no record. What's your thought on that?"

Floyd was dipping his finger and thumb into a can of Copenhagen and looking around the room, checking everything out. "My thought is, fuck the feds, and that's exactly what you need, a little Latina from the hood. Your record with white women is atrocious, pal."

"Thanks, I'll keep that in mind. But what about the plates, do feds register their cars?"

Ray had walked over with a computer printout in his hand and waited.

Floyd was saying, "I don't know. Why don't you check with a DMV investigator. What's the name of that guy we used to use? See if he knows. You still have a number for him?"

"I've got it somewhere," I said.

Ray said, "That'd be good, partner. Let me know what you come up with. This really bothers me now."

Floyd said, "Hey, Dickie, speaking of girls you should meet, you know that little blonde with the gorgeous blue eyes, does the morning news on Channel Five?"

"No."

He rolled his eyes at me. "Yes, you do. I've told you about her . . . Jesus, I know I've pointed her out on T.V. Anyway, I actually met her yesterday, me and Mongo. And I'll tell you what, if I were single like you, I'd be all—"

"The *news* girl?"

65

"Yeah, Dickie, I'm trying to tell you. Me and Mongo were leaving court yesterday and the news van was parked out front. She—this blonde I'm telling you about, Laura something—was standing next to the van looking hot. The side doors were open and a couple guys with microphones and cameras and shit were meandering about, like they were getting ready to cover a story, so I walked up and asked her if they were there for us."

I shook my head and grinned. "Of course you did."

"She says, 'What case are you guys here on?' I tell her whatever case she's interested in, that's what I'm here for. And then I told her I'd be more than happy to give her an interview, now or after drinks. She smiled, and I smiled back while Mongo stood there frowning. Reminded me of you, if you want to know the truth. Another asshole who doesn't like fun. Anyway, that's about it, we just shot the shit for a while and talked about her eyes."

"Her eyes."

"Yeah, Dickie, her eyes, the news, the case they were there covering—some gang murder trial out of Compton—what else? We talked about my tie—which she happened to find quite striking—then she gave me her card and said something about if I had any news, give her a call."

"Oh, I'm sure she did."

"I just happened to notice she wasn't wearing a ring, too, FYI, in the event you would like her number."

"I'm sure you had me in mind when you took her card."

"Of course, Dickie. Why, I'm a married man."

Ray stood behind us now with his notebook and computer printout in his hands, waiting. We stopped chatting and looked at him. Ray held his notebook out for me and said, "Just to double check, partner, this is what you gave me, right?"

I glanced at his notebook while retrieving mine. I looked from one to the other, comparing our notes. "Yeah, five, Frank Edward Tom, three two nine."

He sighed and closed his notebook. "Doesn't make sense."

Floyd said, "Maybe they're mafiosos."

I looked at him and frowned, and then glanced at Ray who just shrugged.

"They looked like feds."

Ray said, "I'd agree."

As Floyd turned to leave, he said, "Just trying to help. You guys don't want to listen to me, I'm going to go check in with the Channel Five News desk." As he rounded the corner I could hear him say, "Come on, Mongo, let's get out of here. It's half-past beer time already."

Ray pulled a chair from a nearby desk and rolled it next to mine. "The man is odd."

"Floyd?"

"No—well, yes—but I meant Chaney."

"He is."

"Now we find out his visitors who looked like feds are driving a cold-plated ride. What's up with all of that, partner?"

I shook my head and thought for a moment before replying. "Everything he said was like it had been scripted, did you notice that?"

"It did kind of seem that way."

"*Kind of,* nothing. It was too clean, Ray. It was like he had prepared for what would be asked. He laid it all out there chronologically—just as you asked him to do—from their first date until the moment he last saw her. No contradictions, no mistakes. Perfectly executed as if reading from a teleprompter. And with no emotion."

"Not perfectly, partner."

I cocked my head.

Ray said, "Did you catch it when he referred to his wife as being dead?"

I began nodding, recalling the conversation.

"It hit me just a while ago, thinking back to the conversation, and I remembered him saying it."

"Yeah, I do remember that, Ray. Something about he knows we consider him a suspect in her death."

"Exactly, partner. 'I know you consider me a suspect in my wife's death.' I think that's pretty much exactly what he said."

"So, what are you thinking?"

"I'm thinking we need to crawl up this guy's ass with a fine-toothed comb, that's what I'm thinking. You?"

"I'd have to agree, Ray. I say we start with the exes."

"Yep, the exes and then the daughter. He never did say why she wasn't there today. He told me she would be there. Something is off with this guy, partner."

I turned back to my desk that held no photographs or files or signs of life, only a lonely blue notebook with a Homicide Bureau logo complete with the bulldog, a case file number handwritten across the top, and the words 'Santa Clarita 187' below that. I sat silent, in thought for a moment, when Ray finally said, "What do you say we call it a day for now, get at it tomorrow, partner?"

I nodded. "Sounds good, Ray. I'll see you in the morning. I'm going to be here for a while tonight, getting settled into my new desk here. I might also play around with this a little more, see if I can dig anything up on hubby, or something with that license plate."

He stood and pushed the chair back to the unoccupied desk. "Sounds like a winner, partner. Mañana."

"Goodnight, Ray."

Before walking out the door, Ray turned back and asked, "Hey partner, you think Floyd was onto something?"

"With the news girl?" I joked.

Ray smiled. "Mafia."

"I don't know, Ray. But it's not beyond the realm of possibility."

---

I WAS PLEASED TO FIND THE BUREAU MOSTLY EMPTY WHEN I WALKED BACK in with a box I'd retrieved from the trunk of my car. I put it on the floor next to the empty desk that I had homesteaded, then sat down and checked the desk phone for a dial tone. You never knew around this place. I called Val's cell, and again there was no answer, only the standard greeting that prompted the caller to leave a voicemail message. Which I elected not to do.

Instead, I sat quietly staring at my new desk. There were no framed photos of loved ones and no awards or fancy name plates. It seemed fitting, in some ways, as I found myself struggling to feel at home here at the bureau with no permanent partner and no assigned team. I was "on loan" to Unsolved Homicides. Great.

To make matters worse, there was no one to go home to or even stay late to avoid.

I pulled open a couple of drawers to find empty files, half-used notepads, miscellaneous pens, pencils, paperclips, rubber bands. I pictured finding a half-empty bottle in one of the drawers and thought that's what I needed right now, but there was no such luck.

I leaned back in my new, old chair and again found myself staring at the phone. It sat solemnly staring back, apparently unmoved by my predicament. I grabbed it and tried again. This time the call went to voicemail quickly, the way it does when someone swipes the ignore button.

At least now I was pissed, not so much worried anymore. If she didn't have the decency to take my call, then so be it. As I stood, prepared to storm out and hit a liquor store on my way home, it occurred to me that our office phones were private numbers. She would have no way to know it was me calling. I retrieved my cell phone from my pocket and tried again, but the result was the same. Now I really was pissed. She wants to be a bitch, so be it. Good for her, I thought, and then for an instant told myself I didn't care if she was safe or not, and didn't need to worry, she wasn't my problem any longer. The fact some psycho was running around whacking real estate ladies in Santa Clarita didn't matter. But the other side of my brain argued that I did still care and that I still loved her.

Jesus, women . . .

I sat back down and tossed my cell onto the desk. Then I propped my feet up, removed my hat, and leaned my head back against the wall. I thought about Valerie, then I pictured the news lady with her blue eyes and saw Floyd at the side of the van laying the charm on her. Before long I was visualizing the scene photos, seeing the woman without a head or hands who may be the late Mrs. Marilynn Chaney, and then I fell asleep, leaving the door to a dark room in my mind wide open and once again vulnerable.

---

EACH TIME HER PHONE VIBRATED ON THE NIGHTSTAND, HE WALKED OVER and looked at its display. The first two calls were private numbers. The third showed 'Richard Cell' and a 323-area code, which he knew to be one of many for the Los Angeles area. He looked over at her motionless body and said, "Dick called." Then he laughed and went to the bathroom where he started the shower. While waiting for the water to heat, he stood in the doorway admiring her curves and the shape of her backside and thought, not bad for an old broad. Valerie lay motionless.

# 13

---

THE COUCH MAY have been new in the eighties, its orange, red, and yellow floral motif dark with stains and reeking of unidentifiable odors from the hundreds of tenants who had used it as their own. Leonard sank deep into its worn cushions. It reminded him of prison, how the mattresses and the bedding and the clothes and socks and everything else smelled like all the convicts before him. Sometimes he wondered about the men who had previously worn his pants or slept on his bunk; what had they done while wearing those pants or sleeping on that bunk? He'd try not to think of it, but he couldn't help himself at times. In the joint, he fought germs by wiping everything down with his bath towel. When issued new clothing, he washed those items in his sink though they had been laundered. He could never seem to remove the stench. Leonard looked around at the furnishings of his temporary home and decided he needed to buy something that would sterilize and remove the odors in this place.

Having finished reliving the moments he had shared with the young Asian girl, he was now angry with himself and wished he hadn't succumbed to the temptation of her young flesh. There would no doubt be more. He had sworn to himself he would fight to abstain from them, though he knew sometimes he would not be able to always resist.

Still thinking about the afternoon with her, he retraced his steps again, this time thinking about evidence he may have left behind. It was possible he left fingerprints as he hadn't worn gloves. He pictured knocking on the front door. That wouldn't have been a problem; she had been the one to open it. Did he push it open with his palm? He didn't remember. He only remembered stepping in as the frightened little girl stepped back saying, "No . . ."

He had spun her around with one hand while putting another over her mouth before forcing her up the stairs and into a bedroom. He didn't think they could get fingerprints from her skin, but he wasn't certain. Once they entered the room, she really began to fight. She squirmed, tried to scream. He had his hand on her mouth. Would that leave DNA? On him, he thought, not her. He was having trouble controlling her. That's when he wrapped his hands around her throat. He knew he wouldn't stop once he started choking her, but so be it; this was always the best part.

The struggle ended and she slumped to the ground peacefully.

He didn't pleasure himself. Not then. Not once she was dead; he wasn't sick like that. Though, the pictures he took, well . . .

Her body had still twitched and gurgled as he removed her panties and explored her body. This was something he very much enjoyed, and he took his time. Maybe he shouldn't have taken the pictures, he now considered. But he dismissed the thought as he lifted his phone and scrolled through the pictures once more. He treasured the photographs. If only he had pictures of all of them—the ones from many years ago. Leonard had learned to use the phone's camera and map, and was glad he had. But he wasn't sure he should keep such evidence stored on the device he would have with him at all times. Maybe he would enjoy them just once or twice more, and then delete them forever.

Leonard recalled his departure, and saw his hand reach to open the sliding glass door that led to the backyard. That may have been his only mistake. *Damnit*, he knew better. He saw himself reaching for the door again, only this time using his shirt or a towel rather than his bare hand. It frustrated him to think he had overlooked such a fundamental precaution.

The phone vibrated in his hand and the display showed *Moses* was calling. He took another pull on his Camel and reached to extinguish it in a gold translucent ashtray that sat on an adjacent table. He pushed the button to answer the phone, raised it to his ear, and waited silently.

After a moment, the familiar, high-pitched, whiny voice said, "You there?"

He calmly replied, "Yeah."

"Well, why didn't you fucking say so? Normal fucking people say '*Hello*' when they answer the phone, or 'How may I help you,' or 'This is fuckface, who's calling?'"

"How may I help you? . . . Is that better, fuckface?"

The phone was silent for a moment.

"Boss wants an update. Did you get the message?"

"Yeah, I got it."

"And?"

"And, what? I got it today."

"Have you located him?"

"Have I located him? You gave me an address. I picked up the message today. I haven't done shit, I've been busy. If he needed it done today, he should have said today, not sometime in the next couple weeks, or thirty days, whatever."

"It was sent four days ago."

"Well, maybe, but I picked it up today. I have twenty-nine days left."

"You have twenty-four."

Leonard frowned across the empty room, seeing a clock on the wall but not a calendar. He didn't need a calendar or a calculator to figure out that Marty fucking Feldman, aka: Moses, or fuckface, was full of shit. "Even if we go off of when it was sent, how the hell do you get twenty-four?"

"Look it, shit-stain, I'm not here to argue. Boss wants an update, I'll tell him you've been fucking off, not doing your job. I told him we shouldn't have hired a squirrelly little prick like you anyway. You're just proving my point."

Leonard pulled the phone from his ear to look at it, as if the device itself were his source of irritation at the moment. He brought it back slowly and held it to his ear while lighting a fresh cigarette and taking a long drag. As he exhaled, he said, "It will be done, don't get your panties all wadded up. Tell the boss I'm all over it. And you should try not being such a suck-ass douchebag."

"Twenty-three days, the clock is ticking, dickwad."

This fucking guy.

"Hey, why the cop anyway?"

"What, are you writing a book?"

Leonard started to ask who it was that wanted a cop croaked but thought better of it. He also thought about saying he needed to double his price for this one, you don't just whack a cop in this town. The cops here will hunt you like a rabid dog and beat you and kill you and then beat you some more after you're dead—you saw it all the time on the news. Nobody gave a shit about most killings in L.A. Hell, yellow tape was part of the landscape. There were too many bodies to worry about a dead bitch here and there, a little Asian girl, or a dead store clerk. But you kill a cop, they're coming for you. He would have insisted on more money had he known he was scheduled for a pig hunt.

"No, I ain't writing no books. But I can tell you one thing, I'm not staying around here after that job. No more jobs on the west coast after that one, you let the boss man know. I'll be on a plane or bus a half hour later headed east or south or maybe north, I don't care. So, tell him I might need a travel bonus."

"Fuck off, little man," was all Moses said before disconnecting the call.

Leonard fumed as he held the phone out and stared at it again. He decided right then that one day he would kill Moses, the pockmarked, Marty Feldman-looking asshole with his squeaky, whiny, little bitch voice. The fucker.

He opened the photos on his phone and began scrolling through them again, trying to get Feldman off his mind. As he did, he began to light another cigarette, but stopped. The cigarette dangled from his mouth as he stared at the lighter in his hand, realizing now he had carried a different one in his pocket, the yellow one. He loved the color yellow. Not the blue one. He hated the color blue. Where was his yellow lighter? Had he lost it? Where? His eyes darted around the room, and he thought of his car, thinking maybe he had left it there. He checked both pockets again, but they were now empty.

Leonard grabbed his keys from the table and went out to his car.

# 14

---

**D**AVEY LOPES LEFT the hotel in Brookings, Oregon, late Friday morning. He was pleased with his conquest, though a part of him wished she hadn't given in so easily.

He had enjoyed the evening, the drinks, the conversation, the mutual bullshitting of one another as they looked into each other's eyes and smiled and laughed while a baseball game played on the big screen. Lopes noticed the patrons that came and went, and he noticed that she, Maria Lopez, was also aware of their surroundings. He assumed she had developed the habit while working as a corrections officer at Pelican Bay. But he also knew she could have just as easily brought the skills with her from the neighborhood. Growing up in *The Avenues* would require street smarts, and she seemed to have plenty of that to go with her good looks and foul mouth.

He'd had a study going, an informal one of course, but one he spoke of with his male partners and friends, usually over drinks. His theory was that all of them were sluts. Every last one. His exes, his girlfriends, his past female partners, hell, even his sisters. Only his mother and his daughters were excluded from this presumed group of the terminally promiscuous. Only they were worthy of an ivory tower, in his mind, so he was destined to a life of bachelorhood.

Maybe it was the age, he had to consider, knowing he was long past the days of meeting untainted women. He understood that, but even so, he did pretty well with the younger ladies—ladies like Lopez *with a Z*—and they too failed the test repeatedly, one after the other. There seemed to not be a mature woman left on the planet who possessed even a trace of modesty when it came right down to it. He decided it was just the day and age, and the influences of pop culture. Which made him feel old. Lopes wasn't old, not in his mind. He was a young fifty-two-year-old who kept himself in excellent physical and mental shape.

He thought about her from last night and smiled through his windshield as the white lines raced past him and the road hummed beneath his rental. He had the window down and was lapping up the fresh coastal air before returning to the city. He did love playing the game, a little cat and mouse with the ladies. He enjoyed it nearly as much as playing cops and robbers. Maybe more in some ways, less in others. He understood *robbers,* but he'd never figure out the *mice.*

He considered it a challenge when a woman would insinuate that he didn't have a chance. Most of the time, he knew that meant his odds were even or better. He actually stood a good chance, as far as he was concerned. It seemed the best strategy was to shrug it off as no big deal, *whatever, lady,* giving the impression it was they who would be missing the prize. It seemed to drive them crazy, and that was the part he loved most. *What, you're not even interested?*

So, when *Lopez with a Z* had escorted Davey Lopes—whose family had apparently changed the spelling of their name to deny their race, according to Z—out of the prison, she asked where he was staying, and if he planned on getting a drink later. He smiled his cocky smile, just a hint of one corner of his mouth turning up and the corresponding eye squinting while the other seemed to sparkle. He had practiced it and knew how it looked in the mirror. The two were facing each other, standing near the gun lockers outside of security at the notorious Pelican Bay prison. Lopes had finished holstering his pistol while looking into her mischievous brown eyes. He snapped his holster closed and pulled a pen from behind his ear and steadied it over the palm of his left hand.

He had said, "You want to give me your number?"

Lopes waited while she looked around the small, enclosed concrete room with walls of lockers and a bank of reinforced, bulletproof mirrored windows that sat above their heads. He figured they were being watched and were probably the topic of conversation on the other side of the glass. He also knew she would realize it too. But the gate was opening to the free world and he was about to disappear. She would have no business-related reason to follow him beyond the sally port, and he knew it. It was now or never.

She had glanced up at the mirrored windows and back to Lopes. "Okay, tell me where you're staying, I don't want you writing something down. They'll know what that means in there."

He stuck the pen back behind his ear with a precise, practiced motion. "Best Western, up the highway. I don't stay local, where all the assholes' baby mamas stay while they're here smuggling drugs into your prison."

"Ah, Brookings," she had said with a nod, "up in Oregon. Good choice."

He turned toward the opened gate as others were coming in from outside. Before he broke eye contact, he said, "Well, you know where to find me. I'm sure I'll be at the hotel's bar most of the evening."

Now he was driving his rental car south to Del Norte where he would be picked up by a private plane and flown back to Long Beach, all on the county dime and time. An old radio car partner was one of the pilots assigned to the sheriff's fixed-wing plane at the Aero Bureau, and he was more than happy to fly homicide guys around for their various investigative needs. But only if the sheriff didn't have something else scheduled for *his* plane. The drive and coastal scenery did little to remove his thoughts of Officer Lopez with a Z.

He thought about her one last time as he pulled into the rental return lane of the quaint coastal airport, and then his mind went back to the business at hand. He had mafia members making moves that would likely impact his county—and already had. He thought about the double murder in El Monte and how Spooky seemed to want to dismiss the notion that it was a mafia hit. There had been another murder in Long Beach he had meant to bring up, and forgot. He would ask him about it on the next visit.

But what bothered him most was when—off the cuff and out of the blue—Lopes had asked him, "What do you know about a bitch losing her head and hands?" and Spooky blinked. It was similar to playing poker, and

Lopes was a better player than most. Spooky had lied to him when he said he didn't know anything about it; Lopes was certain of it.

What did it mean? He didn't know. Maybe Spooky had heard about it, or maybe it was in fact related to mafia work and Spooky withheld that information too, for some reason. He made a mental note to get with Ray and Dickie back at the bureau to talk with them about their case, just in the unlikely event it too was mob related.

Lopes regretted not pressing Spooky more about these cases. But he didn't want to get off in the weeds, either. The double murder in El Monte was what he primarily wanted to ask about. That was a case which had the markings of a mob hit, but nobody had been able to say for certain that it was. Lopes hadn't picked up anything on the wire, and none of his informants had revealed any information to indicate it was. The victims—two Mexican gang members from El Monte Flores—weren't known to have a *green light* on them, a term used by Mexican gang members to describe someone who had made the hit list. *La lista.*

Lopes had talked to investigators from his previous assignment at Prison Gangs, an LASD Detective Division specialized unit, as well as his own department's OSJ—Operations Safe Jails, and OSS—Operations Safe Streets. He had spoken with a contact at LAPD's CRASH—Community Resources Against Street Hoodlums, who usually had good information on the mafia, as well as a couple of his other informants. Nobody knew of the gangsters from El Monte being on the list, or those murders being mob related.

Their gang, El Monte Flores, wasn't on the list either. Lopes had checked. He was well aware that the two gang members could have been killed just for their gang affiliation, if others in that gang had violated any of the Eme rules. But as far as he could tell, EMF was in good standing with the mafia.

His next option would be his best informant, Spooky, but Spooky said he didn't know. Lopes still felt the gangster was holding something back. Lopes had the feeling a lot of shit was going on that nobody was talking about, and it was starting to piss him off.

He stopped the rental in a vehicle return line and grabbed his overnight bag from the back seat. An attendant came toward him, a Hispanic man with tattoos showing on his hands and neck from beneath his long-sleeved shirt.

The attendant said, "Returning the car, sir?"

Lopes smiled widely. "Yeah, homes, just came from the joint. What about you?"

The attendant broke a big smile and accepted the ten-dollar bill Lopes offered. "Nah, man," he said, still grinning, "I don't fuck around no more, *ese*."

LEONARD CIRCLED THE BLOCK ONCE, SAW THE NUMBERS ON THE FRONT OF the house and double-checked the letter he had received with the name, address, and a photograph of his next job.

That's what he called them, *jobs*. The fun of it had left once it became work. It became work when Moses began pushing him around, talking down to him and stressing him with schedules and deadlines, this pockmarked Marty Feldman-looking asshole who seemed to take pleasure in breathing down Leonard's neck. He couldn't think about it without seeing himself drive a screwdriver into the man's throat. Someday.

He glanced from the letter to the house, twice, idling out front and wanting to get away from there before drawing attention. The numbers were a match, but the plaque on the wall had a last name of Lewis; he was looking for Jones. He wondered if the idiot Moses got it wrong, sent him to the wrong place.

He decided he would watch from down the street for a while to see who came and went. He glanced at the time displayed on the radio and thought he'd give it a couple of hours. It was nearly five, the time of night people would start coming home from work.

The house was on a corner. It fronted Sixth Street, but the detached garage and driveway were around the corner on University, close to Bel Aire Drive. Leonard figured that anyone coming or going would park in the garage or driveway, so he parked up the street where he could easily see the garage.

This was better than sitting in front of the house. He was already nervous enough about the job being a cop. How was he going to do it? He didn't know. Maybe run him down in the street, hit and run. He thought the way to do it with this job would be from a distance. But Leonard had no clue how that could work. He didn't know explosives and he didn't know how to shoot a gun. He had never shot one in his life.

Leonard knew how to choke the life out of people. The key was you never let go too soon. You stayed with it while they flailed and flopped and grabbed at your arms and stared into your eyes with fear and hate and disbelief. You waited until they were limp and no longer twitching and then you waited just a little while longer to be certain. He had experienced one girl coming back to life. That was when he was young and inexperienced, and he had to kill the bitch twice. Leonard also knew how to cut them and drain their lifeblood while watching their skin turn blue and their eyes a dull gray. But he didn't see being able to do any of these things to this cop. Cops had guns, for Christ's sake, and he wasn't looking to get killed trying to kill someone.

Thinking of young girls, he again thought of his lighter. He hadn't found it in the car, and he kept thinking he somehow left it at the Asian girl's home. He tried to not think about it.

Nearly two hours later, a sedan pulled to the curb and parked near the driveway. Leonard didn't know why the man wouldn't pull into the garage. Maybe it wasn't the resident. But it was a cop car, the detective type, there was no doubt about that. Leonard sat up and shifted in his seat as he felt his adrenaline rush through him and his heart start to pound in his chest. The man who stepped out of the car was dressed in slacks and a shirt and tie, and he was wearing a hat. Leonard was too far away to see if the man wore a gun, but he knew this was him, there was no doubt. This was the *job*.

The cop walked through a gate into the backyard. Leonard frowned through the windshield. He continued to watch beyond the garage, looking toward the house and waiting to see lights come on as darkness settled over the city. But as he did, he was surprised to see lights go on over the garage. He hadn't even noticed, but now he saw the apartment. A few minutes later the cop walked out and stood on the balcony over the garage, looking beyond him toward the mountains while sipping a can of beer.

Leonard smiled. This fucking loser cop lives on top of a garage. Maybe it wouldn't be that hard of a job after all. He began to light a cigarette but thought better of it while the man was standing there staring off in his general direction. Instead, he carefully slouched lower into his seat to make himself invisible.

---

I WAS STILL GETTING USED TO MY APARTMENT IN BURBANK WHERE THE streets were congested and confusing and there was no easy access to the freeways. The cops here said it was great because gangsters would come up from the hood—South Los Angeles—to pull some robberies or burglaries or just generally terrorize the working class, and then they'd get lost at least half the time trying to get back to the freeway. The crime rate was low compared to the rest of the San Fernando Valley.

Burbank seemed to be a safe little community and it wasn't far from downtown Los Angeles, the hub of all our activity. Also, there was an In-N-Out between my new apartment and the onramp to the southbound Golden State.

There may have been a lesser motivation to live proximate to Santa Clarita. I held onto a sliver of hope that there was still a chance of recon- ciling with Valerie, so I didn't want to be too far from her. Though I also didn't want to be too close; I might be tempted to check to make sure she was safe. And alone. She had bought a townhouse after we sold our home and divided up the money. The divorce wasn't final yet, but we had both acted as reasonable adults thus far through the process.

Thinking of Val only darkened my already bleak mood, so I pulled a cold beer out of the fridge and walked out onto the balcony that offered a beautiful view of the Verdugo mountains to the east. Lights twinkled throughout the foothills as the sun set to the west, casting long shadows over the valley. It was a view most would enjoy, but truthfully, I couldn't have cared less. It was a lonely goddamned place and it didn't feel like home.

A steady flow of traffic went across Bel Aire Drive, which was a short distance east of my new apartment. There was less traffic directly below me on University Avenue, though at this time of evening residents were coming home from their jobs and from school.

I stood leaning on the rail, feeling sorry for myself while at the same time trying to appreciate having a nice apartment that wasn't in a complex full of other people. I couldn't have afforded anything nice while going through a divorce. It was a mother-in-law type apartment, a one bedroom, one bath job built on top of a detached garage at the rear of a three-thousand square foot home. The homeowners—my landlords—were a pair of retired sergeants from the department who married and bought the place on two cops' salaries when Burbank was affordable to the working class. They were friends of mine from many years prior, and when a mutual friend who knew of the apartment had learned of my predicament, he suggested I give them a call. Chuck and Patti were more than happy to have me take the vacant apartment as long as I was able to make friends with their bulldog, Elvis. The backyard was his turf, and the path to my doorstep lay therein. It was a deal. I loved dogs, and four hundred a month was a steal. I promised to keep an eye on the place while they traveled, which they often did, the three of them together.

I turned the can up and drained the final contents of my beer. As I started for the fridge, a car turned onto University from Bel Aire Drive, its headlights washing across a line of parked cars to the east of where I stood. My attention was drawn to the silhouette of a man sitting alone in one of the cars. I stopped and watched, but the lights were now gone and it appeared as just another sedan parked along a row of others on the side of a busy street.

I turned the empty can up to my mouth so it would be obvious to anyone watching that I had finished my beer. My thought was that it would give me time to get downstairs and out onto the street while someone might believe I had only gone to the fridge. I walked inside. Once I was beyond the view from the street, I hurried into the bedroom, grabbed my gun and a flashlight, and went out the door and down the steps into the backyard.

Once I had exited the backyard through the gate and came out next to my county car, I paused for a moment to look up the street and see if I could identify which vehicle it was that had drawn my attention. I couldn't tell from the street level and hadn't thought to get a count of parked cars before leaving the balcony. It seemed to me the car in question had been about five or six cars from the corner.

I briefly debated walking up to the man in his car, or driving my own car to him. But this internal conflict only lasted a brief moment before I followed my first instinct. I slid into my car and peeled away from the curb.

I turned my headlights on, hit the high beams, and veered toward the opposite side of the road where the man had sat in one of a line of parked cars. There was an empty spot, and right away I knew that was where the car had been. Stopped in the middle of the street, I visually checked each of the other cars to be certain. There were no occupants and nothing about the other cars that seemed suspicious.

It was probably just somebody leaving, I told myself. I was being paranoid, the way I always had. The way most cops are. I began to turn around and head back to my apartment, but then I stopped. I threw the car in park and left it running with the door open and headlights shining high as I stepped out and picked up two cigarette butts from the pavement where the car had sat.

Just because I was paranoid didn't mean I was wrong.

Back in my apartment, I made a note on an envelope of the date, time, and a few details of what I had observed, and placed the two cigarette butts inside. They were Camel or Pall Malls, some type of non-filtered cigarette, the type preferred by convicts. There probably weren't many Burbank residents who smoked non-filtered cigarettes.

I went back onto the porch with two beers in hand and a Glock in my waistband to sit in the darkness and watch the street. Traffic was light and activity was sparse. My mind wandered back to Val and I thought of calling her but fought against the urge. I thought of calling Floyd, but I wasn't sure I was speaking to him. He seemed to be pissing me off, though I didn't know why.

My cell vibrated on the small table that stood next to my patio chair. It was Floyd.

"What's up, asshole?"

"I was wondering why you're pissing me off," he said, "thought I'd go right to the source."

"Funny, I was just thinking the same."

"You're pissing yourself off?"

I chuckled. "Actually, yeah, I am. What are you doing?"

"On my way into the office. Me and Mongo have barrel duty tonight, thought I'd call and see what the hell you've been up to. How's that case, the hot broad with no head?"

"How do you know she's hot?"

"I saw the pictures, remember? You had them spread out there on Ray's desk."

"Okay, but she didn't have a head."

"Never mind, Dickie, you're already back to taking this shit serious."

I was staring at the street where a space between two cars still sat empty, wondering if there was anything to it. The cigarettes concerned me; they were a sure sign of trouble in my opinion. Nobody sat smoking cigarettes in a car in a place like that unless they were watching someone, or waiting for someone. And not many smoked non-filters, period. I thought I'd run it by my partner—my ex-partner—and see what he thought. I had nobody else to tell; even Elvis the bulldog was gone with Chuck and Patti.

When I finished telling him the story, Floyd said, "That ain't good, Dickie."

"You think?"

"I don't like the cigarettes."

"Yeah, me neither."

"Chuck around, or are they out of town?"

"Gone to Havasu, Patti and Elvis too."

He made a *hmmm* sound. I waited while he was likely thinking it through. He was good at this type of thing, and he would have a plan. Floyd always needed a plan.

"How about if I have Mongo man the phones, and I'll come out there and drink your beer. That way, if you have to kill someone, you'll have a witness, and someone there to hold your beer for you."

"That's your plan?"

"It's a start. Seriously though, it's not a bad idea. I can respond from your place in Burbank if anything jumps off. Mongo can handle the phones—he always falls asleep at the desk anyway and it pisses me off. The bastard falls asleep during the middle of a sentence. He'll be telling you about something and all of a sudden, I'm like, 'Hey, man, you're snoring.' I could come keep you company and Mongo can sleep on the desk and answer calls."

"You're welcome to come out for a visit if you'd like, but I don't think there's any point. I mostly wanted to see if you have the same concerns that I do. I hate being paranoid, but this seems strange. I mean, the cigarettes, plus the fact the guy split in those few minutes that I was out of his view between the balcony and the street. He probably realized I saw him in the headlights and panicked."

"Who the hell would be watching you?"

"I've got no idea."

He waited a few seconds before saying, "You don't suppose Val would have a P.I. watching you, do you?"

"For what? No, that wouldn't even make sense."

"You're right, scratch that."

"I was wondering about feds, or even Internal Affairs."

"It's not I.A., not smoking non-filtered cigarettes. Now if we found a tampon and bubblegum wrappers on the ground, I'd say there was a chance you were onto something."

I chuckled. "Yeah, good point. I don't know, man, it's just really strange."

"Well, if there's one thing we love, dickhead, it's strange. I'll see you in half an hour. Put on some coffee. I probably shouldn't drink any beer since I have to stay awake all night."

## 15

FLOYD SHOWED UP with a bag that held two burritos. "I'm starving, Dickie, have you eaten?"

"Not hungry, partner, but thanks."

I walked away from the door and directly back to the balcony, hearing the front door close behind me and feeling Floyd's presence at my heels. I took the far chair and offered the closer one to Floyd with a nod of my head. "You want a beer, or coffee?"

He sat down. "Well, I was going to be good and have coffee, but these burritos would go better with beers, so . . ."

"Sit tight, I'll grab a couple."

I returned with two cans of Coors Light, handed one to Floyd, and popped the top on the other. "What do you think of my new place?"

He looked around as if the balcony was the focus. "I like it, Dickie. Pretty cool for a bachelor pad. Think of it like this, you don't have a lawn to mow, don't have much to keep up inside, and nobody's going to give a shit when you leave your dirty socks on the floor."

"I'm definitely living the dream."

We sat silently for a few minutes. Floyd was devouring the first burrito and I was staring up the street, thinking about the car that had sat there an hour or so before.

It had been just over a year since I was shot. Floyd and I had been investigating a murdered prostitute, a transsexual who went by Susie Q, though her birth name was Shane Wright. While investigating Susie's murder, we stumbled upon another dead prostitute who happened to be Susie's best friend. *She*, also a man in the process of becoming a woman, had been killed across the street from where Susie was murdered, at about the same time. We solved the two cases, unraveling a prostitute ring that had evolved into drugs and extortion. Susie and her friend were not happy with their handler and childhood friend, Donna Edwards, and some of Donna's gangster friends. One such friend, Gilbert Regalado, lived in East Los Angeles with his mother and some other relatives including an uncle named Jorge Regalado. Jorge had spent most of his life in prison and had only recently been released. On the night I was shot, Floyd and I had gone to find Gilbert. We did, and when he ran, Floyd chased after him and another gangster. Floyd and I became separated, and I found myself inside the dingy home of Gilbert Regalado, searching for my partner. It was there I found myself in a fight for my life as Jorge and I came face to face, barrel to barrel. Gunfire erupted, smoke filled the room, and the two of us fell to the floor bleeding from gunshot wounds.

A few days later, I awoke in a hospital bed down one kidney but still alive. That's when I learned I had killed Jorge in the shootout and Floyd had arrested Gilbert and physically beaten two other men in his efforts to get to his downed partner inside the home. Gilbert and Donna Edwards were later charged with the murders of the two prostitutes. I spent a year recovering from being shot.

During that year, I had minimized communications with my old partner and friend, Floyd, and had never bothered telling him why. He probably understood, because he knew me better than anyone. There was a good chance I wouldn't be coming back at all, and I needed to distance myself from the job and all that came with it, even the friendships. Or rather, that's what I believed at the time. Maybe I was only feeling sorry for myself, I don't know. The shrink called it depression. During that time, my wife of six years had packed her bags and now I was facing my second divorce. I blamed both failed marriages on the stresses of being a cop, though in all honesty, I'm not sure it was entirely the job.

Floyd broke the silence as he took his last bite. "So, tell me about the dead chick up in Newhall. What the hell was her problem?"

"She lost her head," I joked. "Technically, it's Santa Clarita, out in the industrial area. But to answer your question, there's not much to tell, other than what you know. You saw the scene, the victim photos. You heard Ray's brief of the case. I don't know, man, it's just one of those really bizarre ones. I wish you were on it with me. I wish it was ours."

He waited, watched, and continued eating.

"I mean, who does something like that? And why? We told you about the old man, right? The guy had no emotion whatsoever. His old lady gets whacked, gets her head cut off, and this asshole sits there in his big leather chair telling us he knows we consider him a suspect in his wife's death."

"You guys identified her?"

"No, that's the point. He tells us that—that he knows we consider him a suspect in his wife's death—and says he has retained an attorney. Then he says he'll speak with us anyway, against the attorney's advice."

Floyd stuffed the wrapper of the first burrito into a paper bag and pulled out the second one. He gestured, offering it to me, but I shook my head. Focused on unwrapping his burrito, he said, "He's playing you."

I cocked my head and raised a brow.

"I'm just saying," Floyd continued, "that maybe that's his strategy. Put all that shit out there and play it cool, make you doubt he could be involved with his wife's disappearance. Using that *all the cards on the table* approach, to soften you up."

He was right, it was disarming in some ways. When a man looks you directly in the eyes and tells you he knows he's a suspect, basically says, *let's get this over with, I don't need an attorney,* it makes you feel the guy has nothing to hide.

"Yeah, well, he might be playing us right now, but I'm going to rock him and his attorney's little world here soon."

"You remember that asshole, Wayne McKnight?" Floyd asked. "He had that idiot attorney who kept leaving voicemails, telling us not to contact his client."

My grin answered his question as to whether or not I recalled it.

Floyd continued, "I thought the captain was going to lose his mind. Every time that asshole told us we couldn't talk to his client, we'd go down there and knock on asshole's door. Then he faxes over a letter to put us on official notice. So, we drove down there and knocked on his door again. His old lady was about to lose *her* mind, and she says, 'Haven't you heard from our attorney?' You go, 'Yeah, we don't give a shit about any of that. Where the hell is Wayne?'

"We get back to the office and Stover's marching all over the bureau with steam blowing out of his ears. He sees me first and starts yelling at me, 'What the hell is wrong with the two of you?'"

Floyd was chuckling now. "I tell Stover, 'What?' He says, 'You know goddamned well *what*.' So, I just shrugged and told him he needed to talk to you. I said, 'Go see Dickie, he's the asshole who's convinced the attorney can't invoke the privilege for his client. The hell do I care?'"

He looked over and we were both laughing now.

"He storms over to your desk and starts chewing your ass, telling us we can't talk to this asshole because his attorney said we can't, and you said, 'Captain, you do realize this guy's not in custody, right?' He says, 'Yeah, and . . .' and you go, 'Well, if he isn't in custody, and he hasn't invoked his right to counsel *to us*—which he hasn't—we're going to continue knocking on his goddamn door until he tells us to go pound sand. We've got a murder to solve.'"

I waited while Floyd took a long swig of his beer, finishing it off. "I swear I thought he was going to shoot you. I'm surprised he didn't bench you or send you to Missings after that. He was so fucking mad, I wouldn't have been surprised to see him stroke out right there in the squad room."

I collected the empty beers and went in for a couple more. After handing him a fresh one, I said, "Yeah, I guess maybe I could've handled that better."

"Dude, it was classic Dickie. That's the shit I lived for, working with you."

I sat down. "Yeah, but that's the type of shit that's given me a lot of headaches too, me being an asshole like that. It's no wonder I'm without a partner now, working Unsolveds. Stover hates me."

That hung in the air for a few minutes and neither of us was laughing or smiling now. We were both looking out over a quiet neighborhood scantly lit by sparingly placed yellow streetlights and a budding quarter moon over the mountains to the east.

Floyd finished his burrito and washed it down with beer. He checked his phone and started texting someone and the smile crept back onto his face.

"What's going on, anything important?"

He didn't look up. "Nah, just my new idiot letting me know he's already sent two teams out. Apparently, it's not going to be a quiet night after all. I probably better head back."

"You think you guys will stay together?"

There it was, I put it out there. It popped out against the promise I made to myself that I wouldn't ask. But here I was, alone in my personal life, and alone in my professional life. To say I felt abandoned by everyone I gave a shit about—Floyd and Val—was an understatement.

He finished his text and leaned back in his chair, took another swig and let the question marinate for a minute. "I don't know, Dickie. I mean, I don't want to train anyone else, that's for sure. That's a pain in the balls. He's a good dude, easy to work with, so I don't know . . . I mean, probably, unless something changes."

I looked away without responding. He knew what I was asking and completely avoided the topic. There it was. Same as with Val, the message was *it's time to move on, nothing personal.*

In the awkward silence, he said, "Dude, if we have a chance to get back together, I'd be happy to. But honestly, I don't think Stover's going to let that happen. Know what I mean?"

True or not, it was good to hear it. Something to hold onto. "Yeah, you're probably right. I guess we burned a lot of bridges with him."

He grinned. "And cars."

I nodded.

"Well, brother, I better head to the office before Mongo breaks something. I'm sure he's buried now, handling the phones and paperwork with two teams sent out. Plus, your former lieutenant is bound to show up at the office to write his memos, and wonder where the hell I am."

I nodded.

"You got a to-go cup for that coffee?"

I stood and motioned for him to walk in. "You bet."

After pouring Floyd a cup to go, I followed him onto the landing and waited while he descended the redwood staircase into the back yard. He looked up before going through the gate. "Keep your eyes open, Dickie, and give me a call if you need anything. I can be up here in ten minutes if need be, twenty tops."

"You bet, bud. Have a good night, and thanks for coming out."

He nodded and disappeared behind the other side of the six-foot, redwood fencing that encircled the yard.

COFFEE SOUNDED GOOD, SO I POURED MYSELF A CUP AND RESUMED WATCH from the balcony. I sat and thought about my conversation with Floyd, and I thought about my position at the bureau, which essentially was the role of a utility player at this point. Available for all, committed to none. Like my personal life.

The streets were quiet now with only the occasional car traveling past. I spent a few minutes trying to convince myself I was being paranoid, and then I began thinking tactics. I came inside and closed the door to the balcony and the blinds that covered it. I locked the door and placed a table and lamp in front of it. I closed the bedroom window and blind and did the same in the kitchen. That was it for glass. I went downstairs and retrieved the shotgun from my trunk, along with a box of shells. After securing the gate, I leaned two cookie sheets against it, so that if it was opened, there would be a noise to alert me.

Back inside I killed all of the lights, kicked off my shoes and stretched out on the couch, the shotgun leaned on the arm of the couch near my head and my pistol resting on my chest. I closed my eyes and waited to drift off, thinking about the car and the man and the cigarette butts I found on the street.

But before I found sleep, my mind ran the gamut of possibilities: I thought about the man who had shot me a year before. The Hispanic gangster named Jorge Regalado who I shot and killed in turn. I wondered if his nephew, Gilbert, was still in jail, or could he be out? I made a mental note to run him on the computer back at the office. The mean, ugly face of Jorge stuck with me though as I tried to move past that nightmare in waiting. I could see his snarling face with his bushy mustache and the spittle flying through the air in slow motion, just as I recalled it from that night in

East L.A. The two of us, face-to-face, shooting each other in a room that smelled of burned tortillas, dirty feet, and cigarettes.

*Cigarettes!*

I pictured the cigarette butts collected from the street, and saw the dead convict, Jorge Regalado, with a non-filtered Camel in his mouth. Then Gilbert, same image. I pictured both of them with their tattoo-covered arms and necks and I pictured the body of Shane Clayton Wright, a soft young man who had been changed to a woman, who sold her body on Long Beach Boulevard in Lynwood. Jorge was the one who had killed her, and Gilbert was an accomplice. One was dead; the other should be in jail. I'd been off work ever since that night when Jorge met his maker and Gilbert was taken into custody. I had only returned to my duties two days ago, just more than a year later. Now the whole event and its players again weighed heavily on my mind, considering the situation at hand.

There had even been a crazy vet, a former sniper who, for a long time, had been a prime suspect. We had called him Fudd, and although there would be no motive I could think of, I went ahead and pictured him in the car watching me too. He had watched our suspects in that case—Gilbert and Jorge—and obtained photographs along the way. His work was largely responsible for our solving the case. Would he be watching me now? Crazier things have happened.

But if not Fudd, or a Regalado—or friends or family thereof—then who? Who would be watching me now, and why?

Maybe just coincidence.

No, I didn't buy it. I don't believe in coincidence. Had there not been two cigarette butts, I could move past it and maybe just be aware of my surroundings to be certain. But no, the two butts told me someone had sat there a minimum of fifteen minutes, probably longer. The type of cigarettes told me something about the person who smoked them. Sure, two generations ago servicemen were known to smoke non-filtered cigarettes, even after being discharged. But that hasn't been the case for a long time. Very rarely will you now find someone smoking a non-filtered cigarette who hadn't acquired such a taste in prison.

Floyd had asked about Val. That didn't make sense to me. There would be no value for her in having me watched. Honestly, I doubt she cared what I was doing. I considered briefly the possibility that it could have something to do with Chuck and Patti, or their careers, but I quickly dismissed the notion. They had been retired for quite a while, and their career paths were very different than mine. Patti had worked in the Training Bureau for many years, and Chuck had been a motor cop. People hated getting tickets, but they generally didn't kill a cop over it.

I wished Elvis was here to bark if there were an intruder. Elvis the bulldog, not fat Elvis.

Jesus, was I going to have to go through all my cases from the last decade to see who had been released? In this state, you never knew who would be released regardless of their crimes. I thought about a case Floyd and I had handled in which a man had killed his family after being released from a psych ward. He had spent two years there after killing someone else, but the state had determined he was rehabilitated. Maybe I'd better check his name next, see if he's been rehabilitated again.

Finally, as I grew tired and felt myself finally drifting off, I decided the entire episode with the stranger in the car was unrelated to me or my career. The clarifying moment came to me when I pondered how anyone would find me and realized the answer was, they wouldn't. There were no records beyond my department personnel files that had been updated with my new address. There was no way anyone outside of law enforcement would have access to that information.

And with that reconciled, I slept.

---

THE APARTMENT REMAINED DARK THROUGHOUT THE DAY FROM THE HEAVY blinds that covered the few portals: a glass door that led to the balcony and two windows, one in the kitchen and the other in the small bedroom. It would be a plus after long nights at crime scenes when I'd need to sleep during the day. However, waking up at 11:30 a.m. was not something I generally intended nor embraced, even on a Saturday morning. But sleep had come late and sparingly so I accepted it as it was.

I opened the blind to the balcony and scanned the road. I didn't see anything of concern, though doing so had given me the idea to bring my binoculars in from my county car. I cooked a couple of eggs and a piece of toast and took breakfast and coffee out to the balcony. I would become accustomed to spending much of my time at home outdoors, as I wouldn't be satisfied with occasional checks of the street below. I would watch nonstop while home until I figured this out or eliminated the idea that any threat existed. Apparently, the idea of it being unrelated and not a threat hadn't reconciled after all.

By afternoon I was sipping iced tea and reviewing the case file on Jane Doe, looking at crime scene photos again and reviewing my notes while glancing up at the sound of any vehicle. The review gave me something to do and helped take my mind off of the situation at hand. The truth is, if it weren't for the potential stalker or surveillance or whatever it was I had going on, I likely would have spent my Saturday in the office alongside other detectives who were without spouses and those who had spouses they couldn't stand.

A light rain began falling in the early evening and forced my retreat inside. By nine I was asleep on the couch, and at four in the morning, wide awake. By dinner time Sunday evening I was exhausted and was again questioning whether there actually was a threat or concern. I had diligently watched the street and surrounding area for the entire weekend and hadn't seen anything suspicious. I hadn't slept well in the process, and my sleeping pattern was now a mess.

I went to bed early with the intent of being at the office by six or seven Monday morning to get a jump on what would be a very busy week.

My plans were disrupted when I found myself wide awake again at midnight, having slept only a couple of hours. I had managed to convince myself there was one suspicious noise outside after another. I got up and checked the street from the balcony half a dozen times. The last time I remember looking at the clock, it was nearly five. And finally, I drifted off to sleep.

# 16

AGAIN, I SLEPT until nearly eleven but this time it was a weekday, a regular day at the office. A day I should have been at it for at least four hours by now. I jumped out of bed and started the coffee without even thinking about checking the street. As I prepared to shower and shave, I started running through my mind all that was planned for the day, and it occurred to me I had missed my appointment with the shrink.

Shit!

Well, another week wouldn't kill me. I needed from her a full release, as described by my captain during his pleasant little *welcome back* speech. It wasn't good enough for him that she had released me to return to work, he wanted her to specifically state in writing that I could return to field duty and be back in the rotation for murders.

I pictured her with her new hairdo and softened demeanor, even showing a smile for the first time in the last few sessions. The truth is, I now enjoyed meeting with her. Katherine James, M.D.—Doc J., Doctor James, Big Red. Or simply, the shrink. Big Red only lasted for a few months before she returned to blonde, which I found more attractive but less seductive.

I had seen her off and on over the years, the first being a mandatory

shrink appointment following my involvement in a shooting. I viewed it
—*her*—as a complete waste of my time, and I only answered what I
thought she wanted to hear, assuming it would all be reported back to the
department. Later, there was an incident in which I lost my temper with a
commander at a crime scene. It was apparently inappropriate for me to
explain to the commander just how anatomically incorrect was his posi-
tioning at the time. In other words, I told the ranking officer he had his
head up his ass, in front of other supervisors and peers. That had set me up
for serious discipline, and it was suggested that I use the semi-legitimate
excuse of being stressed in a high-pressure environment to lessen the
blow. So it was back to see the lovely Doc J., though at that time she did
not seem so lovely.

After being shot, my sessions were ramped up, and somehow I
began feeling differently about her. Now I looked forward to my
appointments and our time together seemed to pass quickly. Too quickly.
Maybe going through another divorce played a part in that, or maybe it
was just my need for female companionship, which I certainly lacked.
Previously, I had always considered her the enemy, my foe, or in the
best-case scenario, an unnecessary evil. When she changed from red
back to blonde, I began calling her Blondezilla, but only behind her
back of course. There had been no warmth between us then, but now it
seemed different; something had changed. Which left me even more
conflicted.

After showering, I poured a cup for the road. Coat and hat in hand, I
cautiously made my way to the county car. Before keying it open, I
inspected it for damage or signs of foul play. I wondered if I should look
underneath, but I didn't want to get on my hands and knees in a suit.

I pulled from the curb and drove up the street to where the car had
been parked a few evenings before, scanning each parked car I passed.
Nothing looked suspicious, but I was now determined to know which cars
belonged in the neighborhood and which did not. A couple more days of
paying attention, and anything that didn't belong would stand out to me
immediately. I drove around the block twice before departing the area, and
then I employed counter-surveillance tactics all the way to the freeway and
for the remainder of my drive to the office.

During the midday commute, I called to reschedule with Doc J., but only reached a voicemail. I left a message apologizing for missing my appointment, and lied that I had been out all night on a case.

---

RAY WAS WAITING WHEN I WALKED THROUGH THE BACK DOOR. "HEY partner, d'you have court this morning?"

"No. It's a long story, but I didn't sleep last night. I must have fallen asleep just before dawn and slept solid once I did. Sorry, man, I hope I didn't keep you from anything."

"Not at all, partner. I just walked in myself. I had to handle an evidence hearing in Compton. I guess my old partner was scheduled to appear, but he didn't show. They called me last minute."

I sat down and pulled my hat off. "What's the deal with him, anyway?"

"Lewandowski?"

"Yeah."

"He's just done, partner. I think he only had another year or so before retirement anyway, so when they came down on him for that deuce, he went off on stress and filed for retirement. Now he won't come in for hearings or anything, says it raises his blood pressure."

"What happened on the deuce?"

"It's not resolved yet, but I hear they're going to plea him to a wet reckless and hit him with some heavy fines. Department can't really do much if he isn't coming back anyway."

"That's too bad; he's a good guy. I mean, I don't think I could work with him, but I've always respected him."

Ray presented me with that friendly smile and said, "Well, partner, the way I see it, I've traded up."

I didn't know what to say. It seemed Ray was hinting he would be interested in permanently hooking up as partners. The thought of it made me smile.

My smile faded when Davey Lopes came through the back door and announced, "Cortez, Jones, don't go anywhere. I need to talk to you both. Let me hit the head and grab a cup, and I'll be right back." He was now pointing a finger at us to make his point as he passed by. "Right back."

Ray and I looked at each other and both of us shrugged.

Ray then chuckled and said, "I guess Lopes needs to talk to us, partner."

———

LOPES SAT NEAR RAY'S DESK AND I LEANED AGAINST AN UNOCCUPIED ONE nearby. Ray had turned his chair around to face each of us.

Lopes said, "I need to know everything you've got going on with that murder up in the valley, the dead bitch." He was snapping his fingers as if trying to remember a name.

"Jane Doe," I said, smiling smugly.

"Right. Fuck you, Jones, you smartass."

Ray began filling him in with the details of our case. He told him about the crime scene in the industrial area of Santa Clarita. He explained how she had been discovered and by whom. He told Lopes about the missing person report and how the two cases are linked by the vehicle. Ray described how the victim's head and her hands had been cut off and were yet to be recovered. Then he nodded to me and said, "And Dickie figured out she couldn't have driven herself to the crime scene, though it was clearly staged to appear she had."

Lopes looked at me. "How'd you figure that, seat position?"

I nodded. Then I picked up where Ray had left off. "Interesting thing on this one, Lopes, is the husband of the missing person. This guy says he knows we consider him a suspect in his wife's death, even though we haven't positively identified her. Says he has retained a lawyer who advised him not to speak with us."

"But he did."

"Exactly. It seemed rehearsed though, to be honest. I also thought it strange he remembered our names without having been provided with cards. The whole thing seems strange."

"Then," Ray said, "we're leaving, and two suits show up."

"Feds?"

"That's what we don't know. They looked like feds, and their car looked like something a fed would drive, but the plates come back with no record on file."

I pulled my notebook out and jotted a reminder to follow up on the license number of that car.

Lopes sat silent for a minute, his eyes fixed on something past Ray, probably just the wall. He appeared to be thinking.

I said, "Why are you asking about it, anyway? This have something to do with the mob?"

Lopes drained his coffee and then sucked in a mouthful of air, filling his cheeks. He blew out a prolonged, exaggerated breath and then looked from me to Ray and back. "There's some bizarre shit going on with the Mexican mafia, brother. So who knows?"

Lopes told us about his visit with Spooky from Big Hazard, and how Spooky described that the Eme was not only ramping up their extortion game, but they were moving into the business communities, leaning on legitimate business owners for protection money. He explained what we already knew, that to sell protection, there needed to be fear, so the mob was on a terror spree. He said they were raping, robbing, and pillaging, though I didn't think he meant it in the literal sense.

"What are they moving in on?" I asked.

"He didn't say. He's holding back on me, which also has me puzzled. I own that little bastard. He's a snitch. He's a walking dead man if I don't protect him. Sooner or later, he'll testify to keep from being part of the RICO. You'd think I'd be the last person he'd start lying to."

"You think he knows something about our case? Ray asked.

Lopes hesitated a moment. "I just didn't like his reaction. I asked him about it on the fly. I was literally walking out of the room and it hit me, I don't know why. It popped into my head, so I just blurted out, 'Hey, what do you know about a bitch getting her head cut off?' He said he didn't know anything about it. But he blinked when I asked him, and he looked away when he answered.

"I should have gone at him on it, but I let it go. I was on my way out and the interview hadn't gone well anyway. I about choked him out at one point, lost my temper in there and was about to throttle him. It wasn't good."

He pulled the pen from behind his ear and started tapping it on the desk. "The main thing is, he says they're farming out work."

"Farming out? . . . Who's farming out to whom?"

"Mexican mafia's farming out some of their work. But he wouldn't say to whom. He claimed he didn't know, but said he'll find out. I mean, it's got to be the brand, they're the only ones who get along with Eme."

"What would be in it for the Aryan Brotherhood?" I asked.

He shook his head. "I don't know, man . . . maybe it's just a business deal. Who else would work for the Mexican mafia? I mean, other than all the cholos on the street, but I didn't get the impression that's what he meant."

Ray said, "What about other mafia? Like Italian?"

"Maybe, but I doubt it. I can't see it," Lopes said. "But what the fuck do I know?"

A few moments of silence told me we'd covered the topic at hand. I said, "Hey, Lopes, speaking of the mob, do you know if a dude named Jorge Regalado is hooked up?"

Lopes squinted and said, "That's the dude you killed."

I nodded, wondering how he knew, or why he remembered.

"What the hell does he have to do with anything? Why are you digging up old shit?"

"Just asking. I just kind of wanted to know. I also wouldn't mind finding out about his nephew, Gilbert. They were both involved in that tranny murder Floyd and I handled last year. I was just curious as to whether either of them had any juice with Eme."

"Uh-huh," Lopes said, letting me know he didn't believe me.

"Look," I pleaded, "I never heard much about those two. I guess maybe I didn't care, or just didn't want to know. Now that I'm back on the job, I'm just curious."

Lopes looked at me without responding. His stare had me squirming inside, but I tried not to let it show. I wouldn't want to be interrogated by him; it seemed he could see right through me. I wondered if I had that effect on others, and briefly considered the times I'd been told I do.

I broke the silence. "I don't know what either of them are called, to be honest, or what gangs they were from. I know they both lived in East L.A.," I said, nodding the direction of the city. "That's about all I know."

"Yeah, Dickie, I know where they fucking lived. I spent two days in that shithole house helping process the shooting scene. Shit, me and Lee and what's his face—cornbread over there—on Team Two—"

"Blankenship?"

"Yeah, cornbread . . . Lee wrote the paper on the place and the three of us oversaw the crime scene investigation. They sucked me in primarily for that purpose, to see if those little assholes were mobbed up. I went through everything in the pad: photographs, letters from the pen, clothing—you name it."

I was shaking my head. "I didn't know anything about that. I'm sorry, man, I didn't realize—"

"Their names were Spider and Shady. Both were from White Fence. Spider's the one you killed, Jorge. Shady, Gilbert Regalado, is up in Tehachapi now doing life without. What else do you want to know?"

Lopes had a flawless memory when it came to the gangsters.

"Do either of them have juice?" I asked.

"The short answer is no, neither were mobbed up. Having said that, White Fence puts in a lot of work for the mob, so they could have been considered associates. I would say they were at least in good standing, neither of them came up on the *lista*. What's this all about, Dickie? And don't tell me you're just curious. I might be stupid, but I'm not *crackhead* stupid."

I looked away, deep in thought for a moment. I decided it would be good to tell a few people. Floyd knew, my partner and Lopes should know too. Especially Lopes; if anyone would hear something about it from the streets or prisons, it would be Lopes. "It's probably nothing, but I thought someone might have been watching me the other night. There was a car up the street from my place. When another car came around the corner and its headlights hit it, I saw a guy sitting there in the dark. I was out on the balcony."

"Ah, that's why you haven't been sleeping, huh, partner?"

I nodded to answer Ray, and then looked at Lopes to see what he thought. "Well?"

"Aren't you going through a divorce?"

I chuckled. "Same thing Floyd thought, a P.I."

"Well, it's one of the first things you think of when you've been through a couple of them, like me and your girlfriend, Floyd."

"Val's got nothing to gain by having me tailed," I told him. "That's not what this is, if it's anything at all. I'm certain of it."

Ray said, "Maybe just some dude making a call, or waiting for someone to show up."

"That's what I had hoped. But when I went out, he was gone."

Lopes said, "So how do you know he'd been watching? How do you know he hadn't just got in the car when you saw him?"

"I'd been sitting out on the balcony looking up the street for fifteen, twenty minutes, just kind of enjoying a beer and the scenery. He had to have been sitting there the whole time. Plus, I picked up a couple cigarette butts where the guy had parked, which tells me he was there for a little while, smoking. Also, those cigarettes were non-filtered."

Lopes looked at Ray. They both then looked at me. Everyone seemed to be on the same page. None of us liked that the cigarettes were non-filtered. Everyone silently confirmed that I wasn't being paranoid. Only assholes smoked non-filtered cigarettes.

---

I HAD IGNORED THREE PHONE CALLS DURING OUR MEETING, NONE OF WHICH were from Valerie. One was from the shrink's office, a secretary telling me I've been rescheduled for Wednesday morning as the good doctor would be out of town Thursday and Friday. It was the only slot they had open until the following week. The message said I only needed to call back if that didn't work for me. Sure, I thought, I'd make it work. I needed the clearance for full duty.

The next message was from county counsel letting me know they intended to represent me in a case filed against the sheriff's department for the wrongful death of Jorge Regalado. Me and Floyd were named as defendants. I rolled my eyes at the news and shook my head. I should have seen it coming, but I hadn't. Nearly every instance of deadly force by a cop results in civil action. There were attorneys who specialized in suing law enforcement and who were elated every time we dumped someone. It had been just over a year since my shooting, so they most likely filed the case just within the one-year statute of limitations. I would have expected to find out another way, and before being blindsided by county counsel.

The third call had been a hang up, but the person didn't disconnect in time to avoid leaving a messageless voicemail. The number was private, so I had no idea where the call had originated. In this business, lots of calls were private, and I didn't give it a second thought. If it were important, they would have left a message. Or they would call back.

After I finished checking messages, I tried calling Val. The call went straight to voicemail. I glanced at my watch, but it held no answers to the questions in my head, such as why was she so intensely avoiding me, and what did I do to deserve excommunication? I had no way to explain or understand her behavior lately.

# 17

LEONARD HAD NO idea why they wanted a cop clipped, but he did know that after the first night watching, he now needed a new ride. He was concerned that the cop—Leonard's new *job*—may have already noticed him and would be suspicious of his return. He flicked a lit cigarette out the window while driving across Hollywood Boulevard and immediately regretted doing so. He checked the mirrors to see if any cops were around who might have noticed. He didn't see any. That's all he needed, to get picked up for something stupid like littering.

Driving a beater Oldsmobile with Florida plates would draw too much attention for the work he was now doing; he needed to find a different car. He had stayed clear of the cop over the weekend in an effort to let things cool. He had a month to do the job, regardless of what Moses Fuckface said. During the weekend, he had put a lot of thought into the situation and had decided a new car was a must. But he needed to buy one for cash with no questions asked. Which is why he had driven to Hollywood. An addict outside his hotel had told Leonard where to go and who to see for just such a business arrangement.

Leonard had $19,000 cash, or a little shy of it, having now received four separate wires of $5,000. Separate wires from different institutions and addressed to four individuals, the names for which he had corresponding identifications. He was paid $20,000 for the first two hits, which he thought was a good deal. So far, he had spent less than a grand of it, forking out $250 per week for his room on Main Street downtown, and buying food, gas, cigarettes, and booze. He thought maybe he'd look for an apartment that cost less but he liked the cash deal with no names at the front desk where he stayed. Parking was nonexistent but he had figured out to park at various restaurants in the area and move the car every four or five hours, even overnight. It wasn't easy getting around by foot once he parked, and on one occasion, he had been accosted by a bum and had ended up stabbing the filthy bastard. He worried about it after, concerned he could contract the AIDS virus from the man's blood all over his hands and arms. Leonard had ditched the knife and washed up at a diner before heading back to the century-old hotel. Now he needed a new knife.

He found the gypsy car dealer just outside of Hollywood. He had no sooner pulled into the lot and stepped out of his car than a smiling Russian in bright colors came directly toward him. The man seemed to be determined to live up to the sign on the building behind him that read *Friendly Auto Sales*. Before the man spoke a word, Leonard knew he hated him.

"Velcome," the stocky man said with a heavy accent. As he neared, he offered his right hand to Leonard.

Leonard looked away, scanning the rows of cars around him. He wasn't about to shake hands with this foreigner, or anyone else for that matter. He didn't touch people unnecessarily in order to avoid germs, and he abhorred others placing hands on him and wouldn't allow it. Not only was it a matter of cleanliness, Leonard also worried that through touch some people could know things about you, or somehow feel connected. There was also his concern for safety. He wouldn't take a chance of being pulled into someone's grasp by offering a hand. Martial artists shake with two hands in order to maintain control and be prepared for combat. Leonard had read about that while he and Whitey studied martial arts in their cell, learning from publications they purchased through the mail. The two had practiced their techniques on one another, all day, every day, for nearly a decade. Each had become proficient in hand-to-hand combat. Leonard didn't want to touch anyone, and nobody was going to touch him.

As a good salesman who would not be deterred, the man withdrew his hand and introduced himself. "Grigori, my name . . . is call Gregory for you Americans. Or, you maybe call me Greg, is better, no?"

Leonard looked at him with a sour expression, and still didn't say anything. What he wanted to say is *What the fuck is that smell?* These foreigners and their goddamn cologne.

"You want, I sell you nice car?"

"Look, man, I'm not here to make friends. I don't care what the fuck your name is, and you don't need to know mine. There's a reason I'm here and not down at the Hollywood fucking Ford or Chevy, ya know what I mean?"

Grigori was undeterred. "Yes, is okay. I sell you nice car, I not know your name."

"I've got twelve hundred. Give me something that runs good and looks like all the other cars on the road, if you get me. Nothing that stands out, attracts attention."

"I have jus' da car."

"I don't need no papers or titles or any other bullshit. Just give me something clean that the cops won't pay attention to. All the lights and blinkers better fucking work. And the air-conditioning."

The Russian's smile widened as he held a finger in the air as if to signal he had just the right vehicle in mind for his special customer. "I have plenty car, they all clean title. Clean as Safeway chicken."

Leonard noticed the finger with its gold ring, and he noticed the other gold rings and bracelets on both hands. He took note of the thick, gold rope necklace around the man's neck with a giant Mercedes emblem that was buried in salt and pepper chest hair, enough to weave a Russian blanket.

The man was saying, "For you, my very good friend, I fix up special." He motioned for Leonard to follow and led him to a silver Ford Taurus that looked like a businessman's special. It would work just fine, Leonard told him, and the two headed for the office to seal the deal.

Leonard walked behind the man and noticed a bulge beneath his untucked, button-up, short-sleeved shirt. He knew it was a gun. Leonard thought about asking him about it, thinking he really did need to learn to use a pistol, and maybe start carrying one. Especially if he was going to have to grease this pig named Dick. But he decided he didn't trust the man. How could you trust a Russian? As they walked up the steps into a mobile home that had the word *Office* hand-painted on the door, Leonard pictured the guy pulling the piece on him inside and robbing him for his cash. There would probably be a dozen more hairy assholes that couldn't speak fucking English waiting inside, smoking their cigarettes and smiling at each other like a bunch of simple foreign assholes. These goddamn Russkies were happy just to be in America where they could commit their crimes and nobody killed them for it. American prisons were vacation destinies for these assholes. Hell, they fed you and gave you TV.

He was relieved to see only a large-breasted, bottle-bleached blonde in a low-cut blouse sitting behind a desk, smoking a long cigarette. Her eyes were painted with silver and blue and her lips were bright red. Whatever she had been doing, she stopped and watched the two of them as they filed in and sat at an adjacent desk.

Grigori Kosloff was the name on the business card he tried to hand Leonard after they sat down. Leonard declined by looking away. The man told him that since he didn't want any papers, maybe it would be best to have his card. He said, "Is okay, you have polize stop at you, tell her you jus' tes' the car, you no buy." He winked and said, "I take good care my special friend." He offered the card once more and Leonard took it from him.

The Russian then asked what he wanted to do with his other car, and Leonard said, "I'll give you another hundred to scrap it, make sure it leaves here in a big block of crushed metal."

$1,300 later, Leonard had a fresh set of wheels with plates as clean as some type of chicken—he had no idea what the fucking Russian even meant—and his other car would disappear from the face of the earth with its Florida plates and who knows what kind of evidence that could possibly link him to half-a-dozen murders. He liked the neutral color, and the light tint on the windows would help conceal him if he wore dark clothes and sat low and still. Especially at night. It was his new work car, and he liked it. But it was also one he could walk away from if needed. Leave it where he had to, if it came to that. Disposable cars were the way to go in his line of work.

LEONARD TOOK THE HOLLYWOOD FREEWAY NORTH FOLLOWING THE MAP program on his company—rather *family*—provided phone. He thought maybe when he returned it, he'd leave the pictures of the dead girl on there to give Feldman something to get off on. The map told him to exit on Barham Boulevard. The next thing he knew he was on Olive and driving right through the center of Burbank. It was just past noon and he hadn't eaten since last night, so he stopped at the In-N-Out and waited in a line of a dozen cars or more to get a burger, fries, and a vanilla milkshake.

Burbank was a nice town. Maybe he'd settle down here someday.

He had some time to kill, knowing his *job* wouldn't be back for several hours, if not longer. He hadn't patterned him yet, but with the suit, Leonard figured him for a daytime cop. Probably an admin guy, captain or higher. Maybe a detective, but he didn't look smart enough for that. Leonard pictured the man sitting on the balcony drinking his beer. The more Leonard watched people, the more his contempt for them would grow. He had realized this as a young boy watching people as they slept. He found it equally true—if not worse—in prison. Watching someone for any length of time made the killing easy. People irritated him.

Leonard thought more about the cop as he finished his burger. Then he thought about how the guy looked like a detective, and it gave him an idea. He'd need to find a phonebook, see where there was a place nearby he could buy a suit. Then, find a place where he could buy some cop shit, maybe a badge and a flashlight or something. Where did cops buy their cop shit? Was there a cop shop type of a place? He'd have to figure it out. He chuckled to himself picturing a store with a bunch of uptight assholes with their mustaches buying cop shit, mirrored sunglasses and whistles.

I HUNG UP WITH EDDIE SHORT, AN INVESTIGATOR WITH THE CALIFORNIA Department of Motor Vehicles. Ray was waiting to hear what had been said on the other end.

"Nothing he can find, though it's complicated."

"Complicated, how? Don't they have an *off the record* list of under-cover vehicles, fed cars and such?"

I shook my head. "Apparently not, but he's going to double-check with the Law Enforcement section of the clerk's office. He said he remembered that for a while, back in the eighties, they had to move everything out of the computer system that was considered deep cover after discovering there were some friends of the Hell's Angels working in the Law Enforcement section. These broads had the job of filing cops' confidential records. Can you believe it?"

"Nice."

"Yeah, the Angels were putting their old ladies inside. Brilliant, really. Makes you wonder where else they've infiltrated."

"I've heard the Eme did the same thing with cops, groomed youngsters to stay clean and get on the job. You ever heard that?"

"Never have, but it wouldn't surprise me, Ray."

"There was a new deputy at the jail, just a few months out of the academy, who they caught muling dope in for the Eme. They arrested him, and when they processed him, he said he didn't want protective custody. Said he'd walk the mainline. That might have been while you were off; it wasn't very long ago."

"A cop who didn't go P.C.?"

"Yeah, that's balls there. Or, I guess, confidence. You know you can walk the mainline because you're mafia."

"So he had worn a costume, not a uniform."

"Exactly," Ray said. "Is this guy going to get back to you, the DMV investigator?"

"Yeah, that's the plan. Have you heard anything back from the lab or the coroner's office on our Jane Doe?"

"No, but I have it on my list of calls to make," he said. After a moment he asked, "Hey partner, are you worried about this deal, that guy watching you?"

"I don't know, Ray, I guess a little. I'm more pissed off about it than anything else." I stood and paused before walking away. "You know, I'm just glad it's only me now, nobody else to worry about getting hurt. It makes it easier, to be honest. Someone wants part of me, come and get it. I'm too old to be worried about dying now. That's something these youngsters don't realize. A guy gets to a certain age, and he's been through the shit, and now he's just doing time in a miserable existence, he might actually welcome a bullet. One thing for sure, he won't be running for cover and hiding under a table. At least, not me. Next time I see that prick, he and I will have to have that conversation."

I walked away thinking of Val as I fumbled for the cell phone in my pocket.

# 18

LEONARD HAD A problem that had been eating at him for the last two days since the assignment came in. How do you kill a cop who carries a gun all the time when you don't have a gun yourself? He had considered running him down when the cop went to his car, and that was about the best he'd come up with. He didn't do guns or explosives or poison, so Leonard's options were limited. The problem he saw with running him down was that he envisioned doing it at the man's house. The problem with that was there was no easy way to get back onto the freeway, and the cops were everywhere around that town. The Burbank Gestapo.

He didn't see being able to strangle, stab, or beat the cop to death with a hammer. He needed to come up with something else.

He had finished his lunch and was now driving across Hollywood Way headed for The Cop Shop, a uniform store he had found in the phone book. Maybe if he had some type of badge he would be able to get close to the cop and overtake him while his guard was down. The man looked older and maybe a little heavyset. He was probably soft, out of shape, and wouldn't be much trouble for a man proficient with martial arts and in good shape from years of calisthenics, such as Leonard. He thought of his good friend—his only friend—Whitey Blanchard and how he had walked in and popped two killers. *Bam, bam* . . . and that was it. Turned and walked out. That's how to do it. That was balls. He pictured blasting the cop as he walked to his car one morning, or maybe smoking him when he came home from work, still seated in his cop car. Walk up to ask a question, or maybe look official, a fellow law officer, and catch him flat-footed. *Bam!* Turn and walk away. He pictured Whitey smiling at the news.

When Leonard walked into the uniform shop, an elderly man, maybe the owner, wearing slacks and a dress shirt, noticed him and came toward him directly. "How may I help you, sir?"

Leonard's social skills were lacking. He knew this about himself. He preferred not speaking to nor interacting with anyone he didn't know. He tried to brush the man off with a simple, "Just looking," and walked away.

The old man lingered and trailed along as Leonard slowly browsed the shop, seeing racks of uniforms of various types: police, security, paramedic, even mailman. He glanced back at the old man who quickly averted his eyes and turned to adjust a pair of boots on a shelf.

There were bullet-proof vests and wind-breaker type jackets with police emblems. Leonard wondered if he could buy either one. He didn't know what the rules were for buying police gear but reasoned they must have to control certain sales. He didn't want this to become more awkward than it already was.

Leonard turned up the next aisle and was now along the back wall where a glass case enclosed the good stuff: handcuffs, flashlights of all sizes, canisters of mace, belt buckles, watches, and miscellaneous jewelry with badges and department logos and letters. There was a gold necklace with the bold letters LAPD. Leonard pictured it hanging from the neck of a dainty blonde with manicured nails and saw himself rip it from her neck and laugh over her dead body.

He glanced at the next display case and saw it was full of pistols and revolvers, guns of varying shapes and sizes. He knew he couldn't legally get a gun, so he looked from the firearms display back to the jewelry before him. He chuckled at another piece that was a gold pig on a necklace.

The employee walked up behind him. "Decide on anything?"

Leonard continued looking at the display and said, "Yeah, I'll need a pair of handcuffs, some type of flashlight, and what kind of badge can I buy?"

The man said from behind him, "What kind of work are you doing, fella?"

"Security," he said quickly, and felt proud of himself for his fast thinking.

"Where at?"

"Huh?"

"Where are you working security?"

That stumped him for a minute. "Uh, In-and-Out, over there," he said and nodded back behind him to indicate the direction he believed it was, the direction he thought he had come. He wished he had thought of something better, but he had been caught off guard and his stop for lunch was the freshest on his mind.

The man said, "Oh? I didn't know they had security now. I know all the guys from the PD, right here in Burbank. I'll have to ask about that."

In his peripheral vision, Leonard saw the man walking as he finished saying it. Leonard looked up to see the shopkeeper was now behind the counter, watching him. Leonard looked around the shop. He didn't see anyone else working or shopping. He saw a door to a back room but wasn't sure if that was an office or a supply room, and of course he had no idea if anyone was back there. Leonard followed the man with his eyes as he made his way back toward him, now on the other side of the counter. The two were watching each other closely. Just before the old man was across from him, he reached under the counter. Leonard reached behind his back for his knife that was no longer there, and in that instant, he saw himself throw the bloody knife into a dumpster. He hadn't yet replaced it. Panic began taking ahold of Leonard as he planned his assault. He would jump over the counter and hit the old man, *pow*, land one square on his nose. That should drop him, and then he'd probably just choke him to death. He glanced around the store again to make sure nobody had come in. He placed his palm on the glass top and prepared to jump over just as the man came up with a set of keys in his hand.

The old man said, "Have you picked out which one you'd like?"

Leonard silently let his breath out, removed his hand from the glass case, and pointed to a silver shield that had *Security* in small letters across the top and *Officer* in much bigger letters beneath it. "That one there'll do," he said, "and whichever handcuffs and flashlight you've got that ain't too expensive."

The old man seemed happy and relaxed and now he wanted to visit. He started talking about crime in the city and how it didn't used to be that way, but with all the security now, his business had never been better. Leonard let the man babble as he gathered the badge, flashlight, and handcuffs and set them on top of the glass case between them.

"Anything else, young fella?"

"How much is that Buck knife there, the one with the rubber grip and a sheath?"

---

RAY WALKED WITH PURPOSE THROUGH THE BACK DOOR OF THE BUREAU and into the squad room. He had a case file in his hand. I sat on the far side of the expansive room talking to Floyd at his desk. Ray nodded when he noticed me and angled toward us. When he was within speaking distance he said, "It's not her."

"Wait, what? Our Jane Doe, it's not Chaney?"

He was shaking his head. "Nope."

I stood and met him near the row of desks. Floyd leaned back in his chair, watching while biting at the end of a pen.

"Who is she then?" I asked.

Ray handed me the file. I opened it, and as I started to read it, Ray began: "Lisa Williams. She's a high-priced hooker out of the Marina area, from what I've discovered so far."

Her photograph was printed on one of the sheets that listed close to a dozen arrests, mostly drugs. I noticed several arrests for prostitution and a couple for extortion too. Those caught my attention, but there wasn't much information that accompanied the entry, only the date, agency, and disposition. Most of her cases had been dismissed.

"These extortions, LAPD Venice, two years back, another from Culver City PD . . . those are interesting. You know anything about them yet?"

He shook his head. "No, partner, just came back from the lab. This is hot off the press. In fact, we need to go brief the captain, asap. This is big news."

I closed the file and handed it back to him.

Floyd said, "How'd you ID her, Ray?"

"DNA, believe it or not. But the reason her DNA was in the system is another mystery. Provost is looking into it for me."

"Do we love Doctor Provost?" Floyd asked, of nobody in particular.

"Ready when you are," I said to Ray. Then to Floyd, "Try staying out of trouble, would you?"

"You two are boring the hell out of me. I think I'll head up to the crime lab, have a visit with Doc Provost, find out how her research is coming along."

I reminded him he wasn't actually assigned to our case.

"Hey, I've got my own cases . . . I'm sure there's something around here I can dig up that needs to be resolved by the sexy doctor."

Ray and I walked off with Floyd adding something about me not liking fun and a newswoman with pretty eyes.

---

THE SQUAD ROOM WAS NEARLY EMPTY AS IT ALWAYS SEEMED TO BE LATE IN the afternoon. It was Monday, which meant a third of the bureau would have the day off. That third would be up for murders through the weekend and work through to the following Thursday, ten days straight. Of those who were on a regular work day, some were out in the field investigating their cases, while others had maybe finished for the day and were off to see their wives or girlfriends or both before the bodies started stacking up again. Though there was an on-call schedule, you never knew when a cop would be killed or multiple murders would occur at once and everyone then became fair game for recall.

Ray and I walked into Stover's office but he didn't look up from his computer screen. "One of you better have good news."

I sat down, committed to keeping my mouth shut.

Ray said, "Well, I suppose it is good news to some, bad for others. We have our girl ID'd."

Stover looked up. "Yeah? Is it the missing person?"

"No. It's a gal named Lisa Williams, a high-priced call girl out of the Marina. She has probably a dozen arrests ranging from prostitution and dope to extortion. That's about all we know right now, this ID is hot off the press. Figured you'd want to know asap."

"Jesus Christ," Stover said. "Okay, well . . ."

He seemed to lose his train of thought, or maybe he didn't have one. He wasn't an investigator, and he didn't think like one. He was an administrator. He was likely thinking how this might impact his budget, whether overtime would be involved, is it better that we have her identified, because now we still had the case of the missing person. What would be the political fallout, and how pissed off would the sheriff be to find out this case just got worse?

I watched him and thought about what he might be thinking, and I realized we were probably miles apart in our thoughts and ideas. I wanted to know things about the dead woman, this Ms. Lisa Williams. Was she married? Did she have kids? If she was married, does the old man know she was hooking? Why was she in Santa Clarita if she was from the Marina, and what the hell was she doing getting herself whacked in Marilynn Chaney's car?

The crime scene photos stayed with me as I went through this list in my head, and new questions surfaced: Where was she killed? We knew she wasn't killed in the car from the lack of blood evidence. Also, she didn't drive it there given the seat position. A man or tall woman drove that car there. How tall was Chaney? I had pictured Mrs. Chaney when I first thought it, and then I pictured Mr. Chaney, the tall, handsome, smug sonofabitch in his big leather chair. And where the hell is the lovely Mrs. Chaney, now that she isn't our dead woman in the car? *That* was the real question.

Ray broke the silence. "You don't have a woman disappear only to have her car recovered with a dead woman inside, who isn't her. Not normally, anyway. It doesn't make sense."

"It is unsettling," Captain Stover said, "that's for sure. How did you identify the dead woman?"

"DNA. It's a hundred percent, boss."

"Nothing's ever a hundred percent, Cortez. Have them double-check it. There's something just not right here. When are you guys in the rotation again?"

Stover seemed to be studying a calendar on his desk. It was color-coded to show which teams were on call at any given time. With six teams, each comprising twelve investigators, to provide 24/7 coverage of a 4,000 square mile county and its ten-million residents, came a complex system of scheduling.

Ray said, "Three and Four are up this week. We come up this weekend, Teams Five and Six."

I finally chimed in and wished I hadn't, only because I had told myself to just listen. "Unless it's busy and our teams come up early."

Captain Stover thought about it for a minute before saying, "So, you guys are off today?"

Ray nodded. I stared straight ahead.

"Jesus, you guys and your overtime."

And of course, I couldn't keep my mouth shut now. "I guess we could be off playing golf when the sheriff calls you for an update."

Stover glanced up at me but didn't speak. He leaned back in his chair, glanced through his office window out to the squad room. He seemed to be thinking, and it seemed he ignored my comment. Normally, he and I would go at each other, and a comment like that wouldn't go unanswered. Maybe the captain was getting soft. Or maybe just tired of my shit.

"You guys are going to need some help on this," he finally said. "There's just too much to it, and I have a bad feeling this is headed in an ugly direction. If Three and Four are up, pick someone off of One or Two and have them work this all week with you. No limit on the overtime. Also, tell your lieutenant I said not to put you two up for murders in the next rotation. I don't care if your team is short in the line-up."

I decided to push my luck. "How about Floyd and his trainee, Diaz? I know Floyd could use the overtime."

Stover grinned his smug grin and held it for a moment. "Yeah, I don't care, that's fine. I can't keep you two apart anyway, so I might as well put you together. And where the hell has White been? Is he still working this case with you?"

Ray lied, "Yeah, boss, he's still at it."

The captain's eyes darted around aimlessly as he seemed scattered in his thoughts. Finally, he looked at me and said, "Tell your old partner this is temporary, don't get any ideas. I might leave you on Five if you and Cortez can stand each other. And if you don't crash any cars or kill anyone in the next ten days or so. That'd be nice."

I felt myself actually smile. It seemed for a moment he didn't hate me, but I was skeptical. "Thanks, Captain."

He ignored it and said to Ray, "Keep me posted on this. I'm not saying anything until we have an absolute on the ID, and we have a strategy of how to go forward. No word to anyone outside this office about any of this until I say so. That includes the sheriff. If his office calls, you don't have anything new to report. Same with Santa Clarita. In fact, don't answer your fucking phones unless you know who it is calling and it's neither of them."

I had stood but waited in front of his desk until he was finished speaking. Ray followed suit.

Stover finally said, "That's it. Get at it."

---

LEONARD PULLED OUT OF THE LOT ONTO HOLLYWOOD WAY, LEAVING THE uniform store behind but not the images of all those guns stored in the display case. He thought about smashing the glass and collecting several of them, and then he saw himself doing it in the dark. He would have to think about it. The more he thought about a gun, the more he liked the idea of having one, or maybe more than one. He could teach himself to shoot, that would be no problem. He and Whitey had taught themselves martial arts. He had taught himself to drive. Everything is easy when you're smart.

His car began sputtering when he pulled away from an intersection where he had stopped for a red light. He pushed the gas pedal further down and it sputtered even more. He feathered the gas and it began to find power, but just as he built up speed, the car's engine died. He cranked the ignition over and over as he coasted it to the side of the road and stopped, cursing under his breath. After trying for several minutes unsuccessfully to start his car, he took the keys and walked away, seeing the smiling Russian in his head, and then having a vision of hitting the goddamn Russkie in his fucking head with a hammer.

He walked to the next intersection where he found a gas station that still employed a mechanic and offered a tow service. It was something Leonard found odd—one of many things—after spending twenty-five years in prison: there were no more service stations. Gas stations had pumps but you were on your own, ladies too. You had to go in and pay for your gas before you bought it. It drove him crazy. How the hell would he know how much it would cost? So, he would usually do twenty at a time. He didn't want to have a full tank of gas if he were going to abandon the car somewhere. Which might happen at any given time, if the heat was turned up. Also, he knew it would always take twenty bucks worth. That kept him from having to go inside twice and interact with people and touch door handles that thousands of dirty people before him had touched.

After making some arrangements with the manager, the mechanic told him to hop up in the tow truck and he'd give him a ride back to get his car. The guy was an Armenian or Russian, or one of those fucking gypsy types, and Leonard thought here it goes, he was going to take it up the ass again. The whole lot of them were probably in cahoots.

---

I CALLED FLOYD WHO ANSWERED THE PHONE, PANTING. I PICTURED Doctor Provost in the white lab coat underneath him, and then the blonde news woman with the pretty eyes. But the background noise gave his location away and rendered in my mind the more accurate vision of him at the gym, sweat dripping off of his head, bare chest, and arms, onto blue mats that lined the floor. He was probably looking at the wall of mirrors as he stood speaking into his phone now.

"Working out?"

"Yeah, what's up, Dickie?" he said through heavy breaths.

"You up for some overtime this week?"

"I'm not working the goddamn Gay Pride Parade, if that's what you're asking."

I smiled, recalling a night we signed up to work overtime in West Hollywood on Halloween. It was a freak show, and we both swore we'd never do it again. He always referred to it as the *Gay Pride Parade*, even though it wasn't. I didn't even know when or where any such parade was held, or if there even was one.

"No gay parades, pal. Me and Ray Cortez need some help on the Santa Clarita case, and I volunteered you and your partner. Stover actually went for it."

"Ah shit, Dickie, I don't know, man. The kids have games all week, Cindy's been all over my jock about never being home . . ."

I waited.

"I haven't been to the gym but maybe twice all month, and now you want me to go back to your crazy idea of working around the clock seven days a week. I know you, Dickie."

"So, you're in?"

"Yeah, I guess. What are we going to be doing?"

"Well you heard about our Jane Doe, how that just went sideways on us with the ID, right?"

"Yeah, your dead girl isn't the missing girl."

"Exactly. And that's a big problem for us. We need to get some direction and go at it on several different fronts. Why don't you finish your little Jane Fonda workout, wash your nasty ass, and be back here at the office by seven. We'll brainstorm it then. Oh, and call your goon."

He laughed. "Mongo. Yeah, shit, I'll need to stop him before he gets into the Jack. When we're not on call, that sonofabitch gets drunker than a tent full of Indians."

"No shit, huh? A Jack and Coke guy?"

"No, straight. I thought he was Samoan, by the size of him, then just figured him for a big-ass Mexican, with Diaz for a name and all. Now I'm starting to think the crazy bastard's an Indian, the bow and arrow type, you know what I mean? Tonto, or Chief Firewater, I don't know."

I chuckled. "Okay man, get crackin'. I'll see you in an hour."

He hung up without saying goodbye. I texted him the emoji of a middle finger. I had recently discovered it and had been dying to use it on him, just waiting for the right time.

On my way to the kitchen for coffee I stopped by Ray's desk to confirm our plans. "Just talked to Floyd. He'll be here by seven and hopefully his partner too, if he's still sober. We can brief and brainstorm then."

"Sounds like a plan, partner. Thanks."

# 19

I T WAS NEARLY eight by the time the four of us had gathered in the conference room. There had been phone calls and emails and matters of great importance, such as making a fresh pot of coffee, that preceded getting to the business at hand.

Once we were settled, Ray briefed the case from the beginning. Much of what he said was a repeat from the briefing he had given at the bureau meeting five days earlier. He updated Floyd and Mongo with what had transpired since that briefing, including our meeting with Mr. Philip Chaney, the husband of the missing person, the two men in suits who arrived as we were leaving, the status of their vehicle license having no record, and finally, the news that was hot off the press, that the missing person found dead and decapitated in Marilynn Chaney's black BMW was not Ms. Chaney after all. She was, in fact, Ms. Lisa Renee Williams, a thirty-four-year-old high-dollar hooker with a nose candy addiction and a willingness to commit other crimes for financial gain.

"Like what?" asked Floyd, who sat at the end of the large, dark conference room table, one leg crossed over the other. His shirt collar hung open and he hadn't bothered to put a tie back on. Two Styrofoam cups sat on the table in front of him next to a can of Copenhagen, a notepad, and pen. One of the two cups steamed from the fresh coffee it contained; the other would no doubt be a spit cup.

"She has a couple extortion charges, one out of Venice and another out of Culver, if I recall correctly. We don't have the particulars yet. I think extortion is an interesting charge for a high-dollar hooker. Makes you wonder what she was up to, and then you have to ask if that has anything to do with her losing her head."

Mongo sat to the side of Floyd, his hands folded high on his stomach and his chin tucked down to meet his tie. He watched and listened carefully, though you didn't expect him to say anything. For one, he was relatively new, less than a year at the bureau. He was a fifteen-year veteran on the department with a solid reputation as both a street cop and then a gang detective, but he was still new to Homicide. The other reason you didn't expect him to say anything is he was the type who didn't have much to say. He was more of an action guy, a hands-on guy. The type of man who spent his free time working on the house or cars, making repairs or remodeling if he wasn't coaching sports or lifting weights. He was the type of cop who studied everyone and everything, and although he was slow to act, when he did there would be a big wake behind him.

I sat at the opposite end of the table from Floyd, next to Ray. I said, "Ray, what are your thoughts about how this Williams broad plays into the bigger picture? I mean, the Chaneys are up to their necks in something, there's no doubt about that. How does Mrs. Chaney go missing and a hooker wakes up dead in her car? That's the question. There's just too much going on for it to not all tie in together, somehow. Do you have any thoughts about any of that?"

"I don't know, partner, to be honest." He was studying a DMV photograph of the good-looking blonde with bright blue eyes that was the former Lisa Williams. "I'm still trying to wrap my head around it, the whole deal. It doesn't make sense."

There was silence.

I looked at Floyd and nodded. He thought for a moment and then offered his thoughts. "Maybe it was meant to fake her death—Chaney's—that was my first thought. Have we looked into insurance policies on her yet?"

Ray said, "Yeah, that was one of our first thoughts after meeting with

Mr. Chaney, a financial gain angle. He said she has a million-dollar policy and shrugged as if that was hardly worth mentioning."

Mongo grunted.

Floyd said, "Or else, they screwed something up with the DNA. Have you considered that?"

"That was Stover's concern," I said, "so we've asked Provost to run it through again."

"We love her."

Mongo and Ray both looked at him with question in their expressions. I just chuckled.

Ray said, "Look, there's a lot of possibilities, but until we know for sure what we have here—as far as an absolute ID, Williams's records and a full history on her, et cetera—we're spinning our wheels."

"So that's where we start," I said. "Let's divvy up the tasks and get at it. Our goal should be to have a positive ID by tomorrow night—did she give us a time frame on rerunning the DNA, Ray?"

"Yeah, she said give her twenty-four hours."

"Okay, then that's the plan. Tomorrow at this time we should have everything about Williams, everything about the Chaneys, an absolute on the DNA that confirms it is in fact Williams in that car, and then we can brainstorm plots and motives. What do you guys think?"

"Sounds like a plan, partner."

Floyd said, "Works for me," while Mongo nodded in agreement with his partner.

We made a list of everything that needed to be done, divided the list into bite-sized pieces, and divvied up the assignments. Floyd and Mongo were first going to do a complete background on Williams which they could start now and work on into the night. Then, they would start contacting known family and friends of Williams's during the day tomorrow, maybe into the evening if need be. Ray and I were going to conduct a more thorough background on both Marilynn and Philip Chaney. We all agreed there was more to them than what we knew. We would look into insurance policies, insurance claims, financial records including liens, judgments, bankruptcies, all matters involving civil actions, and get a complete history of residency on them. We wanted to know where they were raised and went to school, where they attended college, past employers, and all known associations. By midday tomorrow we planned to visit the crime lab where we would follow up with Dr. Provost about the DNA report and check in with latent prints to see if they had any results from processing the vehicle. Finally, if all went well, we would check with the coroner's office on toxicology and trace evidence from the body and clothing.

Ray said, "What do you guys think about checking with the feds, see if they have anything going on with Chaney. I'm still bothered by the two suits that showed up with the cold-plated car."

"Feds won't tell us shit," Floyd said.

Mongo surprised us all by speaking. "I have a cousin who's a feebie. She's assigned to the Wilshire field office but she's on a task force working Russian mafia with LAPD out of Hollywood Division. She might be able to get us something as a favor."

Floyd was frowning. "You didn't tell me you had a female cousin who's a feebie."

Mongo shrugged.

"I hope she isn't built like you."

Mongo smiled but didn't reply. Floyd had named him after the character in *Blazing Saddles*, the huge man named Mongo who was simple-minded but strong as an ox. He was a killer of men, sent to take out the sheriff, but the sheriff had tricked him—*whipped him*, according to Mongo —and won his respect. I pictured *our* Mongo hugging Floyd and saying, *Mongo like Floyd. Mongo not kill him.*

"If you could check with her," Ray said, "I think that'd be good. If she can't find anything out, maybe she can hook us up with someone who can."

"We can check with the Fugitive Task Force out of Major Crimes," I said, "there's usually a couple feds working with our guys over there, and because they work around deputies, they're less inclined to be pompous assholes than the rest of them."

Mongo looked up when I said it, but I didn't get a read on him. Maybe he thought I meant it as a dig toward his cousin. No, he wouldn't make that leap, all local cops hate the feds. He wouldn't take it personally. Would he? Maybe he doesn't like me, the thought occurred to me.

Ray mumbled to himself while making a couple more notes. He

looked up, pointed his pen at me, and said, "Okay, and you're still running with the plates, right? Weren't you waiting on the DMV investigator to get back to you?"

"Yeah, I am. But I'm also going to try something else. I was thinking about going to our traffic division, maybe LAPD's too, and having them do a search for that vehicle's plate being captured on traffic cams. I hear they can do that now, that it's all computerized. Maybe if we can see a pattern, we can figure out who they are. You know, like the plate hits the cameras near the FBI building on Wilshire a couple times a week. That would tell us a lot."

"Or on the fifteen, heading back and forth to Vegas," Floyd said.

"Mobsters?"

"Never know, Dickie."

I said to Ray, "You did say you checked LAPD and some of the nearby jurisdictions, right? San Fernando, Burbank, Glendale?"

"White said he checked them. Maybe we should follow up?"

Mongo nodded, and his partner said, "I'd definitely check it again. You can't rely on White, no offense, but also, you can call twice and get two different answers. I say we check. That's something we can do tonight, and me and Mongo can take care of it." He looked over at Mongo who was now writing something on his notepad.

"Good," I said. "Ray, you have anything else?"

He shook his head, and each of us stood without being prompted to do so. As we gathered our notes and cups and prepared to disperse, I reminded the room, "Stover said unlimited overtime, basically gave us the approval to spend his entire budget on this case. I say we try hard to not disappoint him."

Floyd grinned. "Says the guy with no life."

---

AT TEN O'CLOCK LEONARD STILL SAT WATCHING THE HOUSE AND STEWING over the four-hundred dollars he had spent having his car towed and repaired. He sat low in his car, wearing a suit from J.C. Penney with a badge clipped on the belt in the front and a pair of handcuffs doubled over the back. His flashlight sat on the seat next to him. It was called a Maglite, and it was big and heavy. The type of light you could beat a man to death with if you needed to or just wanted to. Leonard wished he had a pistol to complete the look. He had also come to the conclusion that the best idea was to shoot the cop; it was the easiest thing to do.

He pictured the display of guns inside the uniform store and he pictured the outside of the store with its glass windows and door. It couldn't be hard to get in there, smash and dash with a handful—or maybe a pillowcase full—of guns. He glanced at his flashlight and thought about using it to smash the glass door and using its light to help him find his way back to the guns. He'd break the display case glass, grab what he needed, and be out in five minutes.

If the goddamn cop didn't show up soon, Leonard would go case the uniform shop and see if it was doable. He didn't remember what shops or stores were nearby, and of course he hadn't been there at night to see what type of activity there was. Or maybe he'd go find the Russian and kill him instead of killing the cop or robbing the cop shop. That rotten bastard had cost him nearly two grand now, the car and repairs all added together. He could sneak up behind him and cut his throat with his new knife, open him like a fish, take his gun from his waistband and clobber him with it or shoot him in the back of the head. Then he could walk calmly into the office and turn that whore upside down and shake the money out of her big bra. He was certain she'd have a stash there, probably a derringer also, or maybe a little .25 auto.

He would give Mr. Piggy until midnight. The fucking guy was probably in a bar or at a whorehouse, for all Leonard knew. He doubted the man had a girlfriend, from what he had seen of him. Leonard thoughtlessly pitched another burned cigarette out of his window and leaned back on the headrest. It was going to be a long two hours. He hated this part of the job.

---

I RETURNED TO MY TEMPORARY DESK IN THE UNSOLVEDS OFFICE WHERE I planned to make a couple of calls to start checking on those traffic cameras. Before getting started, I tried Val's cell. It rang four times and went to voicemail. She sounded happy on her custom greeting, and I pictured her recording it. I saw her smile fading and her soft eyes narrowing as she made one recording after another, never happy with how it sounded to her. She was a perfectionist, which had been part of the problem. Now she was being a perfect pain in the ass, dare I say a royal bitch, refusing to answer my calls. I guessed she was finished and had moved on. It occurred to me I should try to do the same.

---

LEONARD LEFT AT A QUARTER TILL MIDNIGHT, SICK AND TIRED OF WAITING for the cop. Pig hunting was boring. He grinned, picturing telling Whitey about pig hunting. Leonard had always preferred to have most conversations in his head, other than those he had with Whitey. Even before prison —when he was just a child—he seldom spoke a word to anyone. Not his mother, not other kids at school, and not to the teachers unless forced to do so. Sometimes not even then. He never had friends until he met Whitey Blanchard in prison. Whitey was the only friend he'd ever had, and Leonard missed him terribly since leaving Raiford. He made a mental note to write Whitey a letter. He could tell him things with the code they had worked out so the prison pigs wouldn't know what they were saying. The cops always read the inmate mail before passing it on in either direction. It was their policy. When sending out a letter, you didn't seal the envelope; they did. In twenty-five years, Leonard never sent one out, and he had never received a letter either. Other than legal correspondence. But Whitey had lots of friends and received a lot of mail. It had always made Leonard a little jealous.

He drove past the uniform shop on Hollywood Way and was discouraged to see that once the business was closed, the glass was protected by a wall of wrought iron that stretched like an accordion to cover the entire store front. He pulled to a stop directly across the street and stared at it, feeling more frustrated by the minute.

A couple of ideas came to mind, mostly born from conversations with more experienced, well-rounded criminals while serving time. He thought of one who had told stories of committing burglaries by dropping in through the ceilings. The burglar had explained that once you cut a hole in the roof or removed a vent or fan or some other rooftop contraption, it was easy. Nobody ever secured the roofs of their businesses. Leonard thought of another who told him about pulling bars off of doors and windows. He was a biker and had specialized in ripping off drug houses. He and his biker friends would show up with a truck and lengths of chain. They'd fasten the chains to the bars on the doors and yank them from their structures with the truck. Then the bikers would file in with automatic weapons and take what they wanted. The biker was doing life without the possibility of parole on a murder charge, having killed a man who tried to defend his stash with a nine-millimeter. The biker had zippered him with a Mac 10 .45 caliber machine pistol. The biker had the superior weapon and was more committed to being the victor.

Leonard spent a few minutes thinking about pulling the bars from the cop shop. He could go steal the tow truck of the Armenian down the street who took him for four bills just a few hours earlier. But now this was just getting complicated. There had to be better ways to get a gun.

He drove off and decided he would go back the way he had come, through the Hollywood Hills and down into Hollywood and across to downtown Los Angeles. He liked being able to travel without being on the freeways. He felt more comfortable with his limited experience of driving, and it seemed to him there was less chance of being stopped by the cops.

As he descended into the festive streets of Hollywood, he decided to take the scenic route and check out the prostitutes and drug addicts that lined the boulevards. He found it interesting that some streets were worked by women, others by boys. He thought about stopping to talk to a few who had caught his eye but thought better of it. He didn't need to draw that type of attention to himself.

As he departed the strip, he decided to take a drive by his Russian friend's car lot. The smiling Russkie with his big-titted peroxide blonde. He didn't know if the man lived there at the lot in his trailer office or if the place would be locked up tight this time of night. He assumed the latter, but thought he'd drive by just to check. Somehow, he was going to get some money back from that goddamn gypsy.

Leonard slowed in front of the small used car lot and saw it had been secured with chain link gates that covered the drive. He pulled into the driveway with the intention of seeing if the gates were actually locked, and when he did, he was immediately greeted by two Dobermans that appeared from nowhere and charged the gate. They barked furiously and slobbered at the prospect of eating an intruder, bouncing up and down behind the chain link gate in the lights of his car. No way was Leonard playing games with these two dogs.

He headed toward his little room in the rundown hotel on Main Street, thinking about the Russian and his lady friend. Leonard decided it would be best to deal with them during business hours when the dogs were nowhere to be seen, probably locked in a cage somewhere. Maybe shake a pistol out of the blonde's blouse and cap them each in the head. Whitey would love that story.

# 20

TUESDAY MORNING I woke up on the couch still dressed in yesterday's suit pants and shirt. The jacket and tie were carelessly hung over a dining room chair. There were two empty beer cans on the table next to me, and the TV was still on though the volume had been muted. I checked my watch. 9:15. I did some rough math in my head and figured I'd had five hours of sleep, since I had not come in until well after three and then apparently took the time to unwind before passing out.

I checked my phone but there were no calls. No calls from Val, which was no surprise, and none from Floyd, which was a bit of a surprise. He generally called me when he was headed to the office just to bullshit and pass the time. Maybe he was getting a late start too, though he had left the office two hours before me last night.

After a quick shower, I dressed and was preparing to leave when I thought to check the street from my balcony. I didn't see the car that had been there a couple of days prior, and there was nothing else that looked suspicious. Still, I double-checked my pistol to confirm there was a round in the chamber and the magazine was full and properly inserted into the butt of the gun.

When I picked up my phone, I saw there was a missed call from Floyd.

He must have called when I was in the shower, probably on his way into the office.

I headed out, removing my cookie sheet alarm system from the gate and then balancing a small twig along the top that would fall to the ground if the gate was opened while I was away. I'd just have to remember to check it before going through when I returned home.

As I pulled from the curb and drove past the line of parked cars, I studied each one. I stopped at the sight of cigarette butts on the street in the empty space between two parked cars. I collected the butts and saw they were the same as the others had been, non-filtered. I tossed the envelope containing the newly acquired butts onto the seat next to me and headed to the office, pissed off. I hadn't seen the butts when I came home last night. I had been more worried about the parked cars, and I looked each one over as I passed by twice before parking. Nothing seemed suspicious and the car I had seen a couple days prior was nowhere to be found. But was another car parked where these butts were? I couldn't recall. It seemed I should have noticed, but I hadn't. Maybe too tired. Maybe I was getting sloppy.

The thought occurred to me that I needed to have DNA collected from these cigarettes, but without a case, there was no way to do it. At least not through the department where it mattered. I could send them to a private lab and have DNA extracted for a couple thousand bucks probably, but what good would it do? I needed the DNA submitted and ran through CODIS, the FBI's Combined DNA Index System, to see if there was a match to an existing profile. And the only way to do that was to be acting in the course of an official law enforcement criminal investigation. Not on a hunch or concern.

I could use the case number from the Santa Clarita case. Who would know?

I shook my head and let out a breath. That would be dangerous. Career-ending dangerous. But what was I supposed to do, wait until something happened to start investigating it? I knew what the captain would say, and I knew what would happen if I was caught doing it. With my luck the DNA would be linked to a serial killer and then I'd never be able to conceal what I had done. The crime lab would explode with elation over connecting other cases to the one in Santa Clarita. Only he wouldn't be guilty of the one in Santa Clarita, only of stalking me. But why? Especially if the DNA did come up linked to other crimes, why would that person be outside my apartment? Maybe it was worth the risk.

I felt a headache coming on and decided to grab a breakfast sandwich from Jack-in-the-Box before getting on the freeway. It was the breakfast of champions. My body was a temple, just look at me. Great sleep patterns, terrific diet, regular exercise if you counted sit-ups (from the chair) and jogging (to the refrigerator). Jesus, maybe I should forego Jack-in-the-Box and find a place that serves bloody marys to go.

When I got on the freeway, I called Floyd.

"Where the hell are you, Dickie?"

"On my way in. You?"

"Mongo and I are here at the office, have been for an hour, and the two assholes who we're supposed to be helping with their case are nowhere to be found."

"No shit, huh? Ray's not there either?"

"No, and to be honest, you're both pissing me off. The captain even asked about you guys. I lied and told him we were in the office until four this morning, and you'd be in shortly."

"Thanks, man. Anything cooking?"

"No, but you are definitely starting to bore the shit out of me. Hang up on yourself and get your ass down here."

"Goodbye, sweetheart."

---

RAY PULLED INTO THE OFFICE PARKING LOT BEHIND ME AND PARKED TWO spaces over. We met each other outside our parked cars and I asked if he were following me. He said I should be so lucky, a reference of my current dilemma.

"Have you figured anything out on that?"

Floyd walked out of the back door. "Well, there you two assholes are."

I smiled at my old partner and answered Ray. "No, but I found out yesterday morning I'm being sued over that shooting. I hadn't given any thought about that being related to someone watching me until driving in this morning. I don't know though, it's probably a stretch."

"You heard the good news, huh?" Floyd said, now standing next to us by the two Crown Vics that sat ticking and hissing from under their hoods. "Did they serve you at home?"

"No, were you served?"

"Yep. There was a subpoena for a deposition in my mailbox here at the office. That's as good as served, since some dumbass at the desk obviously accepted it. I thought I told you about it."

I frowned. "No, you didn't. This is the first I've heard of anything. County Counsel called to let me know they'll be representing us, so we have that going for us. A free legal team, the best of the best, probably led by Darden and Clark."

"So, you think that has something to do with someone watching you, you say?" Ray asked.

"What, your stalker?" Floyd asked.

"I don't know, to be honest. But it did cross my mind. Maybe the plaintiff's attorney has hired a PI to watch me, see what kind of dirt he can pick up."

Floyd was shaking his head. "That doesn't make sense for two reasons: the non-filtered cigarettes, and anyone who knows you, knows you're the most boring person on earth. They aren't going to waste time watching you."

"There could be some crusty old asshole PI who works for sleazy lawyers downtown and smokes Camel non-filtereds."

Floyd rolled his eyes at me. Ray said, "I could see it, partner."

"I don't know, you guys, but it's bothering me a lot. He was out there again last night."

"You saw him?" Floyd asked.

"No," I said, and then I reached into my briefcase and pulled out an envelope. "I picked up more butts this morning. I didn't see anyone out there when I got home last night—rather, this morning—but I might have missed him too, I don't know."

"It's time to report it, buddy. You need to let the captain know and give Burbank a heads up."

I knew Floyd was right, but I was reluctant to cry wolf. It could still be a strange coincidence; I had no solid proof that anyone was watching me. It also made no sense to me as there really was no motive that matched up.

Ray said, "You asked Lopes about Eme. Do you think someone put a hit on you?"

I dismissed the thought of it. "No, Ray, I don't think so. I don't think Eme would be sloppy about it. It would just happen, no reason to sit and watch. Besides, Lopes said those guys—Jorge and Gilbert Regalado—aren't connected with the mob."

Floyd was shaking his head as I finished the sentence. He spat tobacco onto the asphalt. "No, that's *not* what Lopes told you. He said he didn't have information that they *were* connected to the mob, but he also said that White Fence puts in a lot of work for Eme, so they could be in good graces, maybe associates."

Floyd was right, and I knew it but didn't want to admit it.

We all stood silent under the midday sun as two secretaries exited the building for their lunchtime walk.

"I'll keep my eyes peeled, don't worry about me."

Floyd turned to walk inside while saying, "You watch your ass, Dickie."

Just then Mongo walked out, the door nearly catching Floyd as he reached for it. Mongo nodded, sign language that Floyd clearly interpreted to mean *what's up.*

"Just finished talking about Dickie's love life, what's going on?"

He shook his head.

"Okay, then let's get crackin'," Floyd said to Mongo. Then he turned to us. "About seven, eight tonight, you think?"

"Yeah, sounds good, partner," Ray answered. "We'll meet you back here. Hopefully we'll have some direction on this thing."

As I walked into the bureau I made my decision. Ray and I planned to check in at the crime lab to confirm the DNA results on the Santa Clarita case. I would submit the butts under that case number and take my chances. There was too much risk now, and for some reason the talk about Eme had me nervous. Old man or not, I wasn't ready to die.

---

THE SQUAD ROOM IS AN EXPANSIVE OPEN FLOOR COVERED BY STAINED blue carpet and bathed in fluorescent lighting. It holds six columns of metal office desks. Each column comprises thirteen desks, two rows of six butted against each other and side by side, capped by one desk that sits perpendicular to all the others at the end. Those are the lieutenants' desks. Their job is to support the investigators assigned to their teams. Most actually try to do that. Sometimes a new one will think his job is to lead an investigation. That thought never lasts long, even in the thickest of skulls. Team Five was led by Lt. Joe Black, arguably the nicest man ever hired by the sheriff's department, and certainly the nicest one to be promoted to the rank of lieutenant.

As we walked in, Joe asked if I had a minute. He was sitting at his desk with mounds of typed investigative reports he was presumably reading for approval. The job of a lieutenant at Homicide is one that requires an enthusiastic reader. I pulled an empty chair next to his desk.

"What's up, Joe?"

In his soft-spoken manner he said, "Well, I wanted to welcome you to my team, for one."

I smiled. "Oh? Am I officially here now?"

"Well, not officially, but we have an opening coming up," he said, and nodded toward the unoccupied desk across from Ray's. "There's no reason you can't have it, if you don't mind working for an old stickler like me." He lifted a stack of papers. "I'm a little tough on the reports. I love reading to the point it's almost a sickness that makes me want to devour every word on a page."

"Joe, I would be honored to work for you."

"Ray says he would really like to team up with you on a permanent basis. He said you're great to work with, and a good investigator. I don't know if you want to partner with Ray and work for me, or if you're set on going back to Two with your old partner."

"You know, Joe, I think I'd like to work with Ray, and for you. It seems like a good change of pace for me and to be honest, I'm having a good time with Ray. The guy's one of the nicest guys in the bureau, easy to work with."

I almost compared Ray to Joe Black when I mentioned how nice he was, but that seemed it would be over the top, dangerously close to the category of sucking ass. It was true, but to say it didn't seem appropriate. I hadn't considered a change, but something told me when Joe asked that this could be just what I needed. Plus, I was a little desperate, to be honest.

"Good, Richard, I had hoped you would be interested. Listen, I spoke with Lewandowski earlier, and he has no intention of coming back. We all knew that would be the case. So, I told him I'd like to have him clean out his desk so we can fill his spot. He said he'd do it one night this week, or this weekend at the latest. As soon as you notice it's empty, why don't you go ahead and move in there."

"Do we have the boss's approval?"

Joe's wide smile and soft, warm eyes were comforting and welcoming. He was like the bureau's designated grandfather and it wouldn't have felt any different if there were warm cookies and milk served during our meeting. "You let me worry about Captain Stover," he said. "He's so easy to get along with, he'll be fine with it."

*Easy to get along with.* Captain Stover. I almost choked when he said it, but quickly realized this was exactly why I needed to work for Lt. Joe Black. He had the ability to get along with anyone. That would be a nice balance to my dickheadedness.

I walked away feeling welcomed and grateful and as if my luck had changed. This could be the new me. I had a fresh start coming my way and I needed to let the two nice guys, Joe and Ray, rub off on me so I could stop being so eager to fight with my peers and supervisors. His last words really resonated with me, and it drove home the fact that Joe was the type of guy who got along with everyone. If he thinks Stover is an easygoing guy, Joe Black could find redemptive qualities in a third-world dictator. I admired that, and at times I was envious of those with that type of personality. We are the way we're born, for good or bad, better or worse. It wasn't easy being me.

I hadn't made it halfway down the hall for a cup of coffee when the idea of submitting the cigarette butts as evidence came back to me like acid reflux. Thirty seconds hadn't passed since I was embraced by big, huggable Joe Black and now I had a dilemma. It was a huge risk to submit that evidence to the lab under false pretenses, and now more than ever I worried about the potential consequences. It occurred to me I didn't want to let Joe down. Not after his warm welcome to his team, and after the nice things he had said to me. It occurred to me this was a mark of a great leader, to have such a rapport with your subordinates that they wouldn't want to disappoint you.

I poured a cup and decided I wouldn't submit the cigarette butts. At least not today. I'd think about it. Which meant I needed to seriously consider reporting the potential problem of the watcher. But to whom? The last thing I wanted to do now was to go back to Joe and let him know he just invited a man to join his team who has all sorts of baggage and drama in his life. No, I needed to keep this quiet for now. I would ask the few who knew about it—Floyd, Ray, and Lopes—to keep a lid on it for now. And hope that they would.

THE FOUR OF US ONCE AGAIN GATHERED IN THE HOMICIDE BUREAU conference room late in the evening, nearly eight o'clock. Lt. Joe Black asked if he could join us and listen in on our meeting so that he could come up to speed on our investigation. "Of course you can join us, Joe," Ray said.

Ray looked at Floyd and Mongo sitting at the far side of the table in the same seats they had occupied the night before. "Well, how'd you guys do today, partner?"

Mongo reached into a thick file and began pulling papers out as Floyd gave us a rundown: "So, Lisa Renee Williams, a thirty-four-year-old Caucasian woman who we all now know worked as a high-priced call girl, lived at the Esprit apartments in the Marina paying five grand a month for a room with a view. Single, lived alone, no children, been at the apartment for two years and from what we can tell, she didn't bring clients to her home. No legal source of income, hasn't paid taxes in a decade, and she drove a Porsche crossover that she bought new two years ago, paying nearly a hundred-thou cash."

"The hell's a Porsche crossover?" I asked.

"SUV for rich people, Dickie. Anyway, where was I . . . Oh, yeah, so, Ms. Williams was a mystery to her neighbors so nothing much to gain there. We've slapped a seal on the apartment and Mongo started paper this afternoon. Our plan is to get a Mincey warrant signed tomorrow and take the lab out there to process the apartment and the car. Yes, the car is there, parked in its assigned spot. That makes us think Williams left the apartment with the killer, or killers, willingly or otherwise—"

"Dead or alive," I said.

"—which gives us pause at searching the place without the warrant. Just in case her killer had legal standing at her residence, we're playing it safe. There's too much we don't know about her. Maybe she has a roommate and he's our killer."

"Good plan, partner," Ray said. "Do you have anything else?"

"That's it for now I think," Floyd said.

I said, "Mongo, did you get a chance to check with your connection over at the FBI?"

"I put a call in, haven't heard back."

Ray looked at the lieutenant. "He has a cousin who's a feebie. We're hoping to find out if the FBI is investigating something that involves Marilynn Chaney, the missing person we thought was our victim until yesterday. When Dickie and I were leaving their home the other day, two suits who looked like feds showed up. We ran their vehicle, no record on the plates. Something is up with that whole deal—that whole family, actually."

Joe nodded. Ray turned his attention back to Mongo. "Let us know."

He nodded.

Ray looked to me. "Partner, do you want to brief everyone on the Chaney background stuff? Then I'll fill everyone in on the ID and lab info."

"So, Chaney is an interesting guy in that, according to his tax filings, he's pulling in a cool mill a year, give or take. We mentioned that million-dollar policy on Mrs. Chaney, and there is a five-million on him. So, given their income, none of that is too strange. Do you have your wife whacked for a year's salary? I wouldn't think so, unless the bitch drove you crazy anyway, or maybe you had something better on the side.

"Interestingly, we can't find much on her. Originally, we were under the impression she had a daughter from another marriage, but apparently, she had no kids. Ray and I plan to revisit Mr. Chaney once we get some more information on the mystery visitors. We have quite a few follow-up questions for him.

"I think that's about it. No criminal history or civil actions on either one. Mr. Chaney is from Indiana, went to school in New York, has a degree in business and appears to be an investor, working as an independent but with a corporate clientele. Oh, it seems maybe the Chaneys met in New York, maybe while dipshit was in college. I think that about covers it. Any questions?"

Floyd asked, "Any indication this guy's a gambler?"

"Interesting question, why do you ask?"

"Just curious. Seems the type, from what I'm hearing, what I'm seeing, maybe just a picture I'm getting of the guy and concerns I have about the two idiots in suits. If they aren't feds, I still like the idea of mafiosos."

"Well, he has books on gambling in his library, but that's all we have. Maybe we'll have to ask him."

Ray looked around the room. Everyone seemed content, ready to move on. "Well, the DNA is an absolute, so in that regard we are where we started yesterday morning. There are partial prints that have been lifted from the victim's car, but nothing that hits a match in the system. At least we have something to compare if we come up with a suspect. There are some fibers and other trace evidence in the car and on the body, so maybe something will come of that. Of course, they're going through it carefully, looking for a DNA source and analyzing each and every piece of evidence.

"There's still no word on Mrs. Chaney or her whereabouts. We've checked cell phone records and there hasn't been any activity since the day she went missing, and nothing interesting on that day. Any questions?"

Floyd said, "What about a warrant on Chaney?"

"I don't think we have enough at this time, to be honest with you, partner. Dickie and I had discussed maybe getting a warrant for his phone records but we don't think there's enough there."

Lt. Black asked, "Have you asked him for the phone records?"

Ray and I looked at each other. Ray shook his head. "Not a bad idea, boss. We'll hit him up. See if he has anything to hide."

"That reminds me, do we have a phone for our hooker?" Ray asked, looking across the table at Floyd who was packing Copenhagen in his mouth.

He shook his head. "Not yet, but we figure we'll come up with something when we search her pad. Then we can just piggyback the Mincey for a phone warrant, get all the records from that."

The room fell silent. I looked up from having jotted a few notes and saw that the lieutenant and Ray were both doing the same. Floyd had his notebook closed and sitting neatly on the table in front of him next to two cups and a can of Copenhagen. Mongo was packing up his files.

I stood and said, "Well, I guess we all know what we're doing for the next day or two. Shall we meet again tomorrow night?"

Floyd was nodding. Ray said, "Yeah, why not, partner."

Lt. Black said, "I think it's a good idea, and I'll plan on attending. My goal on this is to stay informed so I can keep the captain up to speed and you guys don't have to worry with it."

"Thanks, LT," Ray said.

As we began filing out of the room, I halted Lt. Black and said, "Hey boss, just so you know, I won't be at the bureau meeting in the morning."

"No problem, Richard. You guys are real busy."

I had never worried about keeping lieutenants informed of my schedule, or whether or not I'd miss a meeting. There was something about Joe that made me want to have a better working relationship with him than I had had with other team lieutenants. That would be my responsibility; I would be the one who had to change my approach and practices in dealing with supervisors. I said, "Actually, Joe, I have a mandatory with the shrink."

He smiled. "Ah, Doctor James."

I nodded.

"She is such a wonderful lady, and a really great counselor."

# 21

KATHERINE JAMES LET herself into her apartment and tossed her keys in the direction of the small table by the door. She missed, and the keys clunked onto the carpet. Fine, they could stay there; she'd get them later. She ran her hand wearily through her blonde hair—formerly very big and very "done" looking, but now it curled softly at her shoulders. Her new hair, she called it. Easing first one foot, then the other, out of her work shoes—these high heels were killing her feet—she sighed in relief and curled her toes into the thick, plush carpet. Ah, life's little luxuries. The shoes, like the keys, could stay where they were for the time being. It was all about unwinding right now.

A quick survey of the contents of the refrigerator yielded two of her favorite "unwinders" as she thought of them. The chardonnay or the pinot noir, which one would it be? Did she feel like red or white this evening?

The red won, and she poured a generous amount into one of her new wine glasses, part of a set recently purchased. She opened the French door that led to the balcony and settled herself on one of her new chairs, light-weight metal with a floral cushion. "Here's to me and to all the new, here's to the red, the white, and the blue," she said aloud. She raised the glass and took a long drink, and added, "And fuck you, Steve Silverman."

Steve Silverman. The ex-Mr. Katherine, as she now thought of him. It had been two years since he left, two years of pain and near-crippling self-doubt. Two years of not simply being afraid to move on, but of genuinely not being sure she could. *Cheating bastard*, she thought, then, disgusted with herself, said aloud, "Katherine, you are a worthy and lovable person. You are very capable, and *you* choose whether or not to be happy."

She took another sip of the pinot and felt herself relax a bit. Dr. Slayton had told her she would get to this point, that she would one day feel confident again and be ready to move on. And he'd been right. The therapy and the antidepressants had done their jobs, and she, Dr. Katherine James, had emerged relatively whole. She sighed, thinking of the proverb "Physician, heal thyself." She had felt like such a fraud; what would her patients think of her, knowing their shrink needed a shrink? How could she advise them about their problems when she had so many of her own? Who was she to do that? And the doubts had come crashing in.

The rest of the red disappeared from the glass without her really noticing.

Presently, she felt a chill. Rising from the chair, she took her now-empty wine glass inside and considered having another. She needed just one more, she decided.

It really was time to move on. She had a new apartment with a six-month lease, and could take her time searching for just the right home, one that she wanted. She had also gone on several shopping trips and had filled the apartment with new furniture, dishes, appliances, art, and knickknacks. The shelves in the den held whatever books caught her eye, and she had even changed her hair and wardrobe. She was a new person. No, not really a new person, she thought. She was on her way to being the best version of herself.

And she finally felt ready to meet a new man. Katherine had learned the hard way that she needed to be cautious. No jumping right in. And no blinders on now; she was not the starry-eyed young woman she had once been. She had an idea of what she wanted in a man, and definitely knew what she didn't want. Any man she might consider would have to be honest, decent, and able to give her at least part of himself. And faithful, he had to be faithful, that was not negotiable. She wanted a man who was capable of caring about another human being in the deep way necessary for a real relationship. She deserved that, and knew she could give that in return to the right man. Assuming he existed.

The second glass of wine finished, Katherine put the bottle away and rinsed the glass. She walked to the bedroom, picking up her keys and placing them on the table where they belonged, and gathering her shoes along the way. She took from a dresser drawer her new pajamas, light-weight with a pattern of birds and flowers in pinks and blues and yellows. She stepped out of the knee-length, straight skirt she wore, and unbuttoned her silk blouse, hanging both over a chair back. They would go to the dry cleaner tomorrow. This evening would be a cozy at-home one, with left-over Chinese food and the comfortable pajamas. She would sit on the new couch with her new laptop and go over some of her files, make some notes and prepare for her next sessions with various patients. She had respect for all of them, although she did enjoy working with some more than others. Still she knew she gave each of them her best effort and full attention; she could sleep nights knowing that. Katherine glanced at the first name on the list of her clients. She smiled, unaware that she was doing so. She told herself she needed to start with this file, because the patient had complex issues to deal with and she needed to be well versed in all aspects they had covered so far. She had been considering for a few weeks now advising this patient that having sessions twice a week instead of just once would be beneficial. She found she really cared about his progress, and often thought about him and wondered how he was doing.

Katherine's smile widened, and she realized she was smiling and had been thinking of this patient more than any of the names in the other files. She shook her head. No, Katherine, you are not thinking of this patient as special. You are not. You are his doctor. Just do a good job with him and help him to move on. She opened the file, the one labeled Richard Jones.

# 22

I PASSED THE In-N-Out burger on my way home and thought about a burger, having missed dinner and now noticing a rumbling in my stomach. But I silently declined and sucked in my stomach a bit, thinking it was time to lose some weight. The way to lose weight was to avoid burgers and fries, especially at eleven at night. But I also needed to get back to the gym, or at least to running. I wasn't sure I ever wanted to spar again or work out hard the way I always had, having been pushed to do so by Floyd most of my adult life. Maybe it was my age. Maybe having been shot and just not feeling the same physically anymore. But at the very least, I needed to jog and burn some calories and stress.

As I neared my street I rubbed my elbow against the butt of my gun that sat in a holster high on my hip. It's something I often did without thinking about it, a quick check to make sure I hadn't left it behind somewhere. I never had, but the thought that I might was a deep fear I held. Like locking my keys in the car. I never have, but for some reason I'm always afraid I will. I double check before shutting the door. If I get out of the car and leave it running, I roll the window half down first, even if it's raining. No way I'm going to take a chance of being locked out of my car or find myself in a gunfight without my Glock.

When I turned the corner, coming in the back way to my street, my heartbeat noticeably increased at the sight of an unfamiliar vehicle parked along the row of others. I had come to know each car, and this was one with which I was not familiar. It wasn't the Oldsmobile from last week, but still . . .

I slowed and readied a flashlight as I drove up behind it. It had a California license plate which I read aloud and repeated twice in order to commit it to memory. There was nothing remarkable about the car, it was just a typical sedan. A silver Ford Taurus. Half the guys in our bureau drove cars just like it. The FBI had fleets of them as well. They must have been giving them away, all the ones that didn't get bought by rental companies.

The windows were tinted, so as I came alongside the car, I shined my light at it. I didn't see anything so I continued past it. But a thought hit me and I threw my car in park and quickly exited. At the same time, I jerked my gun from its holster, brought it up in one hand to meet my flashlight in the other, and I approached the car pointing both at its interior. The thought went through my head that this was not the smart thing to do, but now I was committed. My tactics were poor: I didn't have backup; nobody knew where I was or what I was doing; and I hadn't even written down the license plate so that if I were killed there would be a clue left behind. Oh well.

I moved more quickly and aggressively when I neared the car, thrusting the barrel of my gun and its accompanying flashlight at the interior of the parked sedan. It was empty. I scanned the interior again to make sure I hadn't missed anything, careful to see the floorboards as well. Nothing. I looked around, up and down the street, making sure I hadn't missed someone outside the car, but the street was quiet. I walked over and placed my hand on the hood; it was cold to the touch. The car had been parked here for a long time. I looked around on the ground but didn't see any cigarette butts. Maybe I was being paranoid.

I drove around the block twice before parking in my usual spot on the street near the driveway to the garage and the gate to the backyard. I sat there in the dark for another five minutes to watch the street. Finally, I went through the gate—noting that my security twig was still in place—and ascended the steps into my apartment. But I didn't turn on the lights. The outside street lights cast sufficient light into the apartment that I could see the placement of furniture and was able to walk through the darkened interior. I tossed my briefcase onto the couch and walked to the balcony, opening the slider and stepping out into the dark.

I looked up the street at where the car was parked.

It was gone.

I hurried into the kitchen using my phone for lighting as I didn't want to turn on the interior lights. I grabbed a piece of paper and wrote the license plate number down before I forgot it and hoped I had remembered it correctly. It occurred to me I should have taken a picture with my phone.

Then I called the office.

"Homicide Bureau, Detective Farris speaking."

Rich Farris, my name buddy.

"Rich Farris, Rich Jones here."

"Hey Dickie, how's it going, man? I heard you were back but haven't seen you around the office yet."

"Yeah, just got back. Listen, I need a plate ran, you got a second?"

"For you, my brother, anything. Shoot."

I gave him the license number and waited. With the sounds of fingers pecking a keyboard, I pictured Rich Farris alone at the desk, his tie loosened or maybe removed, drowsy eyes. Rich always had drowsy eyes, a man who appeared bored to the casual observer. He was a veteran homicide detective who had the respect of his peers and supervisors alike. A man with blinding white teeth set against chocolate brown skin, who had an easy way about him. He also had a taste for bourbon and troubles with women.

After a few moments of relative silence, he said, "Nothing on that plate, brother. You want to read it back to me, make sure I ran it right?"

I did, and it was the correct plate. At least it was the license number that I had committed to memory and recorded on paper once the situation had escalated. I was mad at myself for not taking the photo, or at least writing it down then and there. Now I questioned if I remembered it correctly, and I repeated it in my head while trying to see the plate again.

"Rich, thanks, man, I really appreciate your help."

Detective Rich Farris said, "No problem, brother. Let me know if you need anything else. I'm here all night."

I thought for a very brief moment of asking him to call Burbank PD for me, or maybe asking him to page my lieutenant. I thought of calling Floyd, or maybe even my new partner, Ray. But nothing seemed right to me. It all seemed overdone. I still was unable to convince myself that I was being watched, and that I wasn't just being paranoid.

"Thanks, Rich. Have a good night."

---

LEONARD HAD GROWN TIRED OF SITTING IN HIS CAR. HE HAD BEEN THERE three hours and needed to take a leak. The street was desolate, like a graveyard, all of the lights were off, yet piggy was nowhere to be found. He needed to figure out what this asshole did that kept him out so late. He must have a drinking problem or something.

He glanced at his phone to check the time. It was nearly midnight, time for him to wrap it up. He wasn't going to wait all night. But first, he needed to relieve himself. It was a long drive back to his room. He slid out of the car and climbed a small hill near where he had parked. There were no homes and he could have some privacy. Just as he finished, he heard the sound of a car approaching. He zipped up quickly and flattened out in the tall grass. He watched until the headlights came close, and then he tucked his face into the turf. He waited. He heard the motor winding and the tires crunching on the pavement as the car slowed nearby. He cautiously lifted his head and saw that the car had stopped in the street, next to Leonard's car. It was the cop, and he was shining his light at the parked vehicles, focusing mostly on Leonard's. He felt lucky he had needed to piss and was not sitting in his car at that moment. He'd have to rethink his strategy now too, as the cop had surprised him and came home a different route. Had he not been pissing, Leonard would have been caught redhanded.

The cop started to drive off, but then stopped. He jumped out of his car, the way cops do, and approached Leonard's car while continuing to shine his light at it. Leonard heard the cop curse as he now stood looking around. Leonard ducked his face again when the cop's eyes panned in his direction.

Leonard looked up when he heard the cop drive away. The cop drove past his house and continued to drive down the street and out of view. This puzzled Leonard, who waited patiently, aware of his rapid heartbeat, not sure if he should move or stay put. He could hear the distant sound of the car's motor, and he could hear the squealing of tires every so often. Soon, he heard the car coming back his direction. Leonard looked around and planned his escape. He would leave by foot, over the mountain. It was a disposable car, after all, and for good reason.

This time, the cop drove by slowly and shined his light all around, looking at other cars and toward homes and into yards. He drove past his apartment, turned around and stopped, but then he just sat there. He must have sat there half an hour, and Leonard was getting cold and stiff from lying on the damp ground. Had piggy seen him? Leonard didn't think so. Although the front of the cop car was pointed directly toward where Leonard lay, he had been still, and he had kept his head low. He could only see the cop car from a small part of his right eye. The rest of his head was tucked into the crook of his arm and concealed by the grass.

Finally, the man exited his car and walked into the backyard. Leonard acted quickly. Without hesitation or second thought, he ran to his car and quickly entered it, started it, and drove off blacked out.

Two blocks away he turned his lights on and then yelled in the darkness of his car's interior. "Goddamn, that was close. Whew!" he said, and laughed.

He needed cigarettes. He hadn't had a smoke since he arrived, not realizing he had run out. When he crossed the freeway and was a good distance from the pig sty, he stopped at a 7-11 and picked up a pack of smokes and a tall can of beer. They didn't sell liquor, so beer would have to do. Leonard needed a drink.

---

ALONE IN THE DARK WITH ONLY MY THOUGHTS, I RECONCILED THE situation at hand thus: either I was being watched by the feds, or not at all and I was only being paranoid.

The feds made sense if I had the plate right. Just like the two suits who had arrived at Chaney's house the day Ray and I interviewed him, this vehicle had no registration. That left me asking why. Why would the feds be watching me, and why would the feds be talking to Chaney? Floyd suggested the mob. I didn't see it. To me, the two suits looked like feds, and I doubted the mafia would have unregistered or cold-plated vehicles. Only cops did shit like that. It was too much hassle and another reason to be detained if your car wasn't registered, so why would criminals take that chance? No, it had to be the feds.

Or, I was being paranoid. Nobody was watching me at all. The car that had been out there tonight was unoccupied. There were no cigarette butts. Nobody sitting inside. It had to have just been timing. The driver had visited someone and just happened to leave as I was coming into my apartment. Coincidental, but not impossible. What else made sense? Nothing.

I opened a second beer and returned to my seat on the deck. There was a lot to think about and I knew I wouldn't sleep. Not for a while. Fortunately, I had a respectable supply of Coors Light in the fridge. Respectable by cop standards; ridiculous or maybe dangerous by normal people's.

As I sat and watched I thought about the situation, and I thought about the Santa Clarita murder, and I thought about the missing Mrs. Chaney. I thought about Jorge Regalado and his heavy mustache, seeing it again in my mind, just inches from my face in a haze of confusion and noise and silence as flames erupted from each of our guns. I went for another beer.

Soon I was thinking about Valerie and wondered how she was, what she was doing, and if she had found someone else. Then I wondered if she had had someone else before she left. You never knew, I supposed. I drained the beer and went for another. As I opened it, I wished there was gin in the house, and was glad there wasn't.

I realized there was a lot to do tomorrow, and I needed to get some sleep. The day would start at the shrink's office, the lovely Doc James. Who had been nearly invisible to me before but now I tended to notice her shape, and her smile, her hazel eyes, and a glimmer that hadn't been there before.

Jesus, what was wrong with me?

I went inside and sprawled out on the couch. The thought occurred to me that I had wasted a grand on a bed.

# 23

D R. KATHERINE JAMES saw her patient out, watching his head recede down the back stairs. Because many of her patients were in law enforcement, she was especially conscientious about the privacy of those who trusted her to treat them. Cops tended not to trust "shrinks" and avoided them for the most part; no cop wanted a career-ending diagnosis. The system, therefore, was set up so that only one patient at a time was in the waiting room, and there were separate doors for entering and exiting her office. Katherine noted that her next patient was due in a few minutes. He had missed an appointment earlier in the week, and she hoped he wouldn't miss a second. She *hoped* he wasn't avoiding her.

After making a few quick notes on her laptop, she rose from her desk and stretched. She caught sight of herself in the small decorative mirror she had hung over a plant next to the window. Frowning slightly, she walked closer to the mirror and looked at her face, her hair. Of course, she was presentable; she always kept her appearance neat and professional at work. Still . . .

Rummaging through her purse, Katherine found her hairbrush and used it for a few seconds. There. Better. Glancing at the clock on her desk, she hastily put the brush away and paused at the door to the waiting room.

She brushed her hand across her skirt, opened the door, and smiled into the waiting room at her next patient.

"Hello, Richard, come in."

He chose the same chair he always chose, the one where he could see both doors. He never chose the opposite chair, nor the couch. Katherine settled in the chair across from him, as always, crossed her legs, and smiled encouragingly.

"We missed on Monday, is everything ok?"

"Yeah, fine."

She noted his shortness but wouldn't mention it. "Is it anything you'd care to talk about?"

"Not really, everything's fine."

"How was your first day back at work?"

"It was okay."

"How did you feel going in?"

"Like everyone was staring at me. Like I was a new kid at school."

"Were there parts that felt good, maybe seeing old friends, your old partner?"

He shifted uncomfortably in his seat and avoided eye contact. After a moment, he said, "I don't know. It was a little weird seeing someone else in my desk. Floyd's new partner, I mean."

"What do you think of his having a new partner? How does that make you feel?"

"I don't know, Doc . . . How's it supposed to make me feel? The wife's gone, partner's gone, one of my kidneys is gone . . . There's been a lot more change than a guy like me is comfortable talking about, really."

She smiled at him politely. "Richard, I know you find it difficult to talk about your feelings, but you know this is a safe place to do that. You have complete privacy here with me, and complete confidentiality. I know we have talked about that, but it bears repeating."

"Yeah, I know. I'm trying to be honest about my feelings but I just don't know what you want me to say."

He looked up as if that was it. Katherine waited. She wanted him to expound on his feelings and believed he might if allowed the time to gather his thoughts.

"I feel alone, okay? I'm glad to be back at work, back to having something to do. Maybe it will help. Help me keep my mind off . . ."

She waited, but soon it became clear he wasn't going to finish that thought.

"Keep your mind off what, Richard?"

He looked away, toward the exit door. It seemed he was always ready to leave.

"Everything. Being shot. Ruining my marriage."

"Why do you think you ruined the marriage?"

"It's what I do. Twice now. It's the job. It's my inability to leave it behind. I can't even look at my beautiful wife without seeing crime scenes. How messed up is that?" He lowered his voice and muttered, "*Ex-wife.*"

"Have the two of you spoken?"

"I don't want to talk about *her.*"

"All right, Richard, what would you like to talk about then?"

"Getting a release so I can get back into the rotation. I might have a shot with a new partner, Ray, who I'm helping out on a case right now. Yesterday the lieutenant mentioned I might be able to come to his team and partner with Ray permanently. But I have to be released, according to the idiot."

"Captain Stover."

"Yes."

"I can do that, Richard, but I need you to tell me why you believe you're ready. You seem to have healed physically, but there is much more to being ready to return than that. You've just pointed out several drastic changes in your life, all in a relatively short time."

"I believe I'm ready because it's what I do, it's who I am. It's all I have left, if you get right down to it. I need it."

Katherine uncrossed her legs, and re-crossed them. She looked at Richard, considering.

"I wonder whether you feel you're ready to terminate our sessions completely. You do seem to be ready to return to work, but the personal matters you're dealing with are very complicated and are separate from the stresses of your job. I am concerned that you have not dealt with the feelings of loss in your personal life and at work."

Katherine knew she was thinking of her patient's best interests in telling him that, but she was a little surprised at how much she wanted him to say he would still come in for sessions. She wouldn't push, but she did find herself wishing he would. It's what is best for *him,* she told herself. She sympathized with him; she knew how hard it was to go through a divorce, and Richard was now in the process of his second one. She knew how it hurt him, how it felt to be left by a spouse.

"I don't mind the sessions. I think, maybe—it's helpful I think. If I were to continue coming in, would you be more comfortable releasing me to full duty?"

"I hope you do continue, Richard. But this is about you, what is comfortable for you. As your psychiatrist, I can advise you to continue with our sessions in order to help you with some issues in your personal life. However, I cannot force you to do that, nor is it a condition of my releasing you to full duty." Katherine smiled encouragingly at him.

He smiled back. "Okay, yes, I would like to continue our sessions. Wednesdays work well, it gets me out of the bureau meetings."

She smiled. "Fine, we can book Wednesdays. Now, why don't you tell me some of the things you are doing to adjust to being single again?"

He chuckled. "Mostly not sleeping and eating horribly. Plus, I have to go to a laundromat now. I haven't done that since I was twenty. I sit there and watch others come and go and I wonder if they're happy or sad, lonely or content. I won't leave, I just sit and wait. Because when I was twenty, I had a pair of jeans stolen out of a washer when I went for a burger. How pathetic is that? I need to start eating better and getting some exercise."

Katherine wanted to tell him she understood, how very well she understood. If they were just two people talking, she could reveal her own experiences and maybe be of some comfort to him. But.

She smiled at him again. "Well, Richard, it sounds like you're aware of some things that need to change before they become real health issues. Maybe you can think about that before our next session and we can explore some ways that you can begin making some changes. For now, I will release you to go back to full duty. I'll call Captain Stover and let him know, and follow it up with a letter for your file."

She stood, as did Richard. "I will see you next week, Richard. Have a good day." She smiled again.

He nodded and went to the door. "Thank you, Doc," and then he was gone.

Katherine inhaled, then sighed. Richard. She stood for a moment, then shook herself and went to her laptop to make some notes about their session. She hoped he would indeed continue returning weekly. He was going to have some things to work out, and she wanted to be there for him.

She looked in the mirror and said to the face smiling back at her. "Well, *Doc*?"

---

HER JOB WAS TO FIX ME UP AND MAKE ME WHOLE. GATHER THE DEMONS and drive them into the dark room and slam the door shut. Most times, the demons rested quietly in the recesses of my mind. But then the horrors of the past would burst through the darkness and shatter any peace I may have had. How much of this could I even tell her? I didn't think I could tell her everything, and also keep my job. Sensory recall was evidence of PTSD, and it struck me often. No shrink would leave a cop on the job once diagnosed with it.

Maybe she knew.

Law enforcement as a profession had come to understand the long-lasting, often irreversible psychological effects of continued exposure. Our department, like many others, maintained a large budget for the prevention or treatment of Post-traumatic Stress Disorder, or PTSD. The hope was to instill coping skills in order to prevent, or at least postpone, one from permanently crawling into a bottle or eating his gun.

I was the type to resist counseling. It was one thing to be told by Floyd regularly and often that I was nuts, and another to be officially diagnosed. As such, I had never found the services of our department shrinks to be anything but a nuisance. It did occur to me that if I were willing and able to be truthful without fear of consequences, there might be hope. Though I did not trust I could be completely honest about my emotional state at times.

I found myself thinking about her. *Katherine James.* Maybe even fondly. I was fooling myself at times to believe I could tell her anything.

Maybe not completely, as I still held back to a degree. Could I trust her? I didn't know. I felt I could. Maybe.

There was something else. Something beyond the counseling that I now found myself contemplating, but it didn't make sense. I shrugged it off; it was my imagination thinking there may be some interest there. Both directions. But it couldn't be. Katherine was smarter, more sophisticated, and on an entirely different professional and social plane than me. I didn't see her spending her evenings sitting on a balcony alone, drinking, reflecting on failed relations and professional challenges. No, she would likely go home to an extravagant dwelling and walk out back to see the kids playing in the pool while patting a golden retriever on its head. A refined gentleman for a husband reminding her they had tickets for the opera. Or, if she was single, a sporty lawyer or young executive roaring up in her circular drive, the setting sun silhouetting his broad shoulders as he stepped out of a Corvette or Porsche. Some yuppie asshole I knew I'd hate.

It was absurd to allow my mind to even wander that direction. The truth of it was, she likely found me crass, simple, maybe not too bright. Maybe uncivilized, the type who seemed to find himself entangled in violence more than others. She had likely surmised there was something to that, something more than simple fate or bad luck. As did I at times.

No, the good doctor had no interest in men like me. Men who wore suits and presented confidently before executives, judges, and jurors, yet were more comfortable on a barstool or in a brawl than at the opera.

Never the opera.

Maybe I *was* nuts.

## 24

M Y TIMING WAS perfect. Investigators were leaving the office in the way Dodgers fans flood the exit rows when their boys are losing by three in the seventh. It signaled the end of the bureau meeting. Most were carrying case files and attaches, though some had empty hands. Many would be headed somewhere to work on a case, their most recent or maybe something they've dallied with for years and refused to give up. Others might be headed to court, the coroner's office, the crime lab, the golf course, or the bar. Few actually partook in the latter two, though it was a stereotype which burdened homicide detectives everywhere. After parking in the shade of the tall building, I went inside, the smile and legs of Doc James weighing heavily on my mind.

"What'd I miss, anything of value?" I asked Ray as I plopped down at Frank Lewandowski's vacant desk, which would soon be mine.

"Not too much. An interesting case out of San Fernando, other than that, just the usual gang killings and the captain's weekly sermon on overtime."

"They cutting it again?"

"Not yet. He was warning that it might be coming, so we needed to be more *judicious* with our *time management.*"

I chuckled. We were currently capped at thirty hours per month. At times, they'd knock it to twenty. One callout would cause you to burn through your allotted overtime, and only one callout per month was virtually unheard of. Then, when cases like the Santa Clarita Jane Doe case came along, or when a cop was killed, you'd eat up thirty hours of overtime before the next time you saw a pillow.

"What about the San Fernando case?"

"Little girl was murdered," Ray said. "Thirteen-year-old who's home alone after school until her mother picks her up. Mom and dad own a cleaners in Sylmar, and mom breaks away when she has the chance and picks her up, brings her back to work. The other day—I think he said it was Thursday—mom came home to find her daughter in her room, strangled to death."

"Interesting. Was it a sex crime?"

"They don't know yet. She wasn't wearing panties, but as Farris said, it's the twenty-first century."

"Rich Farris has it, huh?"

"Him and Lizzy, an assist to San Fernando PD."

I nodded and pictured Rich Farris and Elizabeth Marchesano as I had often seen them before my year's medical leave. She was new at the time —brand new—and maybe underqualified. Rich with his easy way about him and a timid Lizzy following behind, afraid to be noticed. Both black. Both attractive and personable and witty. One a tremendous asset to the bureau, respected throughout the department, the other possibly ruined by those trying to make things better under the guise of equal opportunity.

Lizzy had only worked two years in patrol before promoting to sergeant. As a sergeant, she worked in Recruitment. Then she went to Internal Affairs, and from there—with only a couple years of what most would consider questionable investigative experience—she was brought to Homicide. It was the part of equal opportunity that we all tried to ignore, the fact there were often those who were promoted prematurely and ahead of more qualified and deserving applicants. Mostly, it was unfair to them, those who benefited from such action. They were viewed as less qualified when truthfully many were more than qualified, just not yet ready for primetime. Now they would have to work twice as hard to prove themselves worthy.

"How's she doing anyway, Lizzy?"

"She's turned out pretty good, partner. Still a little lost at times—I think—but Farris speaks highly of her, seems to be happy working with her."

"Is that all he's doing with her?"

Ray shrugged. "Well, you know, partner, you just never know. Although, if he is doing more than working with her, he's braver than I ever knew. Lizzy's old man is a swat cop at LAPD, and from what I understand, a bad dude."

"This girl, the San Fernando murder, is there anything about it that might be of interest to us? Anything at all that might overlap with our Jane Doe—rather, our Lisa Williams case?"

"Not that I know of, partner. Everything looks different to me, age, location, M.O. . . . hell, she even had her head about her."

We each smiled slightly at the pun. But he was right, the *modus operandi* differed significantly.

"Did she have a brother, or a boyfriend?"

"I'm not sure, partner."

"Dad accounted for?"

"Don't know. Maybe you should hit up Rich. I saw him in the kitchen a few minutes ago, having a cup. I honestly don't know much about the case, just enough I didn't feel it was worth looking at, as far as having anything to do with our case."

"You're probably right, Ray. I guess I just don't have enough to think about, having been gone a year. I should just worry about ours for now."

Ray had his nose down, thumbing through notes. As I watched him, it occurred to me for the first time his hair was like a baby's, fine and wavy. I wondered if it would be curly if allowed to grow out. I didn't miss the long, curly red hair I wore as a teenager, and truthfully, the thought of it made me cringe. My parents kept embarrassing photographic evidence of those days prominently displayed in their home. The long-haired little Richard who gave up sports in order to keep a job so there would be money for gas and go-fast parts for his muscle car, a 1965 Ford Mustang fastback. My need for speed had nearly derailed my path to law enforcement on more than one occasion. Apparently, some things are just meant to be.

I interrupted his thoughts. "Ray, I think the watcher was back."

He turned his head and looked over a pair of cheaters. "Yeah? What happened, partner?"

I told him the story of last night, arriving home to see a vehicle that was out of place, not the same vehicle, but one I felt didn't belong. I told him it was unoccupied and that there were no cigarette butts, and that the hood was cold to the touch. He watched with an expression that told me he was trying to see how I thought this could be related, given what I had told him so far. I added that the vehicle left as soon as I went inside.

He said, "Well, that could be a coincidence, partner."

"Yeah, but get this, the plates come back no record on file, same as our two friends in the suits who showed up at the Chaney house."

His expression changed to one of consideration. "That's interesting."

"Yeah, I think so. Maybe it's way out there, but can all of this be connected? Is that even possible?"

He thought about it before answering. "I don't know how it would be, partner. I mean, you weren't even on the case until a few days ago, so that doesn't really make sense."

"Well, maybe, maybe not. We need to see if Mongo came up with anything. Have you seen those two assholes today, Floyd and Mongo?"

He shook his head and then looked around the bureau but didn't have anything to add.

I looked down the column of desks and saw Lt. Black look up from his mound of paperwork, peering over the glasses that hung on his nose. He smiled at me, and I nodded.

"Okay," I announced, "I'm going to go see if I can find Farris, or Floyd and Mongo."

"I'll be right here, partner."

LEONARD PARKED AT A LIQUOR STORE ACROSS THE STREET FROM FRIENDLY Auto Sales. He watched as the happy gypsy schmoozed two Hispanic men dressed in double-knit slacks, silk shirts, and gold necklaces, two men who likely had no legitimate means to buy and register a vehicle this side of the border. He was all smiles while patting their backs and shaking their hands. But the two men walked away and departed in the vehicle that they had apparently arrived in, a gold-colored pickup with a Brahma bull sticker on the tailgate. Grigori's smile faded with their departure, and he turned to walk back to the office.

Leonard moved quickly. He slid out of his Taurus and jogged across the street, darting through traffic. He made his way through the parking lot of cars for sale and paused near the trailer that was the office. He looked around before ascending three grated metal steps and going through the door, his new Buck knife held behind his back.

Grigori stood just inside the door; the bottle blonde sat at her desk smacking gum. Grigori was saying, "Theese fawking Mey-hicanos and der flashy fawking sheeit—"

The Russian was gesturing around his neck, apparently about to describe the Hispanic men's jewelry to his secretary when Leonard thrust his knife over Grigori's right shoulder. Grigori instinctively lifted his head up and back to avoid the weapon, which made his throat that much more accessible. Leonard grabbed the Russian's thick head of hair and pulled his head further back. Grigori grabbed Leonard's forearm, but he didn't have the strength to stop the momentum. Leonard plunged his knife into Grigori's throat and pulled it across his neck from left to right, cutting deep through the tissue and muscle. Blood shot outward in a fine mist of crimson spray. But then—in the way a rotted garden hose bursts under the pressure of water looking to escape—a stream of blood burst through the red mist and shot across the room.

Blondie sat aghast, wide-eyed with her mouth open, her hands out in front of her as if trying to deflect the spattering of blood now adorning her white blouse.

Leonard felt the man collapsing beneath him. He released him, the sounds of his final groans and gurgles fading as the Russkie crumpled onto the carpeted floor. A quick check of his waistline revealed no weapon, which Leonard found odd. He was certain the man had had one beneath his shirt the other time they met. No matter, he would never have had the chance to get it if he had it, thanks to Leonard's quick and efficient attack. He stepped over the dead gypsy and walked toward the woman with her big mouth hanging open, a wad of gum dangling at the corner of her bright red lips. She began pushing her chair back, rolling it away from the desk she sat behind. Leonard lunged across the desk with his blood-covered knife leading the way. The blade caught her left breast as she continued to retreat. Leonard was now prone across the desk with only one foot on the floor. As he pushed himself up, he caught the glimpse of an object coming down on his head. She yelled just as something crashed over his head, and the sound of a loud bell rang in his ears. For a moment it was dark, and then the light returned, though he found it difficult to focus. He was aware of movement and he lunged again and grabbed the gypsy woman around her waist.

She yelled and cussed and continued to hit him on his head and back, but now it was only her fists. The heavy object that had dazed him was no longer in play. Leonard knew she would not be able to inflict any more damage without a weapon. She continued toward the door, Leonard holding on and being dragged behind her. But he knew he had her now, she would be his in a matter of moments.

The Russian woman stumbled and fell to the ground. Leonard pounced, like a wrestler overtaking his opponent. It was then he realized the dead gypsy, the crooked Russkie car thief, was beneath her on the floor. It was his dead body she had fallen over. Her boss, or boyfriend, or pimp.

The slutty Russian went limp and whimpered in defeat. There was no more fight in her.

Leonard tossed the bloody knife aside and pulled her arms behind her back. She didn't resist. He reached around his back and removed the handcuffs he had purchased at the uniform store and placed them on her. He had been handcuffed hundreds of times himself while serving time, and he was familiar with the process. Once she was secured, Leonard sat back and rested on her buttocks.

"G'head, you dirty bastard, hev your vay to me," she said, with the same accent with which Grigori had spoken.

Leonard frowned. "*With me* . . . it's 'have your way *with* me.'"

"Vhatever. Just do vhat you hev to do and let me be."

"Shut up, whore. You have nothing I want."

"Oh? Nothing? I hev cash. You can hev it all. You can hev me too, I gladly give you vhatever you vant, and you can take money too. Ve hev cash."

"How much?"

She paused a moment. "Thousand, maybe two a thousand, in the drawer."

"What about the safe?"

"No safe. You take cash, and you do vhat you vant to me. I saw how you look. How you say, hoany. Like you no have voman long time. You come from the jail, no?"

Leonard stood and pulled her up by the handcuffs and a clump of her hair.

"Goddamnit!"

She stumbled over the gypsy as Leonard shoved her toward her desk. He stood her next to it and came around the front of her, now standing face to face. He could see the age beneath her makeup and he smelled the musky scent of her body and liquor on her breath. His eyes drifted from hers to the desk and back. "Where's the money?"

The blonde woman with the blood-soaked blouse pointed to the far side of the desk by jutting her nose in that direction. "Bottom drawer, in a metal box in the back. Under my sveater and purse."

Leonard pulled out the drawer and removed her sweater and purse and lifted a metal box from the back. He set it on the desk and opened it to see it was half full of cash. He picked up one bundle and saw it was hundreds. There were two bundles of fifties, and two more of twenties. There were several identifications at the bottom of the box. He saw that two were the woman's, each bearing a different name, and three others featured Grigori's face with various aliases. Leonard turned the box upside down to dump the IDs on the desk, and returned the bundles of cash into the box. He picked it up and looked at her. She had streaks of black running down her cheeks and smudges of red lipstick around her mouth and on her chin. Her eyes held contempt, not fear.

"Where's the gun?"

She shook her head.

He didn't ask twice. He knew how these Russkies could be. He punched her in the face with a hard right fist and she hit the ground. He stepped over and kicked her in the stomach. She let out a grunt but didn't cry or scream. He left her there squirming on her side, her hands secured behind her, and returned to the desk.

The top right drawer was the first he opened, and he didn't need to open the others. Sitting right on top was a black nine-millimeter pistol. It felt good in his hand, the first he had ever held. He felt powerful, invincible, and he smiled.

He returned to the blonde and pointed the gun at her head. "Say goodbye, darling."

She sniffled slightly, and her body jerked as if she was holding in emotion.

Leonard thought about the sound of a gunshot and wondered how far it would be heard in the city. He had no idea, and it gave him pause. On the one hand, it would be a perfect time to learn to shoot, and to witness first-hand what happens when you blast a cap into someone's skull. But then there was the noise. It was daytime, a weekday, and people were all about. He would need to cross the boulevard and get to his car unnoticed, and a gunshot now might draw unwanted attention. He looked about until he spotted his knife on the floor. He stepped over and picked it up, and then he returned to straddle her head. "Now, bitch, you can say it for real."

But before she said anything he thrust the knife into her throat and watched her eyes pop open in surprise. He held the pistol in his other hand. He looked around but didn't see a place where he could set it that wasn't covered with blood. Without a free hand, he was unable to grip her head to finish the job properly by slicing her throat, So, he pulled the knife out and jammed it back in over and over until he hit an artery and blood jetted out of the side of her neck. Leonard jumped out of the path of its stream and stood back watching until it petered out and only dripped to the floor. He loved the appearance of blood in any form, but he especially enjoyed seeing it squirt from an artery until the pressure was gone and it slowly stopped flowing at all. He was surprised she had been so silent throughout. These Russkies were a tough bunch; he had to give them that.

Leonard removed the handcuffs and wiped the blood from them on her blouse. Satisfied, he stepped over one dead gypsy and then the other. He turned the lights off and walked out into the bright midday Hollywood sunshine, a smile on his face.

The thought occurred to him he should have taken a picture for Whitey.

FLOYD WAS EATING A BURGER AT THE FOOD COURT WHEN I WALKED UP AND saw a blob of ketchup drip onto the tray in front of him. "Easy, killer."

He wiped his mouth with a paper napkin and nodded toward an empty seat. I pulled it out and looked over at Mongo who had nothing other than empty wrappers and a large paper cup in front of him, and his watchful eyes on me. I made a mental note to ask Floyd about him sometime, what his beef was with me. Or maybe he just has a shitty personality.

Then I thought of a reason to make him speak to me. "Have you heard anything from your niece?"

"Cousin. She's looking into it."

I just nodded. *Why bother with this guy?*

I turned my attention to Floyd. "Want to hear about some weird shit that happened to me?"

"When?"

"Last night. Actually, I had some weird shit happen last night, and then some very different weird shit this morning."

He took a swig of his soda. "Well, hell yeah, Dickie. There's nothing we love more than weird shit. Let's hear it."

I started with last night, told the story for the second time in as many hours about the car with unregistered license plates that sat unoccupied up the street but left right after I arrived. He listened without comment, though he appeared to be measuring every word I said. I could see the wheels turning and I knew he'd have some ideas. When I finished, I waited for his response.

But all he said was, "And what about this morning?"

At first, I was surprised he didn't have any commentary on the news of last night, and then I realized he was interrogating me. That's what cops do, all of us. With each other, with our spouses, with everyone. It's one of the reasons most of us were divorced. Floyd would let me get all of it out and then circle back around and ask more questions before offering solutions.

"Nothing exciting like that, it's just something weird."

He waited.

"The shrink."

"Doc James? What, she still thinks you're nuts? Or she revealed to you her feelings for me? She loves me, you know."

I smiled. "Actually, she revealed her feelings for me."

He grinned. "You don't say?"

"I mean, that's how I'm picking it up. Have you seen her lately?"

"I had the mandatory three sessions after our shooting—*your* shooting —but nothing since then. Amazingly, Cindy isn't driving me nuts lately and without you around I seem to be more stable. So, no, I haven't bothered going. Why do you ask?"

"She's changed her hair color and maybe has lost some weight. Not that she was ever fat, but now she looks terrific, fit. Also, she seems to focus on my impending divorce and asks weird questions like how am I adjusting to being single. Also, she encourages me to continue our sessions."

"That all sounds like normal shrink shit to me, Dickie, as far as normal shrink shit goes. I never thought of her as fat."

"Her skirts seem a little shorter and she seems to move her legs around a lot, crossing one over the other and switching, constantly, as if begging me to have a peek."

Now I had his full attention. "No shit, huh? What'd you see?"

"I was afraid to look. I mean, she's staring right at me, looking me directly in the eyes, but I can see her legs going back and forth. It's like she's daring me to glance down."

"She wants you to look, Dickie, the trampy little crazy cop doctor. I wonder if she's single. You suppose she's single?"

I shrugged.

"Well," he said, as he stood and began gathering his trash, "we have a lot of ground to cover on this piece of shit case of yours. We're meeting Gentry at the dead broad's apartment at two."

"You better get crackin'."

He glanced at his watch. "I'm on overtime, Dickie. From now until at least midnight, maybe later. I bet I write 120 hours this month, just to piss off your captain."

I smiled, knowing he always at least doubled what they allowed and somehow got away with it. He was shooting to quadruple it this month, and I didn't doubt he would.

He lowered his Ray-Bans over his eyes and walked away with Mongo in tow. It occurred to me I had screwed up by mentioning the doc. Floyd could never concentrate on anything other than women while in their presence or while speaking of them. If I knew my ex-partner, he would ponder the Doctor James situation for the next two hours or so, and then he'd shift to my problem with the possible watcher. Once he processed and analyzed the information I provided, and then reanalyzed it, he'd give me a call.

Meanwhile, I'd pay close attention to my surroundings.

# 25

THE APARTMENT WAS decorated in white carpeting with contrasting black furniture, leather sofas and chairs and metal framed tables with glass tops. Black framed mirrors adorned all except one wall which was constructed of glass from floor to ceiling, offering an unrestricted view of the ocean. The pièce de résistance was the bar, and that was where Floyd stood enjoying the scenery outside. He eyed the Bombay and thought of his old partner, Dickie, who did occasionally enjoy his gin. As did he, on the rare occasion. Fancy dinners required it. Floyd would enjoy a glass of red wine with a steak, usually something bold like an old vine California red zinfandel, or a cabernet. But before dinner—while posing at the bar in his suit and tie or a cardigan—he'd have one or two gin and tonics while enjoying a conversation with his guest or a neighboring patron or bartender. He found himself more open to conversation with strangers at five-star restaurants where he mingled with a different class of people. Floyd enjoyed listening to someone tell of their business ventures, their accomplishments or connections, and then seeing their faces when he answered the question that would always follow, "So, what do you do?"

Other times he might enjoy a gin would be on a Saturday afternoon while tending his barbecue, shirtless, in the backyard. As long as he wasn't on call. When on call, he was disciplined; he'd never consider having anything to drink. Other than maybe a couple, four, or five beers. Occasionally more, but not always.

Floyd wasn't entirely opposed to having a gin while working, but it was early in the day and there was still plenty to do once the search of Lisa Williams's Marina apartment was concluded.

His attention was drawn to a blonde who seemed to appear from nowhere, standing on the dock not far from where Floyd gazed through the glass. Standing in her bikini bottoms and a cutoff t-shirt, she seemed to be looking directly at him through the wall of glass. He smiled and batted his eyes, but then she turned away.

Mongo came up from behind him and set a legal-sized envelope on the bar. There wasn't much in it. "I think we're done here, boss."

Floyd looked around at Mongo, then he pushed away from the bar and surveyed the apartment. It occurred to him that this was just what Dickie needed, a place at the Marina. Floyd could visit him on the weekends to escape the constraints of family life now and then. Though he loved his wife and kids, he almost envied his partner for being single and having virtually no responsibility. He thought of Dickie sitting on his balcony, and recalled the situation with someone possibly watching him. He thought about the news of a different vehicle being outside Dickie's apartment last night, a car with cold plates, according to Dickie. Something had been bothering him ever since Dickie told him the story, but he hadn't yet put his finger on what it was.

He looked back toward the dock but the bikini-clad blonde was gone. His eyes quickly scanned the yachts and sailboats but she was nowhere to be seen. Well, then, back to business.

"What do we have for evidence?"

Mongo reached into the envelope. "Not a lot. An address book is probably our best bet. At least maybe we can find someone who knew her. Other than that, a few odds and ends." He began lifting one item at a time and replacing it with another as he summarized his findings. "Got a toothbrush for DNA, an old phone that is dead and probably has no service, a charger so that maybe we can power it up, a few sex toys from the nightstand—"

"Sex toys?"

"I was thinking maybe DNA."

Floyd made a sound like "Hmpf" and leaned over to peek inside the envelope.

Phil Gentry from the crime lab appeared in the hallway. "I think we're done here, boys."

"Photos and prints, everything wrapped up?"

"Everything," he said, answering Floyd while his eyes scanned the room. "I don't know how much good we've done. There are a lot of latent prints, but you know how that goes, most of them will probably be hers."

"Hey, we do the best we can. You want to do the car here or should we have it impounded?"

"It's up to you," Phil said, "either way."

Floyd looked at Mongo who shrugged, signifying his thoughts on the matter.

"You know what, Phil, we probably better go ahead and impound it. I don't know what else Ray and that idiot ex-partner of mine are going to want to do with it other than prints. You never know with those two."

Phil was smiling. "Richard's back?"

"Yeah, Dickie's back alright, and he's knee-deep in this bizarre case. Plus he has someone following him around, his wife's left him for another woman, and he's in love with his shrink. For fuck's sake."

Phil chuckled. "I haven't seen him around," he said, and then paused. "Wait, did you say his wife left him for another woman?"

"It wouldn't surprise me, Phil."

Lab Technician Phil Gentry slung his camera bag over his shoulder and turned toward the door. Before he stepped out, he looked back at Floyd. "You know, they should make a movie about you two."

"Me and Mongo?"

He grinned. "Okay, maybe all three of you."

---

My cell rang as I sat alone in Unsolveds thinking about Valerie. It was Floyd. "What's up?"

"We're finished at the hooker's pad."

"How'd it go?"

"There's some hot babes around here, I'll tell you that. Her apartment has a nice view, and I'm not talking about the boats, Dickie. You should look into getting an apartment here; it could be a constant source of adult entertainment. Maybe you could get her pad, now that it'll be available, and I could be your part-time roommate. You want me to check and see if they're taking names, starting a list or anything?"

"Like I could afford it. Did you guys get anything?"

"No, not really. I mean, it doesn't seem like someone lived here, to be honest. Are you sure she didn't hook out of this place?"

"I'm not sure of anything. You're the one who said it didn't appear she did."

"I was basing that off of a couple neighbors who had told us they didn't see people coming and going. No parties or gatherings, rarely if ever did they see Ms. Williams. Maybe I had it wrong."

"Yeah, maybe it is where she tricks. I mean, if she's high-dollar, how many clients does she see a day, or a week?"

"Good question, Dickie. Something to look into, that's for sure. Looks like a stopover pad, someplace to spend a few hours here and there. Or maybe a few nights. I mean, it's furnished, the bar is stocked, the dresser and closets have plenty of clothes. But you know what's missing?"

"What?"

"Every day wear: sweats, shorts, flip-flops, a bikini. There's plenty of evening wear, pumps, designer jeans, silky blouses, and several drawers of lingerie. She has trinket boxes with plenty of nice jewelry—earrings, necklaces, bracelets, and rings—but nothing to tie a ponytail to go for a run. No earbuds or running shoes or spandex. I'm just saying, if you were a hot chick living at the Marina, you'd have that kind of shit in your apartment."

Davey Lopes had walked in and looked at me as Floyd was finishing up. He nodded and sat down at his desk, pulled the chain to turn on a desk lamp, and was now fishing around for his reading glasses in his shirt pocket.

"That's interesting," I said into the phone.

"Maybe. Or weird. I'd go with weird, since you're involved."

I told Floyd he was beginning to bore me, and I'd see him when he got back to the office. Then I hit the end button. I wanted to ask Davey Lopes about his informants and what, if anything, he had heard.

"What's up, Lopes?"

He glanced over. "Nothing, man. What's up with you? Did you guys solve the headless bitch case?"

"Not yet. We did get her identified though. Had you heard that?"

"Yeah, Ray mentioned it in the meeting this morning."

"You were there?" I said, shocked to hear it.

"Yeah. Where were you?"

"With the shrink."

He snickered. "That's a good place for you."

A few seconds passed. "Hey, when are you going to be talking to some of your gangsters again?"

He settled back against his chair. "I don't know, why? What's up?"

"Just wondering about this case. It's been on my mind, what you said about Snoopy up there acting strange when you asked about it."

"Spooky."

"Whatever."

"I don't know, maybe in the next week or two. Did I tell you about the little cha-cha girl I met up at the Bay?"

"Pelican Bay?"

He smiled. "Yeah, my escort. Hot little Latina who walked me in to protect me from the bad guys."

I chuckled.

"She ended up paying me a little visit that evening at my hotel. This, after playing hard to get all day at the prison," he sneered, seemingly pleased with himself.

"No, you didn't tell me, you dirty dawg."

"Well, anyway, she's coming to see me this weekend."

"Oh?"

"Technically, she's coming to see her family—or so she says. But she wanted to make sure I had time to see her while she's here. What do you think?"

"Sounds good. She have a sister?"

"She'd be too young for you if she did," Lopes said, grinning. "You guys don't have any direction on that case?"

"None. It's just bizarre."

"Well, that's probably why you're on it. Don't you and your little sister over there, Floyd, specialize in bizarre shit?"

I grinned and nodded and then looked to the door when Ray poked his head in. "Hey, partner, we have to roll."

"What's up?" I asked, as I stood and started gathering my briefcase, coat, and hat.

"Gentry wants to show us something at the lab. He said we'd need to see it for it to make any sense. Come on, I'll drive."

"Later, buddy."

Lopes tossed his chin in the air. "Later, homie."

———

THE CRIME LAB, FORMALLY CALLED SCIENTIFIC SERVICES BUREAU, IS located on Beverly Boulevard just outside of downtown Los Angeles. We parked curbside near the front door. It was not yet five, so we'd be able to walk in through the front doors and sign in. After hours you had to be buzzed in through the back door and sign in on the log. Ray signed us both in, quickly scribbling *Cortez/Jones, Homicide,* the time, and our destination, *Latent Prints.* The receptionist knew us by sight the way she knew all the faces of Homicide, frequent visitors of the lab. The Homicide Bureau and Crime Lab should have shared a building or been located next door to one another. Homicide detectives made numerous trips each week to visit the various sections of the lab: *Latent Prints, Photography, Firearms, Biology, Narcotics, Polygraph.* Those were the most commonly utilized services, but there were many others. She buzzed us through the door not bothering to ask if we knew where we were going.

Phil Gentry sat at a stool looking at two large computer screens. We walked in and gathered behind him, knowing the images thereon would be the focal point of discussion.

"What do you have for us, partner?"

Without looking up, he pointed to one of several images of fingerprints on one of the monitors. "These are prints I lifted today at the apartment of your victim, Ms. Williams. When I got back here, I ran them through right away. Floyd said you had a rush on this case. While waiting for the return,

I brought up these," he said, moving his finger to the other monitor and waving it across the screen, indicating those were the images he referenced. "It only took a glance to see that these prints are all from one person."

Ray pointed to the second monitor, "So, what are these images from?"

"The vehicle."

"Which vehicle, Phil?" I asked. "The one you did today, or our Beemer with the dead woman?"

He glanced over. "The BMW at the scene. We didn't do Williams's vehicle yet."

The three of us stood staring at the two monitors. I saw that our Jane Doe case number—now corresponding to the name Lisa Renee Williams—labeled each of the images displayed on the two monitors. To me—and likely Ray and anyone else without the training and experience of Phil Gentry and those like him—the images were nothing more than a collection of latent prints.

"Okay, Phil, you're going to have to elaborate. We know she was in that car, it's where she was killed."

"Or at least discovered," I added.

Ray nodded.

Phil pointed to the second monitor and specifically directed our attention to the two images at the bottom of that screen. "But I lifted these two prints from the registration papers for that car, which were secured in the glove box."

Neither of us spoke. Ray had his thumb on his chin while using his index finger to pet the sparse hair over his lip he referred to as a mustache. My mind was racing with the possibilities: she'd been in the car before, they were friends, maybe both were hookers . . .

I pictured the headless and handless woman in the BMW and wondered, *why*? Other than the obvious attempt to conceal her identity, why would someone cut off her head and hands? I couldn't think of a reason. I pictured Mr. Chaney in his plush library office with his smug face and tried to find a connection there. Nothing. Then I saw the two suits in my mind's eye again, and this time they looked more like gangsters than feds. Or was I just seeing what I wanted to see?

Why the hell would Lisa Williams's fingerprints be on the registration papers of the car she was found murdered in, which happened to belong to a missing person who is still nowhere to be found? The evidence indicated to me that the scene was staged, that she was killed elsewhere and placed in the driver's seat of the BMW at the secondary crime scene, the location of recovery. But why? And now, the bigger question would be, why would Williams's fingerprints be found on the registration papers? How would they get there, given she had no hands? Was the killer so clever that he purposely caused that to happen? Or did Lisa Williams ride in that car before she was killed?

"Was there any blood detected on any items inside that glove box?" I asked.

Phil shook his head as Ray said, "No."

"Not a bloody print, then?"

"Nope," Phil said, "there was nothing visible at all. Those prints were developed through iodine fuming. We got lucky."

"On the back of a registration."

He nodded.

"Which is only handled by the owner, presumably. I can't imagine someone other than the owner of a car handling the registration unless they were driving a friend's car and were stopped for a traffic violation and cited. They would have to hand the cop the registration. Other than that, there'd be no reason for her prints to be there."

Ray said, "Well, we know she wasn't cited in that car. In fact, she didn't have any traffic citations on her record at all."

"Maybe she was stopped driving that car at some point, but not cited," I said. "Gave the cop her license, registration, and some cleavage, and was sent on her way."

"That night?" Ray asked.

"Maybe. Or maybe on another occasion. There's the problem, how do we connect Lisa Williams and Marilynn Chaney?"

"Or do we?"

I didn't know. There were no answers that made sense. "What are we missing, Ray?"

"I don't know, partner . . . I don't know."

A FEW HOURS LATER THE CONFERENCE ROOM WAS FILLED WITH THE familiar faces: me and Ray, Floyd and Mongo, and Lt. Joe Black. We were also joined by Davey Lopes who said he had nothing better to do when I asked if he wanted to sit in, see if he had any thoughts. One of the very best practices of a skilled homicide detective is to recognize the skills and experience that surround him. There were eighty investigators in our bureau with an accumulation of tens of thousands of death investigations, and centuries of experience. You didn't have to be a genius to be a good investigator here, if you were smart enough to learn from all of the talent that surrounded you.

Ray started the briefing as he always would, recapping the basics of the case, then following up with recent developments. Ray and I had few things to talk about other than the latent print information, which Ray only mentioned briefly and said he would come back to after we heard from everyone. I brought up the license plate search through traffic cameras and broke the bad news: nothing came of it. Floyd asked if we had thought to do the same with the BMW, and I made a note to check. Then he said, "Well, while you're at it, why not check the victim's Porsche and the license plate of that asshole who's been following you around."

Joe Black looked over and frowned, but then looked away. I could see in his eyes it had registered, and I expected we would be speaking about it in the near future, probably privately.

I looked over and glared at Floyd to make certain he was aware of the mistake, and then I made another note in my notebook, jotting down his ideas.

Ray said, "Mongo, anything?"

He shook his head.

"What about your cousin?"

"She was supposed to get back to me but hasn't. I called her a couple hours ago and she couldn't talk, said she was at a murder scene in Holly-wood. One of the Russians they were investigating got whacked."

"Fucking Russians," Lopes added.

"I think Floyd has some interesting thoughts about Williams's apart-ment," I said.

Everyone listened as Floyd talked about the apartment, its location, the contents which gave him the impression that the tenant was not a full-time resident, that it was more likely used only as a place to do business. He said that they had originally thought otherwise, had misinterpreted the comments from neighbors about it being quiet there and that they rarely saw her. The more he thought about it, he said, the more he was convinced this is where she would bring her clients, probably wealthy businessmen or sheiks and princes or dirty politicians. He concluded by saying that was about it, unless Gentry comes up with anything in the way of prints or something from the Porsche.

The room grew silent while some jotted notes and others stared across the walnut table, deep in thought.

Lopes said, "So, let me get this straight, your dead girl, the headless bitch with no hands, is this Lisa Williams bitch, who is a hooker by trade and lives in a fancy apartment in the Marina—"

"She probably doesn't live there," Floyd reminded him.

"Yeah, I get that, whatever. Anyway, she's found dead in a BMW in Santa Clarita. The Beemer belongs to that Chaney what's-her-face, the asshole's old lady who went missing—" he was pointing his pen around the room as he spoke, addressing each of us at various times. "—and that bitch is never found, but Williams's fingerprints are on the registration papers in that Beemer."

We were all nodding along, everyone other than Joe who watched attentively.

Ray said, "Yes."

He grunted and continued to look around the room. All eyes were on him, and he seemed to engage one person at a time while in deep thought on the topic.

"Same bitch," he said.

"Wait, what?!" I exclaimed. The idea of it stunned me. The DNA had confirmed the dead woman was Lisa Williams. It was Lisa Williams from Marina del Rey who was killed in Marilynn Chaney's car. But then when Lopes said it, and in the moments that passed quickly after, it occurred to me that one fact did not necessarily exclude the other.

Lopes said, "Did anyone check DNA from the missing person, this Chaney broad, against that of the dead woman?"

Ray looked at me.

"We had talked about getting something from the husband, a toothbrush or something. I think his demeanor threw us off. I never thought of it once we were there."

"I didn't either, partner," Ray said, "it completely slipped my mind."

Lt. Black said, "Well, if anyone cares what I think, I'd say that should be a priority." He nodded toward Davey Lopes as he said, "David presents a very interesting theory."

Silence again fell on the room. After a minute or so of silent brainstorming, Ray announced the meeting would be adjourned, and he suggested we meet again tomorrow night. He said, "We might just want to plan on pow-wowing every evening until we get somewhere solid, or the captain shuts us down."

Lt. Black said, "I don't think that's going to happen. I'll bring him up to speed when I see him in the morning, and I'll emphasize the complexity of the case."

Before walking out, I had to check. "Hey guys, just to make sure I'm up to speed here—I missed the bureau meeting this morning—but there's no other noteworthy murders we should know about, right? Nothing else of interest?"

Ray said, "Just the Asian girl in San Fernando. I think I mentioned it to you, the one Farris and Marchesano are handling. That's about it, and it doesn't seem related. There were a handful of gang murders over the weekend, but nothing else was briefed this morning."

Mongo said, "And the dead Russians in Hollywood."

Floyd said, "Nobody gives a shit about dead Russians."

# 26

HAVING NOBODY TO go home to caused my indifference to time. No longer did it matter where I was or when I got there, unless a subpoena mandated otherwise.

I could stay in the office all night trying to solve the only murder case I'd been allowed to touch in a year, and one of the best of my career. It was intriguing, a real mystery, the puzzling disappearance of one woman and the savage murder and decapitation of another. It had my full attention, and it had felt good to hit the ground running on a case like this one.

There were always a couple of detectives found lingering in the office past the witching hour and into the early morning hours. Usually, they would be working on cases because they had nothing else to do with their lives. They were single—meaning divorced, at this stage—or miserably married. There were exceptions, like the workaholics who had difficulty putting down a file at any given time. There was always something else to do on your cases; that was the curse. But at a certain hour of the night, the office would settle as the stragglers filed out and large sections of fluorescent lighting would be dimmed.

Tonight, the conversations and laughter had died, and the phones had stopped ringing. In the scant light and eerie silence, the office fittingly felt like a graveyard. A place where spirits lingered, hovering over files that told their stories through collections of words and photographs, waiting for the day they could peacefully rest. Too often, that day never came.

For me, there were few options. Stay in the office and work, go home to an empty apartment, or go out for a drink.

There were cop bars throughout the county, some of which I had been known to visit on occasion. All of which—at times—offered the possibility of companionship for cops. But mostly for the young, fit, handsome cops, those who worked patrol or gangs or maybe SWAT, and told great stories of fights and shootouts and car chases through the housing projects. Any such companionship would be devoid of anything meaningful. For the most part, the ladies were pathetic, discarded women called groupies— or donut dollies, badge bunnies, *sucias* (which is Spanish for *dirty girl*), or maybe more to the point, punchboards. There is a radio code, *924,* which translates to *Station Detail.* This code is used over the radio to assign a particular unit some sort of detail that needed to be taken care of but wasn't directly related to police work. Such as a chow run for the desk crew, or to transport a drunken captain from the local watering hole to his home or back to the bunk room. Somehow, the code *924* became synonymous with the *sucias,* and it was not uncommon to hear on the car-to-car (Charlie) frequency, that someone's *924* needed them to call or come by. There had been an occasion when two Spanish-speaking young ladies had driven into the back lot of Firestone Station, an area designated for radio cars and personal vehicles of employees. All others were forbidden access into this area. The two ladies drove in displaying a cardboard sign with the numbers *924* boldly displayed across it. The sign was effective; the two were treated as guests, welcome to park and stay as long as they'd like.

Many times, these wayward ladies were only searching for a thrill, a good time, or a story. Other times, they were in search of a dental plan, an insurance card, direct deposit twice a month. Which is why some cops simply referred to them as their future ex-wives.

The last thing I needed were more complications in my life. So, work it was. I opted to go see Mr. Chaney. Maybe I'd ask him about that toothbrush for his wife's DNA. While I was at it, maybe I'd ask about the two suits who had visited him.

LEONARD COUNTED IT OUT: $3,740. NOT BAD, BUT NOW THAT HE thought of it, there had probably been more. He should have had a better look around the place, checked all the drawers and cabinets and looked for secret compartments in the walls or beneath the floor. Those Russians were sneaky bastards. But he knew better than to spend a lot of time with dead people, especially when it was he who made them dead. After counting the cash, he sat back in his chair and held the pistol up to have a good look at it. Beretta. He assumed it was Russian but wasn't sure. He didn't care. It was a nine-millimeter, he saw that on the barrel. After playing with it for a while he figured out how to release the clip—that's what they called it in movies he watched in prison—and saw this clip was full of bullets. He wasn't sure how to remove them from the clip, though he didn't think it would be necessary to do so. All that mattered was there were bullets in it and all he had to do was pull the trigger. He was fairly certain of that, though he thought better than to try it.

He began thinking about the cop in the hat, the *job* he now had about three weeks to get done, 23 days by his count, 18 if he went by Feldman's calendar. Which he wouldn't. He didn't care what that asshole had to say, and he was glad he hadn't heard from him in nearly a week. It'd be okay with Leonard if the prick never called again. They could send him his assignments and leave him be. Which made him think about checking the PO box. He needed to do that, just in case something had come in. Like a change in plans.

He chuckled at the thought that with his luck, he'd whack the cop and there'd be a notice in his box telling him the hit was off. That's all he'd need. Then he'd be arguing with that pockmarked prick about what day the letter was sent in order for him to get his money out of them. Plus, he'd have every cop in the county looking for him, out to gun him down or beat him to death. That's what they did out here. There were movies about it.

Leonard lit a Camel and blew a cloud of smoke at the dim light that hung above his head. It occurred to him it would be easier to continue whacking these foreigners and stealing their cash than taking out a cop and having that kind of heat come down on you. Maybe he would retire, go into business for himself. What's Feldman going to do, come looking for him? Leonard smiled at the idea of it as he envisioned driving a knife into the mobster's throat. But, it would be steady work if he kept whacking for the mob, so he'd kill the pig and wait for the next job.

He thought back to the single-wide trailer that made the Russian's office and saw the bodies still lying there in the dark. He had been smart to turn the lights off. It would be days before anyone discovered them, and by then they both would stink. He thought of the dogs and wondered where they were kept during the day. Had he thought of it, he could have pulled the gate closed and let them out, left the trailer door open so the dogs would have something to eat. He had read one time that when someone dies and can no longer care for their dog, little Smoochie will start feeding on their flesh within a couple days. The reliable little companion eating away the face of their former caretaker. So much for *man's best friend.* But he hadn't thought of it, and now that he did, it bothered him to think where the dogs might have been. Not because he was worried that they were locked away and there was no one to feed them or provide fresh water, but because had he thought of it, he might have put a bullet in each of them for trying to eat through the fence and kill him one night. Leonard hated dogs.

Now he just needed to figure out a way to kill the damn cop. First, he had to figure out a way to watch him without being seen. The man was careful to notice people and vehicles in his neighborhood, that was for sure. Leonard had thought about how watching the cop from the grassy knoll that night seemed to work well. He could park a few blocks away and hike in next time, since the cop seemed to be looking for his car. He could buy an outfit from the army surplus and sneak in like a special forces guy. He pictured war movies and documentaries he had seen and now had an image of himself dressed in camouflage with some black paint on his face. The cop would come home as he always did, looking carefully for suspicious vehicles, and when none were found, he'd go inside and sleep soundly. Leonard could sneak in behind him and cut him the way he had cut the Russian and his big-titted girlfriend. He would give this more thought, because he felt he might be onto something now.

Again, he thought about the need to check his mail. He snuffed out a cigarette and looked through exhaled smoke to the wall with no calendar. Leonard needed to get to bed so he could start early tomorrow, say ten or eleven, and not waste the day away. In the meantime, he would be thinking of ways to get the pork job done. He was tired of being in L.A. now; there were too many foreigners.

---

I PULLED TO THE CURB ACROSS FROM CHANEY'S, A COUPLE PROPERTIES down the street, and sat to watch for a few minutes before deciding on if and how to make an approach. The thought of Ray being annoyed that I would do this without him weighed on my mind. I wasn't going to call him this late in the evening when he would be home enjoying his large family; four children, a wife, and a mother-in-law all lived in apparent harmony beneath the same roof. It was something to be admired, if not coveted. But with the images in my mind, I was careful to consider his time away. I reminded myself that some cops do have lives other than the job. As odd as it seemed.

The scant interior lights gave me the impression nobody was home. After watching for half an hour, I decided to ring the bell. The street was silent with only an occasional vehicle traveling past. It was almost nine, and most people in this neighborhood would be settled in for the evening. *Most.*

When I closed my car door, a dog barked from a nearby yard. It occurred to me that you didn't often hear dogs barking in neighborhoods nowadays, now that most people's dogs lived inside with the family, not outside on a chain or in a shabby wooden house. At least in most communities.

After ringing the bell and waiting a minute, I moved around the front of the house trying to steal a peek inside. There was nothing notable and the home appeared uninhabited. It was furnished, and dimly lit, but there was something that felt abandoned and lonely about the place.

I pulled away in my car and watched the windows as I did, just to be sure. But there was nothing to see, no movement or signs of life. It occurred to me I should find out which day the trash is collected here and come back the night before for a trash run. I was big on stealing trash for the purposes of gathering intelligence, and the courts had upheld that once the trash is set out on the street, it is fair game. Which means that without a warrant you could take what you wanted. Usually, when I planned a trash run, I would empty the contents of my trunk—all of my equipment and tools of the trade—and line it with plastic tarps. Sometime after midnight, and after watching the target's home and surrounding residences for a short period of time, I would swoop in, grab several bags from the garbage containers and throw them in the trunk. I'd be back on the road in seconds. Floyd and I were known to meet at one of our homes—wherever the target was geographically located would be the deciding factor—and then once the collection was made, we'd spend the next several hours drinking beer and sifting trash with latex-gloved hands. It was surprising what one could learn by sifting the trash of another. I'd have to mention it to Ray.

When I turned onto Valencia Boulevard I was going the wrong way. Not the wrong way against traffic, but the wrong direction to get home. I was headed toward Valerie's but not readily admitting it to myself just yet. Once I turned onto her street, I could no longer deny it to myself. I reasoned that it was only to check on her welfare, make sure she was okay. There was a vicious killer nearby, and separated or not—soon to be divorced, or not—I still cared for her. I still loved her.

Sometimes I hated myself.

# 27

T HERE WAS NO correspondence from Feldman; however, there was a letter from Whitey. Leonard smiled widely at the sight of it and rushed back to his car where he would read it before doing anything else. He was giddy at reading the words of his best and only friend.

In the car he tore it open and quickly checked his surroundings, checking the rearview mirror, the side mirrors, and looking out all of the windows.

*Dearest Leonardo,*

*I trust this correspondence finds you in the best of health and highest spirits. Please do forgive the time elapsed since my last letter; however, you must know the discovery of your whereabouts is arduous at times. Thankfully!*

*But, I think of you daily. At least we can write to stay in touch. Cruel though it is, we may never see each other face to face, but we will always remain connected in our hearts. Know that I miss you dearly. Outside must be glorious, no? Family. Friends. Beaches replete with bikini-clad girls. Ocean waves crashing against their sandy shores. Seagulls circling while cawing for their loved ones. Sun rays that kiss the golden-brown skin of those who adore her, while the damp, salty air caresses one's face. But for me, these sensations are but dreams. Or are they? You, the liberated between us, must live these dreams for us both.*

*It would be unwise to speak of the many adventures that freedom has brought you, as our discourse will surely be scrutinized by the custodians. However, I do hear you are gainfully employed and excelling at your job. Did you know your CEO has a daughter? She is but a rotund thing and awkward, though loved dearly by her father and his son-in-law who stays by both of their sides. Sir Leonardo, I must apologize for the brevity of my friendly note, but you see, I have long days now, working as the librarian of the warden's study. I find the assignment pleasurable, in that I have access to more literature than I could read in two lifetimes, which, ironically, I have been awarded for past transgressions. I now find myself awakening daily with renewed energy and a sense of purpose.*

*Be well, my friend.*

*Whitey*

Leonard smiled, hearing his friend's voice and seeing his smiling, handsome face. Whitey fancied himself as the character of *Doc Holliday* in *Tombstone*, an educated gentleman of a killer. He had often quoted lines from the movie: *Ed, what an ugly thing to say; I'm your Huckleberry; Why, Johnny Ringo, you look like someone just walked over your grave; You're a daisy if you do.* The two of them had watched it dozens of times in their cell on DVD, and Whitey had memorized every memorable line. He claimed to have used the line, *I'm your Huckleberry,* when he walked into the diner and killed the two mobsters over their lunch plates. Though it had not been confirmed, Leonard didn't doubt that he had.

Fond memories aside, now the message. Leonard studied the middle paragraph. He read aloud the first letters of each sentence. B, A, C, K, O, F, F, B, O, S, S, B, O, Y. He repeated it twice, putting the words together in his head, and muttering them to himself. BACK OFF BOSS BOY. That was the message? What would it mean? Back off the boss's boy? He must be referring to Stretch, the nameless, pockmarked, Marty Feldman lookalike. Moses. But why? What had his friend heard? Clearly, there had been grumblings about the tension between the two. What a pussy, Leonard thought. Feldman had been whining to the boss that he's been disrespected by a hired man. Somewhat of a cryptic message, yet a clear warning. Fine. He would try to show more respect. No, he couldn't. Okay, he would try to show less contempt. There.

He read the letter again, skipping over the middle paragraph babble because there was no meaning beyond the message. Whitey heard he had done well at his job. That was something to put the message in perspective. They are pleased, just don't be such an asshole. Leonard smiled as he pictured Whitey working in the library, as he knew this would bring him great joy. Whitey loved to read, and to be surrounded by books would have to be the best possible scenario for a young man who would never again experience freedom.

The reference to the CEO's daughter had escaped him, but as he read it a third time he realized the message was connected to this passage. Feldman had married the boss's daughter. Which would make him indispensable in all but the most egregious scenario. Whitey was warning him to back off, nothing good could come from his conflict with the right-hand man. Feldman.

He smiled while folding the letter back into its envelope. He dropped his shades over his eyes and pulled out of the lot with one thing on his mind: murder.

# 28

THURSDAY AFTERNOON, MARIA Lopez landed at Burbank Airport and was picked up by her uncle and one of his friends. They didn't park the SUV and they didn't get out to greet her. They waited while she approached, both men watching her carefully through dark sunglasses, their expressionless faces telling her nothing about their moods.

She was growing tired of the pressure her family put on her, and at times she wished she could escape and just live a normal life. Why couldn't she?

The back hatch of the Land Rover popped open and slowly lifted automatically as Maria stood waiting. She tossed her one suitcase into the rear compartment which was immaculate. The carpet appeared as it would have when brand new, and the plastic shined from some type of protectant coating. There was a strong scent of fresh pine, likely an air freshener. It occurred to her, knowing her uncle, there was probably some young *vato* assigned to detail the car weekly, wash it daily. These guys had an image to protect, and they loved their cars.

She climbed into the back and slid into the slick leather seat. *Tio* looked back from the driver's seat. "How's our favorite hack?" He smiled and glanced at the gangster who rode with him before pulling away from the curb.

*Hack.* She hated the reference, especially at home. It was one thing at the prison—it was expected there, the common term for prison guards— but she sensed the underlying distrust when it was used by family members. Especially from Lazy E. That's what she secretly called him growing up. The gangsters in the neighborhood called him "Big Ed," or "Big E" for short. But they didn't grow up seeing his fat ass sleeping on their couch for a decade—when he wasn't in prison. How he became a *carnale*, a made man of La Eme, she didn't know. She thought of him as a loser, but she knew he put in a lot of work. What the gangsters call work: killing other gangsters or at least always being willing to try. That was her Uncle Ed. Big Ed. Lazy E. Lazy other than when it came to killing.

"*Mija,* you ever met my homie from Florence, Pelon?" He looked to his sidekick who craned his neck around the seat to see her.

Maria only lifted her chin a bit as a way of greeting and forced a quick smile. Neither spoke. Big Ed said, "We were down together at Tehachapi, my last stint. He's a *carnale*, eh?"

Who wasn't, it seemed. At least in this family and its circle. It's why she had dropped her dad's name, Santos, and had taken her mother's, Lopez. But changing her name hadn't allowed her to change her life. She had visitors at all times reminding her of her roots. Reminding her they would never forget her. Reminding her she was part of them and pres- suring her for something else. There was always something else.

"He's in charge of collecting from all those *Florencia vatos,* which is no easy task. So, we work together most times. I ride with him down there, and he backs me up in my hoods. I got *The Avenues* and most of *East Los*, eh."

Pelon looked back again, only this time she didn't smile at him. She knew what he wanted. It's what they all wanted, and it had always been that way, since she was thirteen. All the older homies and their friends, and even good old Uncle Ed had tried once. *Lazy E*. But Ed's little brother —Maria's father, God rest his soul—explained to him she was off limits. He had explained it by beating him unconscious with his fists. They had called her old man Boxer. He too was from *The Avenues*, and he was killed by *18th Street*, a rival gang, when she was only fifteen.

Lazy E was still speaking. He would only stop after a barrel of heroin was loaded into his veins, and that would only slow him down for a few hours.

"When we ride down south, we sometimes go through *18th Street*, and I think of *mi hermano*, and them cockroaches that gunned him down." Big Ed removed his hat briefly as a sign of respect, and then glared at his homie, who sat quietly. The man riding shotgun reacted by removing his black Los Angeles Dodgers ball cap to reveal his bald head. *Pelon.*

"One of these days," he continued, "I'll see that little bitch, *Rascal,* from *18th Street,* and I'll get some payback for Boxer. That motherfucker ain't nothing but an addict now, anyway. But somehow, someday, I'll catch him slipping and put a cap in his junkie ass."

She thought of her father and the night he was gunned down in front of their home. There had been a gathering that evening, and it had wound down to just the closest relatives. And the homeboys. All of her father's *carnales.* It had been her *quinceañera*, a celebration of her fifteenth birthday, her passage into womanhood. Though it was only a formality, as her *womanhood* had been realized years prior. Her dress was covered by her father's blood when it was over. The cops loaded all of them up and hauled them to the station as if they were suspects in the killing. It was hours before the detectives took her statement and finally allowed her to return home. Like all the others, she had said she had no idea who was responsible. It was as if none of the thirty people present heard the shooter yelling "18th Street" before he opened up. Big dumb Ed was in jail at the time, probably sleeping. She had always wished it would have been him, not his brother, who was there to take the bullet.

"Drop me off at *Nana's,*" Maria finally said, tired of his droning on. Of all her family, she loved her grandmother the most, and she always looked forward to seeing her.

He glanced back again, and said to her in Spanish, "Your mother will want to see you. Are you not planning to visit?"

Her mother. A *hood rat*, by Maria's definition. A punchboard for the gang ever since her father was killed. Who knows, maybe even before. Maybe that's why her father had stayed stoned and occasionally knocked around the little *chola* he had married at seventeen. She hated her mother, though she pretended not to. Truthfully, she hated the entire family—other than her grandmother—and all of their friends. *The neighborhood*. She only wanted out, away from them all. But there was no way out. With that, she had come to terms. Mostly.

"If I'm meeting with the cop, I don't plan to stay in the neighborhood," she replied in Spanish. Then she switched to English: "*Nana* is the only relative we have who isn't a fucking gangster. What if he—this cop —wants to pick me up, or drive me home? Am I going to have him bring me into the hood, introduce him to my gangster uncle and *chola* mother?"

Her uncle's mouth tightened behind his heavy black mustache. Though his eyes were concealed by dark shades, she could feel them penetrate her as he watched her in the rearview mirror. He too returned to speaking English. "You watch how you speak of your mother."

Great, she thought. Uncle Ed has probably been hitting that shit too. Bedding down with her mom, his sister-in-law. He was such a pig.

They rode in silence for a minute while coming into East Los Angeles on the southbound I-5. She was looking out the window at the train tracks and concrete bridges painted with bright colored graffiti, and the faraway buildings that stood tall against a smoggy sky. In the distance she could see the stands of lights of Dodger Stadium, and for a moment she reflected on childhood memories of going to games with her father. And the gang. Always the gang. They sat in the cheap seats out in left field and the *vatos* drank their beer and talked shit and sooner or later—but always—they would jump someone from another neighborhood and beat him down. Half the time they would end up going to jail and the women would drive home without them. She hated L.A.

He said, "So, you want me to take you into Whittier, when we ain't even packin' heat?"

She shrugged. "You'll be fine. Aren't you a mobster?"

He reached down and fumbled for his cigarettes in the console, then extracted a Camel and lit it with a Bic lighter. He cracked the window and exhaled a plume of smoke toward it. "Whatever you say, *Officer Lopez*."

---

THURSDAY NIGHT THE WHOLE CREW GATHERED AGAIN IN THE HOMICIDE conference room. Floyd and Mongo, me and Ray, Lt. Joe Black, and

Davey Lopes, each of us gravitating to the seats we had claimed earlier in the week. Cops were resistant to change. Something as petty as temporary seats in an anonymous room claimed by no one would become permanent, structured, unspoken seating arrangements. We were joined by the captain who seldom was seen in the office after five. He walked in and pulled out one of the four remaining chairs at the table without speaking to anyone.

Lt. Black greeted him. "Captain."

"Good evening, Joe. I thought I'd join in tonight."

Joe smiled.

Without further ado, Ray took it from there, bringing all in attendance up to speed.

There had been no luck with the license plate search through traffic cameras. Nothing showed up. Not for the victim's vehicle nor for the sedan with the two suits who had visited Chaney. There was still no sign of the missing person, Marilynn Chaney. I found it interesting that neither Ray nor Lopes brought up the possible theory that Lopes had referred to last night, that maybe the two of them—Marilynn Chaney and Lisa Williams—were one and the same. Ray talked about the apartment, Floyd's theory that it was uninhabited other than for the purposes of business, and he restated that there had been no similar murders that we were aware of. He looked at me and said, "Right, partner?"

"Right. From what I understand, you have the young girl murdered in the valley, which was probably a sex crime. It happened inside her house right after school, so it may have even been a student. Or maybe a boyfriend, or some gang initiation. But there's nothing that overlaps with our murder on that case. So, other than a handful of gang killings, we have nothing else. Oh, and I guess LAPD had two Russians whacked in Hollywood. I can't imagine how that would have anything to do with our case."

Floyd said, "Unless it was a Russian mafia hit on our girl in the Beamer."

The room fell silent for a moment. Ray said, "What are you thinking?"

He shrugged. "I don't know. Just thought I'd throw it out there, muddy the water a little more."

Captain Stover grunted and rolled his eyes. "That'd be great."

Floyd continued. "You know, weirder shit has happened. It's not your normal, everyday pervert that goes around chopping women's hands and heads off. This almost feels like a message, or revenge. Unless that was done just to conceal her identity."

"Except we have DNA," I said.

"But what killer would think of that? I mean, unless you have a hunch who the victim is, what would you compare it to? Our victim was only in CODIS because she took a felony rap after the law passed, Prop 69, which mandates all felons will have their DNA collected and put into the system."

Captain Stover asked, "What felony did our victim commit? I thought she was just a hooker."

"Extortion," Ray said.

Which triggered the thought I had had a few times but continually forgot to ask of anyone. "Has anyone ordered the extortion cases from records? There might be something there, maybe a hint about how she got herself whacked."

Floyd spoke up. "They're ordered, should be here next week at the latest."

"So back to the Russian," Ray said, looking at Mongo, "what do we know about that murder?"

He shook his head. "Nothing other than that my cousin is working on it. She's on a task force that's working the Russian mob, so I assume the victim must be a mobster. Unless they think he's the victim of a mob hit. But I don't know."

It was the most I had heard Mongo say in one sitting.

"We can look into it, Ray," Floyd offered.

"That'd be good," Ray said, and quickly jotted a note. Then he looked around the room. "Okay, anything else?"

Captain Stover asked, "What's the deal with the missing and her husband? That seems to be a big part of this that can't be explained. She's still gone, hubby's a mystery, and our girl gets herself killed in the missing person's car. Something is wrong there."

I looked over and saw that it bothered Floyd too. His expression told me his brain was processing all of it, and his eyes told me he knew that he and I were likely on the same page, that there was some type of connection between the two women. Or, as Lopes had blurted out in the previous night's briefing, maybe they were one and the same.

Lt. Black asked, "Have you guys done anything to get that DNA sample on our missing?"

I spoke up before Ray could say that we hadn't. He didn't know I had been out there the night before, and by revealing it now it would at least show we had made an effort since the lieutenant first suggested it. "We tried last night, Joe, but Chaney wasn't home. I'm thinking about a trash run."

Ray glanced over, seemingly pleased with my answer.

"Are those still legal?" Captain Stover asked.

"Yep."

"I thought I had heard—"

"Case law," I said, "once it's out on the sidewalk or street, courts have ruled it's good to go."

Ray said, "Sounds good, partner, thanks for that." Then he looked around for a moment before settling his gaze on the veteran who was slouched and silent in his chair. Lopes had checked his phone often during the meeting and he was uncharacteristically quiet tonight. Not that he was ever loud and obnoxious, or even the vocal, opinionated type, but when working on a case, he didn't hold back his thoughts and ideas. Tonight, though, he didn't seem to have anything to add or questions to ask. He seemed anxious or otherwise distracted. "Lopes?"

Lopes shook his head. "Nothing, man."

"Okay then, guys, let's wrap it up. I guess we'll see how tomorrow plays out and whether we think we need another briefing."

"Before we go," Stover interrupted, "I need to give something to the captain at Santa Clarita in the way of an update. They are under the gun on this. What do you guys think we can tell them that they can give to the local media up there without jeopardizing anything you're working on?"

Ray looked to me. I didn't hesitate. "We *tell* them nothing. We *ask* for their help. They just want a story. Recap old information: 'We have a woman who was killed in a car. The car belongs to a missing person'—go ahead and put out her name and photograph—'but we have not been able to confirm that the body recovered in that car is that of Marilynn Chaney.' That will give them plenty to talk about."

"But that's a lie, right? We know who was killed in that car."

"Well, Captain, actually it's not necessarily a lie," Ray said. "We are in fact trying to confirm whether or not the woman in the car is Marilynn Chaney."

"I'm confused. I thought we had ID'd her as Lisa Williams."

Ray said, "Lopes came up with a theory last night that maybe it's just the one woman, two names."

"Jesus," he said. He stood and picked up his notebook, glanced around the room as we all followed suit. "Keep me posted on this."

Lt. Joe Black assured him *he* would.

---

I CAUGHT UP WITH LOPES IN UNSOLVEDS. HE WAS COLLECTING HIS belongings. "You in a hurry tonight? You seemed a tad distracted."

"I told you about Maria, from the Bay?"

"Prison guard."

"That'd be the one. She's in town, that's all." He smiled. "We're going to have a drink, and no, she doesn't have a sister."

"Have fun, buddy. I'll see you tomorrow."

"I'm off for the weekend, but you guys can call me if you need anything."

I reminded him the checkbook was open on this case, and told him if he's bored to come on in. He said he didn't expect to be bored this week-end, and smiled.

---

TEN MINUTES LATER LOPES WAS ON THE PHONE GETTING DIRECTIONS FROM a friendly and flirtatious Maria Lopez *with a Z* as he headed east on Slauson toward Whittier. He asked if she was hungry, or if she just wanted to go out for a cocktail. She said maybe both. He suggested a Mexican restaurant just down the road from her in Norwalk.

"Norwalk Trese?" she asked, citing a known street gang in that area.

It silenced him briefly. The way she had said it bothered him.

Maybe it was from working at the institution, he reasoned. Cops were the same everywhere, adapting some of the language of the gangs. Some would speak in similar fashion as they became accustomed to communicating with them more than others in society. You could listen to cops tell stories over drinks, and you would hear them use words like *gats, biscuits, heat,* and *piece,* when referencing guns. They might refer to their girlfriends as *homegirl, concha, chica, or jaina.*

Lopes also knew that no matter how much she tried to distance herself from the neighborhood where she was raised, there were pieces of that culture that would remain a part of her foundation. Growing up in *The Avenues,* or any other barrio or ghetto, had lasting effects on a person. Though she had said she was never affiliated with gangs, and she had described her childhood as that of typical immigrants (overcrowding a small home, men who worked each day and slept under the same roofs with their extended families), she would know the streets. Or, in her case, *The Avenues.*

But she had reactively cited the correct gang of the area in which Lopes had suggested. *Varrio Trese Norwalk,* or, as she had correctly abbreviated it, *Norwalk Trese.* He wondered if that was a coincidence, and as he thought of that for a moment, he thought of the bigger question: Did she know that *Norwalk* and *The Avenues* were at war? Is that the reason she blurted it out?

"What," he said to her, "you can't go there?"

"Come on now, Detective," she said, "I already told you I'm not affiliated. Why would you say some shit like that?"

He waited for a moment. He pictured the glimmer in her eyes, her bright smile, and the dimples that had drawn him in. Lopes said, "Just messing with you. I'll see you in about twenty minutes, unless I hit traffic."

"Okay, I'll be ready to go, sweetie."

*Sweetie.*

Lopes glanced in his rearview and checked his tail. He always checked his tail. He had been instrumental in taking down many gangsters, including made members and associates of the notorious La Eme prison gang. They were not to be taken lightly, and hits on cops were not unheard of. Satisfied, he relaxed in his seat and thought about the pretty girl he was headed to see. He felt himself smiling at his memories of her from the first time they met. Pelican Bay. She walked confidently through the halls as she had escorted him to an interview room. Eyes would turn with each person she passed, inmates and faculty alike. She was hot, and she likely knew it. She was also probably fifteen years younger than he, or better. His smile faded, and cynical Lopes questioned, *why him?* All the young studs around, yet she hooked up with him the first time they met and was now bringing him to Whittier to pick her up. He hadn't even checked her out or checked out the address she provided to see if there were any notations of gang affiliation. He was slipping.

*Norwalk Trese.*

He quickly started thinking of the Lopez families he knew that were connected to the mafia. There were several. None from Whittier that he knew of, not off the top of his head. What about from *The Avenues*? He didn't know.

He was being paranoid. Or was he?

Lopes dialed the office.

Something was eating away at him.

# 29

MARIA LOPEZ SET her phone on the bathroom counter and smiled as its light faded, the name Lopes disappearing from the display. She looked at her reflection in the mirror and fussed with her hair, throwing it all to one side but then letting it settle back on both shoulders. Frustrated, she fumbled in her purse for a ponytail holder, digging around past the hairbrush, several lipsticks, her cigarettes, a lighter, her folding knife, and several snacks: a package of peanuts, a box of Chiclets, and a packet of cinnamon-flavored gum. She found one and put it between her teeth, pushed her hair back with both hands, and combed through the thick black mane until it pulled tight the skin of her forehead. She held the ponytail with one hand and took the band from her mouth with the other. When finished, she turned each way quickly, the ponytail swinging with the motion. Were her earrings too big? That was the question now that her hair was pulled back. After a moment she concluded they were fine. She had bigger hoops, but she didn't want to look *ho-ish*. She had tamed the eyeliner, knowing cops were more conservative. This Lopes may like his cha-cha girls, but he probably wasn't looking for a *hood rat*, a *sucia*. Though, she *could* be one at times, and had been, she silently acknowledged. She smiled at the *sucia* staring back at her. Then she laughed, accentuating her prominent dimples. She had learned at an early age that the dimples would always draw them in. All of them, young boys and older men. Cops and gangsters alike. Lesbians too. Though she had no use and little tolerance for the latter, all the others she had experienced.

They called her "Dimples" growing up in her neighborhood, *The Avenues*. And when she was young, she had spray painted it on fences and buildings. She had written it on papers and book covers. Using a marker, she had tagged her backpack, her tennis shoes, parts of her clothing with the given moniker and more: *Dimples. Avenues. Aves. Surenos 13. Sur 13. RIP Boxer* . . .

She applied a dark lipstick, ran her tongue across her teeth, and then smacked her lips. Maria leaned into the mirror to check closely. Perfect. She tugged the bottom of her blouse to lower the neckline a little, and then she pushed her breasts up while straightening her posture. There, just right, just enough cleavage showed for a first date.

*First date.* Who was she kidding? She went to his hotel after he visited Pelican Bay, had drinks with him in the lobby, and ended up in his room. This cop named Davey Lopes. Spent the night in his bed, made love to him that night and again in the morning. She had brought with her an overnight bag. Now she pictured his smile, the glimmer in his squinting eyes as he had later teased her, telling her he knew she had wanted him.

This was no first date.

Maybe a redo.

She could tell him, "Look, Lopes,"—no, she would call him Davey now. She liked that. Davey. "Look, Davey, that night in Brookings, the hotel, well, I don't normally do that. I mean, I'm not really that kind of girl . . . I'm no *hoochie mama*." No, she silently argued to her reflection, that's stupid. That's what bimbos say, white girls. And actually, she knew she *was* that kind of girl, and he likely knew it too. Maybe—she saw herself leaning into him, running her finger down his chest, "Look, I like you, Lopes—*Davey*. I need a redo, because, well, I deserve one. Every girl does from time to time. Let's call this our first date, okay?"

Maria sighed at herself. She wasn't sure what to say. Or maybe not say anything at all. Really, what was she even thinking? This couldn't ever be a thing. Or could it? No, impossible. Her family would never allow it.

Even if they did, Lopes would never accept her for who she really is. He could never even know. Which is why it would never work.

It wasn't her fault she was born into a fucked-up family of gangsters. But it was her cross to bear nonetheless.

Disgusted, Maria threw the burgundy lipstick into her purse.

She frowned at her reflection, and then she smiled. She checked her teeth once more for lipstick stains, and then made the sign of the cross on her forehead before turning from the mirror. She stopped briefly before walking out to check her bra strap for her stash. Even going out with a cop, she wouldn't trust not needing cash. She reached for the light switch but paused to check her ass in the mirror. Satisfied, she flipped the switch and turned into the hallway where she was greeted by the smell of warmed tortillas.

In the living room, Maria's grandmother sat in a straight-backed, wooden chair with a blanket over her lap. Folded tortillas and a serving each of beans and rice steamed from a plate on the TV tray next to her. There were no utensils, because grandma—"*Nana*"—would fold the tortillas into triangles and scoop the rice and beans. On the wall behind her hung a large Jesus hologram with eyes that glare back at you and a stare that no one can escape.

A proud and strong woman, *Nana* (who, like her granddaughter, is named Maria Lopez—Maria Guadalupe Lopez Sanchez), wore a thrifty but clean dress with a wooden rosary necklace, although she had no place to be and was in for the evening. She wore her hair pulled tight to the scalp with braids held together by silk ribbons. She was knitting and didn't seem to notice the sights or sounds of the nearby television as Jeopardy played beneath a shrine of flickering rosary candles: Lady of Guadalupe, Sacred Heart, and Jesus, alongside candles to assure health and prosperity. Maria didn't know if *Nana* paid any mind to the program on TV, or if she used it to fill a void, a way to not feel alone in the quiet home.

Maria passed through the living room, saying, "I fucking love that show."

Her grandmother didn't like her using that word. "*Mija!*"

When she returned from the kitchen, having sneaked a shot of *Patron* to calm her nerves, Maria listened as Alex Trebek announced the next category: "Gangsters."

"Check it out, *Nana*, fucking *'Gangsters'* right now on the show." She stepped back and lowered herself to the edge of the couch, watching with anticipation. Maria smiled as she silently played with the theme, imagining Trebek giving the questions: *This vato was killed at the county jail after he ratted on La Eme . . . Who was Flaco from Tiny Winos?* Or, *In order to raise money for a vato's funeral, the homies gather on a Saturday to do this . . . What is a carwash?* She would totally nail the Gangster Jeopardy.

Her grandmother began to speak, looking up from her work and saying "*Mija—*"

Maria shushed her, holding up a hand while focusing on the TV. "*Nana, esperate!* (Wait a moment.)"

Trebek read the first question as a graphic displayed it across the screen: "This good-looking gangster was named the Robin Hood of the Cookson Hills."

Maria jumped from the couch. "Fuck, that's easy—"

"*Mija, por favor . . .*"

"Who is Pretty Boy Floyd!"

The contestant answered, "Who is Pretty Boy Floyd?" and Alex Trebek affirmed it.

Her grandmother shook her head while Maria danced around the living room, pumping her fist and exclaiming, "*Te dije, te dije!* (I told you, I told you!)"

Grandma was no fan of this "*Yepordy*" show. "*Mija*, I hope dis cho end soon, es me *novela* come on right now."

Still giddy, Maria handed her grandmother the remote as she leaned in to kiss her on the forehead. "Adios, *Nana, te quiero mucho.*"

Her grandmother reached for Maria with frail, shaky hands, arthritic from a lifetime of chores and cooking. "*Cuidate, Mija.*"

"I'm always careful, *Nana*," she said as she stepped away. She blew her a kiss and turned to the door.

Maria stepped outside to wait for Lopes. *Davey.* She wanted a cigarette, and *Nana* didn't allow it in her home. She knew Lopes didn't smoke and probably wouldn't allow it in his car. She sat on the front steps and lit a cigarette using a knockoff Zippo with a picture of the Virgin Mary, as if that would lessen her grandmother's disapproval of the filthy habit. As Maria sucked on the cigarette and filled her lungs with smoke, she looked past the glow of its cherry and silently questioned the identity and purpose of two boys walking toward her. They were the gangster types, each dressed in dark, baggy clothing with hoodies worn over their heads. It was no surprise to her, not in this neighborhood. Not in any neighborhood where she had lived until a few years ago when she settled into the small community of Crescent City, not far from the prison where she worked. There she lived with the father of her children though they seldom slept together. Maria preferred sleeping in the second room of the small rented home with their two children, Rafael and Rosalva, ages three and five. Someday she would leave him. She would take her kids and start over, leaving all of these gangsters and their insane lives behind.

The boys drew nearer.

Maria noticed they were coming toward her, purposefully it seemed.

She had started to say, "What's up," but the words were stuck in her mouth as the two boys stopped just feet from where she sat.

Silently, each raised an arm and pointed at her.

She saw the pistols.

Grabbing the banister rail, she tried to stand, her first step to escape the nightmare unfolding before her.

"NO!" she yelled. But the word stuck in her head and hadn't come out. She would try again. She needed to tell them to stop, that she was not from around here, that she didn't fuck around, she didn't bang. "*I'm from nowhere!*"

It was too late.

Brilliant flashes of light shattered the darkness, bursting from one boy's hand and then the other's, like two sets of fireworks dancing in the sky, competing against one another.

Maria fell back. A burning sensation consumed her, but only for a moment. Her pain subsided and she felt nothing at all as she slumped onto the cool, concrete steps.

As darkness closed around her, Maria pictured her two children and then her grandmother, the only ones she truly loved. She saw *Nana* in the chair where she had left her, and in her mind, Maria saw her grandmother looking up from her work, gazing toward the front door with sadness filling her eyes. She would know what had happened outside; their family was accustomed to premature, violent death.

Maria silently said, *Que Dios te cuide* (God be with you), and fixed her stare against the darkness that befell her.

———

RICH FARRIS WAS WORKING THE PHONES BEHIND THE COUNTER OF THE front desk. I passed through on my way to the kitchen. "Mr. Farris, what is happening, my friend?"

He lowered a newspaper and smiled at me. "What's up, Dickie? Working late, I see."

"Yes sir. And I'm going to brew a fresh pot for the occasion. Can I bring you a cup?"

"Sounds good, man. Black. Like my women."

I smiled and turned into the hall, thinking Rich Farris probably had an assortment of women, all colors. He was a handsome black man, a sharp dresser, a smooth talker, and he drove a black convertible Corvette when not in his county-issued Crown Vic. He had been through at least one divorce and the last I knew, he was single. Though, around here, marital statuses were changed more often than neckties.

I returned with two cups of hot, black coffee and handed him one. "Your night in the barrel, huh?"

"Every rotation, it seems. No matter how long I've been around here, no matter how many kids come in behind me, I still get the shit end of the stick."

"Where's your partner?"

Rich Farris was sitting up straight now, the paper folded on the desk. He spun his chair to look through the window area that offers a view of the squad room. He came back with a questioning look on his face. "I don't know. Probably on her way. She's actually got a life, unlike you and me."

I glanced at my watch. 8:45 p.m. He was working the desk on the early morning shift. Which was the 10 p.m. – 6 a.m. shift that became the 9:30 p.m. – 5:30 a.m. shift that became the 9:00 p.m. – 5:00 a.m. shift, all without a spoken or written word on the matter. It happened by detectives being friendly and relieving one another earlier and earlier over the years. When Floyd and I were partners, he was trying to take it back to 8:30 p.m., showing up earlier each time we worked the desk. The problem was nobody wanted to make the dayshift relief at 4:30 in the morning, so me and that dummy would end up putting in at least an extra half hour. It appeared Floyd had recruited Rich into his push for 8:30.

"How's she doing, anyway?"

"Lizzy? She's good, man. She's a cool chick with a good attitude, just needs some seasoning is all. She maybe could've had a little more experience when she came here."

"She's okay though, huh?"

He nodded. "I like her. A guy could do a lot worse around here, if you know what I mean."

I agreed. "Hey, what's up with that case you guys caught out in the valley? I wanted to ask you about that."

"The Asian girl?"

"Yeah."

"Were you here for the meeting yesterday?"

"No, but Ray was, and he gave me the Reader's Digest version. I was at my mandatory shrink meeting."

"Who do you see, Dr. James?"

"Yeah."

He smiled. "Now, *she* is a sexy thing, you ask me. I hook up again, that's the way I'm going, get me a professional woman, someone makes a little bank and doesn't break yours and rob you of your retirement when she leaves."

"You know, you might be onto something, Rich. Now, tell me about the Asian girl."

The phone rang. "Homicide, Farris . . . yeah, what's up Lopes? Yep, hang on." He tucked the phone beneath his chin and said to me, "Lopes needs me to run something in CalGangs. Give me a second here, Dickie."

"I thought he had a date tonight. The hell's wrong with that guy?"

Rich started laughing. "Lopes heard you man, said tell Dickie shut the fuck up."

I smiled.

"Okay, Lopes, go . . . uh-huh . . . Lopez, with a Z . . . hang on . . ."

Rich Farris was typing and glancing back and forth from the screen to the keyboard, pecking one letter at a time. "Okay, first? . . . Maria . . . M-A-R-I-A. You running your girlfriends again, Lopes?"

I could hear his voice on the other end but couldn't understand the words. At least not most of them. Farris was laughing, and then he said, "Okay, hold on . . . Jesus Christ, man, the hell? Okay, address, go . . ."

Rich Farris repeated the address as he typed it into the CalGangs program, a law enforcement database with a collection of data related to more than 150,000 gang members and their associates. The data was mostly compiled through arrest bookings and intelligence gathered by gang investigators. A name inquiry could provide a photo, moniker, vehicles, associates, and more. An address search would provide records of any gang activity attributed to a particular location, including the names of any gang members who have listed the address as a residence, or were contacted at the address by law enforcement. Any crime reports with the address listed in any manner—location of the crime, or the residence of someone involved, whether it be a victim or suspect—would be revealed in an address search. The information could range from warnings for law enforcement to general information and intelligence associated with the address.

As I waited, I grew more intrigued. Ten minutes earlier Lopes was headed out the door to pick up a woman he had met at Pelican Bay, a corrections officer who by description was Latina and hot. Now he's calling in to check a name and address of a Maria Lopez. There was no doubt in my mind it was related to his planned date. But why? Lopes had good instinct. What was it that had him decide now, on his way to pick her up, that he'd better check her out? Maybe just applying additional caution. Maybe a gut feeling.

"Nothing, man . . . no hits on either one," Farris said into the phone. "You bet, brother, anytime."

He hung up the phone and said, "The Asian . . ."

Lizzy walked in, squeezed behind Rich's chair and sat in an adjacent chair, offering only a smile to each of us. Rich was telling me that the case didn't appear to be a sexually motivated murder, unless something went wrong. There hadn't been any penetration and the medical examination determined the victim was still a virgin. Rich also told me what I had previously heard, that she was found by her mother strangled to death in an upstairs bedroom. She wasn't wearing panties. She didn't have a boyfriend. There were no brothers or cousins and nobody else should have been at the home. There was no evidence of forced entry, so she must have let him in. Which, Rich said, caused him to think the killer was someone she knew, or at least someone she trusted.

Lizzy said, "Like a cop, or mailman."

Rich Farris glanced over and nodded. "The thing about it is, we've got nothing to work on. And brother, I mean nothing. No DNA, no prints. There was a lighter found in the pad, on the floor in her room. Nobody in the family smokes, so we think it's likely our killer's. But, as luck would have it, no identifiable prints on it."

"Did you run the dogs?"

He paused a moment, apparently in thought. "No. What are you thinking, Dickie?"

"I'd have Ted collect scent off that lighter and run his dogs out there, see what you pick up. Might take you right next door, some fifteen-year-old doper with a hard-on for Asian girls. Maybe Ted's coonhound would ID the mailman, if you timed it right. Who knows, maybe he'll follow a trail to the local high school and jump in the janitor's lap. Those dogs are awesome."

"Coonhound? What the hell, man?" Rich said, chuckling.

"Basset hounds, bloodhounds, coonhounds, whatever the hell they are, big, droopy-eared sonsofbitches that look like they need a nap, like Floyd's new partner."

Lizzy laughed and we both glanced over at her.

Rich said to me, "It's been damn near a week, man."

"Call Ted. I think they can run those dogs for a couple weeks on a scent trail. It's worth a try, especially if you have nothing else."

Rich and Lizzy looked at one another and each shrugged, both with a *what do we have to lose* expression about them.

Farris said, "You got his number, Ted's?"

I smiled and pointed at the list of frequently called numbers displayed in plain sight but often overlooked. Rich's empty coffee cup sat near it. I said, "Hand me that mug and I'll fill you up, I'm headed back there myself. Meanwhile, you can call Ted and get him scheduled for the morning. You don't have anything else to do tomorrow, do you?"

"Not a thing, man . . . nothing other than sleep."

Walking away, I suggested they could catch some sleep during their shift if the phones stayed as quiet as they had been the last few days.

---

LOPES HAD HUNG UP AFTER SPEAKING WITH FARRIS AT THE DESK AND found himself in a somber mood, deep in thought. He still had a bad feeling about something. No hits in the CalGangs, but it seemed there was something more to this sexy little corrections officer. It was something he felt in his gut and couldn't put a finger on. He thought about all of the conversations the two of them had had—they'd spoken on the phone half a dozen times since meeting a week earlier at Pelican Bay—and he realized there was one thing that had bothered him. It occurred to him she had asked more than once what the deal was with Spooky, why Lopes was going all the way up to Pelican Bay from Los Angeles to talk to a "poser" like Spooky.

*Poser.*

Why would she call him that? Just tough talk from a corrections officer, or did that come from the street side of her? More importantly, why had she been so interested in Lopes's relationship with Spooky? Was she trying to find out if Spooky was informing on the mob? He had to consider the possibility.

For only a moment, Lopes considered the possibility of something much more troubling about her inquiries, a relationship between guard and inmate. It happens, far too often. He pictured Spooky and then saw the pretty officer Maria Lopez and shook his head. There was no way she would have anything to do with that *vato*.

It occurred to Lopes he had slipped up at the prison. Actually, it was Spooky, but Lopes had failed to clean it up. In front of Maria, Spooky had reminded Lopes to put money on his books. Both were comfortable with Officer Maria Lopez to say such a thing in front of her. Lopes should have caught it, and told him, "Whatever, dipshit," or something along those lines to play it off as a joke. But he hadn't. And Maria Lopez may have considered the statement afterwards, and questioned why a cop would be putting money on a convict's books. There was only one reason. Lopes knew that had been a mistake.

Davey Lopes was startled from his thoughts and concerns about his date with the corrections officer when two cop cars sailed past him, lights and sirens in play. He hadn't even seen them coming up behind him, and now they were flying by. It was as if he'd been in a trance. He watched the cars fade into the night ahead of him and turn right at a distant intersection. A minute later Lopes was turning onto the same street. He saw the two cop cars sitting in the street with open doors, their lights casting red and blue beams throughout the neighborhood. Cops were moving about with urgency near the front porch of a modest but tidy home on the south side of the street. One of them had a roll of yellow tape and he began stringing it across the front.

Lopes had stopped behind the cop cars and was looking at the numbers on the curb when he realized he had arrived at Maria's grandmother's home.

Two paramedics were hunched over a body near the front door. A cop stood watching, his flashlight adding light to the dimly illuminated porch. Another cop scanned the ground in the immediate vicinity, shining his light on the ground as if looking for something lost.

As Lopes walked briskly toward the scene he saw the body of a young woman curled up on the concrete steps, motionless. At that moment, he realized what his instinct had tried to warn him: there was more to his relationship with Maria Lopez than a chance encounter, a casual date. His gut had told him, but he ignored it. Now he knew what CalGangs hadn't been able to reveal to him; there was more to Maria Lopez than dimples and a great ass.

# 30

7 60 MILES NORTH of Whittier, the Pelican Bay State Prison consumes 275 acres of pristine real estate just outside of Crescent City, California. Surrounded by forest, the location is near the border of Oregon and only two miles inland from the Pacific Ocean. Built to house 3,319 inmates, the state's only "supermax" prison opened for business in 1989. It is home to the most violent and dangerous prisoners in the state, many of whom are affiliated with one of the four primary prison gangs: The Mexican mafia (La Eme), Nuestra Familia (NF, or Ene), The Black Guerilla Family (BGF), and the Aryan Brotherhood (AB).

Cellblock C, or *C Block*, is a designated Special Housing Unit (SHU) reserved for the most dangerous of the prison's population. Their activities are rigorously monitored as they remain in their cells 22 hours each day, seven days a week. Each day they are allowed access, one or two at a time, to an exercise facility the inmates call the dog run. It is a small, narrow concrete box with walls fifteen feet high. Nearly half of its occupants are serving life sentences; most—or more likely, all—are killers, convicted or not.

Victor Hernandez, also known as "Little Spooky" from Big Hazard, a Hispanic street gang located in East Los Angeles, had been housed in C Block for nearly six years. A known associate of the prison gang, La Eme,

Hernandez had killed two gang members from Whittier for failing to pay taxes to the Mexican mafia. It was learned the two victims had taken over drug sales in their neighborhood after several others were sent to prison, the result of gang and drug enforcement sweeps. The two murdered gang members had been counseled twice (they were jumped on two separate occasions, one of which resulted in one of the two being stabbed repeatedly), yet their unwillingness to pay the required taxes had persisted. Spooky, accompanied by three of his fellow Hazard gang enthusiasts, had gone to the home of one of the soon-to-be-victims. They abducted him at gunpoint, drove to the business partner's home and scooped him up too, and then the three gangsters drove with their two prisoners thirty miles north to the Angeles National Forest. There, the two were taken from the car, placed on their knees, and shot to death with a shotgun, two nine-millimeter pistols, and an AK-47.

One of the accomplices to the murder, Juan "Joker" Torres, had recently become Spooky's new cellie. The arrangement came as a surprise to Spooky as the four defendants had each been housed separately since their convictions. For the first three days they talked nonstop, like two girls at summer camp. They chatted day and night as they sat or lay on their bunks in the two-man cell, a small concrete enclosure with stacked bunks, a toilet, and a sink. The cells are too small for two men who don't get along well; one of the two would eventually kill the other if not compatible. But these two gangsters had been friends and *homeboys* all of their lives, and Spooky was glad for the company. They spent their time catching up on prison gossip and talk of the streets: who had been killed and who was locked up, which homegirls were still down for the hood, providing sexual favors for those on the outside and bringing in dope to the *vatos* inside. Finally, Joker got to it, asking his codefendant, homie, cellie, and friend, Spooky, "What do you hear about the mob, eh?"

Spooky filled him in, telling him everything he had heard as far as current criminal activities, how they were using some white boys connected with the Irish mafia to do some hits on the outside, how he had heard they were moving in on legitimate businesses now, not just taxing gangsters dealing dope. The goal was to bring in more money. Money equaled power, he was told. Spooky also told him he heard about a woman who was killed and had her head and hands chopped off, and he had heard that Eme might have had something to do with it, but he didn't know. He asked Joker if he knew, and Joker shook his head. Spooky said he recently heard there was a green light on a hack, a sheriff in Los Angeles, but said he didn't know what that was all about, either. He said, "I mean, goddamn, talk about bringing the heat, eh?"

When Spooky finished, Joker asked how he knew about all of this when he was locked down so tight. He replied, "All I do is listen to the conversations, man, it's all I've had to do in here till you came, eh. I been kickin' it up in here by myself for the last what, three or two years, eh."

In the quiet of the third night, Joker and Spooky were both lying on top of their beds; it was too warm in the SHU to do otherwise. Joker quietly asked his new cellie—old "crimie"—what ever happened to his little girl. He said, "Do you see her, or hear from her?"

Spooky told him no, he didn't see her or hear from her, and then he told him his ex had kicked him to the curb and was now hooked up with— and he lowered his voice— "That *puto*, Peanut from Puente, eh, a *carnale*. He got her wrapped on his leg, eh, and she ain't got time for me no more. My baby girl is almost grown up now, eh, and I don't even know her."

For a few minutes after he said it, neither of them spoke. Finally, Joker said his last words of the night: "You should know better than to fuck with the *carnales*, homie, La Eme."

That was it. No reply. Neither said goodnight. Nobody ever said good-night in prison, unless you were a bitch.

On the morning of the fourth day, long before the 6:00 a.m. wakeup, Joker lay wide awake listening to Spooky sleep soundly above him in the dark. There were dim lights outside of the cell that weakly illuminated the module and provided enough light to move around in the darkened cell as needed. He could tell Spooky was in a deep sleep and would not easily awaken. Joker quietly slid off the bottom bunk, removed the strips of bedding he had prepared days before and concealed beneath his mattress, and climbed carefully onto Spooky's bunk. He had the strips of cloth wrapped around Spooky's neck before he awakened. Joker pulled the liga-ture violently and held tight through a barrage of fists hitting his head. He stayed atop of his cellie who was now bucking his hips and twisting and turning his torso and legs, desperately trying to free himself. There were muffled sounds of grunts and groans and then it was over. It had taken less than a minute, but Joker continued to choke him for another to be safe. Soon he smelled the release of bodily functions and felt the last involuntary convulsions of Spooky's body.

Joker slid off the bunk. He stood solemnly at the cell's door in his white boxer shorts, his muscular and tattooed body glistening with sweat. He took a moment to calm himself, to control his breathing, to relax. While doing so, he wiped sweat from his head and body with Spooky's shower towel; Spooky would no longer be needing it. Joker pushed his face against the bars and called out in the direction of the officer's booth. "Hey, yo, officer . . . we got a man down on Baker row, man down."

The familiar voice of a neighbor bounced off the concrete walls, not much more than a whisper in the shadows. "Is it done?"

"Yeah, it's done," Joker said softly.

———

LEONARD AWOKE LATE FRIDAY MORNING WITH A HEADACHE. LIKELY TOO much Cuervo and too many cigarettes after a long night of watching again and getting nowhere. The cop hadn't come home. Now Leonard moved about in the quiet room he called home, a worn bed, a couch and table, and a kitchenette. He plopped down on the sofa with a box of donuts and a quart of orange juice he had bought at the corner market from the foreigner who wore a sheet wrapped around his head. His phone vibrated and flashed light against the coffee table. He reached for it and saw the display said Moses. The Marty Feldman of the Irish mob. He ignored the call.

Five minutes later the phone rang again, but Leonard's head still hurt, and he had no news and no desire to speak with the boss's boy, Feldman.

When it rang a third time not five minutes later, Leonard gave in. "Hello, fuckface."

Silence.

"Hello?"

A gravelly voice, one Leonard had never heard on the phone but recognized immediately from his one meeting with the boss. "Excuse me?"

"Sir . . . Mr. McFarland, I didn't know—"

"Please do not use my name."

"Sorry, Mr., uh, sir."

"Why are you not answering your phone when my assistant, Mr. Lomeli calls? He has complained of your attitude on several occasions. Is there a problem between the two of you, something I need to address?"

Leonard pictured the distinguished man, his gray hair slicked back, the jewelry on his wrists and hands. He could see the boss man twisting the emerald ring on his left hand while he waited for the answer. "No sir."

"Good. Make sure it stays that way. Now, on to business, where are we on the assignment?"

Leonard reached for a cigarette and began searching for a lighter. "Sir, I've not had much luck. I'm not so sure he even lives at that address I was given."

"Why would you say that? Haven't you seen him there?"

"Yes, twice, but—"

"Then what is the problem?"

"He's hardly ever there. I'm starting to wonder if it's a crash pad or something, maybe somewhere he meets his girlfriend."

"He has a girlfriend, does he?"

"No—I don't know. I'm just saying, it doesn't seem he lives there. This isn't going to be easy with a, um, person like that . . . I need to see his routine in order to have a plan. There's no routine. The guy's a fucking weirdo, man—I mean, sir."

After a brief pause, the boss said, "It's a good address. It came straight from his departmental records, courtesy of our fed. He lives there, we are certain."

"Yes sir. Okay, well . . . I'll continue to wait, and watch. I have three weeks to get it done still."

"Two."

These guys and their fucking math. "Yes sir, two weeks. Thank you."

The phone went silent and Leonard tossed it on the table. He needed something to go with his O.J.; maybe he'd walk down to the corner and buy a bottle of vodka. This working for a living—having a boss telling you what to do and when to do it—wasn't playing out the way he had hoped it would. In fact, it was a pain in his balls. He pictured Whitey in his cell, maybe lying on his bunk or doing pushups on the concrete floor.

At times, Leonard just wanted to go back to Raiford. It was home. The only home he ever knew, really. The only place he had a friend.

---

I HAD JUST COLLAPSED AT MY DESK IN THE HOMICIDE BUREAU, HAGGARD from the night's work. It had started shortly after Lopes had called in and asked Farris to run a check on the corrections officer. I was still visiting with Farris when Lopes phoned again and said he needed two teams, the crime lab, scent dogs, SWAT, and a lieutenant to respond to Whittier. He provided an address. I could hear Lopes over the phone as he spoke with Rich Farris, and his voice had an urgent tone, though he remained composed. It reminded me of the night Lopes's partner was shot in Firestone, and Lopes put out a broadcast on the radio. The exigency was there in his voice and tone, but he remained cool under fire and was able to deliver the message methodically. I felt there was a similar urgency in this call.

Farris had scribbled an address onto a pad of scratch paper that sat by the phone, and while Lopes still spoke into the phone, Farris pushed the paper toward his partner and told her to page their lieutenant. I leaned over to see the address upside down, and wrote it on the palm of my hand with a pen.

I said to Farris, "I'm rolling," and walked away.

Farris's voice and a sudden increase of phones ringing faded behind me as I hurried toward the rear door. I didn't know what had happened, and it didn't matter. Lopes was asking for help and I was ready to roll. With the red light and siren parting the way, I could be there in 10-15 minutes.

My tires squealed and the engine roared as I turned out of the lot and headed east. A box of files sailed across the back seat and crashed against the door. I glanced over my shoulder to see its contents had spilled all over the backseat. It didn't matter. What mattered was Lopes walked into something. The phone call Lopes had made on his way to pick up his date told me something was on his mind. But what? What had suddenly bothered him about his date? And now, what had he walked into?

A setup had crossed my mind. Lopes lured into a deadly encounter through a pretty girl. It was our weakness, all of us. Mankind. We haven't really evolved all that much.

I slowed for a red light, looked both ways, and then floored it again. Had he walked into an ambush? Had he dumped some asshole, forced into a shooting situation by falling into a trap? He had asked for the world to roll, as we would call it; send everyone, and someone better pitch three tents because the circus would be coming to town. I hit the brakes and swerved around the front end of an obviously drunk driver's vehicle which had drifted into my lane of traffic. Again, the backseat contents scrambled.

The address Lopes had provided took me into a quaint, older Whittier neighborhood that had once hummed with the hustle and bustle of families who worked and attended school and pursued the American dream. Now the homes were secured as fortresses and decorated with graffiti. Cars and pickups littered driveways and front yards and crowded the curb space, leaving nowhere to park. I had left my Crown Vic double-parked on the street behind several emergency vehicles, and moved toward the activity two doors ahead.

A uniformed deputy sheriff had stood guarding the front yard that was encircled by crime scene tape. I glanced at the dimly lit front porch while walking up to introduce myself and sign in on the crime scene log. From where I stood, it didn't look good. There were the telltale signs of a death scene: rubber gloves on the bloodstained concrete, empty packages and containers from medical supplies, personal belongings scattered about, an indication the owner would likely not return. The volume of blood is what told the story; survival of the victim was not likely when most of one's life blood is spilled onto the ground. There was a purse, a pack of cigarettes, a lighter, and a cell phone that I could see across the lawn. It was a woman who had been shot. She had sat on the porch smoking a cigarette. That was my first impression based on the evidence at hand. I didn't see shell casings, but I didn't expect to at that distance and in the relative darkness. I scribbled my name and wrote down the time and "Homicide" next to it. Handing the clipboard back to the deputy, I had asked, "Where's Lopes?"

He nodded his head toward the back of the house. "He's inside, sir. There's a back entrance."

"Everything's been cleared?"

"Yes sir. Everything is clear. Suspects are GPA. Just an old lady inside, I think a relative."

The suspects were gone prior to his arrival. Of course they were. Was it a drive-by? Who was the lady inside? "The old lady, is she a relative of the woman who was shot?"

The deputy seemed surprised. "Yes sir. How did you know it was a woman?"

I had walked away without responding and went in through the back door, announcing my presence as I did. Because the house had been cleared and the suspect—or suspects—were said to be gone prior to arrival, didn't mean Lopes wouldn't be on edge.

Lopes had called out in response, "In here, Dickie."

That's when I first met Mrs. Maria Guadalupe Lopez Sanchez, the despondent grandmother of Corrections Officer Maria Lopez.

After an interview of the grandmother—or as Lopes had called her, *Nana*—I accompanied him to the hospital where we spent the rest of the night waiting for the news. That she had not yet expired surprised me, not just from what I saw, but also from what Lopes had told me: she had received multiple gunshot wounds, had lost a lot of blood, and was unresponsive. He had thought she was dead, but the paramedics found signs of life and worked feverishly to keep her alive as they rolled her to the hospital.

When I left the hospital later in the morning, the staff had informed us she was critical. Lopes said he was going to wait; he wanted to be the first to talk to her if she was ever able. I sensed there was more. We didn't discuss any of it then, but I was confident we'd discuss it when he came back to the office. It would be one of those days—possibly weekends—that all of us went without sleep.

I put my feet up on my desk, removed my hat, and laid my head back. An hour or two would provide all the rest I needed to get through another day. An hour or two and then a gallon or so of coffee.

# 31

AN HOUR LATER lights were turned on and low levels of chatter echoed through the chambers of metal desks and stained blue carpet. I glanced at my watch: 7:29. It was Friday, and a few people were getting an early start. My eyes were heavy and the lids fell closed again regardless of the budding activity around me. Nobody would care that I was asleep at my desk, and nobody would find it odd. This was the home of homicide detectives; everyone in the place had, at one time or another, slept at their desks, on the floor near their desks, in their county-issued department sedans, and at times, places where maybe they shouldn't have.

There is a leather sofa in the ladies' room at the bureau that makes for a nice bed. Like most men in the bureau, I didn't know why it was there, but I knew of its existence. Most detectives first learned of it from a senior partner while still new at the bureau. It would happen on an early morning shift, what many call graveyard, when the seasoned detective would inform the newly assigned. For me, it went like this: "Partner, I think you can handle the phones for the next hour or so, I'm going to lie down. There's a bed in the ladies' room and that's where I'll be if you need me." Subsequent to new guy status, two partners on the desk would likely take shifts using the room, so to speak. I hadn't opted for the ladies' room this morning as it was already too late in the day and I didn't want to sleep soundly only to be awakened by one of the females of the bureau coming in to use the facility. These women are armed.

After half an hour, I surrendered. The phones were ringing, the chatter about the place seemed more urgent than usual, and detectives were scurrying about. I could sense it all and it kept me from sleeping.

When I passed the front desk headed for coffee, I was glad to see both detectives on phones. I wouldn't have to speak to anyone until I was properly caffeinated. It was the dayshift now, and these people had presumably just come off of a full night's sleep. I could not equal their level of awareness, enthusiasm, or willingness to communicate with the world. In fact, it might be said that my disposition at this point rivaled that of a rattlesnake who has been suddenly pulled from his shelter and peaceful sleep.

Fully aware of my unpleasant disposition, I grabbed a cup of coffee and went into the men's room with the travel bag that stays in my trunk. Ten minutes later I emerged freshly groomed and with the appearance of a living human. I drained the remainder of that first cup and cringed at the conflict it had with the fresh mint flavor occupying my mouth. After filling a second cup, I worked my way back to the front desk where the two dayshift detectives stood speaking to their lieutenant—my former lieutenant when I worked with Floyd on Team Two—Ed Jordan. The three stopped speaking as I walked in, and now they all seemed to be focused on me.

"Good morning."

"Long night?" Lt. Jordan asked.

"Yeah, Lopes's deal."

"What's the word on it, any idea?" he asked.

I sighed and set my coffee on the counter that separates the desk personnel from the lobby. "I don't know a lot, boss. Lopes met this gal up at Pelican. She's a corrections officer. I guess they hit it off, and she was down here visiting her family so they were going to hook up, go out. We had had a briefing last night on the Santa Clarita case—you've heard about the gal that had her head cut off, right?"

"Yeah, you and Cortez are working it, and you stole your old partner back to help with it," he said and smiled.

"Yeah, so we've been having these nightly briefings, those of us working the case—me, Ray, Floyd, and Mongo—and then Lopes has been joining in, kind of just staying up on it with us, paying attention in case there's something about the mafia that factors in."

"You think the Mexican mafia was involved in it?"

"We're not sure, boss. But in our briefing last night, Lopes seemed distracted—that's the whole point. He kept checking his phone and he didn't really participate. He was distant, I'd say. Then, after the briefing, he takes off. He said he was taking this gal out, this corrections officer. So, he splits. I'm hanging around here because I pretty much don't have a life, and I was bullshitting with Farris and his new partner, Lizzy, up here at the desk when Lopes called in asking Farris to check this broad out on CalGangs—"

"Who? Check who out?"

"This corrections officer."

He frowned.

"Yeah, that's what I thought. What the hell made him think to run her —and the address he was going to—through CalGangs? But I was standing right there when he did it. Farris checked it out, nothing came up on either one—the name or the address—but I really was puzzled by it. Lopes has good instinct. He was bothered by something during our briefing, and now, on his way to pick this lady up for a date, he decides to run her through the system.

"Anyway, I'm still here a half-hour later—no, it wasn't even that, maybe fifteen minutes—when he calls back, asking for two teams and a lieutenant and a SWAT team and whatever the hell else he asked for—the world. I knew it was serious, so I grabbed the address and started rolling that way without knowing what had happened. I figured he might have dumped someone, to be honest. In my mind, I saw Lopes with a smoking gun in one hand and his phone in the other. I didn't have any idea what the hell could have happened out there, but I knew it wasn't good."

All three were quiet, attentive, waiting for more. I swigged the remainder of my coffee and looked at the bottom of my cup as if it were another mystery to be solved.

"That's about it, other than what you probably already know, that Lopes arrived to pick her up and saw what had happened. Someone had walked up and smoked her while she was having a smoke of her own. I stayed with Lopes while he talked to grandma for quite a while, waiting for the teams to show up. Stringer and Jackson showed up first—I guess they have the handle on it—and after Lopes gave them a brief statement, he headed to the hospital. I went with him. I didn't want to leave him alone, especially not knowing what any of this is about. He doesn't know either, boss. We talked a lot at the hospital. He's dumbfounded. As far as the reason he ran her, she's from *The Avenues*. Something about that bothered him. She's from *The Avenues* but had him going to Whittier to pick her up. I guess that gave him pause. He also mentioned that she had asked a lot of questions—or seemed to anyway—about what he was doing up at Pelican, why he was talking to a gangster named Spooky, who is giving him information about the mob."

Jordan was nodding. "Where is he now?"

"Spooky, or Lopes?"

"Yes."

"Spooky's in Pelican, Lopes stayed at the hospital. Said he was staying until she was able to talk. He's dead set on it, wants to know what happened and he wants to be the first to hear it, directly from her if possible."

There were more investigators filing in, though slowly and sporadically. Being a Friday, it would be a light day at the office. A third of the bureau would be starting a three-day weekend after working ten straight and covering the previous weekend on call. Teams Five and Six, now up for murders until Monday morning, were already scattered about the county; four investigators were in Whittier handling the shooting of Maria Lopez. Though it was not yet a murder, it would be handled as if it were, for three reasons: it could very well end up a murder, the victim is a corrections officer, and Lopes insisted on it. He carried considerable weight at the bureau and nobody would second-guess his concerns about the situation. It wasn't about him and her, it was about much more than that. Lopes hadn't yet laid it out—maybe he hadn't yet entirely figured it out—but he instinctively knew there was more to this than a random walkup shooting. Two other teams had been sent out in the night, one for a gang murder in Compton (we could always count on Compton to keep the stats high) and another had been sent to my old stomping grounds, the Firestone District, now policed by deputies out of Century Station.

"They've sent her phone back from the lab already," Jordan said. "It's been printed and swabbed, blood samples taken, finished with the forensics. I've got it on my desk, if you want to start going through it. I doubt they'll mind, the handling team."

"Jackson and Stringer have the handle, right?"

He nodded.

"Who's assisting?"

Jordan glanced over at the whiteboard that hung on the wall behind the front desk. It changed rapidly, nearly daily, and had all the information about which teams were up, who was handling which case, and the names of the recently departed. Jordan must have drawn a blank at the question because he had to have known who he had assigned to handle and assist on the Maria Lopez shooting case; the board was his reminder. "Martinez and Blair."

"I'll give one of them a call, just to make sure, boss. I don't want to step on anyone's toes, but yeah, I'd like to have a look at that phone, maybe start writing paper on it."

Jordan burrowed his brows. "If we have the phone, why would you need a search warrant?"

"We're going to need a certified copy of the records, all her calls and texts for the billing period, maybe three billing periods back, just to be safe. Not everything is going to be on the phone, or, I should say, it might not be. Either way, if anything ever goes to court, we'll need more than a report of what I find on the phone itself; we'll need all of the records. Also, once we have a search warrant for the phone, it's easy to piggyback that warrant for all the subscriber information and records of the numbers we find on there. I have a feeling a lot of this is going to be relevant."

He sighed. "Yeah, Lopes's number will be all over it too; that's not going to look good."

"She's a corrections officer. She's single—presumably—as is Lopes. It's okay that they met and hooked up, boss. Even if she's dirty, that's not going to matter. He's not. He had no idea she was. *If* she's dirty; that's just a possibility at this point."

His eyes bugged out. "Wait, you think she's a dirty cop? That's what this is about?"

"I don't know what it's about, boss. I'm just saying, *if* that's how it plays out. The only reason that even crosses my mind is that Lopes had something bothering him about the whole thing. I wouldn't be surprised."

"You don't think he was walking into a setup, do you?"

I shrugged. "I don't know what to think. I don't know if he was walking into a setup, or if it's all a big coincidence. Hell, for all I know, Lopes gunned her down himself when he got there and found some other *vato* with her."

"Jesus Christ," Jordan said.

I patted his shoulder and smiled. "Just kidding, boss. That's the only thing I'm sure *didn't* happen."

Before walking away, I asked that the desk crew page one of the four detectives out on the Whittier case and transfer them to my desk when they called in. Being old-fashioned, I still trusted landlines more than cell phones at times like this.

---

LEONARD ARRIVED AND PARKED UP THE STREET FROM THE COP'S residence, the apartment over a garage in the backyard of a big yellow house with a manicured lawn and shade trees and shrubbery. Though he had been reluctant to watch again from his vehicle, he didn't think hiding on the hillside would work during daylight hours. He'd have to take his chances in the car.

A man he'd never seen before was in the driveway of the detached garage beneath the apartment, washing a boat. He wore shorts and a tank-top, and his skin was tanned. Leonard could tell he was a cop. He was older, but as is the case with many cops and convicts, he appeared to be physically fit, stronger than many his age. The man in shorts, *beach boy,* Leonard thought, also had the watchful eyes of a cop, looking up when Leonard pulled over and parked, and looking up every few minutes since. It made Leonard uncomfortable.

After drying the boat, the man backed it into the garage beneath the apartment, unhooked it from his truck, and drove around to the front of the house, out of Leonard's view. Two ladies jogged by and peered at him. The whole fucking neighborhood was on alert, it seemed, like these goddamn people didn't have anything better to do with their lives than worry about people sitting in cars.

When a few minutes had passed, Leonard's nerves got the best of him and he pulled away from the curb. But he didn't turn around and leave the back way as he normally would; rather, he drove around the corner to see the front of the home. As he did, the tanned cop, *beach boy,* stepped out of another garage—one that was attached to the front of the home—and walked down the driveway alongside his shiny silver pickup toward the street. His eyes seemed to drill into Leonard behind his mirrored cop glasses.

Leonard panicked and floored it.

He heard the man yell, "Hey!" and Leonard glanced in his side-view mirror to see beach boy at a trot in his turquoise shorts and flip-flops. His arms were waving and Leonard could hear faint sounds of shouting as he pulled away.

*Shit!*

Leonard made his way back to the freeway as quickly as he could without drawing attention, and headed south to L.A.. Once he settled, Leonard came to the decision the job was off. He wasn't going to do it. He'd call Moses later today and tell him so. Better yet, he'd say, *Put the boss on the phone, douchebag,* and tell old man McFarland himself. He didn't need this shit, these fucking cops that seemed to pay attention to everything even while they're drinking beer and washing boats.

But then he remembered he had no way to call them. That was part of the deal. *They* would contact *him*. Great.

Well, he could send a letter and split. They'd figure it out when they got it. Maybe put the letter in a box along with the phone with the dirty pictures of a dead gook, see how Mr. Fuckface liked that.

But that would likely result in a hit being put on him. Leonard wouldn't even be able to return to prison and walk the yard, not with a mafia bounty on him. This made him think of Whitey, and he realized if he failed the family, their friendship would be over. What a pickle. He wished the goddamn judge would have sentenced him to life; he would be much better off in prison.

When he walked into his hotel room it was time for tequila. Still not yet noon, but he didn't care. He was done for the day and he wouldn't dare go outside again. He had even parked a few blocks further away in the event the buffed beach boy pig got his license and called it in. He didn't want any cops sniffing around his room if they found the car nearby.

As Leonard loosened up with the medicinal aid of Mr. Cuervo, he considered his options: he could allow himself to be caught and go back to prison. No, not in California. He had heard tales of the prisons here. Ran by Mexicans, mostly, and overpopulated by blacks; he wanted no part of them. He needed to get back to Florida and commit a crime there that would secure his future incarceration. But no, not if he didn't finish the job at hand. Again, the hit on *him* would then be on. Leonard took a long pull off the bottle and as the warmth rushed over him he came to terms with what he had to do: kill the damn cop as instructed and get the hell back to the east coast where he belonged. Simple enough. Just find the pig. *Jesus*.

AS I SAT AT MY DESK STARING AT ITS BLOTTER DEVOID OF ANY EVIDENCE of life—no photographs of family or friends or hobbies of fishing or hunting or playing golf in funny outfits—I tried sorting it all out in my mind: the headless woman, the missing woman still unaccounted for, the watcher—someone seemingly stalking me—and now this, a corrections officer getting whacked. A female Hispanic corrections officer who grew up in *The Avenues*, arguably one of the most mafia friendly geographical regions of the southland, who is probably twenty years Lopes's junior but moved in fast to be with him, and then she wanted to see him again a very short time later, a long way from her home. I thought about all of this and my conversations with Lopes about Jorge Regalado, the gangster I had shot and killed just over a year ago, and his nephew Gilbert who was facing a life behind bars for two murders, thanks in part to the efforts of Dickie and Floyd. Did it all connect somehow?

My cell phone vibrating on the desktop jarred me away from my reflection. It was a text message from Chuck, my landlord, asking that I call when convenient. My first thought was he was evicting me. Maybe the mother-in-law was moving in. Or I forgot to close the gate and Elvis escaped and Chuck had had it with me. Then I thought maybe something worse had happened, and my stalker came to mind. I regretted not informing Chuck and Patti of the suspicious person and activity, but I still had not completely accepted that it was a reality. I should have told him anyway.

When I called, Chuck described an incident that occurred a short time before. Someone had sat up the street from the residence, east of the detached garage and my apartment. Chuck had been washing the boat before putting it away when he noticed the man and thought him suspicious. Then, after putting the boat away, Chuck drove around to the front of the house and parked the truck in the driveway. He went into the garage, planning to go inside, and it occurred to him he needed to check the mail. As Chuck walked out to get the mail, the same vehicle drove past, and its occupant was eyeing him closely. He yelled at the guy who sped off. He was unable to get a tag, but it was a California license plate on a silver Ford Taurus.

I knew the car, I could see it in my mind parked up the street. My stomach suddenly felt queasy.

"I just thought you should know, in case you see that car around. Have you happened to notice anything strange around here while we were gone?"

"Chuck, I should have told you . . ."

I started filling him in, providing the details of the encounters with the watcher. Just as I did, Floyd and Mongo walked through the back door. They peeled apart, and Floyd came toward me while Mongo veered toward their desks on the other side of the squad room. Floyd pulled out a chair and waited, frowning as I finished with Chuck and awaited his reply.

Expecting anger from Chuck, I avoided eye contact with Floyd. He would no doubt be staring at me, wanting to figure out who I was talking to and wanting all the details. Having no patience, he would nod, and mouth the words "Who is that?" not willing to wait until the call ended. I couldn't deal with him and take the ass-chewing I had coming from Chuck.

Chuck said, "Well, I'm glad you're around here. I'd be afraid to leave with this shit going on if you weren't here."

"But, it's probably me that brought the trouble to you, Chuck. I'm really sorry. I'll figure it out, and get it fixed."

Chuck, in his deep voice, said, "Hey man, no worries. We see the little bastard around here again, we'll kill him and call it in, let Burbank clean it up. They don't like assholes in their town and they don't mess around. The chief—who Patti and I happen to be friends with—would probably pin medals on our chests if we smoked some asshole in his city."

I smiled and said, "Thanks, Chuck. I'll keep a close eye when I'm there."

"Sounds good, buddy. Hey, while I've got you on the line, Patti and I were going to ask if you could watch Elvis for a couple days. We have a wedding down in San Diego next Friday, leaving Wednesday. Apparently, the snooty assholes don't allow bulldogs at the ceremony. Can we leave him with you?"

"You bet, Chuck. I'd be happy to have the company."

I ended the call and looked to my old partner. He said, "Chuck?"

"Yeah."

"Where's Ray?"

"I don't know, haven't heard from him. It's been a crazy night."

"Well, let's hear it. Then, when Ray shows up, I want to bounce some thoughts off you guys about this piece of shit case that's got me lying about overtime. What the hell happened last night?"

---

RAY WALKED IN AS I TOLD FLOYD EVERYTHING I KNEW ABOUT THE NIGHT before. When finished, I didn't allow Ray to ask about the details he missed before joining us. I looked at him and said, "Apparently, Floyd wants to bounce some thoughts off us about the case. This should be good . . . good and demented."

Floyd looked at Ray and said, "I think Lopes may be onto something with this *one and the same* theory, the idea that our missing girl is also the dead woman."

# 32

FLOYD OPENED HIS case notebook and began flipping back and forth through a few pages nearly halfway into it. The notebooks were supplied to us and we went through them quickly. Every case required a fresh notebook, and in many cases an investigator would fill several of them. They were designed to fit in a suit coat or rear pants pocket, and the covers were printed with the Homicide logo, a bulldog that appeared ready to fight. An article had appeared in the Los Angeles Times back in the seventies that had labeled the L.A. Sheriff's Homicide detectives as bulldogs, and ever since we had embraced the sturdy breed of dog as our mascot. The notebooks made me think about Elvis, and it made me want to get on better terms with him. If we became buddies, I could bring Elvis to the office when I watched him for Chuck and Patti next week. Maybe let him piss on Floyd's chair.

The pages of Floyd's notebook were filled with words written in black ink with important notations accented with red ink or highlighted in yellow. I had worked with him long enough to know this was not unusual; this was the product of his undiagnosed obsessive-compulsive disorder. Any detective could pick up a notebook from his desk and dictate a report that was as accurate as if they had been with him on scene or during the interviews. I had done so on many occasions. I would sometimes bargain with him since he never wanted to drive: "You drive, I'll dictate."

Working on a fresh case, we always tried to stay up with the dictation. It wasn't his favorite thing to do, but I didn't mind as much. I was never big on talking to strangers unless I had to, and I wasn't even the most talkative around those who knew me. I could spend hours in the same room with someone in comfortable silence. But I didn't mind speaking into inanimate objects or conversing with dead people. Homicide was the perfect assignment for me.

He lowered the notebook and leaned back in his chair. "Okay, ready?"

Ray and I glanced at each other. I asked Floyd, "Should we have cocktails for this?"

"It wouldn't be a bad idea, Dickie. It's *never* a bad idea. Anyway, here are my thoughts on this fiasco you've gotten me into. I think there's something to Lopes's theory that they are one and the same, this Lisa Williams and Marilynn Chaney. That the dead woman *is* the missing person, who was also living large as a high-class hooker. One woman living two lives. Well, you know how I feel about hookers, so I figured this warranted a more detailed inspection—"

"No surprise there," I said.

Floyd grinned. "Where is that asshole, anyway?"

"Who, Lopes?"

"Yeah, Lopes, dickhead."

"He's still at the hospital, far as I know."

Satisfied, Floyd continued: "Well, I started thinking, maybe old *what's-his-ass*, your missing's old man, found out his wife had a second life, a secret life where she's giving it up for big bucks and not sharing the wealth. I mean, that limp-dicked S.O.B. probably doesn't miss the action —if he's even straight—but he's pissed to find out she's got this place in the Marina and a hundred-thousand-dollar car he didn't know about. You have to figure, if she's been hooking enough to support that lifestyle on the side, she's not home very often, if at all. The marriage is likely just a façade. He probably has his deal on the side too, maybe a little pirate hooker or a young Asian boy, someone with very little facial hair. Who knows?

"Which leads me to my next *ah-hah* moment . . . So, running with

Lopes's theory, I had to wonder how that would work. If Marilynn Chaney and Lisa Williams are one and the same, would it not make sense that each vehicle should have evidence of one woman's presence—DNA, hair, fingerprints? We know that the DNA from the corpse was identified as a match to DNA in CODIS attributed to Lisa Williams. But there was no other source of DNA compared to that of the corpse. The lab had collected trace evidence which included hair, but nobody had asked for any other samples to be compared to the DNA from the corpse. Or, Lisa Williams.

"Now," he said, and pointed at me, "I took the liberty to push for a rush on all collected DNA evidence from your crime scene, as well as the Marina apartment and Lisa Williams's badass Porsche. If they are not one person, we should find a second profile somewhere, right? Something? Anything? There's no way you don't leave a trace of evidence behind when in your personal vehicle.

"Lastly—and I've been thinking about this a lot—if she was killed elsewhere and put in the vehicle to make it look like she had driven there, for whatever reason, and the dead woman is Lisa Williams—*not* Marilynn Chaney—then there shouldn't be any evidence of Williams in that car, other than her body and her blood. Her head and hands would have been removed elsewhere, if you guys have it right. Yet, Gentry found Williams's prints on that registration."

He looked at me. "Dickie, how the hell do you get fingerprints on anything when you don't have any hands?"

Before I continued, he answered his own question. "You don't. Lisa Williams was in that car before she was murdered. Given that the prints are on the registration, I would say she was in the car many times before she was murdered. In fact, I would say—as Lopes surmised—that she is the owner of that car. She—Lisa Williams—is Marilynn Chaney.

"Finally, if Lopes is right, there shouldn't even be hair belonging to Williams in that car. But there should be hair from our missing person in that car, right? Marilynn Chaney should be all over that car—hair, prints, DNA. But I bet we don't come up with anything other than Williams. I think Lopes has it right."

The three of us sat quietly for a moment in contemplation. I was thinking about the two women, the DNA, hair, latent prints, a woman living two lives, or two women with a connection. Ray was likely processing everything Floyd had said in similar fashion. Floyd had likely moved on and was wondering about lunch or what the hell Mongo was up to or thinking about some reporter with pretty eyes.

"When are they going to have results, partner?" Ray asked. "Did they say?"

Floyd's hazel eyes darted back and forth from me to Ray as he answered. "I don't know. They know it's a priority case, but I didn't push a rush. Nor did I ask. Do you want me to ask?"

"Yeah, partner, if you wouldn't mind. I have to be honest, this is intriguing, this idea of it being just the one woman living two lives. I'd like to know about that as soon as possible. So, yes, if you wouldn't mind, Floyd, maybe get an answer to their ETA and urge them to expedite. They know—I've previously told them—that the sheriff is keeping his eye on this case. That should be more than enough motivation. If not, we'll have Joe make a call."

I nodded, agreeing with Ray. Floyd stood and faced the two of us in a fighter's stance, absent raised fists. It was his natural stance from years of training and practice in the gym and near anything that reflected his image. He looked at us smugly and said, "Okay, bitches, I'm out of here!"

He walked away shadow-boxing and mumbling: "Where the hell is Mongo? Has anyone seen my Mongo?"

———

LATER THAT DAY WHEN I HAD FINISHED REVIEWING THE CALL LOGS FROM the cell phone of Maria Lopez, I typed an affidavit of probable cause and its accompanying search warrant and drove to East Los Angeles Municipal Court. I walked into Department 3 on the second floor and paused inside the heavy wooden double doors to remove my hat. The Honorable Judge Porfirio Vazquez peered at me over reading glasses that sat on the end of his nose and were secured by a chain around his neck. With two fingers he motioned for me to approach even though a trial was in progress and a witness was being questioned. The prosecutor, an attractive Hispanic lady in her thirties wearing a bright red dress and black nylons, stopped her line of questioning as I approached the bench. The jurors seemed distracted by it as well. The judge motioned for the prosecutor to continue, and she did.

Judge Vasquez received the warrant and affidavit over the front of his bench and raised his right hand slightly as a cue for me to do the same. The questioning continued in the background while the judge accepted my silent oath and carelessly flipped through the pages I had handed him. He scribbled his name on the appropriate pages of my search warrant and affidavit. He had signed dozens of my warrants over the years and no longer scrutinized my probable cause declarations. I had also testified before his court on many cases. He knew of my assignment and trusted that if I sought a warrant while he was in trial, it was urgent. I quietly thanked him, wishing to explain that the other courts were now dark, there were no other judges available in the courthouse, and I didn't have time to get downtown. He likely knew it anyway. Judge Vasquez only nodded while handing back the stack of papers which was now disheveled and no longer clipped together. I walked through the two sets of doors and stopped in the hallway to reorganize the search warrant and affidavit.

I decided to forego filing the papers and drawing a warrant number from the clerk. I would do it later when I presented Judge Vasquez with a Return to Search Warrant. I didn't have the time nor inclination to worry about clerical matters late on a Friday afternoon. I returned to the office and faxed the telephone search warrant to the Custodian of Records at Verizon Wireless. That completed, I set the file and evidence-held cell phone aside. That was all I could expect to accomplish until Monday, absent a more urgent cause such as a hostage situation, a kidnapping, or a matter of national security. At least as far as Verizon Wireless was concerned. For us, weekends were no different than Mondays or Wednesdays, other than the welcomed absence of administrators.

I returned to find the bureau had once again dwindled down to the few of us who had too much work or nothing better to do. My eyelids were heavy as I stared across the sea of desks, focused on only the far window showing a darkening sky. I leaned back in my chair and rested my head against the wall behind me, pulled my hat forward to shield my eyes, and drifted off to sleep again.

LEONARD LIT A CIGARETTE, CRUMPLED THE EMPTY PACKAGE, AND TOSSED it onto the coffee table where his feet were propped. He was bored. In prison all he could think about was freedom, but it was overrated. Free to do what? The only thing good about being outside was the predator to prey ratio. Inside, he was always on guard. Two out of every three men were predators and if given the chance, they'd cut you or stab you or choke you to death for your clean towel or newer tennis shoes. Out here, predators were a drop in the bucket. The sea was full of fish and you rarely saw sharks. Leonard could roam freely and confidently without fear of his fellow man. Even if he crossed paths with another predator, there would be no reason to fear him. Predators only prey on other predators when that's all there is to choose from, or when they are forced to do so as a manner of survival. Never for a wallet or tennis shoes or sex.

Now he wished he hadn't killed the goddamn Russkies. He needed a different car after his encounter with *beach boy,* the tanned and somewhat buff boat washer, obviously a cop like the other dipshit. Leonard couldn't risk driving back into that neighborhood in his Taurus. He wished he knew how to steal one. Well, he could cut some bitch's throat and steal hers. That would be the way to do it, he supposed, when you didn't know how to hot-wire a car. Hell, he didn't even know how to break into one unless he smashed a window. Nobody wanted to drive around in a stolen car with a smashed window though. He wondered about the car lot and the two dead Russians, and he pictured them rotting in the trailer and stinking up the neighborhood. Not likely, he decided; they had probably been discovered and there was no way Leonard was going back to a murder scene for a car. Though if they were still there, he wouldn't mind going back just to see how they would look and smell now, and to see the bugs crawling over them and getting fat on their flesh. Everyone had to make a living, even maggots.

He puffed a series of smoke rings toward the ceiling and thought about Whitey. If Whitey were with him, life would be perfect. They could work together and hang out together and do whatever they wanted, whenever they wanted to do it. But Whitey would never be free, and once again Leonard pondered if he wouldn't be happier back in prison. He sat up against the soft, worn couch cushion and mashed his cigarette into an ashtray that needed to be emptied. Then he flopped back and stared at the ceiling until he fell asleep.

———

I awoke to Lopes pulling a chair up next to me. When I lifted the front of my hat and looked into his weary eyes he said, "Didn't mean to wake you."

"No worries, buddy," I said, sitting up and trying to collect my wits. "Well?"

He shrugged. "She's basically in a coma and living on machines. They don't know. It doesn't look good." That hung in the air for a few moments. "Come on, man, let's go get a cup."

I followed Lopes into the kitchen and we drained the remaining coagulated black liquid from the bottom of a scorched glass coffee decanter, its brown handle indicating the contents were *leaded*. There were three carafes at the coffee station and only one with an orange handle. It was for the administrators, or maybe secretaries. Nobody working cases would settle for decaf. He started another pot, dumping the old grounds into a tall metal trash container and refilling the filtered basket with mounding scoops of Folgers. As he did, I told him about the phone, that I had gone through and made a list of all calls—incoming, outgoing, and missed—from the call log. And that I had written a search warrant for phone records and served it on Verizon, adding that I didn't expect anything back until at least Monday. I told Lopes that Floyd was running full steam with the one woman Lisa Williams/Marilynn Chaney theory, thinking maybe changing topics would be beneficial for us both.

He watched the coffee dripping into its carafe without responding for a moment. Finally, he looked up at me and said, "You want to go to Pelican with me?"

"When?"

"Tonight."

I glanced at my watch; it was nearly eight now. "Can we get the plane?"

"Probably not this late on a Friday," he said, "but we can go commercial. Take a redeye and get some sleep on the plane, be at the prison bright and early so I can beat the sleep out of Spooky's beady little brown eyes."

"Why not? I don't have anything else planned for the weekend."

"It would be good to have you up there with me when I wrap my hands around that little asshole's neck. I want some answers on this deal with Maria, and if he doesn't have any, he had better fucking get some, the little prick."

"I'd be happy to go along, but I doubt you'll need my help in there."

"I might need you to keep me from killing him."

"Okay, let's do it. You going to make a call, let them know we're coming up?"

"No. I'm going to drop in and surprise him. I don't know that I can trust any of the guards to keep quiet about it. I don't want him warned. I want to walk in and look him in his eyes; that will tell me if he knows or not. If he does, you're going to have to keep me from killing him. Got it?"

I nodded, and we filled our cups with fresh coffee and walked silently back to our desks.

# 33

THE NEXT MORNING we stood in a large room that echoed with our every footstep or movement. Neither of us spoke though both of us were perplexed by the greeting we had just received. When Lopes spoke through the intercom, presumably to those who sat behind a wall of mirrored glass, he identified us and stated we were there to interview Victor "Spooky" Hernandez in C-block. There had been silence for a few moments before a male voice instructed us to wait there, that someone would be out to speak with us.

I didn't know what Lopes was thinking but I knew I didn't like the reception we had received. Having interviewed hundreds of inmates in custody facilities throughout the nation, I was familiar with odd occurrences and nothing surprised me anymore. But this had a different feel to it, something I couldn't pinpoint and didn't like. I could tell by the look in Lopes's eyes he didn't like it either.

After what seemed to be half an hour but was only five minutes, a heavy door was keyed open and a man in casual attire—khaki pants and a polo shirt—walked through and immediately made eye contact with Lopes. The logo on his shirt identified him as a gang investigator for the California Department of Corrections, Institutional Gang Unit. The corrections department logo features the scales of justice, a torch, and equal parts of sea, mountains, green pastures, and the big city. California was the perfect geographic location for quality living. At one time.

Lopes nodded and the short, stocky investigator—a white man with a gray mustache and goatee against a tanned narrow face—called him by name. "Davey, how are you?"

"What's up, Morgan? The fuck's going on here?"

The investigator glanced at me but didn't introduce himself. Lopes was otherwise focused. The man called Morgan said, "Spooky's dead. He was found yesterday morning in his cell."

Lopes glanced at me with intensity in his eyes. He looked back at Morgan. "Murdered?"

Morgan nodded. "His cellie strangled him. An old associate of his, Juan Torres. They were supposed to be compatible, Lopes. I'm sorry."

"Joker. He's from Hazard too," Lopes replied. "That's a hit, from the mob. Joker wouldn't kill Spooky if he had a choice. Those two have been homies since they were little kids."

"We're working it, but nobody is talking."

"How fucking rare," Lopes said. He turned and stared off at the horizon beyond the glass doors and the three of us stood silent. He turned back and said to Morgan, "I want to talk to Joker."

Morgan shook his head, saying, "No can do, Lopes. I'm sorry man, that's down from the warden. It isn't going to happen."

Lopes huffed and turned to walk out. I shrugged at the man I had never been introduced to and turned to follow Lopes. Outside under the coastal sunlight and blue skies, walking rapidly toward our rental car, I said, "What now?"

He didn't look back and didn't answer. We rode to the airport in silence and dropped the rental. Finally, he spoke. "Well, we have three hours before our flight back. Let's get through security and I'll buy you a beer."

I glanced at my watch. It was a quarter till nine and breakfast sounded better, but I wasn't going to say so.

IT WAS MID AFTERNOON WHEN LOPES AND I WALKED THROUGH THE BACK door and into the squad room to find Rich Farris and his partner, Lizzy, saying goodbye to Ted Hampton and his floppy-eared hound he calls Rocket for reasons that escape me. Lopes veered off toward the front desk without speaking to anyone. I assumed he would be checking the medical status of Maria Lopez and the progress of the investigation. I greeted Ted and patted Rocket on the head before they walked out the back door. Rich Farris sat waiting.

"Well, how did it go?" I asked.

He bobbed his head in a combination of shaking and nodding as if the result had been a mixed bag of good and bad, or better than nothing, or worth a try but probably not anything that was going to solve the case of the strangled Asian girl in San Fernando. He said, "Well, we think we know where he parked, that's about it."

"Oh?"

"Yeah, the dog picked up a scent trail from the bedroom where she was killed, followed it downstairs, out the back door, around through a side gate, down the sidewalk to the middle of the street where the sonofabitch just stopped. He looked left and right, walked in a few circles, and then looked up at Ted like, *This is the end of the line, my brother*."

"Interesting."

"Yeah. So, we knocked on some doors, but nobody remembers seeing anything suspicious or made note of any cars that didn't belong in the neighborhood. Most of the adults were working and the few kids we spoke with just shrugged. They didn't know shit, probably came home and started playing video games and eating chips and picking their noses."

"You think he got in a car there."

Rich Farris nodded. "There was a cigarette butt right where the scent trail ended. It was about ten feet from the curb, right about where someone would step out of a vehicle and drop a cigarette on the ground as they walked away. Ted collected scent from it and said Joe's dog can do a scent lineup or some shit, see if the lighter and the cigarette have corresponding scent. We'll bag the butt for DNA but we might wait until we see what the dogs do on the scent."

My mind raced. I could hardly contain myself with the obvious question, but I didn't want to interrupt. As soon as he finished, I asked, "What type of cigarette, Rich?"

He shrugged. "I don't know, just some kind of non-filtered, probably a Camel."

Could I have been so lucky? No, I'm never that lucky. But I also couldn't talk myself out of the possibility, even though I had no way to make it work in my head. How could I possibly make a connection between a young girl being murdered in San Fernando and my stalker in Burbank? It was a long shot. "When's Joe coming in for the scent lineup?"

"He's on his way. Ted said he was going to go get a burger for him and Rocket, said they were both starving. I guess that hound dog eats hamburgers."

"Probably just cheeseburger snacks," I joked. "Listen, Rich, I want to try something when they come in, if you don't mind."

"What's that?"

"I've got some similar cigarettes from another case I'm working. I'd kind of like to have the dogs sniff to see if there's a match between those and the one you've got, or that lighter."

"Yeah, no problem, Dickie. What do you have, another little girl murder?"

I shook my head. "No, it's probably unrelated. Nothing even similar, other than the smokes. It seems to me we don't see these non-filtered cigs very often. But still, it's probably completely unrelated."

Rich nodded but his eyes said he knew I wasn't telling him the truth.

"Okay, Dickie. I'll shout at you when they get here."

I found Lopes standing in silence at the front desk while an investigator was busy on the phone. "Any word?"

"He's checking with the hospital now," Lopes replied, nodding toward the investigator on the phone in front of us. "Nothing from Martinez or Blair on the investigation, no workable information. Nobody saw shit. Two shooters from the pattern of spent casings, all nine-millimeter. What's up with Farris and the dog? What do they have going?"

"He's working that case from San Fernando, the little girl."

Lopes nodded.

"I'm going to give them a hand doing a scent lineup here in a bit, and

I've got some follow-up to do on our Santa Clarita case until then, if you don't need me for anything."

"Nah, man, thanks."

I went back to my desk and opened the bottom drawer where two envelopes were buried in the back beneath some files. I pulled them out, opened each and peeked inside to make sure they were the envelopes with the cigarette butts I had collected from the street outside my apartment. They were. I kept one and secured the other back inside the drawer.

Farris called out, "Back lot, Dickie," as he passed through the door to the parking lot with Lizzy on his heels.

Evidence in hand, I crossed the squad room and followed them out back where Ted stood talking to Joe, who held a yellow lab at his side on its leash. We shook hands and I looked at Ted. "I have something I would like to include in the lineup, if you don't mind."

"Sure, what do you have?"

I opened the envelope and positioned it so that Ted could see inside. "A couple of similar butts from another case. Can you pull scent off those? I need to keep them for DNA though, so . . ."

"No worries."

Ted retrieved his scent collection device from his van. It was basically a battery-powered, hand-held vacuum like a Dust Buster. A sterile pad that functioned as a filter would be placed between the inlet and the collection chamber, and it was from this pad that scent would be introduced to the dog. Ted asked me to hold the envelope containing the cigarette butts. He turned the vacuum on and held the mouth of it against the envelope's opening. With gloved hands, he removed the newly made scent pad and placed it in a Ziplock bag but didn't seal it closed. He handed me the baggie and said, "Go put it out there somewhere with the others."

There were six similar plastic bags strewn ten feet apart across the mostly empty parking lot. I walked to them and looked back at Joe and Ted and Rich Farris and Lizzy who all watched from fifty feet away. I said, "Hey, don't let Joe or that mutt watch, I don't want any cheating."

Joe laughed, then turned so that he and his dog were faced away. I quickly rearranged a couple of bags and put mine in the middle. Once ready, I gave the okay. Joe introduced his dog to scent that had been collected from the cigarette lighter. He then took the dog to the field of baggies containing scent pads and asked the canine to check them one at a time. The dog showed no interest in the first three bags, and then after sniffing the one that I had placed in the middle, he sat and looked up at his handler. Joe praised him and threw a tennis ball across the parking lot. The dog ran and fetched it; that was the reward.

Joe looked at me. "That was yours, I take it?"

I nodded.

"It's a match." He looked at Rich Farris and said, "Okay, let's do yours next."

The same process took place with similar results. Joe's Labrador retriever had indicated that the scent from the cigarette lighter found inside the dead girl's residence contained scent that corresponded with that from the cigarette butt found outside of the crime scene, as well as with scent from the butts left by my stalker. It was the first time I had ever witnessed a successful identification process and didn't rejoice. In fact, I hoped to not throw up, as I was suddenly overwhelmed with a sick feeling, a rapid heartbeat, and a rising body temperature. A serial killer was stalking me.

---

THAT NIGHT WE HAD A BRIEFING THAT ONLY INCLUDED MYSELF, RAY, Floyd, and Mongo. Lopes was nowhere to be found, and we didn't bother him. He likely had returned to the hospital or maybe had gone home for some sleep and to freshen up. Lt. Black was not around, and we didn't expect to see him on a Saturday evening. Same for the captain, to my great delight.

For the first ten minutes we talked about the Maria Lopez shooting. It was the topic *du jour*, so I told everything I knew about the victim, the shooting, and to a lesser degree, the connection—or *relationship*—between Maria Lopez and Davey Lopes. When finished, Floyd said, "Well, if they need any help on that case, we're available. I mean, either way I'm lying about a shitload of overtime this weekend."

I then told them about Spooky being killed up at Pelican, and how Lopes and I had gone up to maybe get some answers on the Maria Lopez shooting. I told them Lopes was convinced it was mob related. Nobody commented.

Ray took over and recapped what Floyd had told us the day before as far as his theory on Williams and Chaney being the same person. Mongo had not been there for the conversation, though it was likely Floyd had discussed his thoughts with him. Still, Ray wanted to hash through it again, and as he did he checked off parts of a list he had before him and added notes to the bottom of it.

"What about your cousin, Mongo?" Ray asked.

"That deal is all Russian mafia shit. The guy that got whacked was vin switching and cold-plating cars and selling them to illegals, or people who need untraceable cars. Probably a wetback did him in."

Cold-plating cars rattled around in my head as Ray said, "Okay, so nothing of interest. Oh, how was he killed, this Russian guy?"

"Had his throat cut by a knife, nearly decapitated him. But the woman had her throat hacked to pieces, not sliced. Probably two different killers, completely different methods."

Now I had *cold-plating* and *decapitated* both rolling around in my head.

Ray said, "Definitely nothing to do with our deal then, right?"

Mongo affirmed it with a slight nod. Floyd was looking at him. Everyone looked at me when I said, "Not so fast."

And then: "First, I wouldn't assume there are two killers based on what Mongo described as far as the murders. One may have been more spontaneous than the other, or the killer had more of a fight with one of the victims than he had had with the other. Since there were two people killed, maybe the first was caught off guard and was quick and easy, and the second was combative."

"Okay," Ray said, "but the point is, this doesn't have any overlap with our case."

"Except the cold-plated car, and maybe the near-decap."

I could see he hadn't previously considered it. I looked over and saw the same expression on Mongo's face. Floyd was with me; his relaxed expression confirmed it. He likely had reached similar conclusions before I mapped it out. We seemed to always be on the same page, even now after a year's sabbatical and no longer being partnered.

"I don't like coincidences," I said, and looked to see Floyd nodding in agreement now, "and the fact that two suits showed up at Chaney's has bothered us throughout this investigation. One, because we don't know if they're feds or mobsters—"

"I've said mobsters all along," Floyd interjected.

"—and two, the car they drove was cold-plated. Now, I don't want to get way out in left field, but I need you guys to hear me out on this and follow along. You all know that one of the cars driven by whoever the hell it is watching me is also cold-plated. I hadn't filled you in on this, but Chuck saw him at the house yesterday." I looked at Mongo and said, "Chuck owns the main house of the apartment I live in, and he and his wife are both retired deputies."

I looked over at Floyd who was frowning, probably because this is the first he'd heard of this. "Yeah, the same guy was watching the house yesterday. Chuck got a pretty good look at him as he drove past. Interestingly, he said it was a white guy, maybe forty, blond hair. Didn't get a plate but it had to be the same guy. He had been parked in the same location where I had seen him previously. Chuck yelled out at the guy when he drove past and the guy took off like a bat out of hell. He called to tell me about it, and I told him the whole story about being watched. But it gets worse.

"Rich Farris had the dog alert on a cigarette butt on the street at the end of a scent trail, up in San Fernando on that Asian girl murder. It was non-filtered, like the ones I found after this asshole had been around my place. So, they do a scent lineup today, and I throw my hat in the ring, have them check those butts I recovered. I'll be a sonofabitch if that lab of Joe's didn't ID them. Same scent on butts at my house and on the lighter and butt from the Asian girl murder."

"Unreal," Floyd said.

I nodded. "Look, I can't wrap my head around this, but when Mongo said 'cold-plated car,' something grabbed me. Then, when he described the 'near decapitation,' I about lost it. I mean, can you imagine if this is one guy out there doing all of this killing? To nearly take someone's head off with a knife, that puts that asshole in the ballpark of sawing off someone's head and hands. Same type of person. And those people aren't just all over the place."

Ray said, "Man, what are you thinking then, partner?"

"I don't know, Ray. Maybe a professional, and all these are contracts being filled."

"Wait," Floyd said, "but the Asian girl was strangled."

"Yeah, I know. But, maybe . . . I don't know, maybe a pro has several ways he likes to do his hits. Maybe he's a pro that does hits but gets off on little girls on the side, I don't know."

"But then why would he be watching you," Ray asked, "if this is all one guy, and he's a pro?"

I was shaking my head as I drew in a deep breath. "I don't know, Ray. The only thing at all I can think of is if it's related to Regalado, the asshole I killed a year ago, and his family. Maybe they put something out on me. I hit up Lopes and he didn't find any connection to the Mexican mafia, but he did say they were down with White Fence, and that White Fence puts in a lot of work for the mob. I don't think it's too far a stretch to say they asked for a favor."

"But the guy watching you is white, you said."

"I know, Ray . . . I know. Some of it doesn't work."

"And our victim in Santa Clarita is white," Ray said, "and higher class at that. It doesn't look like Mexican mob stuff to me. And then the car lot guy is a Russian. This thing is all over the place, and although there are some overlapping suggestions, it doesn't add up. Plus, partner, I'll be real honest with you, I don't put a lot of faith in those dogs."

Maybe he was right. When you said it aloud it didn't make sense; there were too many holes in it. But then there were too many connectors too: the cold-plated cars, the decapitation, the scent. I wasn't convinced, but I wasn't ready to dismiss it either. I said, "What about throwing my cigarettes into the DNA mix? Have them tested against—" and I realized we didn't have DNA from a suspect on any of the other cases. "Never mind."

I sat deflated for a minute. Floyd said, "Wait, you may be onto something."

I perked up. What had I missed? "What?"

"Let's submit your evidence for DNA and see if we get a profile. If that asshole is in CODIS, the pieces might fall together. Think about it, we get a CODIS hit, we'd have a photo, prints, criminal history, associations, locations—the whole shebang. Let's ID this asshole and work it backwards, see if he connects to Regalados, see if he likes little girls. Maybe he has skin crimes on his rap sheet and he'd show up as a registered sex offender. Let's see if he's connected to Russians for any reason, or to the Mexican mafia by chance. Shit, Lopes may know the asshole, or know more about any association between Mexicans and Russians, if there is one. I think you might be onto something. It might also be way off course, but what does it hurt to try?"

"How? How do we submit the DNA on something that has no case number?"

Floyd laughed. "What, suddenly you're worried about the rules? Buy me a beer after and I'll drive you up to the lab and we'll tell Gentry to get it done on the sly. It will only matter if the parts come together, and then we'll worry about procedure."

Ray was rubbing his head and had a concerned look on his face. He leaned back in his chair and exhaled a heavy breath. "I don't know, guys."

"Trust me," Floyd said. "We'll keep you clean on the whole deal. We don't have time to fuck around with policy when someone's trying to kill Dickie."

And with that he stood as if there would be no further discussion. Mongo followed him out the door.

I looked over at Ray, wanting to apologize but the words escaped me.

He said, "I'm not sure if I'm glad Joe Black wasn't here tonight, or if I wish that he had been."

I smiled. "Don't worry. Floyd does crazy shit all the time, and he always lands on his feet. You watch."

# 34

TWENTY MINUTES LATER Floyd and I were driving out of the lot together in his black Ford Taurus, but he went the wrong way, assuming we were going to the crime lab.

"Where are you taking me?"

"The crime lab, and then out for a burger and beer, but you're buying."

"Do you need directions? I can tell you how to get to the lab, if you need me to."

"We have to run by my house first."

"Oh, well that's a bit out of the way, like thirty miles and two hours traveling."

"We're on overtime, Dickie, in a county car that runs on county gas. Don't you worry about it."

I removed my hat and stretched my arm across the back of his seat. "Okay, I don't have anything better to do. Plus, I haven't seen the kids for a while. Have at it, pal."

He glanced over and smiled.

After a minute passed: "Okay, I can't stand it. Why are we going to your place?"

"I need to pick up a couple of things."

"Like?"

"Well, BDU's—camouflaged of course—combat boots, spotting scope, extra mags for the H&K, my scoped AR-15, maybe a tomahawk."

"Are we going to the crime lab, or Afghanistan?"

"Crime lab, Dickie. And then your place. I'm staying with you the rest of the weekend until we figure this out. I was thinking of having you stay with me, but we have Chuck and Patti to consider also—"

"And Elvis."

"—and Elvis. If there's a pro looking to kill you, I say we kill him first, fast, and repeatedly."

"Kill him repeatedly?"

"Yes. Repeatedly. As in multiple times. A multiplicity, a plethora, a conglomeration of various and assorted methods, manners, and fashions, with an overabundance of glee in our hearts. Kill him dead, deader, and deadest, so that we send a message to the next sonofabitch who gets the idea to commit such un-Christian-like dastardly deeds upon us."

"Why the BDU's?" as if everything else made perfect sense.

"In case we need to hide in the bushes, Dickie. Jesus."

---

WE DROPPED THE EVIDENCE AT THE CRIME LAB WITH A TECHNICIAN WHO had the night duty. Floyd asked that he put it on Gentry's desk with a note to call him ASAP for direction. We pulled away from the curb and made a U-turn on Beverly Boulevard heading west.

"Where now?" I asked.

"Tommy's. I told you I'd let you buy me a burger and beer. Well, let's grab a Tommy's; I have a box of beer in the trunk. It'll be like the old days."

"Jesus, man, we aren't twenty-five anymore. That shit will kill a couple old men like us."

"Where is your sense of adventure, Dickie? Besides, if anything's going to kill us, it's going to be boredom. You're driving me insane."

I chuckled. "Okay, you're the boss. What'd Cindy say about you moving in with me for a couple days?"

"She started to give me some shit until I gave it to her straight."

"Straight."

"Yeah, Dickie. You know, I'm seldom serious about anything. On the rare occasion I am, it has an effect on people. It's something you should try. Lighten up a little, then, when you get serious, people will pay attention. Nobody pays attention to you cause you're pissed off all of the time. Everyone just thinks it's normal shit. Anyway, Cindy saw it on my face when I told her there might be a contract on you and I wasn't going to leave you alone to get yourself killed. She started to say, 'Bring him here,' and I explained the Chuck and Patti thing—"

"And Elvis."

"—and Elvis, and so now she understands."

There was a heaviness in the ensuing silence. Then Floyd lightened up. "Besides, I told her you'd sleep through your own fucking murder if I wasn't there to wake you."

---

Leonard had driven past the used car dealer and saw that it now appeared abandoned, not a single vehicle left on the lot. There was crime scene tape on the gate and again at the office. The dead Russkies had been discovered. He fondly recalled the feel of slicing the man's throat, and the final spasms of his body and gasps for air. It must be awful to die that way, he thought, but there were worse ways to go. He imagined a sharp knife wouldn't cause much pain, but the shock of knowing it was all over would be surreal. Knowing you were a dead man and there was nothing you could do about it. Seeing your life blood shoot across the room at a dumb, big-titted blonde, who sat chomping her gum, and knowing that bitch was the last thing you'd ever see.

Now, she, on the other hand, had died a violent death. Leonard smiled as he pictured himself stabbing her repeatedly in the throat until finally he hit the jugular and made it happen. He preferred to be more kind in killing, such as the way he had let the little girl go quietly in the still of the afternoon. It had been such a pleasant experience, for them both, he was sure. It was very pleasurable when he was able to explore her body thoroughly in the privacy of their moments together. He remembered the photos on the phone and thought he would look at them again soon, when he wasn't driving. The idea of it thrilled him.

The bloody scenes had their own appeal, but he relished the violence more when the person was deserving, as was the case with the two stupid Russian gypsies who had ripped him off with the piece of shit car they sold him. It was far less pleasant to employ such violence against less deserving souls, those who were destined for death but not necessarily justifiably so. Some people had to die to benefit others, Leonard knew. Especially now that he had gone professional.

Take the hooker. What a lovely lady she had seemed to be, all the way up to the moment he sawed off her head. Which had been oddly intriguing, and made for an interesting experience. He found that his knife cut cleanly through the tissue and muscle, and when it hit bone, with just a slight adjustment in its trajectory, he was able to work the knife through the cartilage and discs. When the head came off, he couldn't believe it. He laughed out loud as he now recalled it, picturing himself holding the head by its hair, the two of them looking each other directly in the eyes. Hers were wide open, intense. The thought of kissing the headless woman had amused him, so he did it. The hands had come off in similar fashion, just a little maneuvering and *voila*, the knife sliced cleanly through. He didn't like handling the woman's hands but didn't mind holding her head by a lock of hair. He now pondered that phenomenon but had no answer. The left hand was to be mailed back, and it was. But why? He didn't know. It occurred to him that perhaps the client wanted proof of a wedding band, or to see the absence thereof. But there was no wedding band, only a tattoo where a wedding band would be worn, and it had nothing to do with matrimony. It was a simple word surrounded by two red hearts: *Sisters*. The remaining parts were to be discarded, which was easy enough. The head and other hand were accompanied by several large rocks and placed in a suitcase and tossed into the nearby ocean. That was all that had been required of him. That and mailing back the one hand. Two men had arranged the rest, collecting the body and her car and driving off in tandem in her car and theirs. The dead hooker rode in her trunk wrapped in plastic. He had wondered what they would do with her but dismissed it as unnecessary knowledge. His job was completed. Next.

Now this cop. Jesus, this had been a nightmare all around. And now when he needed a car, the fucking Russians were dead and all their cars were gone. Leonard figured the cars would be at a police impound where they would discover that they were all stolen, and then see that their deaths had been justified. Nobody liked thieves.

He dropped down onto Santa Monica Boulevard. Boys Town, where the sissies hustled rich men who had grown tired of the old hags they'd married and could no longer get a young woman. Boys were easy, no bullshit. Twenty bucks and the little junkies would get you off and they never even tried having a conversation. Some of them were predators though and would rip the men off because they knew the men would never report it to the cops. Leonard normally avoided those boys. Not tonight though. Tonight, he felt like teaching one a lesson. He would find a predator—he could spot them easily by the look in their eyes—and that would be the one he would date. And kill. It was Saturday night, and this was a day off, a night for selfish pleasures. Tomorrow he would be back to work finding a new car. And then he would get back on track, back to hunting the pig.

---

IN THE APARTMENT, FLOYD SAID I NEEDED TO SPRUCE THINGS UP A BIT IF I were planning to stay, make it feel more like home. He also said if I were going to have a woman guest, he would recommend buying some plants, or a fish. He said it would make it seem like I was civilized and mature, give a woman the impression I wasn't the giant asshole he knew me to be. He said, "Look, a couple Bonsai trees and maybe a salt-water tank, but don't fill it with sharks. Get something pretty that doesn't live to kill other shit. It's all about presentation, Dickie."

"Bonsai trees?"

"Yeah, you know, those Japanese miniatures, little trees the size of plants. You can prune them this way or that, make them grow up or flow out to the sides. Oh yeah, Dickie, there's all kinds of things you can do with them. I've always wanted one. It'd be cool to have a couple as a hobby, something to do indoors when it's raining or a serial killer's watching your house and you can't go out. I'd probably end up pruning mine into a gigantic penis though, accidentally. That would be my luck. I'd trim a little here and there and the next thing you know, I'd have this giant green erection on the coffee table. Cindy would be cocking her head left and right, trying to figure out what the hell it was supposed to be.

Maybe, if I do ever get one, I'll get me a little Japanese girl to take care of it, kind of a house girl. Tell Cindy she's just here for the tree, honey. What do you think?"

"You're not right in the head, man."

"Right, evidenced by the fact I'm having a sleepover with you. Two grown men spending the night together hoping to kill someone. Hey, speaking of you trying to change your image, how's that going with the shrink? Are you two dating yet? I think she'd have a whole different outlook on your mental stability if she saw you were into Bonsais, or at least had a fish."

I was shaking my head. "Dude, honestly, you kill me. No, I haven't got anything planned with Dr. James—"

"Oh, it's *Dr. James* now, is it? Not *the shrink.*"

"—she's my doctor, and I'm pretty sure there's rules about that for her. Besides, she's out of my league."

He laughed. "They're never out of your league, Dickie, not unless you let them think they are. Next time you see her, tell her, 'Hey, doc, how about we get a beer and I'll introduce you to my Bonsai tree.' She'd love that. Worse she could say is no, and if she says no, she'd tell you there's rules against her dating a patient. It's not like she's going to tell you you're ugly or fat or have bad breath. Hey, let's kill the lights in here and have a couple beers on the balcony. If he doesn't show up by two or three, we'll take shifts sleeping."

# 35

AN HOUR BEFORE dawn Sunday morning, Leonard drove his newly acquired vehicle through the empty parking structure not far from where he stayed in downtown Los Angeles. The area was currently impacted by the Urban Renewal Revitalization Project, the queer had told him. There were abandoned, demolished, and under-construction buildings, homes, parking structures and more, all over the area. The old, crime-ridden, poverty-stricken, gang-infested neighbor-hoods from downtown Los Angeles to Hollywood were being rejuvenated and attracting new businesses—including clubs and restaurants—as well as investors, residents, tourists, and hipsters on the hunt for new nightlife crazes. There were new parks with walking and jogging paths and water features that gave people a sense of tranquility. As if fresh buildings and neon signs displaced a quarter-of-a-million gang members who kill each other and random Angelenos when not raping and robbing them or supplying them with drugs.

The queer had pulled alongside Leonard at a stoplight. He had licked his red lips and asked if Leonard was looking for a good time, and if he really wanted to pay one of these street hustler queers when there were lonely, legit gays who gave it up for free. Leonard hadn't spotted the right one yet, the type he had been cruising for, so he quickly considered and then accepted the offer. The queer appeared fragile and weak, a thin young man with slicked hair and the face of a boy; he probably had AIDS. He was driving some sort of sporty little car, black with tan leather interior. An AIDS-ridden trust-fund fag, or maybe he still lived with his rich dad and a mom who thrived on Valium and red wine. He was perfect. Leonard would satisfy his desire to snuff the life from another and at the same time resolve his need for a new car.

"What do you have in mind?" Leonard had asked. The boy said he'd show him a good time and said to follow him; he'd take him to a place nearby where they could be alone. So Leonard had done just that, smiling all the way, knowing it would be him who showed the queer a good time. His last good time.

Leonard might have let the boy pleasure him on the top of the vacated parking structure had he not feared the boy was sick with the AIDS. He was sick with something, and Leonard wasn't a desperate man. He had learned to live without family or friends and he had never had a relationship or any meaningful companionship other than his cellie, Whitey Blanchard. Sex was easy to forego, easier than food, water, booze, and cigarettes. He lit a Camel as he turned onto Sunset Boulevard and drove toward downtown. The streets were empty now, the night finally over even for the most enthusiastic of revelers. Leonard thought back to the moment on top of the structure when he and the queer first embraced outside of their cars and then Leonard clamped both hands on the boy's fragile neck and began squeezing. The boy's eyes were wide open yet soft and pleading as he gasped and resisted, but only slightly. His weak body had been no match for Leonard, who was much stronger than he appeared. The distant sounds of cars and jovial voices from the streets below had replaced the sounds of choking and gasping and gurgling as the boy finally slumped onto the hood of the car. Leonard had carefully lowered him to the cool concrete and after another minute—to assure his death—released his grip of the boy's neck. He had then leaned against the car and lit a cigarette as he looked across a blanket of softly glowing lights that ended downtown where blinking red lights marked the tops of skyscrapers.

Leonard contemplated the idea of switching cars and leaving the dead boy in the piece of shit sedan he had bought from the gypsy. The cops would find both—the boy and the car—and the boy would then be thought to have murdered the Russian and his girlfriend, the bottle-bleached blonde who had hardly whimpered as Leonard punched the blade of his knife into her throat. Leonard had admired her resolve, and as he thought more about the way he had efficiently killed them both, he realized he didn't want the fag to be credited with their deaths. He dropped his cigarette and lit another, filling both lungs to capacity before allowing the smoke to drift from his nose and mouth. His face muscles relaxed and gave way to a budding smile brought on by a revelation: the cops would never know the boy was a queer, if they never knew who the boy was.

With that, Leonard had set to work using his recently acquired skill of removing the head and hands of a fresh corpse with his sharp knife. It was easier this time than it had been with the woman. The hooker. The great looking broad with expensive jewelry and a delightful fresh scent that seemed natural to him. He allowed the blood to drain from the queer, and then the newly severed parts were placed in a shopping bag Leonard found in the back seat of the dead boy's car. The bag was then stored in the trunk for the drive south. He would bypass the city and head down the Long Beach Freeway, straight for the ocean, where he would say goodbye to gay boy but not kiss him because he was certain the kid had AIDS.

Leonard stalled the car while turning onto the freeway onramp. It was the third time. He had never driven a car with a standard transmission before, but knew he could easily learn to do so. Like learning martial arts or how to make *pruno* from fruit cocktail and warm water in a plastic bag in your cell. He pushed in the clutch and restarted the car. This time, he gave it more gas as he slowly released the clutch. The engine whined but then the transmission caught, and the car jumped forward and roared up the onramp.

The freeway was mostly empty as the sky to the east showed its first signs of light. Leonard would have to hurry to discard the bag before the light of day was upon him. He moved over two lanes and settled in at 65 mph, careful not to draw attention. Leonard pictured the queer sitting behind the wheel of his abandoned car without his head or hands. He glanced at his reflection in the rearview mirror, his face lighted by the soft glow of the vehicle's cluster of gauges, and he laughed.

AT NOON I AWOKE SUDDENLY TO A LOUD CRASH IN THE LIVING ROOM. I rolled out of bed, instinctively grabbing my pistol from the nightstand. I quickly moved to the threshold and brought the gun up as I stepped through the short hallway and into the living room. Floyd looked over and said, "Nice shorts, Dickie."

"What the hell? . . ."

He stood near the coffee table leaning on a golf club. My eyes drifted from his grin to the club—it was a nine iron—to the coffee table with a shattered glass top. When my eyes met his again, he shrugged.

"Practicing my swing, Dickie, while you're in there sleeping. Do you know you snore?"

"Do you know you break shit? This is why we can't have nice things."

"Like a fish tank," he said, "or Bonsai trees."

"Exactly."

"Well, Dickie, as much as I love seeing your fat ass half naked, I'd prefer you got dressed and ready to go. You've bored the hell out of me again."

"Where are we going?"

"I was thinking we'd get some lunch. I'm starved. Then head to the office; we've got shit to do."

He gripped the club with both hands again and took his stance, lining up the imaginary ball with the patio door, apparently playing through. He didn't look up when he said, "Let's go, Dickie."

I retreated to my room shaking my head and mumbling about Floyd being a bull in a china shop. After I shaved and showered, I dressed in Sunday casual attire: slacks and a sports shirt. This would allow me to be somewhat presentable if something came up that required us to be out among the public. We started down the stairs descending from my apartment to the back yard of Chuck and Patti's home, and Elvis waddled up to meet me at the bottom. I bent down and patted his head and ran my hand gently over his soft, rumpled face. He licked at me and wagged his bobtailed butt. "Okay, little buddy, I'll see you tonight."

"That dog hates you," Floyd said.

"How do you figure? Did you see that? Did you see him run up to me and wag his tail when I petted him?"

"Only *you* would consider that running. As a matter of fact," Floyd said, now leading the way to the gate, "you two have about the same build and you run in similar fashion. Maybe he does like you. Maybe he thinks you're his dad or something."

He stepped through the gate and turned to face me while holding it open. I walked past him and immediately looked up and down the street. "Yeah, well, he might think you're his mother."

Floyd closed the gate and gave it a tug to make sure it latched. "Should we take two cars?" he was saying, but the sounds of his voice slowed and became garbled in my brain as time seemed to stop. Floyd's persistent grin had disappeared and his eyes popped wide and his face tightened into a grimace as he stared past me. He shoved me aside and reached for his gun. I followed his gaze as I stumbled away with the force of his push, but my movement felt as if I was stuck in molasses. Nothing could be rushed now, no matter how I tried. A car was stopped in the street adjacent to where we stood. The driver had his hand extended from its window, a gun pointed at us. I didn't hear the shots, but I saw muzzle flashes erupting from the barrel of Floyd's gun. The driver pulled his arm back into the car as he ducked away from the open window, leaning toward the passenger's seat. As I drew my weapon the car started moving. I could see bluish smoke rise from the asphalt and I could smell burning rubber and gunpowder. I now saw the action in real time as bullets struck the rear window of the fleeing car, one burst of glass after another. Floyd continued sending hot lead down range as I stood with an unfired weapon watching the action unfold before me.

Floyd yelled, "Sonofabitch!"

The little black car faded from view as Floyd ran to his car, shouting over his shoulder for me to get in. He flipped a U-turn and we gave chase, but the car was nowhere in sight. Floyd asked where it went, if I was hit, and told me to call 9-1-1 as he raced to each intersection, stopping to look both ways in search of the shooter's car. I realized my gun was still in my hand. I hadn't fired it, and now as we raced through the streets, I wondered why. I leaned toward Floyd to holster my weapon on my right hip. We were driving at high speeds on a major boulevard, darting through traffic.

Floyd's county car had no siren; most of the detective cars were no longer equipped with them. We didn't need them, they had said. But captains and above somehow did. Floyd was on the horn, yelling and cursing through the open windows, but everyone else was oblivious to our emergency. Finally, we skidded into an intersection where our vehicle was nearly struck by a firetruck turning in the direction we had come from. Floyd yelled, "Fucking firemen!" and remained there until horns began blaring from all directions. He swiveled his head one way and then the other before jerking the wheel and accelerating through the intersection, reversing our direction of travel. We were headed back toward my apartment.

Soon two cop cars sailed past us, lights and sirens activated, and Floyd slowed and steered to the right. When they passed, Floyd accelerated again and began following them.

"Headed to my place, I'm sure."

He glanced over. "Did you fire any rounds?"

"No."

He had looked back to the road but glanced over at me again after I answered. "Why not?"

I shrugged but he hadn't seen it. "I don't know. It happened fast. The guy was gone when I came up with my piece."

He didn't say anything, and moments later we arrived at my house and pulled in behind the two Burbank police cars, a firetruck, and a para-medics' rig. Chuck and Patti were outside, both wearing shorts and t-shirts, comfortable retiree attire. Chuck started our way as we exited Floyd's car. The firemen were pulling away now in no hurry.

"Are you guys okay?"

I nodded. "Yeah, is everyone okay here?"

"So far, it looks that way. Elvis is okay, that's all I care about. I guess they'll have to check all the neighbors' houses." Chuck then smiled and said, "Half of them I don't care if they took a stray round. What the hell happened?"

I started to answer but Floyd beat me to the punch. "That asshole who's been trying to kill Dickie four-seventeened us."

"Did he cap rounds or just four-seventeened you?"

Floyd shook his head. "I don't think he got any shots off, Chuck. But I looked right down the muzzle of his pistol. He was definitely four-seventeen."

I said, "Yeah, he definitely had a gun. I never saw muzzle flashes from the asshole's gun, only from Floyd's. But he definitely had a pistol in his hand, and he pointed it right at us. I never heard any shots, not even his," I said nodding toward Floyd. "It was weird."

Chuck said, "I sure as hell heard them. It sounded like about ten shots or more to me."

I leaned against a parked car and waited as one of the uniforms approached. I nodded to Floyd. "I saw the gun, partner. I don't know if he shot at us or not, but he pointed a gun at us."

"Shit yeah, he did. I know that much. I'm not worried about the shooting."

Chuck smiled as he greeted the approaching officer. "Hey, Mike, good to see you. It's been a while since you've stopped by, you little prick."

"Jesus, Chuck," the officer said, "what the hell happened out here? We've had a dozen 9-1-1 calls saying there were shots fired. I hope this is clean, not some kind of drunken cop bullshit."

Chuck assured him it was, and then he introduced us to the officer and suggested we go inside. Once inside, Chuck said, "Can I get anyone an iced tea or lemonade? Or maybe you guys would prefer bourbon or tequila, something to help take the edge off."

"Now you're talking," Floyd said.

---

LEONARD HAD THROWN THE GODDAMN GUN THAT DIDN'T SHOOT WHEN HE pulled the trigger right out the window while speeding away from the location, and immediately regretted having done so. Now he waited outside of the uniform shop watching the front door where two young men had walked in just as he arrived. They appeared to be in the military, or maybe new cops, with their short-cropped hair and white t-shirts tucked into jeans. Each of them were lean and muscular. Leonard figured he would wait until the pair left, then go in. He'd pop the old man with a fist and knock him on his ass. Then he'd make him show him how to use a goddamn gun so the next time he tried to kill the damn cop he wouldn't feel stupid sitting there pulling the trigger with nothing happening, and then having the fucking cops shoot back at him. Jesus. After the old man showed him how to properly use it, he'd practice one time at the back of the old man's head. He had just about had it with this assignment. He needed to get it over with and kill that sonofabitch with the hat and his pretty boy partner too if he got a chance, the sonofabitch who shot the back window out of his brand-new fucking car.

# 36

THE LIVING ROOM was comfortably furnished in brown leather sofas and chairs and hardwood tables. Chuck and Patti sat on one of the sofas, and Floyd and I sat on another. Two officers sat in floral-patterned Queen Anne chairs across the glass-topped table from us. The glass was intact, which made me recall Floyd playing through in my living room. I pictured him breaking the glass on this table and saw in my mind Chuck taking the club away and attacking him with it. One of the officers opened a notebook and hovered a pen over it. "I just need everyone's names and a brief synopsis of what happened. Your agency will have the lead on the investigation, according to my watch commander."

This would be short and sweet, just the basics for his "first" report of the incident. The shooting investigation would be the formal, recorded statement, conducted by two homicide detectives from our unit. Their investigation would be monitored by Internal Affairs and the Force Review Board. To me, there was nothing to be concerned about. It was cut and dried. A man pointed his gun at us, and Floyd shot at him. The only concern I had was the question of why I hadn't fired my pistol. And chances were, I wouldn't be the only one to worry about it.

Floyd provided some background, telling the officers about someone watching me, telling them about the Regalado shooting a year ago, telling them about a possible connection between all of it or otherwise we had no clue why someone would want me dead. He said, "Dickie's a hell of a nice guy, once you get to know him."

The young officer didn't know Floyd and didn't catch the attempt at humor. I told the officer that what Floyd had said was the long and short of it, and added that when we came outside, there were no cars driving on the street, and that I hadn't noticed any parked cars that appeared suspicious. It was as if the suspect had appeared out of nowhere and had done so instantly. One second, the street was clear, the next, a man was twenty feet away, pointing a gun directly at us. They asked if the suspect had fired his weapon. Floyd shook his head as I shrugged and said I wasn't sure. The officer looked from Floyd to me and then at Chuck and Patti. Chuck told him they weren't outside and didn't see anything. I said, "I know he pointed a gun at us."

Another Burbank officer appeared at the door. Everyone looked up. "No casings on the street other than those near the curb. There are fourteen expended nine-millimeter casings in a group on the sidewalk, parkway, and in the street near the curb. That's it."

The officer interviewing us thanked him. I watched as he retreated through the door, and noticed the black Crown Vic pulling up in front of the house. Lt. Joe Black stepped out of it, as did Captain Stover.

I looked at Floyd. "Well, so much for the good times."

---

Leonard watched the two young, buff men leave The Cop Shop in a black Jeep. They turned onto Hollywood Way and disappeared into traffic. Leonard didn't hesitate. There was no time to. He needed to get a gun, he needed to get the cop killed, and he needed to get out of this goddamn city and county and state and get back to Florida where life made more sense. Maybe back to Raiford where a daily routine provided less stress, and where Whitey Blanchard, Leonard's only friend in the world, would spend the rest of his life.

Leonard walked directly up to the same older gentleman who had helped him the last time he was in, nearly a week earlier, and punched him in the face with a closed fist. But the old man bobbed his head to avoid the punch the way a trained boxer might, and the blow glanced off of him with little impact. Leonard didn't see the hard, walloping punch, but he felt it. The man's fist came in low and landed squarely on Leonard's chin, knocking him backward and momentarily stunning him. Before he could recover from the first punch, the man hit Leonard two or three more times in the face and once or twice in the abdomen. This old man's hands were lightning fast, and his punches hard and accurate. One of the low punches sent a wave of pain through Leonard's body and he fell to the ground. He curled up with both hands covering the part of his body where the pain persisted, over his liver. He recovered quickly and realized he would need a weapon. He dug into his rear pocket for the knife he had purchased at this very store and had used to cut two Russians' throats and saw off a queer's head and hands. But as Leonard struggled to his feet with the knife in hand, the old man produced a pistol and pointed it directly at him. Leonard turned and ran. He heard the sonic crack of bullets whizzing past him, each immediately followed by the sound of a gunshot. He pushed through the door and ran into a man who was walking in, knocking him down onto the pavement. Leonard ignored the yelling from that man and the old man with iron fists who was now trying to shoot and kill him. Leonard jumped into his car and sped from the lot.

He needed to get the hell out of Burbank. Get back to downtown Los Angeles where it was safe.

---

LATE SUNDAY EVENING WE FINISHED PROVIDING OUR INDIVIDUAL statements of the incident to investigators from our office and to Captain Stover and Lt. Joe Black. After the Burbank cops had received all they needed from us for their reports, we left Burbank and drove back to our office. Joe told us repeatedly how glad he was nobody was hurt. The captain said he was glad that for once we hadn't killed anyone nor had we even wrecked a car—at least not any of *his* cars. Then he chewed my ass for not informing him about the situation with someone watching. I told him it hadn't been confirmed, and I was reluctant to jump to conclusions. He said, "We don't take chances with things like this, Richard," and left it at that. I walked out of his office starting to believe he had both heart and soul.

I rounded the corner into Unsolveds and found Davey Lopes at his desk. He looked up with tired eyes, but then looked back down. I could see he was going over phone records.

"Those the phone records?"

Without looking up he said, "Yeah, I pulled them off the fax machine. Came in a couple hours ago."

Nothing was said for a minute, so I walked out. He didn't want to be bothered; that was plain to see. More than likely he didn't want to talk to anyone, and I wouldn't take it personally. But it did make me wonder what had happened. I walked back toward the front desk to see if there were any updates on Maria Lopez. Maria Lopez with a Z, as Lopes had called her, and always smiled when he had. I wondered if the story behind Lopes's current disposition would be found at the desk, written in pencil on a Homicide Bureau *Dead Sheet*.

# 37

MONDAY MORNING TRAFFIC had me dreading the drive to the shrink's office though I looked forward to speaking with Dr. Katherine James. After yesterday I had much to discuss, and I had thought of it all night until the moment I fell asleep, and again first thing this morning. So I called Dr. James's office and asked if I could slip in to see her on short notice, and said it was urgent. Her receptionist had checked with Dr. James and said it would be no problem, she would move some things around for me. Now I was thinking about all of it again, everything that had happened the morning before, and all of the self-doubt and serious concerns it left me with. I made a silent vow to be truthful with Dr. James in order to get an expert opinion on the matters. I needed some answers, badly. She was the only one who would be able to help me now. This was potentially a matter of cowardice, and I wasn't going to discuss it with anyone else. I needed her to help me figure out why I hadn't fired my weapon. What had happened to me?

When I arrived at her office the receptionist smiled and offered me coffee, which I gladly accepted. There were no sign-in sheets or billing issues or any other normal healthcare considerations at this office. It was comfortable enough that I considered booking it for the whole day, or maybe the week.

I took my mug of coffee and had a seat at the far edge of a sofa nearest the entrance to Dr. James's office, and furthest away from the front entry. It was quiet and softly lit. I hadn't brought my reading glasses and I had no interest in the magazines scattered about the room.

I was thinking about yesterday afternoon when the door to her office opened.

She smiled and greeted me warmly. "Hello, Richard, please come in."

Our eyes met.

She stepped back into her office and held the door, gesturing for me to step inside. I had to turn slightly to avoid brushing against her as I entered. She smelled fresh, as if she had just bathed in a bouquet of wild flowers. I walked across the carpeted floor and took my usual seat where it would be her back to the door, and not mine. I wondered which chair she would choose if I allowed it. But I didn't. Ever. Not in any circumstance other than dining with someone whose skills I implicitly trusted. Like Floyd. Or Lopes. Maybe a very few others. I watched as she approached and took the other chair; this placed our knees just inches apart. She glanced at my lap, causing me to look down also. Both hands held a half-empty, oversized mug, and the remaining coffee was sloshing around inside. I realized my hands were unsteady, and she had noticed.

Her eyes met my gaze again, and she indicated the table to the side of my chair. "You can put the cup there, Richard, if you like."

I set the cup on the table and leaned back in my chair. I scanned the room as if I had never seen it before.

"Richard, you seem uneasy today. Is there something on your mind, something bothering you?"

"Is it that obvious?"

"Do you think you would feel better if you talked about it?"

"Someone tried to kill me yesterday."

"Richard!" Her eyes widened and her hand flew to her chest, as if she were shocked. Then, seeming to realize she may have reacted more impulsively than professionally, and immediately regretting having done so, she smoothed her blouse a bit and dropped her hand to her lap so that it joined the other. She drew a deep breath and slowly exhaled. "My goodness, that must have been quite an experience. Tell me about it."

Good cover, I thought. And Dr. Katherine James was back to being professional. Dr. James was always professional.

"It's a long story. Someone has been watching me. It took a while for me to allow that truth to settle in. But some things have happened, and I've been concerned, and then Floyd decided to stay the weekend with me because everything started adding up. To make a long story short, we don't know who it is or why he wants me dead. For that matter, we don't even know if *he* is the one who wants me dead—the man who's been watching—or if someone else has sent him to do it. Though after yesterday, I can't imagine he's a pro."

Katherine, Dr. James that is, gazed steadily at me for a few seconds, her face giving no indication of what she might be thinking. I couldn't tell if she was merely deciding on the best way to handle this information for me as my shrink, or if maybe—*maybe*—she was considering things on a more personal level. Just as I was dismissing the thought, she spoke. "Why do you think he's trying to kill you, Richard?"

"I have no idea."

As I looked at the floor I could feel her eyes on me, and then I heard a sharp intake of breath. She let a beat go by. I looked up as she spoke again. Dr. James, professional, in control. "Why don't you tell me more about what happened, Richard."

"I messed up. I held my fire, and the circumstances dictated I should have shot him."

"Why do you think you elected not to shoot at him when you could have?"

"That's the problem, Doc. I don't know. I froze. Maybe that's not the right way to describe it, but I didn't react quickly. I couldn't. My mind didn't allow it. Floyd pushed me out of the way—" I stopped and thought about that for the first time, realizing he was shoving me out of the kill zone like I was a woman or a child or an unarmed man, while he remained and took on my fight. I took in a slow, deep breath, squeezed my eyes closed for a moment and then opened them, hoping there was no sign of moisture gathering. "The man had a gun pointed directly at us from the window of his car, but I didn't think he had fired it. He hadn't, as it turns out. But at the time, that went through my mind. Even as Floyd began shooting I was thinking this guy hadn't shot at us. It was as if I was trying to reason that our lives were not actually in danger."

"Well, Richard, can you tell me why this upsets you? It sounds like you made a good decision not to shoot."

"Because it's wrong. I screwed up. When a man points a gun directly at you, you don't wait to take a bullet before shooting him. That's not how you win a gunfight. But that's exactly what I did. Not Floyd; he emptied his gun into the asshole's car."

"Did you and your partner arrest him?" Her voice remained calm, steady.

"We never found him. We chased him but he got away. Burbank PD responded, and they put it out on the radio, told everyone to be on the lookout. I guess Glendale cops rolled also, and their helicopter was even up looking for the car, but it was never found. So, here I am, lucky to be alive, but with no idea who it is that wants me dead, or why. And I'm not sure if I will be able to defend myself if it happens again. I froze up. Like a coward."

There was silence for a few beats. Then she spoke.

"'Coward' is a strong word, Richard, and not one I am sure fits the circumstances. Have you had anything like this happen before, to you, or maybe to someone else in a situation you have investigated?"

"I had something similar happen one other time, back in my patrol days. There was a pursuit that ended and LAPD started shooting at the guy in the car we were chasing. Then my partner and another deputy shot also. I didn't shoot because I didn't perceive a level of threat that justified it. That happens. But, in that instance, I didn't regret it at all. It turned out the guy was an old drunk and anything he did was incidental to his intoxication and not an intent to kill us. In other words, the guy would have just continued driving down the road drunk and happy had we not been there to impede his travels. He was trying to get away from the cops. I'm not saying the actions of others that night weren't justified, I'm just saying I didn't perceive the same level of threat, and I refrained from joining the ranks of the shooters, in that instance. Truthfully, I was more worried about the crossfire situation than I was about the threat or the suspect. We all did days off behind that incident too. Suspended for a variety of reasons, none of which stated the shooting was unjustified.

"I've investigated many shootings where the perception of threat varied from one officer to another. That perception dictates the action of the cop. That's a good thing; contagious fire is never good. So, as long as officers act on *their* perceptions, I have no problem with it. There are so many things that factor into the equation and it happens in an instant, though it seems like minutes or hours at times. I have no problem with one officer shooting and another holding his fire. Truthfully, it validates the premise we argue in the defense of many officers whose shootings are scrutinized. That premise is that we all have our independent perceptions, based on many factors, and each of us processes those factors and the resulting threat individually.

"There's no doubt in my mind that Floyd did the right thing. I wish he had killed the sonofabitch. I'm just bothered that I didn't fire my weapon. Even as the suspect fled, and enough time had passed that I should have known the shooting was justified, I wasn't able to shoot. And *that* has also happened to me before."

"You are telling me, Richard, that police officers act on perceptions. It seems that your perception at the time was that it was not appropriate to fire at the man with the gun. Maybe you were not sure it was a real gun, have you thought of that? Maybe you noticed something at the time that you haven't realized yet. Tell me about the time before that you didn't shoot."

I felt she was somehow relieved that I hadn't shot at the man in the car, as if I would be in the wrong if I had. I found myself starting to get irritated, but decided to give her the benefit of the doubt. She did smell so nice, after all, and there was a lot to admire about her.

I grinned. "Well, once I had a dog bite me and run off. Some of my colleagues asked why I didn't shoot it. I told them it would be stupid to shoot the dog once he ran off, and I argued that the dog was only doing his job—I was on *his* property at the time. But it always puzzled me how some deputies questioned that and boasted how they would have shot the dog anyway. Why? I don't ever want to shoot a dog. I like dogs. I don't want to shoot another human either, if I can help it. And I don't even like people. Not most, anyway."

Dr. James smiled. I felt I was back in her good graces, if in fact I had ever been out of them. Maybe I was imagining things. I decided to tell her more.

"There was another incident when a man pulled a gun on me, and as it turned out, he had pulled the trigger but the gun malfunctioned. Thankfully, or you'd be talking to me over at Forest Lawn, not in your office. It was dark, right at the mouth of an alley, and he was dressed in all dark clothing, wearing a large coat. When he jumped out of the car, I thought he was going to run, but he didn't. He turned to face me. I had already left the cover of my car and was running directly at him. When I realized something was wrong—that rather than running, he had turned to face me —it was at that instant I heard the sound of a gun hitting the ground. Then, he ran. I didn't fire my weapon. Because, believe it or not, in that split second, my brain processed the fact that he had been trying to kill me, and my mind said *Shoot*. But in the same nanosecond, my mind told me *Don't shoot*, because I knew he had dropped the gun and the deadly threat had passed. I actually processed all of that in microseconds. It seemed like minutes. That's the difference between good guys and bad guys. We have a conscience, they don't. That, coupled with my training, kept me from shooting at that moment. And it pisses me off to this day."

"What do you mean? How does it anger you?"

"Well, as I chased the sonofabitch down a dark alley, my anger grew. He had wanted to kill me. He had *tried* to kill me. There was a gun lying on the ground back there, which, by the way, turned out to be a fully-automatic machine pistol, an Ingram MAC-11. This is what they call an open-bolt gun. Open-bolt means the bolt is only closed when there are no bullets left to fire, or in the case of a misfire. The bolt on this gun was closed on a live round. Which means he had pulled the trigger on me, and the gun had malfunctioned. The 32-round magazine was full. That gun can empty its magazine in less than two seconds, all 32 rounds with one squeeze of the trigger. I should be dead. If not for a malfunction, I would be. Of course, I didn't know all of that when I ran after him, but I knew he had tried to kill me. I had seen the look in his eyes, the surprise, which later I realized was his reaction to the gun malfunctioning. So, it angers me that I didn't shoot him when I should have, when I could have. Because I didn't, he probably went on to kill someone else on another night. Maybe a cop, I don't know. He was the type. I mean, think about it: he made the decision to shoot it out with the cops, and he pulled the trigger. There's no doubt he had killed men before, not a doubt in my mind. As I ran behind him, all of this was clear to me. And I knew I had failed."

Her silent gaze encouraged me to continue. I didn't want to, but for some reason I couldn't stop telling this story. A story that had kept me awake many nights over the years.

"So, I tried to kill him. I shot at him as we ran through the alley, long after the immediate threat had been removed." I chuckled, though some-what awkwardly. "It's harder than you think, hitting a moving target while running."

Her expressionless gaze erased my grin.

"I missed. He got away."

"What if you hadn't, Richard? What if you had killed the man in anger while he ran away?"

That hung between us for a moment. I looked into her eyes and knew she was evaluating this in a way that could determine her final analysis of me. Her opinion of me meant more than what I might have been willing to admit. If I didn't care on a personal level, it wouldn't matter to me how she viewed what I just told her. Everything I said here was confidential. I didn't worry about any departmental recourse. But I knew from the way she watched, waiting for the reply, that this mattered to her. Maybe more than it should have.

I hoped the time it took for my response would be interpreted as me processing the question and answer, giving careful consideration and self-evaluation about how I might have felt. As if I had never considered it before. But in truth, I already knew the answer. I had always known the answer to that question. I had asked myself the same question thousands of times. *What if I had killed him?* Shoot/don't shoot scenarios stay with you until the day you die. Either way, I would have second-guessed myself for the rest of my life. The guy with the machine gun, and others. Now this one too, this situation in front of the house where I froze. It was part of the price we pay for doing the job. We may not remember Christmas gifts or anniversaries or sometimes our own phone numbers, but we remember every detail of these types of situations. I remember that night as if it were last night, and I remember the feelings I had at the instant it happened, and all of the thoughts and feelings I've had in the twenty years since. The truth of it was I still—to this very day—regret not killing that sonofabitch. I wish I had instinctively gunned him down, even knowing he had dropped his weapon. Some cops may have. I should have. I hate that I didn't. In my analysis over the years—and to answer her question—had I hit him when I fired two rounds as he pulled away from me running down that alley, I could live with it. What would it matter? Either way, it stays with you. At least I would have found solace knowing he would never have pulled the trigger on another cop. That's what it boiled down to for me; he had pulled the trigger on me. I might kill him today if I knew who he was and where to find him.

But there was no way I was telling her any of that.

"I would have felt awful," I lied, "and I'm really thankful I missed."

She kept her gaze neutral for a moment, then glanced at the clock on the wall. Then she gave me her usual smile, professional but kind. "All right, Richard. We're out of time for now. You've done a lot of work here today; I hope it has helped. We can continue with this next week; I think there is much more to explore here."

She stood, and I followed suit, turning toward the door.

I felt her follow me across the room. I paused at the door having made my decision in that instant. I turned to face her and surprised her with a question of my own. On my terms, the two of us standing face to face, not seated in chairs playing the roles of doctor and patient. "Are you disappointed?"

She seemed startled by the question. Then she glanced past me, looking at nothing in particular, considering. After a few seconds, she looked up at me. "Richard, remember, this is not about what I or anyone else may think. You are here because you want to clarify some things in your life and be able to move forward, to have some peace and understanding, to come to terms with everything that has led you to this point. What I think is irrelevant." Her gaze flicked away and her hand brushed a non-existent speck of lint from her shoulder.

Now I knew; it was crystal clear. It was no different than knowing you had the right man during an interrogation. The moment they averted their eyes while answering a question or squirmed in their seats at an accusation. Sometimes it would be the manner of speech or the words they would utter. There was always some hint, a minute tell that an experienced investigator could read and which would provide clarity on an issue. Dr. James had not only answered the question at hand, but she allowed me to see inside her soul, if only for an instant. I knew at that moment there was something more between us.

"Do you like Chinese?"

"I'm sorry, what?" She looked at me, puzzled at what to her was an utter non sequitur.

"I was just thinking maybe we could have dinner."

Her eyes widened slightly and her mouth opened just a little, then closed. She looked away at nothing again, then back at me. I saw a hint of a real smile, I was certain of it, and her cheeks had become slightly pink. Katherine showing herself. Then she rallied, and there was that Dr. James smile again, kind but professional. Nothing personal here, Dickie!

When she finally answered, her tone was calm and neutral, as always. "Richard, that is a nice offer, thank you. But I am your doctor, and it would not be at all ethical for me to socialize with you."

I waited, saying nothing. It was a technique I found effective with the toughest of opponents. She continued, as I had been sure she would.

"That is, I cannot become personally involved with you or with any patient. That could compromise my ability to be objective, and that, in turn, could jeopardize your much needed treatment."

I waited again. The professional smile was faltering a bit.

"It's a matter of ethics, Richard, my job, your job…" her voice trailed off. She looked at me, saying nothing.

"I'm not saying I want to run out and get married, Doc, but I am craving Chinese food and a cold beer. There's a place in Chinatown, and I was thinking . . . I just thought that maybe, well—never mind. I'm probably out of line here."

I put my hand on the door knob, but didn't otherwise move.

*Come on, Doc . . . Katherine. It's just dinner. Come have drinks and find out what I'm really like. Trust me, I'm a cop.*

I gave her the pathetic smile, the hangdog one that almost always worked. This time it wasn't insincere. "Sorry, Doc, I didn't mean to offend you. I just thought it would be nice to have some company at dinner. That's all." I gave her a beat to answer, to move, to respond at all.

She didn't.

Deflated, I turned to go. I opened the door and started through it, but paused. "Thank you, Dr. James, I guess I'll see you next week."

No response. I kept moving, now just wanting to get away.

I looked over my shoulder just before starting down the stairs. I expected to see a closed door—and wasn't that ever a metaphor for my life right now—but to my surprise, Dr. James was standing in the doorway. Embarrassed at being caught looking, I turned away quickly and started down the stairs. I was halfway down when I thought I heard something. I stopped, my heart beating oddly fast. I waited.

She appeared at the top of the stairs. "What is the name of the place, Richard, the place in Chinatown?"

*Katherine* was back.

# 38

I T WAS ONLY noon, Monday, the start of a new week following a chaotic weekend. I drove to the office with nothing other than Dr. James on my mind. *Katherine.* But when I swung the nose of my Crown Vic around and backed into an empty parking space near the back door, all of that changed. Floyd walked briskly toward my car with an uncharacteristically serious look about him.

I stepped out. "What's up?"

He had stopped a few feet from where I parked and waited. "Everything. Come on, they want to have a meeting." With that, he turned on his heel and headed back to the bureau.

I followed along in silence, wondering what had happened or was about to happen. Floyd didn't look back until he held the door to the squad room open, waiting for me. Our eyes met as I walked past him, but we didn't speak. I veered toward the kitchen and he said at my back, "Conference room."

For some reason, I found myself annoyed with him. "I'll be there after I grab a cup."

I noticed others funneling toward the hallway that leads to the conference room and felt a vibe that didn't always run through the office.

Passing through the desk area did nothing to lift my spirits or calm my nerves. Two investigators sat silently, purposely not noticing my presence. It suited me fine. The fewer people I talked to today, the better. I feared there would be questions about the shooting incident and the stalker who was following me, and quiet speculation about my performance yesterday afternoon—or lack thereof. I poured a cup and glanced at my watch. It was going to be a long day.

Mongo and I rounded a corner together on the way to the conference room. He nodded.

"What's going on?"

His arms swung wide as he propelled himself through the hall. I gave him a wide berth. "Everything, apparently. Your stalker, the shooting, some asshole killing people all around the county." He stopped and looked up at me before opening the door. "They're even looking at that Russian murder now, the one in Hollywood, maybe being related."

I frowned. "Related?"

He nodded and pulled the door open.

The room was packed. Everyone seemed to notice our entry. Ray stood at the end of a large table; there were a dozen chairs around it and more along two walls of the room. He looked at me when I stepped in. "Squeeze in here partner, it's standing room only."

I stepped in and stopped. Once Mongo cleared the threshold, I closed the door and stayed there. It would make for a quick exit, an option I would leave open throughout the meeting.

"Okay," Ray said, scanning the room, "I'm going to bring everyone up to speed. Some of this is repetitive, but some of our guests here today don't have all the facts."

I glanced around the room for the first time. I saw that Dr. Provost and Phil Gentry, both from the crime lab, were present, along with the captain, Lt. Black, Detectives Rich Farris and Liz Marchesano, and Dwight Campbell, a sergeant in charge of one of our department surveillance teams. He was flanked by two other undercover detectives, one who looked like a heavy metal band guitarist with his long, straggly hair and beard and tattooed arms, and a petite black woman who appeared too young to be a deputy, much less a member of the surveillance team. All three wore their badges on chains around their necks for identification. Dwight's had the backdrop of a *Malcom X* t-shirt. His cover was being a radical inner-city brother, and he played it well. We went way back, and I was glad to see him. It occurred to me for the first time since the incident that I might have around-the-clock companionship for a while after the attempt on my life. Notably absent was Davey Lopes.

Ray first brought the newcomers up to speed with the basic facts of our case and those on the peripheral, as well as the situation with my stalker. Then he paused a beat and looked over at me. "Sorry you're hearing some of this just now, partner, but with everything going on with you yesterday, I haven't had time to fill you in on this new information."

I nodded and waited with great expectation of the news to follow.

"Late Saturday night I received a call from a woman who identified herself as the adoptive mother of Lisa Williams. She gave us a history of her daughter's life up until the time she dropped out of school at seventeen and ran away from home. There isn't much information after that. The mother told us Lisa was a troubled girl who was blessed—or maybe cursed—with fabulous looks. Lisa apparently used those good looks to get whatever she wanted in life. The mother—her adoptive one—said the first time she heard from Williams after she had run away was when Lisa called saying she was in jail and needed help. It had been two years since they had heard from her. She had been arrested for prostitution but told her mother it was a false charge. The mother said she knew immediately that it wasn't, and said that she wasn't surprised at the news of her arrest. She and her husband told Williams she was on her own and asked her to never contact them again. She had been a real problem child.

"The takeaway here for us is that she was adopted. I started thinking about that and wondered if it could mean anything, and I called the mother back and asked if she knew anything about Williams's biological family. She said she didn't know much, just that she was one of three children removed from the biological mother at young ages and adopted out. This morning I obtained a warrant to unseal the adoption records and I'm waiting for the word that I can go view those records.

"Now, we're going to leave that there for a moment and cover some other cases that might all tie together. A couple days after our murder, a young girl was killed in San Fernando. They asked for our assistance as they had had an officer-involved shooting and their detectives were buried in work. Rich Farris and Elizabeth Marchesano handled the case. There wasn't much to work on, and no reason to think it might be related to ours, as this girl was strangled in her home, which of course is a completely different M.O. than our case.

"Fast forward. Dickie starts noticing someone suspicious in and around his neighborhood. He feels he's being watched. He never gets a good look at the watcher, but he knows it was an adult male, possibly Caucasian. There have been a couple different cars used, and on one occasion, Dickie was able to get a license plate. However, the plate came back no record on file. Now, in our case—the Santa Clarita murder—we saw two men in suits approach Phil Chaney's home. We obtained the license number of their car and it came back with no record. We assumed they were feds. Dickie started thinking maybe he was being watched by the feds. He was recently served with a subpoena for a federal civil rights case against him for his shooting last year of that gangster in East L.A. However, a couple days ago, Chuck Lewis, a retired deputy who owns the house where Dickie lives, saw a suspicious man out front and had a minor confrontation with the guy. The car is described as the same one Dickie had seen. The driver, however, was no fed. Chuck said the guy was a convict. Not tatted up or dressed down, just a white boy with slicked back blond hair. But Chuck said he looked the man in his eyes and knew immediately he had done significant time in the joint. I don't doubt Chuck Lewis on something like that.

"Now, during all of this, a Russian couple is killed in Hollywood. LAPD has the handle, and the case has drawn the attention of a task force made up of LAPD and FBI who are investigating the Russian mob. These two had their throats cut; the male was almost decapitated. Interestingly, these two Russians specialized in selling untraceable, cold-plated cars. We originally didn't think much of this, but as Dickie pointed out, cutting someone's head off and nearly doing so are in the same playing field as far as M.O. The cold-plated cars just add to the intrigue of these cases being related.

"Bear with me here. Not far from the car lot where the Russians were killed, a young man was murdered sometime Saturday night or Sunday morning at the top of a parking structure. He was decapitated, and his hands were cut off. Those body parts have not been found—nor have the body parts of our Santa Clarita victim, Lisa Williams. But this young, headless man on the structure was found seated in a sedan that matches the description of the sedan Dickie saw at his place, and the one that Chuck had encountered."

I looked around and saw that half of those present were taking notes. I knew most of this, but some of it was news. I didn't have a notebook and would have to have Ray recap later. Which was okay; we were partners.

Floyd said, "Ray, were there plates on that car, the one in the parking structure?"

"No, the license plates had been removed. But here's where things get really interesting. The car driven by the man you shot at yesterday, the guy who pointed a gun at you and Dickie, was described by both of you as a smaller, two-door black sedan with tan interior. LAPD is currently working on a case of a missing twenty-four-year-old male who was driving a black Lexus two-door coupe."

Floyd went to work on his phone, feverishly.

Ray went on, "We are waiting for DNA results on the body and donor samples provided by his—"

"That's it!" Floyd exclaimed. "That's the car, Dickie." He stood from his seat and walked through the crowded conference room holding his phone up for me to see.

I squinted at it as he approached, and then took it from him. It was an image of a Lexus two-door coupe from some type of internet search he had done. I looked at Ray and nodded. "That does look like the right type of car."

"So, if that's the case, it all ties together. Now, for those who haven't yet heard, we also have scent evidence tying some of this together. Dickie collected non-filtered cigarette butts from the street on two separate occasions when he believed he was being watched. Rich Farris and Lizzy ran a scent dog from their crime scene based on scent from a lighter. That lead them to a non-filtered cigarette on the street. The dogs say the scent on those items is a match to those from Dickie's caper."

"We need to run those dogs on the car," I said.

Ray nodded at me with his brows scrunched down over his eyes, seemingly looking for clarification.

"The car on the structure. If that's our boy—the one who tried killing us, and the one who killed the Asian girl—the dog should be able to identify his scent from that car. If LAPD will let us do that as soon as they're done with their examination, that would be good. If they find DNA from hairs or whatever in that car, we can compare that to our cigarette butts too. Doc, are there any results yet on the DNA?"

She shook her head. "Not as of an hour ago when I drove down. I'll check when I get back to the lab, and I'll be sure to let you know as soon as anything comes in. I'm personally monitoring it."

"Is everyone with me so far?" Ray asked the group.

"If this is one guy on a killing spree, I have several questions," Rich Farris said. "First, how does your Santa Clarita murder tie into any of these others, other than the decap and the two suits in the cold-plated car? That seems a stretch. Any physical evidence that could be compared to the others?"

"No, that's all we have so far on that."

"Okay, and what about the Hollywood deal, same thing?"

"The car lot is the same so far, just the cold-plated cars and a near decapitation that have us looking at it. So far, there's no physical evidence to tie it to anything."

"And the proximity to the decap in the parking structure," Floyd added.

"Yeah. Actually, *on* the parking structure, technically. It was found on the very top, open level, just to be clear."

"Got it."

"Anything else?"

"How did the mother of Lisa Williams know to contact you?" Floyd asked.

"Once we had the DNA checked again to confirm her identity, the ID was released. It's been all over the news, partner."

Everyone looked around waiting for someone to speak. Nobody did. Ray said, "Captain?"

Stover stood up from his chair and made eye contact with me. "Dwight's team is covering you until further notice. They're going to split up in order to provide 24/7 coverage." He motioned with his hand toward the three undercover detectives. "This is your starting crew. Three others will take their place at three am. When we break from this meeting, you will all get a list of their vehicles and photographs of the undercovers.

"Farris is going to liaison with LAPD on the Hollywood murders—the Russians and the kid on the parking structure—and he can also take care of the request for dogs and coordinate anything that needs to be done with that." He nodded at Floyd. "I want you and your partner to be on speed-dial with the lab. Dr. Provost, if you would please make sure you have both of their numbers and notify them first and immediately with any information on the DNA. The second we get that news," Stover said, staring at Floyd, "You're to call me on my cell. No matter the time of day or night.

"Lastly, nothing to the media on this. Any of it. Clear?" He scanned the room. Most were nodding, nobody opposed him. He glanced at his watch. "We'll play it by ear from here forward. I don't want to schedule another briefing on this case at this time. We'll call another when something breaks. Let me know if we need any other investigators or other resources."

With that, he pushed his chair in and began wading through the bodies toward the door. It occurred to me that he was different than he used to be. Maybe it was me. I know he had been turned down for another bump, a promotion to Commander. That may have made a difference. He was now likely watching the calendar. I heard he only had two years to go. As he passed by, I said, "Thanks, Captain." He lightly patted my shoulder and walked out.

Dwight passed by and he also patted my shoulder. He said, "Where's your desk now, man? We'll get with you and go over the plan and details."

I pointed toward the wall where Teams Five and Six occupied two columns of desks on the other side. "I'm on Five now, with Ray. You know where he sits?"

"Yeah, generally."

"I'm next to him. I'll be back there in a few. I need to talk to Ray and Floyd and grab another cup. It's going to be a long day."

"Okay, man, I'll see you back there in a few."

"Thanks, D."

Ray waited for the room to empty. Floyd waited too. Mongo stood his ground as well. Once it was just the four of us, Floyd said, "Fuck."

"Uh-huh."

Ray said, "Let's go see about those court records. There's nothing else we can do right now, and that will get our minds off everything else while we're waiting."

"Okay," I said. "I just need to check in with Dwight first. I think they have to follow us everywhere we go, doing counter-surveillance for us."

"For you."

Floyd smiled and said, "I'm going to hit up Doc Provost and give her my number. All of them. Cell phone, office, home, pager . . . I might even give her Cindy's cell as a backup, tell Cindy if a sexy black woman who says she's a doctor calls looking for me, direct her to the jacuzzi at once. And bring cold beer."

I shook my head. "You amaze me."

He grinned.

"Has anyone seen or heard from Lopes?"

Ray answered me. "Someone said the corrections officer is pulling through. He's probably at the hospital."

"Damn, that's good news," I said. "That's a whole other cluster we have going."

"You bet, partner. But thankfully, that case has nothing to do with all the others."

"As far as we know."

Mongo nodded and the two of them walked out. As they disappeared around the corner, I heard Floyd say, "I have to go say hello to that new secretary. I'll see you in a few."

---

AT 7 P.M. THE OLD MAN WHO RAN THE UNIFORM SHOP IN BURBANK locked the glass door and began to pull the accordion-like wrought iron security gate across the front of the building. Leonard walked up behind him, smiling with anticipation. The old boxer might have gotten the best of him last time, but he wouldn't stand a chance this time. He wouldn't even see it coming. Leonard dropped his cigarette to the pavement in his final steps, his eyes opened wide with anticipation and rage. The boxer turned and appeared startled to see Leonard there. Before the man understood what was happening, Leonard stepped into him, his knife leading the way. The man instinctively raised his hands in defense, but it was too late.

The blade flashed and sank deep into the old man's neck. Leonard pulled the knife across the man's throat and watched it open up. Blood sprayed, then streamed from both sides of his neck, spraying a fine mist of red across Leonard's face as he tried to pull his knife out. It was as if the knife had become a part of the man, and as Leonard held onto it, he fell to the ground with the dying store owner. Once on the ground, Leonard had better leverage and was able to pull the knife out of the man's neck. He stood over him and watched as the old man's stare became dull and his body limp.

Satisfied, Leonard straightened and took a look around. Nobody seemed to have noticed. He took the keys from the man's clenched fist and quickly found the one that opened the glass front door. It had a red plastic tab on it. Once the door was opened, Leonard stepped over and grabbed the store owner by the collar of his blood-soaked shirt and dragged him inside. Then he went to work. He pulled a duffle from one of the shelves. It had *POLICE* printed boldly on both sides. Leonard went shopping and filled the bag with four handguns, ten boxes of ammunition, four knives—Leonard loved his knives—and a nylon jacket that also had *POLICE* printed on the back in large letters and again on the front in smaller letters over a silkscreened badge. He also grabbed a hoodie from a shelf.

Leonard found the restroom. He removed his shirt and washed his face, head, and torso with warm water, and dried off with a hand towel that hung on a peg. Then he slipped on his new hoodie sweatshirt. Dark blue, it was emblazoned with a pig's head wearing a cop's hat with a badge on the front.

Leonard paused at the door and sorted through the keys until he found the Ford key that he presumed was for the van at the far side of the parking lot. Only the van and Leonard's recently acquired Lexus remained in the parking lot. He looked back at the blob of boxer now lying on the ground and said, "Adios, motherfucker," and walked out.

# 39

D WIGHT FOUND A place to edge in right across from Yee Me Loo's on Spring Street in Chinatown. He said on the radio: "The fuck's he doing here?"

"I hope you're on simplex, sarge," replied one of his investigators. On simplex their radio traffic would be car-to-car, not through a repeater and heard everywhere. It was Kelly. Steve Kelly, the longhaired white boy Dwight considered his right-hand man. They had been in the shit together, and Dwight considered him one of the best he'd ever worked with. It didn't matter if it was fists or bullets, the man was at the top of his game, and he never sweated anything.

He chuckled. "Yeah, no worries, Kell, I am. But seriously, I didn't even know cops drank here anymore. This guy's a fucking dinosaur."

Brandi chimed in. "You two are dinosaurs too, so you might want to check yourselves."

"You, Detective Gil, are a rookie. We'll let you know when we want to hear from you."

"Whatever, Kell."

Dwight said, "Where y'all at?"

"I'm a hundred yards north of you, D, same side of the street. I can see the front doors but that's about it. Parking sucks around here."

He waited but the *rookie* female didn't answer. "Brandi, where're ya at, sister?"

"Oh, so you *do* want to hear from me?"

The airwaves were silent on simplex for a moment. "Yes, Detective Gil, please bless us with your sultry little voice."

"I'm around the corner. I can't see either of you, and I can't see the front of the restaurant."

"What *can* you see?" Dwight asked.

"Well, if someone tried to sneak in the back door and walk up to his table and shoot him over his plate of noodles, I'd see the entrance and the exit of our suspect. I might even be able to take him out and wrap this all up for y'all."

Dwight smiled at his radio. "This ain't *The Godfather*, honey."

"Never know."

"Wait," Dwight said, and then there was radio silence. After a moment he said, "I think Dr. James from Psych Services just walked in there. You suppose Dickie has an appointment, or ya think this is *her* watering hole too?"

Steve Kelly replied: "She went into Yee Me Loo's?"

"Uh-huh."

"I think someone's getting a little extra couch therapy."

---

KATHERINE SCANNED THE ADDRESSES—THE ONES THAT COULD STILL BE read, anyway, on the buildings that had them at all—trying to find the place she was supposed to meet Richard. She had misgivings about meeting with him, to put it mildly. Where *was* the damned place anyway? She decided that if she couldn't find it in the next sixty seconds, and park in the sixty seconds after that, she would simply drive away. That was what she should do, she told herself. The Universe was trying to tell her to call this off, not to make what would surely turn out to be a bad decision. She didn't need any problems professionally, not after finally getting to the point that she felt fit to practice, and she most certainly didn't need to court problems of the heart. Those always seemed to find *her*.

Just as she had decided to listen to the Universe after all, she saw the sign displayed boldly at the top of the building: *Yee Me Loo*. And, miraculously, or maybe horribly, a car was just pulling away from the curb in front of it; a perfect parking space had opened up right in front of her. Astonished, she pulled her Audi Q-5 to the curb and turned off the engine. She sat for a minute, telling herself *run away, Katherine, run away.* Then she pulled down the visor, checked her face in the mirror one last time, and got out of the car. She shut the door a bit harder than she meant to —*resolutely*, she told herself—and strode toward the entrance door. Beyond it, she knew, lay uncertainty, upheaval, and possible unhappy consequences. And Richard.

---

LEONARD DROVE BY, SAYING, "FUCKING CHINAMEN EVERYWHERE, YOU can't find a place to park." And answering himself, "Right there, dummy." He wheeled the Ford van to the curb. It looked like something a serial killer would drive. He laughed at the thought. *Serial killer.*

After waiting nearly an hour, Leonard looked at the time displayed on his phone—*how long does it take a pig to finish his slop?*—and wondered if he was actually there to eat, or if this was where he came to drink. He had wondered why the asshole was never home. Now he knew. The prick drank all night and probably shacked up with a Chinese woman. He glanced at his phone again. He'd give him a half hour. That's it. If he didn't come out in thirty minutes, Leonard would walk in Whitey-style and blast the man while he ate his chow mein. Right there in front of everyone. *Bam, bam.* Or maybe *pew, pew.* He laughed.

This was it. He could feel it. Everything lined up perfectly, and his brilliance had paid off. After numerous trips through the nonsensical road patterns of Burbank, he finally figured it out. There were only two ways to get on the freeway in the whole damn city, and only one that made sense from the cop's apartment. So he decided to stake out the route, not the house, and it had paid off. Leonard had just driven his new van from the uniform shop across town, found a spot to sit—expecting to see the cop coming home from work—when he noticed the Crown Vic driving toward the freeway onramp. At first he thought there was no way, he couldn't be that lucky, but when he saw that the driver wore that stupid hat, his gangster fedora, Leonard knew that was his mark. *The Job.* It was time to finish the job and get the hell out of California. Florida was calling his name.

It had been easy trailing the cop to the restaurant in this crowded part of town because Piggy drove as slow as a ninety-year-old man. For some reason, the area was full of Chinamen and Chinamen-women. They were everywhere, these Chinese people, and they drove horribly, pulling out in front of you, never looking where they were going, putting along like they had nowhere to be for a month. They parked no better.

Leonard opened the duffle next to him and pulled out one of the pistols. It was a nine-millimeter. He knew that because it was printed on the side of the gun. He had made sure when selecting the ammunition that it would all match up. It took him a minute to figure out how to release the *clip*, but once he did, he found it easy to load. Leonard did this with two identical pistols. Then he racked a round into the chamber of each, having realized that he had failed to do that with the Russian's gun, and that that had probably been the problem when he tried to shoot the cop and his buddy yesterday. He had seen enough movies and shows to know you had to rack a round into the chamber. Then he pulled the hood of his piggy sweatshirt over his head and leaned back to wait. He checked his phone. It had been five minutes.

---

I HAD JUST HUNG UP WITH FLOYD WHEN SHE WALKED IN, TEN MINUTES late. I almost didn't recognize her wearing a Yankees ball cap. She had changed out of her professional attire into jeans and a blouse, and topped it off with the hat. Perfect! Hopefully the surveillance team wouldn't notice her either; I was sure at least two of the three watching had met her before in a professional setting. Dr. Katherine James had agreed to meet me for a drink but she had been tentative about doing so. The idea of it went against all manner of ethical conduct, she had said, though she had a warm smile when we parted company. Against my better judgment, I had just told Floyd all about it. He would have killed me if I hadn't, and I was nervous about the whole setup now with a team on me. About that, Floyd had said, "Who gives a shit?" When I told him that she and I were meeting at Yee Me

Loo's, he had said, "You're taking her to *our* place?" Then he said, "Hey, have fun. Maybe I'll pop in accidentally in an hour or so to see how things are going. You could buy me a gin and tonic. Besides, Doc loves me."

I asked that he not, and then said, "Here she is, gotta go."

I stood to greet her and pulled a stool away from the bar to offer her a seat. "Doctor." I realized how corny it sounded the second it came out of my mouth.

"Katherine, please," she said.

She slid onto the stool and swiveled it my direction. I took my seat next to her. "Would you rather sit at a table?"

She looked around the small bar crowded with businessmen, lawyers, cops, and local citizens. A layer of smoke hung above the bar though smoking inside any establishment—including bars—in California had been outlawed more than a decade before. There were no tables in the bar. If it were a garage, you could fit two cars in long-ways, but not side-by-side. A jukebox sat against one wall. Though there were country and pop available as selections, it usually played vinyl classics such as Sinatra, Dean, the Beach Boys, and Elvis. From where we sat you could see into the dining area. It wasn't much larger than the bar, and it appeared to be equally as crowded. Katherine said, "It looks like we're lucky to have these two seats," and glanced at the back of the man who leaned against the bar next to her, his light blue dress shirt showing wrinkles and sweat stains on its back.

"What would you like?"

She glanced at my drink. "Gin and tonic?"

I smiled. "Good guess."

"It's not a guess, it's data. You told me two years ago that you and your partner, *Floyd,* would come here for gin and tonics occasionally."

"When we shoot someone."

She nodded, but the smile dissipated. "I'll have a glass of Chardonnay, whatever they have."

I signaled the bartender, a small and frail older Asian gentleman with gray hair tight against his leathery face. He glided effortlessly down the bar that is dimly lit by tile lanterns hanging on the wall along with statues of various immortals of Chinese lore. I asked for a glass of his best

Chardonnay and signaled for a refill on mine. He nodded politely and disappeared, moving like a cat behind the bar.

Sinatra was singing about doing things his way when she leaned closer to speak over Frank. "This place is an interesting little dive."

I smiled. "It is a dive, but a classic at that. This place—Yee Me Loo's —has been here for fifty years or better. Serving cops, lawyers, business-men, writers, artists . . . who knows, maybe a shrink or two." I winked, and she smiled. Her wine was delivered so we lightly clinked our glasses, and each took a drink.

"You know, if anyone who knows me saw us together, this would be really bad. Career-ending bad."

"Would you rather go to My Place?"

Her eyebrows shot up. "That's a little forward, Richard."

"It's a bar out in the valley, another place I occasionally visit." I smiled, and I could see her relax. "I just thought I'd throw it out there as a suggestion. Also, to see what type of reaction I'd get."

She narrowed her eyes at me, but her mouth turned up slightly, enough to show she wasn't bothered by any of it.

"So, how's that work. If we date, I mean. Do I still see you profes-sionally?"

"I'm not sure we can date, Richard. I don't know why I agreed to meet you. It was foolish, honestly." She put her hand on my forearm. "It's unprofessional at the very least. Doctors are never supposed to become involved with patients on any emotional level, even after they stop treating the patient. Although I do hear from time to time about a doctor and an ex-patient establishing a more personal relationship." She took a sip of her wine, then looked at me, considering. She sighed a little, and looked down at the floor, then directly at me. I wondered what was going on in her head. She let a beat go by, then spoke. "Richard, I will be completely honest. I do find myself . . . I find that I think . . . I find you interesting." Katherine had definitely taken over, the always-professional Dr. James in full retreat. I was drawing a breath to answer her, or to ask a question, or to speak to her somehow—I had no plan really—when she continued. "I am attracted to you, Richard." And then more softly, "God help me."

"Hey now."

She smiled. "Well, tell me I'm wrong. You're a wreck."

"I know. I need to find a new doc, someone who can get me all fixed up."

"So, you're already cheating on me."

"Touché," I said, and we clinked our glasses gently again.

———

HE LOOKED AT THE PHONE. TWENTY-FIVE MINUTES. HE WAS TIRED OF waiting. Leonard pictured Whitey walking into the diner and blasting the two hitmen as they sat with associates. He saw it in his mind the way he always had from the first time Whitey told the story. He was riveted by it. Then and now. And here was his chance to give Whitey something to be riveted by himself. Walk in and do the cop in front of everyone. Walk out. Anyone tries stopping him, they get smoked too. Jesus, he thought, if only he was being paid for all the assholes he had had to kill just to finish this one job. He needed to ask for a raise. A raise, and a transfer. He'd had all he could take of Los Angeles.

Leonard tucked both guns into his waistband and left the van at the curb with the keys dangling from the ignition. He didn't want to have to look for them when he returned. He crossed the road, weaving through slow-moving traffic, and headed directly to the front door.

———

DWIGHT LOOKED AT HIS RADIO AS IT CRACKLED AND THEN PICKED UP A conversation in progress. It was Steve Kelly. "—on the freeway, now headed into the restaurant with a hoodie up over his head."

"Come again, Kell, you were broken."

"The guy crossing the street right now, he's right across from you . . . Do you see him, wearing the dark hoodie?"

"Yeah, I see him—"

"He just got out of a van I swear I had eyeballed on the freeway. It was hanging back, and I tried to get a look at the driver, but could barely see in. But the van, I'm certain this is the same van. I remember the stickers on the back window, NRA and something else about supporting police. This doesn't feel right, boss."

"He's almost at the door. He's going in. Let's go. Brandi Gil, did you copy?"

"Copy, I'll cover—"

---

FLOYD SAW DWIGHT CROSSING THE STREET TOWARD YEE ME LOO'S AND said in his otherwise empty car, "I'll be damned. I guess surveillance guys get thirsty too." Then he saw Dwight drawing his gun. In Floyd's peripheral vision he caught another man running across the street. This one was white. It was Steve Kelly and he was carrying a sawed-off shotgun. His badge—hung by a chain outside of his shirt—bounced beneath his scraggly beard as he jogged toward the door. Floyd abandoned his sedan where it stood in the middle of the street and started for Yee Me Loo's. He yanked his nine from its holster and called out, "Behind you, Kell." He didn't want to run up and startle a man wielding a sawed-off shotgun.

Kelly glanced back. "Blue hoodie, white male. Nothing confirmed yet, but he just stepped inside, right ahead of us. Dickie's in the bar."

---

LEONARD SAW HIS TARGET AT THE FAR END OF THE BAR FACING THE FRONT door. It was as if he were waiting for someone to arrive, watching as Leonard walked in. He felt the cop recognized him instantly. Now the cop was standing, his eyes showing intensity as he shoved a woman off her barstool and—*Jesus*, now this cop is pulling his gun.

---

"GET DOWN!" I YELLED ACROSS THE BAR AS I JERKED MY GUN. THE second I saw his face I knew it was him. It flashed in my head from yesterday, and I saw him in my mind pointing a gun at me from his car directly in front of my apartment. Now here he was, coming for me again. There was no doubt in my mind as the two of us locked eyes across the crowded room as if nobody else was there. But they were there, a lot of people, innocent bystanders, and I knew this was going to get ugly. He was reaching under his sweatshirt, going for a gun. I was sure, but I couldn't shoot. Once again, I couldn't shoot. Would he actually pull a gun and shoot at me here in this bar crowded with civilians, innocent people? It would leave me no choice.

The door flew open behind him and he spun to face it. Gunshots rang out and muzzle flashes brightened the dark room like fireworks against a moonless black sky. Time slowed to nearly a stop, as it always seemed to do during shooting situations. The players all froze. Silence fell. There was nobody between him and me, at least nobody I could see. Everyone was likely on the ground now. Glasses, bottles, and ashtrays full of burning or smoldering cigarettes littered the surface of the bar. But there were no patrons, none that I could see, though moments before there had been standing room only. Now, nothing stood between me and the man who, for reasons unknown to me, had been stalking me, waiting for the chance to kill me. His back was to me. As had been the case twenty-some years earlier when I chased through a dark alley another man who had tried to kill me. This time, though, I wasn't trying to take aim while running, and the threat remained. I had a clear view and a steady aim. The man in the hoodie stood shooting toward the door, but at whom, and why, I had no idea. I knew he had come in looking for me; there was no doubt about it. He would be shooting at me next if he survives the battle at the door. This time, I wasn't going to spend the rest of my life regretting the outcome. I had a shot, and I took it.

I pulled the trigger twice. I paused a beat, and fired twice more. I could see the bullets striking him in his back. He jerked with each shot but continued to fire his pistol toward the door he had just walked through. Gunfire continued from the smoke-filled doorway. There were steady bursts of light and then a larger flash that accompanied a concussion. It had to have been a shotgun blast. The man in the hoodie staggered back-ward in my direction and his arms went up in the air. A muzzle blast from the pistol in his hand went toward the ceiling. His momentum carried him several strides, and then he collapsed.

As time and sound slowly returned to normal, I became aware of men crowding the front door. I was surprised to see Floyd was one of the men. The others were Steve Kelly and Dwight Campbell. They were approaching the man on the ground with their guns pointed at him. Floyd searched the room until our eyes met across the bar. We held our gaze for a moment. People began rising from the floor, gasping, shrieking, and some were crying. They crowded one another, pushing and shoving while they funneled through the back and into the adjacent restaurant; it was their only path of escape from the dark shooting gallery that was Yee Me Loo's.

Katherine's hand was on my arm. I hadn't noticed until I moved it to holster my weapon beneath my suit coat. I looked at her. She was frightened, but also sad. I said, "Welcome to my world."

# 40

A GENTLE BREEZE persisted from the west. Katherine gave up and pulled her hair back, tying it in a ponytail.

She said, "I like the view."

I saw the mountains to the east with only a hint of smog yet to be blown out of the valley. Although an hour of daylight remained, a new moon showed itself on the horizon. My eyes fell on the street below and I thought of Leonard Freeman, the serial killer-turned-contract killer who had sat watching and plotting my death. I pictured him as I last saw him, over on Mission Street, lying on a cold stainless-steel table with his scalp peeled back and his skull sawed open. His brain had been removed and plopped into a bucket where its weight was recorded before it would be stored for further analysis. They had opened his chest like a canoe and removed his breast plate by cutting through the ribs with large pruning shears. Some of his ribs were already severed and splintered from the violent impacts of lead projectiles. Much of his thorax had been destroyed by multiple nine-millimeter projectiles and double-ought buckshot that had cut through his flesh, organs, and bone. He had been hit more than a dozen times by gunfire from me and three other shooters: Floyd, Dwight Campbell, and Steve Kelly. His demise had been quick. Before the smoke had cleared, LAPD, Sheriff's Homicide investigators, and two prosecutors

from CAPOS—the L.A. District Attorney's Crimes Against Peace Officers Section—had descended upon Chinatown. The yellow tape had been
strewn across the front of the business as Leonard Freeman worked to
achieve room temperature on the floor of my favorite watering hole, Yee
Me Loo's.

I felt her eyes on me and turned to meet her gaze. "It's beautiful, isn't
it? It seems more peaceful now that . . ." I didn't finish. Neither of us had
spoken about the killer who had watched from the street below. Though he
was no longer a direct threat, he had also left no answers to the questions
of why, and whether someone else would be sent. Each time this crossed
my mind I pictured Jorge Regalado and that night in East Los Angeles just
a year before when we stood face to face, our eyes locked while our
pistols erupted into one another's torsos. I couldn't help but believe that
that incident was the catalyst to this one. Why else would anyone want me
killed? Sure, I had put many men and a few women in prison for the rest
of their lives, but many cops have. It was a rare occasion when retaliation
followed. There were always threats—both implicit and explicit—but it
was one in several thousand or more who followed through and tried to
exact revenge.

She smiled with her eyes and turned back to the view. We sat in
comfortable silence for several minutes.

"What now?" she asked.

"As far as?"

"Your job. Will you go back?"

I looked down at the tumbler cupped in both hands on my lap. It was
down to ice and a wedge of lime, begging to be refilled. "Of course I will.
This week was on the county—courtesy of my new shrink who is not at all
hot like the old one."

She smiled.

"Our team is off for the weekend, but I'll be back at it Monday.
There's going to be a lot to do now, wrapping everything up. There's still a
lot of unanswered questions."

After a moment, I said, "I truly needed a week off though."

"I agree."

"Usually, I don't. Believe it or not, I'm normally better off to stay in
the game."

"At least you think so," she said softly.

I looked into her blue eyes, paused a beat and said, "You know, it doesn't bother me that I killed him."

She nodded. "I know."

"In fact, I'm glad he's dead. I'm relieved by it, honestly."

"Richard, I'm not here as your counselor."

"I know." I took our glasses and left her on the balcony with the new wicker chairs, the wild flowers, and a planted Bonsai tree that looked like a miniature juniper and at times allowed a forest-like aroma to flood my senses. It would take me away from the city and all of her evils, if only for moments at a time. I should have bought one years ago.

Katherine called out behind me that she was good, indicating she didn't need a refill. I set the two glasses on the counter and briefly considered the implications if I *did* need a refill—if I *wasn't* yet good.

I returned with a fresh gin and tonic that she glanced at as I reclaimed my seat next to her. "Tell me, doc, what's a shrink do when she experiences a life-and-death situation and the carnage that follows? I'm sure you've never seen anything like it, right?"

She shook her head.

"So, do you need to see a doc? Does it help? Are you a true believer?"

"Are you?" she asked, staring off in the distance.

A moment passed as I carefully considered my answer. "I'm not sure I'm a true believer of anything anymore, other than maybe life and death, good and evil. But you just played the role of my shrink and turned my question around on me. I honestly want to know; does it bother you what happened? You were there when a man was killed. Seeing something like that can cause trauma—"

"I didn't actually see it happen. I was on the floor."

"But you *experienced* it. You were there. You hit the floor. You heard the shooting and heard the screams and saw the aftermath. You felt the fear and for a moment must have wondered if you were going to die. That's natural during these types of incidents. Then, when it was over, you saw a dead man lying on the floor in a pool of his own blood. Blood that I spilled. At least in part, I was responsible for his death."

Her eyes came back to me and narrowed as she retorted, "He tried to kill you. *Us*, maybe. It didn't bother me that he was dead, or that I saw him that way." She looked away, and her tone softened. "Maybe I was relieved that he was dead. Maybe that's the part I've always missed about you guys and your shooting people. I've always expected my cops to have some sort of regret for taking a man's life, yet it is seldom that I've seen it. I generally wrote it off to virility—"

"The hell is *virility?*"

She looked back to me and smiled. "Machismo. Manliness . . . It had never occurred to me that there was a true sense of relief, or gratitude. That you—or whomever—had encountered a deadly incident and survived, and were only grateful to be alive." She looked away again, contemplating. "I believe this experience will have a profound impact on my ability to help officers going forward. And that's a good thing."

"If you keep your job."

She dismissed the notion with a wave of her hand. "It's all a formality. The board will ask a few questions. I will provide the answers, and life goes on. I'm not worried about it."

"But if . . . What . . ."

"Us?"

"What?"

"You trailed off. You were going to ask about us. What if we keep seeing one another. What if we date. What if there is a future, a relationship. How do I take my cop boyfriend—a former patient—to the holiday party, right?"

"Boyfriend?"

"I'm just saying, if we were to continue whatever it is we're doing."

I sipped my gin and smiled as I thought about whatever it was we were "doing." It was Friday evening, four days since the shooting in Chinatown, and she and I had spent parts of the week together. Monday night went into the early morning hours of Tuesday with the processes of officer-involved shooting cases: interviews, statements, debriefing, blood draw for blood-alcohol testing, and a lot of waiting and drinking coffee. Late Tuesday afternoon she had called and asked if we could meet. Privately, not at another one of my famous barrooms, she had said. I suggested my place. She declined, stating she had some concerns about that given the scrutiny I might be under after yet another shooting. So, her place it was. She lived in a modest townhome in an affluent part of Pasadena, not far from Burbank. It was warmly decorated and very obviously the home of a single woman. We had sat on her balcony and visited for a few hours over lunch and iced tea. The afternoon had turned to evening. The drinks turned from tea to wine and beer. We moved from the balcony to the living room sofa where comfort had offered closeness, and that too became something more. I stayed the night and it was comfortable for us both. Wednesday morning we went for breakfast and I called Chuck to tell him I'd be home in a couple hours. They were leaving for San Diego that afternoon and I was set to watch Elvis. Katherine politely declined my offer to accompany me to my apartment, stating she had a lot to do the rest of the week, which included makeup sessions for cancellations she had made Tuesday. It had been just a few hours ago, Friday evening, when I finally convinced her to come see me at my apartment. I had used Elvis as an excuse, though truthfully, I wanted her to see this part of me. The simple life of a middle-aged homicide detective and soon to be second-time-around divorcee. I had cleaned all week and bought some new furnishings and mentally made the decision to move on with my life. I still hadn't heard a thing from Valerie, not a single returned phone call or message.

What *were* we actually doing? Me and the doc. Was it something with potential for growth and sustainability? Or, was this the reaction of two survivors with no intimacy in their lives when they needed it most? Were we only drawn together as the result of a shared traumatic experience, a sort of bond of war? Were we two lonely souls who yearned to escape the realities of their near-death experience, and found comfort in one another's arms?

Floyd and I had been partners for years and had experienced many life-threatening experiences; our friendship had been cemented by each one. We were close now in the way of brothers. We were two men who had fought together. We knew one another's darkest secrets, greatest strengths and weaknesses, and the few fears each had. The more violence and mayhem we experienced, the tighter was our bond, not dissimilar—I presumed—to what war veterans experienced. The unintended consequence was the narrowing of our inner circles. He and I spoke of it at times and both acknowledged there were no others we trusted with our closely guarded thoughts and emotions. I wondered if that was what Katherine and I were experiencing, a small slice of it. Maybe her more so than me. I needed the female companionship and I was sexually attracted to her.

*Whatever it is we're doing.*

"Currently, I'm enjoying the evening with a drink and my favorite shrink. How could it be any better than that?"

"Well, to answer the question you never did get around to asking, you are no longer my patient. We did not date when you were. If we date now, it's just one of those gray areas that nobody ever really addresses. It happens. Even shrinks are human."

I grinned and took a long drink of my gin. It went down smooth and made me feel better, more relaxed, less concerned with everything going on in my life. It allowed me an escape that left me in peace, enjoying her very pleasant company.

In the silence that followed I heard Elvis whining outside. "Elvis."

"He probably wants in. He's lonely. Does he live inside when they're home?" she asked.

I nodded. "He does. But he can't get up and down the stairs to come into my apartment. Bad hips, I guess. He's an old guy, like me. Though my hips are still okay."

She smiled.

"So, he spends a lot of time at the bottom step waiting for me. I put a little blanket down there for him—you might have noticed it—so he'd have a comfy place to hang out, sleep."

"You could carry him up and down, bring him in, the poor baby."

It hadn't occurred to me, but it was a great idea. I went out and brought him in. When I set him down inside the doorway, I straightened up and groaned while stretching my back. "Maybe that wasn't such a good idea; he's heavier than you'd think."

Katherine watched Elvis follow me out to the balcony. He circled three times before curling up at her feet and lying there contently, panting and drooling and looking about with baggy, bloodshot eyes. We had a few things in common, me and Elvis.

She leaned down and patted the old boy on his head. "Elvis is such a cutie-pie."

# 41

O N MY WAY into the office Monday morning, I called the desk to ask if anyone had seen Ray Cortez this morning. I had not been able to reach him at his desk or on his cell phone. Rich Farris picked up the phone. After harassing him for drawing desk duty again, I asked for Ray. Farris told me Ray was in a meeting with the sheriff. "*The* sheriff?"

Yes, he said, *THE* sheriff.

"What in the hell is going on? What has happened?" I demanded.

"I've got no idea, man," Rich said, "but your captain was running around the office with his ass on fire. Something's going down, brother."

I thanked him and disconnected while shifting in my seat and picking up speed. This had to be about the Santa Clarita case. It just had to be. But what would bring the sheriff to the bureau? Usually, if he wanted a personal briefing on a case, the involved investigators would pull the knots of their ties up tight and find a suit coat and—along with the team lieutenant—accompany the captain to the big house on the hill. The administrative megalopolis known as Sheriff's Headquarters. Or, the house of fairies, as I called it. The sheriff didn't come to you. Almost never. I punched in Floyd's number on the speed dial.

"What's up, Dickie?"

"Are you at the office?"

"Not yet, why?"

I told him. He said, "Holy shit." We both agreed to haul ass, and I told him he had failed us on the intel today. "No shit," and we hung up.

When I pulled into the lot behind the bureau I saw Ray hustling to his car. I stopped alongside him. "What's going on, Ray?"

He looked over at me through aviators and said, "Park it and jump in; we have to go!"

The tires of my Crown Vic squealed as I swerved head first into the nearest available spot. It went against my grain to not back in, but this was clearly urgent. I grabbed my briefcase and suit coat—knowing the sheriff was somewhere nearby—and stepped to Ray's car. It sat waiting at an angle, halfway out of its parking space, the wheels cranked and passenger's door open. As I got in, Floyd pulled up and blocked our path. He flipped us off, never taking anything seriously, and Ray hit his horn and waved him out of the way. He jerked his car to the side and stuck his head out of the window. "What's going on?"

"Tell him to get in," Ray said.

"Park your car and jump in, hurry up!"

His reaction equalled the urgency in my tone. He too pulled nose first into a nearby parking space and in a short moment was sliding into the backseat behind where I sat in Ray's car, now with a serious expression. "What the hell is going on?"

"We're both about to find out. Ray?"

Ray wheeled onto Eastern Avenue and picked up speed heading for the freeway. He glanced over at me and then into his rearview, lifting his head slightly to pick up Floyd in the reflection. "The shit has hit the fan. Chaney's barricaded in his house."

I turned in my seat to look at Floyd. He smiled and nodded, indicating he was ready for action. Floyd spent his entire life preparing for action and praying it would come. Ray was checking his mirrors while passing cars and maneuvering through traffic.

I asked him, "This is Chaney's house we're talking about? *Our* Chaney?"

"Yeah, William Chaney, husband of our missing girl. Apparently there've been shots fired too. Smack-dab in the middle of beautiful Santa

Clarita. SWAT's rolling, the location is secured, they have a negotiator en route, and we have two birds up top. I'm sure the media is crawling and flying all over the place too."

"Jesus. What the hell happened?"

"That's the crazy part. Davey Lopes knocked on his door about an hour ago and apparently told him he was going down for murder, in the way only Lopes could. It didn't go over well—"

"Atta boy, Davey," from the back seat.

"Is that why the sheriff was at the bureau?"

Ray glanced over. "You heard?"

I nodded, but he didn't see me.

"Yeah, apparently Chaney has some powerful connections, the idiot governor being one, our sheriff another. I guess what happened is Lopes went there on a tear—let me back up. Did you guys hear about the corrections officer, the lady Lopes was going—"

"Prison guard out of Pelican, was shot a week or so ago."

"Right. So, you guys heard she's pulled through, right? She is out of the woods now, stable and doing good." He craned his head again as he looked into the rearview mirror for an answer.

Floyd said he had heard she was still critical, just the other day.

"Well, Lopes now has her in witness protection and she's rolling over on the mob, big time. I guess she's hooked into them, has family members who are confirmed *carnales*. Apparently, our Santa Clarita case was a mob hit, hired by the husband of the victim, Chaney. She didn't have a lot of details but said she had heard talk about it and knows that was the case."

"Jesus," Floyd said, "he hired his old lady killed, had them cut her fucking head off?"

He nodded. "That's what this corrections officer is saying. So anyway, Lopes tells me this yesterday, and he and I drive out to talk to Chaney. Again, no answer. I tell Lopes the guy hasn't been around since our first interview with him, that you and I have both tried coming out and he's never here, and that we don't know if he's skipped town or what. Next thing I know, shit's hit the fan. Apparently, Lopes drove out there by himself this morning and knocked on the door. He didn't get an answer, and Lopes talked some shit, telling him he can't keep hiding, that he was coming for him. You know how Lopes can get. Anyway, Lopes drives off but sits down the street watching for a while. A few minutes later, Chaney starts backing out of the garage. Lopes races in and skids up behind him, blocks him in, and bails out of his hoop. Chaney sees him, panics—"

"Wouldn't you?"

"—and floors it back into the garage, throws his car in park, and runs into the house with Lopes on his heels. Lopes kicks the door and goes in behind him—I don't know what the hell he was going to do if he caught him—but the guy is already going up a staircase when Lopes rounds the corner, and Chaney busts a cap at him!"

"Wait, what?!"

We were sailing through traffic now, the emergency red light and siren clearing a path in the number one lane of the Golden State freeway, headed north. I glanced over to see we were doing 80, average. Debris flew up from the pavement as Ray crowded the median, hinting for drivers to move out of our lane. He was saying, "Yeah, and Lopes returned fire, but then he backed out of the house, probably realizing this had gone to shit."

"Jesus," Floyd said. "Did he hit this Chaney asshole, or do we know?"

"We don't know. I mean, this is just what we got from Lopes on the phone. That's the crazy part too, all of this happens right as the sheriff came down to the bureau to have a piece of my ass, and the captain's too, apparently. Chaney had called this morning and complained that we keep harassing him, said we were up there last night banging on his door and the neighbors were now talking about it, and in essence, we were tarnishing his good standing in the community. He claimed we've been stalking him, and now his neighbors all think he has something to do with his wife's murder. Literally, the captain comes through the bureau and grabs me and is looking for Lopes—Lopes was helping me all last week while you were off—and I tell him I hadn't seen Lopes yet this morning. He's fuming and tells me to get my ass into the conference room. We walk through the front desk area and the captain yells for someone to get ahold of Lopes and get him in there.

"I walked into the conference room and there's the sheriff and his driver—that big redheaded kid who used to work SWAT—and the under-sheriff, and some other asshole I'd never seen. Before we could be introduced, we get word that Lopes is in a shooting in Santa Clarita. I about shit."

Floyd was shaking his head, but still grinning. "This ought to be good."

I said, "All this just happened?"

"Yeah, partner, like the smoke hasn't cleared yet. Lopes backed out and was about to put out a call for help when the front desk called—trying to get ahold of him per the captain's order—and he's still panting from all the action. He tells Farris at the front desk what happened, which is where I got it from. When we all met up and tore out of there, the sheriff was still at the bureau. He might be on his way up to Santa Clarita now. This is a real mess."

"Wait a minute," I said, "That wasn't Chaney's wife in the car. It was Lisa Williams, confirmed by DNA, right?"

"Unless Lopes had it right all along that there is only one woman, that Lisa Williams and Marilynn Chaney are one and the same."

Floyd said, "I hope one of you two assholes thought to bring an extra vest. I don't have shit with me but Vanessa and two extra mags for her."

I turned in my seat. "You just keep Vanessa holstered, pal; I think we've had more than enough action for the month."

"We'll see about that, Dickie."

---

WE WERE UNABLE TO TURN ONTO CHANEY'S STREET DUE TO THE NUMBER of emergency vehicles parked at the end of the road: sheriff's radio cars, some from Santa Clarita station, others that were driven there by responding SWAT team members. There were detective vehicles, firetrucks, and two ambulances which were left parked at the edge of a strip of yellow tape that had been strewn across the street. An armored transport was also present, and a dozen men in olive-drab green uniforms with green and black patches stood about in helmets with automatic weapons slung over their shoulders. Lopes stood off to one side of the gathered SWAT cops and was speaking to a captain in uniform. I didn't recognize him, but I assumed he was the captain of Santa Clarita station.

Lopes had his tie loosened and his cuffs turned up; his hands were resting on his hips.

Ray parked his car across the driveway of a nearby house. Up and down the street in both directions people stood outside of the yellow tape, watching. There were no complaints that we left our vehicle across the driveway. The three of us walked directly to Lopes and the captain. After a slight nod to acknowledge the captain, Ray got to it: "What the hell happened out here, partner?"

Lopes was shaking his head. "You got me, buddy. I just thought I'd check again, see if I could catch shit-stain at home early in the morning. Well, I did. I actually saw him inside, but he wouldn't answer the door, so that pissed me off. I talked some shit to him through the door, told him I was coming for him. The rest is pretty much history. Fucker took a shot at me and I dumped about six at him. I hope he's up there leaking to death."

"I guess this confirms what the lady corrections officer told you, that he hired it out. Why else would he behave this way?"

"There's no doubt, buddy. She's shooting straight now, wants out of the life. She's lucky to be alive and knows it. I've got her in protective custody now, and I had some cops up north secure her kids. Everyone's locked down and safe. Now she's singing a pretty tune."

"I'm glad she's okay, Lopes," I said, "but how are you?"

"I'm okay."

He watched me for a moment. I said, "She was dirty, uh?"

"Yeah, kind of. I mean, she was raised dirty I guess. She didn't have a way out. She told me she's been looking for a way out and was thinking about coming clean to me. I don't know, she's probably full of shit, playing more games. You know how they are. I don't know, man."

I nodded. "Has she fully debriefed?"

He shielded the sun from his eyes as he glanced up. A helicopter was right above us, and Lopes waited for its chopping rotors to fade away. "No, not as far as the mob stuff, just answering questions we need answered about these murders, and that asshole you assholes killed in Chinatown. She knew about him being sent to kill you, but she has no idea why they tried to take her out too. She's convinced it was a hit on her by the mob, not some random gangster bullshit. She didn't know they had taken out Little Spooky, but when I told her, she wasn't surprised. She said they knew he was a rat."

"Yeah," I said, "because she told them he was."

Lopes glared at me and I realized I shouldn't have said it. He knew it too, but it was a low shot that didn't need to be taken. I said, "On this deal with the Chaney broad, did she have any details?"

"No, nothing. She heard about it, said Eme farmed it out. They heard some freak was doing it, some white boy who works for the Irish. I guess the guy's a pro."

I looked at Ray and then Floyd, each of them stoic behind shades under a bright morning sun. Floyd said, "Your boy Leonard."

I nodded. "It had to be him, I'd say."

Lopes said, "It's what I was thinking too. Don't we have him linked to three or four murders now, Ray?"

"He's linked by DNA to the gay kid who was killed in Hollywood, and by prints to the little girl out in San Fernando. There were partial prints on the lighter that hadn't been sufficient to run through the index, but we had them compared to Freeman after he was killed. That's about it, so far, though there's a strong suspicion he's good for the double in Hollywood, and of course this one, Chaney."

"Williams," I said.

"Well, it now seems certain they are one and the same," Ray argued.

I only shrugged. I wasn't yet ready to buy it. Something bothered me about the premise of it, though I couldn't quite put my finger on it. Why would Marilynn Chaney live a double life, a housewife in Santa Clarita and a hooker in the Marina? She didn't need the money; her husband was loaded. So without needing the money, why would an attractive woman choose to sell her goods? I had met a lot of hookers in my life—all professionally, of course—and I didn't know a single one who would continue to work if they married money. But it was a bigger leap yet to think they were two separate people, and that the hooker, Lisa Williams, was driving Chaney's car when she was murdered. Besides, where was Marilynn Chaney? If that were the case, if Lisa Williams, the high-class hooker of Marina del Rey was murdered in Marilynn Chaney's car, then why? And where the hell was Marilynn Chaney?

The sheriff arrived with his driver. As he walked toward us, a gunshot rang out. It seemed to have come from the Chaney residence. All of us stood silent for a moment, everyone looking around as if one of us might have an explanation. As it turned out, one among us did. A SWAT member stepped out of a mobile command vehicle and announced they had lost contact with the suspect, and there had been a gunshot inside the residence.

Lopes asked him, "Are you guys going in?"

The man in green was next to us now, and for the first time, I noticed the discreet black lieutenant bars on his uniform. He answered. "We'll run the robot in first with a camera to see what we have. Stand by, it won't be long now."

A second gunshot stopped us cold, and silence followed. Even the helicopters seemed to have disappeared or frozen for that long moment. After the first shot, I envisioned the suspect dead on the floor with a self-inflicted gunshot wound to the head. It was likely every cop on scene had had the same thought. But then there was the second shot, and that changed everything.

I considered the possibilities: hesitation? There were suicides where a victim would lose his courage and pull the gun away on the first attempt. So, it was possible. A miss? It is less likely that he either completely missed with the first shot or wounded himself and needed to take a second. Or, he hadn't shot *himself*. Had he shot at someone else? There was no gunfire directed toward us at the command post. There were no reports of shots fired from the deputies on the containment who were closer to the home. If it had been a deputy who shot, that would have been quickly reported by radio.

Did Chaney kill someone else inside the house?

I looked at Lopes and broke the silence. "Any chance someone else was in that house?"

He shrugged. "I didn't see or hear anyone else, but who knows? I was busy being shot at and returning fire."

"I know the feeling."

IT TOOK NEARLY AN HOUR BEFORE THE ROBOT COULD ENTER THE PREMISES. As is the case with every operation involving SWAT, there's always some house-fairy that has to question each and every step of the tactical operation, always with liabilities in mind. How will it be sent in? Can't go through the garage because the passage was too narrow from where Chaney had abandoned his vehicle when Lopes chased him into his own home.

"What about the front door?" one SWAT member had asked.

"We're going to assume it's locked," the lieutenant had said, "so we have to count on damage. We can pull it off or blow it off or ram it with the armored truck. Whichever way we go, the home is badly damaged."

Nobody gave a shit about the robot.

Once the door was breeched and the robot was sent in to clear the location, the rest of us huddled outside the command vehicle peering through the opened back doors, trying to see the activity on the computer display inside. The footage was grainy, and the camera seemed to jerk and bounce regularly as the robot began climbing stairs. It made it to the top and leveled out, and then turned sharply to the left after bumping a table and knocking a vase off of its top. The robot continued along a hallway and then turned into what appeared to be a master bedroom.

"What the—"

"Jesus, is that—"

The lieutenant keyed the mic of his radio and announced, *"240 Lincoln, there's two down in the location, repeat, two down. Appears to be one male, one female, both Caucasian, both apparently deceased. Prepare the team for entry."* He then turned to us and said, "I'll be goddamned."

# 42

---

I T WAS MARILYNN Chaney.

She lay dead next to her husband, William Chaney. We would have to wait for the autopsies to confirm it, but the collective years of experience that stood in the threshold this morning agreed it was a murder-suicide. Marilynn Chaney was the shooter. It appeared William Chaney had suffered a single gunshot to the chest, nearly dead center. The ten-ring. Likely close-range. The autopsy would determine that based on the presence or absence of soot or stippling. The woman lay dead a short distance from him. She was on her back, face up, with a .38 caliber revolver near her right hand. Her eyes were open and clouded, holding that stare I had seen a million times. Not that I had seen a million corpses—far from it—but of the several hundred I had, their images had been permanently warehoused in that dreadful dark room in my head, and they were often involuntarily recalled, complete with sight, sound, and smell. Marilynn Chaney had suffered a gunshot to the right temple. The wound was round, its edges seared. There was the slightest amount of blood at the entrance, though a volume of blood had gathered on the opposite side of her head, turning her blonde hair into a dark red and black sticky mass. There would likely be an impression of the muzzle tattooed on her skin that would present itself once she was cleaned up at the coroner's office; it would confirm it as a contact wound.

Lt. Joe Black accompanied Captain Stover up the stairs behind us. Ray, Floyd, Lopes, and I stood quietly, contemplating. There were many secrets snuffed out by two gunshots on an otherwise promising, sunny day in Los Angeles County. Santa Clarita, one of America's safest cities. Lt. Black said, "We have two teams from Team Four coming out to handle this. You guys figure out what else you need to know from here, and then head back to the office."

Floyd holstered his pistol. *Vanessa.* "Well, Dickie, I for one am glad to have you back. You've been a constant source of entertainment the last couple of weeks."

"Yeah," Stover sarcastically said, "it's been great."

Lopes silently turned and descended the staircase, disappearing through the front door at the bottom. Ray and I turned to follow. Floyd was saying to the captain, "I think you need to put Dickie back on Team Two where I can keep an eye on him. It's pretty clear he needs constant supervision."

---

THE AUTOPSIES OF WILLIAM AND MARILYNN CHANEY WERE GIVEN priority at the coroner's office because of the media circus the event had brought about. Early the next morning the two who had been bound by marriage up until death *did* they part were ushered into a room and situated side by side on matching stainless-steel tables. Each had been bathed, photographed, x-rayed, and prepared for final examination. Looking at the pair it occurred to me they were the epitome of everything wrong with our society: greed, lust, hatred. The pursuit of self-gratification at all costs. What had happened here was yet a mystery, but the motives would no doubt be in this realm. Their exit, side by side, naked and unabashed, was no story of Adam and Eve.

As predicted, the medical examiner determined the manner of death of Marilynn Chaney a suicide; the mode of death a single gunshot to the head. As for William Chaney, his death was ruled a homicide. The mode of death: multiple gunshot wounds.

"WAIT, *MULTIPLE* GUNSHOT WOUNDS?" LOPES QUESTIONED AT THE NEWS.

I pulled a chair out next to his desk at the office, removed my hat, and set my notebook down. "Yep. Dr. Wang recovered a .38 caliber projectile from the thorax which had entered his chest and penetrated his heart. This was determined to be the fatal wound. However, doc said he would not be able to say with certainty that the gunshot to his buttock wouldn't have killed him."

He leaned back in his chair, looking up at me as I provided the details. His permanently squinting eyes seemed to twinkle slightly, and a grin crept onto his face. "You're serious?"

I nodded. "Doc recovered a 9mm projectile from his lower back. The trajectory was sharply upward, entering the left ass cheek and traveling through a kidney before taking out a few vertebrae and lodging in his spine. Good expansion on the hollow point round, apparently. He said that injury could have been fatal had the wife not intervened. The internal bleeding alone might have finished him off had he remained barricaded a few more hours."

"Good," he said, "I'm glad to hear it. The sonofabitch busted a cap at me when all I wanted to do was talk to him. He deserved to suffer for a while."

Floyd had walked in behind me. "Yeah, good job, Lopes. You shot the poor bastard in his ass."

"You want to be next?"

"Whatever, man."

Lopes grinned. He said, "I have some news for you, from Maria."

I frowned. "Maria?"

"Maria Lopez, the corrections officer from Pelican."

"Oh, yeah . . ."

"She was in better shape this morning, and we had quite the conversation. She has a lot to say and wants immunity to testify against the mafia. I'm meeting with Brennan and Thompson from Hardcore this evening, and some federal prosecutor who is assigned with them at the D.A.'s office. It will probably be the kickoff of another RICO against the mob."

"Sounds fun," I said. "What'd she have to say? Hopefully something about that asshole Leonard Freeman."

He nodded. "Eme was using the Irish mob for some of their work; she has no idea why. She didn't know anything about Freeman, but she had heard the Irish sent some crazy white boy out here from the east coast. He apparently did a few hits and he had been given yours also. She did know the *why* part of it, why there was a hit against you."

My heart rate quickened and I suddenly felt hot in the cool room. Lopes watched me in the moment of silence, waiting. I could feel Floyd's eyes on me too. Both were probably waiting for me to ask for the details. The *why*. But did I even want to know? Of course I wanted to know. But for some reason I was frozen and unable to ask what he had learned. Maybe it was because I knew. It had been all I could think of for the last couple of weeks, since the first time I had felt I was being watched. I'd been thinking about nothing other than the *why* ever since the confrontation on the street in front of my apartment, the incident that resulted in Floyd unloading his gun on a fleeing car. Every path I took in my head ended at the same place. A dreary living room in East Los Angeles on a cold and rainy night not much more than a year ago. *Familia Regalado*. One dead, the other in prison, likely for life. Each associated with a gang known to be affiliated with the Mexican mafia. I had concluded some time ago that the serial killer Leonard Freeman had been contracted to kill me because of that night. What else could it have been?

I picked up my hat and notebook, stood, and walked out of the office without a word.

---

FLOYD WATCHED DICKIE WALK OUT, HIS EYES TRAILING HIM TO THE BACK door of the office. He looked back to see that Lopes had also watched the departure. Their eyes met, and Floyd shrugged, as if he couldn't explain Dickie's response. Lopes said, "He knows."

"It's the shooting, right? East L.A.?"

Lopes nodded. "That's what Maria told me. She said what we already knew, that White Fence puts in a lot of work for the Eme, and this was done as a favor."

"Jesus, that's some heavyweight shit, man. No wonder he walked out like he'd seen a ghost."

"I know how he feels. I had a green light on me once—"

"I remember," Floyd said.

"—and there's no worse feeling. You think we're normally paranoid as cops, try being on the mob's list. You check behind the shower curtain before taking a leak. I could see it on Dickie's face, that uncertainty. He knows that if one was sent another could replace him. He just realized this might not end here. That's why he responded the way he did. He knows."

"What can we do?"

"Like I said, I'm meeting with the shot-callers over at Hardcore tonight. They already have something cooking at the D.A.'s office, a joint task force deal with the feds. I'm sure this will become a big part of that. We'll go after them. Don't worry, they won't be sending someone else once we start taking people down. Chances are, they couldn't anyway. Not after a failed attempt. They're probably wishing they'd never got involved in that bullshit now. They know the heat's coming."

"I'm in, Lopes. You get that RICO going, I'll be with you going through doors. We'll make these sonsofbitches think twice about putting a cop on their list."

---

FLOYD WALKED UP AND STOOD NEXT TO ME WHERE I LEANED AGAINST someone's Crown Vic parked near the rear door. It was shaded by the building, but I was sweating nonetheless. I held my hat in my hand and continued wiping my forehead and brows every few moments. He said, "Ray's looking for you."

I nodded as if to ask what that was about. He understood the gesture. "Debriefing in a half hour up at Headquarters."

"The sheriff's office?"

He was putting a pinch of Copenhagen in his mouth. Once finished, he said, "Yeah, all the fairies want the details. Better tighten up that tie, Dickie, make yourself presentable."

"It's going to take more than a pretty tie, partner; I'm a wreck."

He stepped toward the door and paused. "I know. Come on, I'll buy the gin tonight."

------

CAPTAIN STOVER INTRODUCED ALL OF US FROM THE BUREAU: LT. JOE Black, then me, Ray, Floyd, Mongo, Rich Farris, Elizabeth Marchesano, and Davey Lopes. He was addressing a gathering of various executives who sat around the long, dark table that was situated in the center of a narrow room with photos of past sheriffs, as well as a prominent one of the present sheriff, adorning the walls. We were apparently expected to know each of the attendants as the introductions were one-sided. I recognized the sheriff of course; I'd known him for a lot of years and he was on the news regularly, more so now than ever before due to a number of scandals hitting our department. The undersheriff was also easily recognizable for all of the same reasons, plus the added fact that he had worked the streets of South Central back when I was a patrol cop. Only he hadn't spent much time doing it. He was born to be a politician and only stayed somewhere long enough to pad his resume and shake a lot of hands. The captain of Santa Clarita was there, and sitting next to him was a lady whom I had seen at that station but hadn't met. The others were a bit of a mystery. I recognized the faces of some, which told me they were likely either Internal Affairs or part of the Force Review board. I always felt these meetings would be more appropriately held under a tent like every other circus.

Once Stover sat down, Ray took over.

"I'm Raymond Cortez, assigned to Homicide. Richard Jones is my partner. The other detectives here have all worked on the case we are briefing today and/or cases that are somehow related to ours. By *ours,* I am obviously referring to the murder of Lisa Renee Williams, the person identified as the woman who was decapitated and dismembered and ultimately found in the industrial area of Santa Clarita. I will begin with that case as it makes sense to do so chronologically."

He went on to tell the assembly the gruesome details of the recovery. He said we had never identified the location of the murder, but we were confident that it didn't happen where she was found. He said we also didn't believe she was killed in the car. He then began explaining the car, how it was the registered vehicle of Marilynn Chaney, who, at the time of this investigation, was a reported missing person. He told how Lisa Williams had been identified by DNA, reminding the audience there was no other way the victim could have been identified. "We were lucky she had been arrested, or we might not have ever identified her." Ray described her lifestyle, her arrests, her apartment, her expensive vehicle, the fact she had been adopted at birth, and then he paused, looked over at me and said to the group, "And currently we are in the midst of running with a theory that she might in fact be related to Chaney. The two may have been twins."

Ray went on to say the theory began at the crime lab, and he credited Phil Gentry and Dr. Provost. They were discussing the theory Lopes had proposed that the two were one and the same, that Chaney lived a double life as a call girl in the Marina. That prompted Gentry and the doctor to consider the possibility that they were identical twins, and as such, they would have identical DNA profiles. He said when this theory was presented, it made sense to him and Lopes, and they came up with the following theory: "William Chaney was in financial trouble, though at first glance it appeared otherwise. He has a million-dollar insurance policy on the wife. She and her sister must have learned of each other's existence recently, somehow. We know that the two must have had *some* type of relationship, as Williams's fingerprint was found on the back of the regis-tration papers in Chaney's vehicle. She had been in that vehicle when she was alive, and likely more than once. At first," Ray explained, "we theo-rized that the two of them—Mr. and Mrs. Chaney—were in on it together. They were going to stage Marilynn Chaney's death to collect on the insur-ance. To do so, they would kill her sister, Lisa Williams, and put her in Marilynn's car. They likely believed it would be an assumption that it was Chaney in the car, and not too much else would ever come of it. Part of that reasoning would come from the fact Williams lived the type of life that she likely wouldn't be missed for a long time. It would also be reason-able to think that the Chaneys looked down upon her for her lifestyle. All of this of course is based on the premise that the two sisters didn't know each other until recently, both being adopted as infants. Now, however, we are starting to rethink the idea that it was both Mr. and Mrs. Chaney who devised the plan to kill the sister. We're leaning toward the theory that this was Mr. Chaney's idea and the missus reluctantly went along with it initially, but later couldn't live with herself—or with him, for that matter —after her twin sister was murdered.

"Early on there was mention of an adult daughter. None exists. The only theory we can come up with for that early statement by Mr. Chaney is that after the initial missing person report was made, Mrs. Chaney must have appeared back at the house for some reason. Maybe she was seen by a neighbor or Mr. Chaney worried she might have been. Either way, we think perhaps he felt the need to prepare for any such sighting being reported to us by a neighbor. He would be able to shrug it off and say it was their daughter, that the two are mistaken as sisters when together, or some such thing. That's our thought on it, anyway.

"The murder-suicide is essentially caught on audio. Hostage negotiators were on the line with Mr. Chaney, trying to get him to come out. He mentioned at that time that he had been shot, which we didn't know until the autopsies this morning. He said he didn't know why a crazy Mexican was chasing him into his home, and that he had shot at the man believing him to be an intruder. In his dying moments, he still stuck with the story and maintained his innocence. However, a female is heard in the background. Her voice is faint, but the tech crew enhanced the recording and what comes across clearly is her calling him a bastard. He only says her name, weakly. Almost pleadingly. *"Marilynn."* Then a gunshot. Based on the forensic evidence, coupled with the recording, there is no doubt Mrs. Chaney surprised Mr. Chaney with her presence and then shot him in the chest, killing him. After a few moments, she turned the gun on herself. We don't know what the delay was, probably contemplation. She shot herself in the head, which is unusual."

One of the suits asked, "What do you mean by that, Detective?"

"Women seldom shoot themselves in the head or face to commit suicide. If they use a gun at all—which is low percentage—they might shoot themselves in the heart, believe it or not. The head is a better, more effective, and probably less painful way to do it. Either way, she did it; there's no doubt about that. It was a contact wound to the right temple. She is right-handed. The gun was near her right hand. There is substantial gunshot residue on her right hand and arm. He was shot from a distance of probably three feet or less, and he was positioned lower than the pistol. There was a slight downward trajectory. Given the severity of the other gunshot wound, it is likely he was seated on the floor when she killed him."

"The other gunshot wound, that was us?" the undersheriff asked.

Ray nodded, turned and glanced at Lopes who sat expressionless to his right. "Yes, that was us. Detective Lopes had pursued the suspect into the home. As the suspect ran up the stairs, he turned and fired at Detective Lopes. Detective Lopes returned fire, striking the suspect once in the buttock. The bullet traveled in an upward trajectory into his lower thorax area, severing a kidney along the way. That trauma may or may not have resulted in his death, according to the medical examiner. It is likely he would have died if he went a long time without treatment.

"Are there any other questions to this point? We have a lot more to discuss, but I want to make sure we're all on the same page." He looked around the room. The various executives sat silent, some of them shaking their heads in response to his inquiry. Ray glanced down at his belt and fumbled with his cell phone. "Excuse me just one second, I've been waiting for something pertinent to this briefing to come in as a text." He quickly read a message on his phone, and put it back in its holster. He looked at me for a moment before continuing.

"It has been confirmed through DNA, Chaney and Williams were identical twins."

Floyd's voice carried more than he probably had anticipated in the suddenly silent room when he said, "Holy shit."

I glanced at him and he just shrugged.

Ray continued: "As for the murder of Lisa Williams, there is no physical evidence linking the serial killer, Leonard Freeman, to her death. At least, not yet. However, there are similarities in a case being handled by LAPD. More on that in a minute.

"We know through an informant that the hit on Detective Jones was contracted by the Mexican mafia through the Irish mafia."

"Who's the informant?" someone asked.

"The corrections officer who was shot in Whittier two weeks ago Thursday. She survived and is talking, giving everything up. Apparently, she was a dirty cop. Her family is heavily tied to the Mexican mafia."

316

I glanced at Lopes who stared blankly across the room. It seemed he had focused on something faraway, something beyond the walls of this room. Or perhaps he had gone to a place we all knew to well, a place of pain, darkness, and regret. Either way, he could have been holding aces or deuces, you would never have guessed which.

"We believe Freeman was sent here for the hits on both Lisa Williams and Detective Jones. We know he is tied to the Irish mafia in Florida as we recovered a letter he carried with him from a known hitman for the Irish mob, Whitey Blanchard. It turns out Freeman and Blanchard were long-time cellmates in Raiford, and from the letter, it appears they are very good friends. The letter itself seems to be in code to a degree. Lara over at Prison Gangs is working with it to see if they can decipher any instructions hidden in the message.

"We know that Freeman killed a young girl in San Fernando. That murder seems to have been for nothing other than personal gratification, as far as we can tell. There were photographs of the victim on his cell phone, and he was linked to the crime scene through fingerprints. We expect that case will also be linked by DNA. Detective Farris is going to give you more detail on that in a moment.

"LAPD is investigating three murders in the Hollywood area we believe to be linked to Freeman. One is a young man found at the top of a parking structure. Like the Freeman murder, his hands had been cut from his body and he was decapitated. The other two was a double murder in Hollywood. Two Russians at a car lot were found stabbed to death, throats slit, one nearly decapitated, just a couple weeks ago. The biggest link to that murder at this point is the car Freeman drove. See, Freeman was linked by DNA and prints to the murder of the kid killed on top of the parking structure. That victim's car was found in Chinatown just down the street from the bar where Freeman died in a shootout with our guys, and Freeman's prints are in it. The victim—the young man who was decapitated—was found in a Ford Taurus which turns out is the vehicle previously driven by Freeman. That vehicle has been linked to the dead Russians through paperwork recovered in their office. It is a cold-plated, vin-switched car, as were many of the cars on that lot. It was the retail part of an elaborate Russian auto theft ring. But, that's how all of the cases seemed to be linked together. We don't know if the Hollywood cases are contract murders or something else."

He looked at me. "What have I missed?"

While I was thinking, Lopes said, "You want to explain the hit on Dickie, what we got from Maria Lopez?"

He nodded and turned back to the group, still standing at the end of the table near his vacant seat. "The reason for the hit on Detective Jones, according to the same informant, is retaliation for a shooting he was involved in just over a year ago, right over here in East L.A." Ray nodded toward the east-facing wall as he said it. "Many of you probably remember it. Detective Jones was wounded during the shooting, and in fact, he only returned to work a few weeks ago. The person who shot him —the one Detective Jones killed—was a White Fence gang member. They put in a lot of work for the mob, and it is said that the attempted hit on Detective Jones was a favor to the gang. As a result of the attempted murder of Detective Jones, and other information the corrections officer is now providing about the Mexican mafia, Detective Lopes is working with the D.A.'s Hardcore office and the feds. They will be putting together another RICO on the mob."

The sheriff nodded with intensity as if he greatly appreciated the idea of it. "Good. I want to be kept up to date on the progress of that." He looked at his undersheriff. "Make sure I have at least weekly briefings on that operation." The undersheriff made a note on the pad in front of him.

After a moment, Ray asked again if there were any questions. One of the executives asked how Chaney would have been able to go through the Mexican mafia for a hit, if he did in fact have Lisa Williams killed.

"I have to be honest, sir, when Marilynn Chaney killed her husband and then turned the gun on herself, she took their dirty secrets to the grave with her. The only saving grace is that with both of them and Leonard Freeman all dead, we don't have to know. Of course, we will continue investigating, looking at all of their friends, associates, business records, et cetera, to see if anything further is learned or anyone else is culpable. But at this point, we just don't know. Chaney was into gambling, so maybe there's a connection there. Hell, these casinos around here are breeding grounds for the underworld. We'll be sure to reach out to Organized

Crimes and Gaming also, see if any of our detectives in those units can help us connect any dots."

The executive who asked the question just nodded. Ray looked around quickly and then settled his eyes on Rich Farris.

"With that, I'm going to turn this over to Detective Rich Farris. He and Detective Marchesano investigated the case of the little girl killed in the valley, so he can provide more detail on that. I believe he is also going to brief about two other cases that might be related to Freeman, a homeless man who was murdered downtown, and a storeowner out in Burbank. Thank you, gentlemen."

Nobody clapped. I was tempted to, but realized that only Floyd would appreciate the humor of it.

Farris stood and cleared his throat. As he began to speak, Detective Raymond Cortez—my new partner—took his seat next to me. He leaned over and whispered, "Everything's going to be good, partner. You watch and see."

# 43

I 'VE BEEN WORRIED sick about you. Have you heard about everything going on in Santa Clarita?"

It was Valerie. I probably sounded a little over the top excited and quickly regretted answering the phone that way. I hadn't spoken with her in weeks. I was worried, and it showed. But I also knew the second I finished saying it—in that brief moment of silence that followed—that this part of me is what had driven her away. I was too intense, all of the time. She was the opposite, believing nothing would ever happen to anyone she knew or loved. Even at times when she *should* have been worried sick about me, she remained unaffected. During the 1992 L.A. riots we had worked around the clock. Violence consumed every hour of every shift. The city was on fire, her citizenry out of control. Once in a while she would check in, seemingly oblivious to what might be going on around me. *How's work?*

*How's work? Well, I'm standing on a bed of ash, the remains of which comprised Griff's Liquor down here on Firestone Boulevard. I'm looking for a gun some asshole tossed right after he shot at us and my partner lit off two rounds of double-ought buck from the window of our unit. We were patrolling with our lights off when he ambushed us from the ruins of the same store his mama likely bought his diapers and formula, and up until two days ago, he would buy his single cigarettes and malt liquor. Our window was blown out but we're okay, how's everything at home?*

*Oh, okay, I had dinner with the neighbors . . .*

"Richard, I'm calling to tell you I need you to stop checking on me. There's a reason I am not answering your phone calls, and I know you've been by my house several times. Please, this needs to stop. *You* need to stop."

"I still care about you, Val."

"Richard, there's someone else now; you need to know that. It's awkward when you call and we're together. Twice you called while we were away on vacation. It would be best for all of us if you just accepted this and moved on. Really . . . *Please*."

I pulled the phone away from my ear to see who was calling through. It was Katherine. I didn't answer her call. I also didn't say goodbye to Valerie. I powered off my cell and tossed it onto the seat next to me and redirected the Crown Victoria toward Chinatown. Pasadena and Dr. Katherine James would have to wait while I sorted things out. Hopefully she would.

———

TONIGHT, THE PLACE STOOD EMPTY. ZHONG—WHICH HE HAD TOLD ME long ago translates to *loyal, steadfast*—reached for the blue bottle of Bombay, and I nodded. He noticed me looking around. "It's been this way in here a week now. Nobody comes in, ever since . . ."

He met me at the end of the bar where I took my seat furthest from the door with a wall at my back. It's where I sat. Always. *That* night. He set my drink down and lazily swiped at the bar top with a towel, working his way to the other end. Leaving me alone in my misery, marinating in regret, reflection, and deliberation. *The demons.*

Oldies played from the jukebox but even Sinatra provided little distraction as I recalled the images of a killer whose life I ended one week ago. The man who had been sent to kill me and died on the floor I had just walked over with neither reverence nor contempt. As I sat staring at the door he had walked through that night, the scene played on a continuous loop in my head.

*He stepped through the door and quickly assessed the room. His villainous eyes found me watching him, closely, contemplating . . . But only for a brief moment. And in that moment, we knew . . . We both knew.*

*The door banged open behind him, and he turned.*

*Flames burst in the darkness. Fiery lead whistled through the smoke-filled, dingy room. The killer jerked and staggered as he fired toward the door, his back now to me. I took careful aim. The patrons had all disappeared, dropping low and ducking beneath the bar. It was only him and me, and someone outside the front door. I squeezed the trigger twice, and then twice again, and I watched him flinch as my bullets struck his back. A brilliant flash of light filled the doorway, sending the killer stumbling backward. He fell and crumpled onto the floor. His body twitched—but only a couple of times—and then his eyes fixed on something seemingly intangible, something far beyond his reach. Then it was gone. Whatever it had been, he let it go.*

I thought about Lisa Williams, a girl who seemed to have lost her direction at birth. I wondered if she had felt whole after discovering her twin sister, all of these years later. Marilynn Chaney had been the more evil of the two, as it turns out. She had been willing to murder the one with whom she had shared a womb, all for money. It would have been the perfect crime had Williams's DNA profile not been in CODIS; we would likely never have discovered the truth since the two had identical DNA profiles. Mr. Chaney had been smart to not offer items containing his wife's DNA for comparison. He knew we would come up with something on our own or eventually ask him for her toothbrush. The DNA would have matched perfectly, the missing person case would be closed, and Chaney would have been smiling all the way to the bank.

Another gin and tonic arrived without being ordered. Zhong: *loyal, steadfast.* He collected the empty glass and swiped his towel where it had sat. He paused a moment, appearing deep in thought. But then he looked me in the eyes and only nodded, subtly, as if to say it would be okay. *He knew.* We exchanged smiles before he turned away, and it was then I realized the demons had quieted and retreated into the darkness.

For now.

As Zhong meandered to the other end of the bar, I lifted my glass and softly said to the small man's back, *"Everything's going to be good, partner. You watch and see."*

———

Independent authors count on word-of-mouth and paid advertising to find new readers and sell more books. Reviews can help shoppers decide about taking a chance on authors who are new to them.

I would be grateful if you took a moment to write a review on Amazon.

Thank you!

Danny R. Smith

I love staying connected with my readers through social media and email. If you would like to connect, find me on BookBub, Amazon, Goodreads, Facebook, Instagram, and Twitter. You can also sign up for my newsletter and receive bonus material, such as the action-packed short story, EXHUMING HER HONOR.

As a newsletter subscriber, you will receive special offers, updates, book releases, and blog posts. I promise to never sell or spam your email.

Danny R. Smith

Dickie Floyd Novels

# ALSO BY DANNY R. SMITH

**THE DICKIE FLOYD DETECTIVE SERIES**

- A GOOD BUNCH OF MEN
- DOOR TO A DARK ROOM
- ECHO KILLERS
- THE COLOR DEAD
- DEATH AFTER DISHONOR
- UNWRITTEN RULES
- THE PROGRAM
- THE FIRST FELONY
- HARD-BOILED: BOXSET - FIRST THREE DICKIE FLOYD NOVELS

**THE RICH FARRIS DETECTIVE SERIES**

- THE OUTLAW

**DICKIE FLOYD SHORT STORIES**

- In the City of Crosses
- Exhuming Her Honor

**AVAILABLE AUDIOBOOKS**

- A Good Bunch of Men
- Door to a Dark Room
- Nothing Left to Prove

**NON-FICTION — MEMOIR**

- Nothing Left to Prove: A Law Enforcement Memoir

The Following is a preview of Book 3 in the Dickie Floyd Detective series.

## ECHO KILLERS

---

**THE KILLERS WALKED** in dressed in black boots, pants, turtleneck sweaters, and ski masks. Only their eyes were visible to the witness, but he insisted both were Caucasian. *"You could just tell."*

The larger of the two carried a "machine gun," the young witness said, hanging from a sling over the man's right shoulder. The other cradled a sawed-off shotgun, the barrel resting in the crook of his right arm, his left hand holding the grip. This second man appeared small next to the other, the two of them filling the doorway as the glass doors closed behind them. The big man swung the rifle up and fired. *"Pop-pop-pop!"*

Cedric continued: "The other one turned sideways so that his shotgun was pointed at the *chino,* and then he blasted it twice. *Bam, bam!"*

Floyd looked at Mongo with his brows raised. Mongo only shrugged. Back to the kid, Floyd said, "And you saw all of this, little man?"

The boy's green eyes sparkled when he smiled. "Yessir."

"You said, '*chino*' . . . they shot the *chino.* What did you mean by that?"

"You know, *chino.*" The boy then placed his index fingers at the outside corners of his eyes and pulled the skin back, making both eyes slanted. "The people who own the liquor stores."

"Did they see you, these two men with the guns?"

Cedric straightened in his chair. "Sure they did. They seen me when I ran past them, out the door."

Floyd glanced at his partner again, the big Hawaiian-looking Mexican named Diaz whom Floyd and now everyone else at the Homicide Bureau just called *"Mongo."* Always one to limit his expenditure of unnecessary words, Mongo nodded.

"How *exactly* did you run past them?" Floyd asked.

Cedric rubbed a hand back and forth over his short-cropped natural hair, and ran his tongue back and forth over chapped lips. "I just ran right by, super fast. They di'nt see me till I was right there at the door. And then the big one cursed, said something to the other'n about gettin' me. I kept going, and right as I went around the corner of the building, *BAM!* Another blast from that shotgun.*"*

"They shot at you?"

"Yup. But I ran up the alley until I heard them peeling out, and then I jumped over a fence and hid in someone's back yard, underneath a boat."

"Under a boat?"

"One of them metal ones. It was upside-down on the grass, and there was like an opening at the back, a part of the metal that's cut away where I think a motor goes. Anyway, there was plenty of room to crawl through there, so I did. Stayed there 'til the next day, 'bout froze my nuts off. I might'a died if it weren't for Snuggles."

"Snuggles?"

"He's my puppy. I found him under the boat, and he followed me when I left the next morning."

Mongo surprised Floyd and the boy both when he said, "You stole the puppy?"

"He di'nt have no food or water in there and he was on a chain. He snuggled with me all night long, 'cause he likes me. So I kept him."

Floyd shrugged, no big deal. "Okay, so you kept Snuggles."

"Yeah. You want, I can show him to ya."

Floyd stood and Mongo and Cedric followed suit. They stepped out of the interview room into a tiled hallway where a steady stream of uniformed deputies passed in both directions, their police radios crackling.

Floyd put his arm around Cedric and led him toward the front lobby where a woman waited to take him home.

Floyd said, "Alright, little buddy, I'm going to look into all of this, and then I'll be coming down to your house to see you. Deal?"

Cedric smiled, and Floyd raised his hand for a high-five.

"Will you come tomorrow?"

Floyd chuckled. "Maybe, buddy; we'll see. Okay?"

"Okay, sir."

Floyd rubbed the kid's head and guided him toward the lady who waited. When he turned back, Mongo stood grinning.

"What are you grinning at, asshole?"

———

**THE BIG MAN** blew smoke rings into the air, but the twirling fan destroyed their shape and redirected the haze in the flickering light of the television set. "We have to find that green-eyed little bastard, and kill him." He stabbed his cigarette out in an overfilled ashtray while searching his partner's eyes for an answer. None came. He only saw apprehension, doubt. The pussy. The big man grunted and rose from his chair. Turning toward the kitchen, he said over his shoulder, "Want another beer?"

———

Danny R. Smith spent 21 years with the Los Angeles County Sheriff's Department, the last seven as a homicide detective. He now lives in Idaho where he works as a private investigator and consultant. He is blessed with a beautiful family and surrounded by an assortment of furry critters whom he counts among his friends.

Danny is the author of the *Dickie Floyd Detective Novel* series and the *Rich Farris Detective* series. He writes about true crime and other topics in his blog, The Murder Memo.

He has appeared as an expert on numerous podcasts and shows including True Crime Daily and the STARZ channel's WRONG MAN series, and is the host of *Unsolved Murders with Danny Smith* on the Dr. Carlos Crime Network podcast.

Danny is a member of the Idaho Writers Guild and the Public Safety Writers Association.

facebook.com/Dickie.Floyd.Novels
x.com/dickiefloyd187
instagram.com/dickiefloyd